HOT
Italian
DAYS

MELANIE
MILBURNE

CATHY
WILLIAMS

CHANTELLE
SHAW

MILLS & BOON

HOT ITALIAN DAYS © 2024 by Harlequin Books S.A.

HIS INNOCENT'S PASSIONATE AWAKENING
© 2020 by Melanie Milburne
Australian Copyright 2020
New Zealand Copyright 2020

First Published 2020
Second Australian Paperback Edition 2024
ISBN 978 1 038 93568 7

THE UNCOMPROMISING ITALIAN
© 2014 by Cathy Williams
Australian Copyright 2014
New Zealand Copyright 2014

First Published 2014
Third Australian Paperback Edition 2024
ISBN 978 1 038 93568 7

A BABY SCANDAL IN ITALY
© 2022 by Chantelle Shaw
Australian Copyright 2022
New Zealand Copyright 2022

First Published 2022
Third Australian Paperback Edition 2024
ISBN 978 1 038 93568 7

Published by
Mills & Boon
An imprint of Harlequin Enterprises (Australia) Pty Limited
(ABN 47 001 180 918), a subsidiary of HarperCollins
Publishers Australia Pty Limited (ABN 36 009 913 517)
Level 19, 201 Elizabeth Street
SYDNEY NSW 2000
AUSTRALIA

MIX
Paper | Supporting
responsible forestry
FSC® C001695

® and ™ (apart from those relating to FSC®) are trademarks of Harlequin Enterprises (Australia) Pty Limited or its corporate affiliates. Trademarks indicated with ® are registered in Australia, New Zealand and in other countries. Contact admin_legal@Harlequin.ca for details.

Printed and bound in Australia by McPherson's Printing Group

CONTENTS

His Innocent's Passionate Awakening

Melanie Milburne

Melanie Milburne read her first Harlequin novel at the age of seventeen, in between studying for her final exams. After completing a master's degree in education, she decided to write a novel, and thus her career as a romance author was born. Melanie is an ambassador for the Australian Childhood Foundation and a keen dog lover and trainer. She enjoys long walks in the Tasmanian bush. In 2015 Melanie won the HOLT Medallion, a prestigious award honoring outstanding literary talent.

Books by Melanie Milburne

Harlequin Modern

The Tycoon's Marriage Deal
A Virgin for a Vow
Blackmailed into the Marriage Bed
Tycoon's Forbidden Cinderella
The Return of Her Billionaire Husband

Conveniently Wed!

Bound by a One-Night Vow
Penniless Virgin to Sicilian's Bride
Billionaire's Wife on Paper

Secret Heirs of Billionaires

Cinderella's Scandalous Secret

The Scandal Before the Wedding

Claimed for the Billionaire's Convenience
The Venetian One-Night Baby

Visit the Author Profile page
at millsandboon.com.au for more titles.

Dear Reader,

When my editor first approached me about doing a Sleeping Beauty theme for my next book, I was so excited. I adore classic fairy tales! I enjoyed the challenge of incorporating some of the essential elements of the Brothers Grimm fairy tale while doing my own spin on it. No pun intended! Alas, there are no spindles in my story, but I did make my heroine, Artemisia, a talented embroiderer living in an ancient ivy-clad castle. And of course, my hero, Luca Ferrantelli, is the dashingly handsome prince who awakens her with a kiss.

In the Brothers Grimm fairy tale, Sleeping Beauty is asleep for one hundred years in a glass coffin due to a curse put upon her as a child. Artie, in my story, suffers from severe social anxiety and hasn't left the *castello* for a decade. She is psychologically asleep to her potential, and it is only when she meets Luca that she is able to gradually break free of the curse of guilt that has contained her since she was a teenager.

Something rather spooky happened as I was writing this story. I suddenly realized I didn't just have one Sleeping Beauty in my novel—I had three! Luca was also a Sleeping Beauty and so, too, was Artie's friend and housekeeper at the *castello*, Rosa.

Social anxiety is a crippling condition and is notoriously difficult to overcome, but it can be done. Some people very close to me have suffered from it, and their courage in trying to overcome it has always inspired and impressed me.

Best wishes,

Melanie XX

Dedicated to Rachel Bailey—a fellow dog lover, romance writer and awesome brainstorming partner! Thanks for being such a wonderful friend xxxxx. Licks and cuddles from Polly and Lily, too.

CHAPTER ONE

ARTEMISIA BELLANTE STARED at her father's lawyer in abject horror. 'But there must be some mistake. How can Castello Mireille be...be *mortgaged?* It's been in my father's family for generations. Papa never mentioned anything about owing money to a bank.'

'He didn't owe it to a bank.' The lawyer, Bruno Rossi, pushed a sheaf of papers across the desk towards Artie, his expression grave. 'Have you heard of Luca Ferrantelli? He runs his late father's global property developing company. He's also a wine and olive producer with a keen interest in rare grape varieties, some of which are on the Castello Mireille estate.'

Artie lowered her gaze to the papers in front of her, a light shiver racing down her spine like a stray current of electricity. 'I've vaguely heard of him...' She might have spent years living in isolation on her family's ancient estate but even she had heard of the handsome billionaire playboy. And seen pictures. And swooned just like any other woman between the ages of fifteen and fifty.

She raised her gaze back to the lawyer's. 'But how did this happen? I know Papa had to let some of the gardeners go to keep costs down and insisted we cut back on housekeeping expenses, but he didn't mention anything about borrowing money from anyone. I don't understand how Signor Ferrantelli now owns most, if not all, my family's home. Why didn't Papa tell me before he died?'

To find out like this was beyond embarrassing. And deeply hurtful. Was this her father's way of forcing his shut-in daughter out of the nest by pushing her to the verge of bankruptcy?

Where would she find the sort of money to dig herself out of this catastrophic mess?

Bruno shifted his glasses further up the bridge of his Roman nose. 'Apparently your father and Luca's father had some sort of business connection in the past. He contacted Luca for financial help when the storm damage hit the *castello* late last year. His insurance policy had lapsed and he knew he would have no choice but to sell if someone didn't bail him out.'

Artie rapid-blinked. 'The insurance lapsed? But why didn't he tell me? I'm his only child. The only family he had left. Surely he should have trusted me enough to tell me the truth about our finances.'

Bruno Rossi made a shrugging movement with one shoulder. 'Pride. Embarrassment. Shame. The usual suspects in cases like this. He had to mortgage the estate to pay for the repairs. Luca Ferrantelli seemed the best option—the only option, considering your father's poor state of health. But the repayment plan didn't go according to schedule, which leaves you in an awkward position.'

Artie wrinkled her brow, a tension headache stabbing at the backs of her eyes like scorching hot needles. Was this a nightmare? Would she suddenly wake up and find this was nothing but a terrifying dream?

Please let this not be real.

'Surely Papa knew he would have to eventually pay back the money he borrowed from Signor Ferrantelli? How could he have let it get to this? And wouldn't Luca Ferrantelli have done due diligence and realised Papa wouldn't be able to pay it back? Or was that Ferrantelli's intention all along—to take the *castello* off us?'

Bruno leaned forward in his chair with a sigh. 'Your father was a good man, Artie, but he wasn't good at managing finances, especially since the accident. There have been a lot of expenses, as you know, with running the estate since he came home from hospital. Your mother was the one with the financial clout to keep things in the black, but of course, after she died in the accident, it naturally fell to him. Unfortunately, he didn't always listen to advice from his accountants and financial advisors.'

He gave a rueful movement of his lips and continued.

'I'm sure I wouldn't be the first person to tell you how much the accident changed him. He fired his last three accountants because they told him things had to change. Luca Ferrantelli's offer of financial help has meant you could nurse your father here until he passed away, but now of course, unless you can find the money to pay off the mortgage, it will remain in Luca's possession.'

Over her dead body, it would. No way was she handing over her family's home without a fight, even if it would be a David and Goliath mismatch. Artie would find some way of winning.

She *had* to.

Artie did her best to ignore the beads of sweat forming between her shoulder blades. The drumbeat of panic in her chest. The hammering needles behind her eyeballs. The sense of the floor beneath her feet pitching like a paper boat riding a tsunami. 'When and where did Papa meet with Signor Ferrantelli? I've been Papa's full-time carer for the last ten years and don't recall Signor Ferrantelli ever coming here to see him.'

'Maybe he came one day while you were out.'

Out? Artie didn't go *out.*

She wasn't like other people, who could walk out of their homes and meet up with friends. It was impossible for her to be around more than one or two people at a time. Three was very definitely a crowd.

'Maybe...' Artie looked down at the papers again, conscious of warmth filling her cheeks. Her social anxiety was far more effective than a maximum-security prison. She hadn't been outside the *castello* walls since she was fifteen.

Ten years.

A decade.

Two fifths of her life.

As far as she knew, it wasn't common knowledge that she suffered from social anxiety. Her father's dependence on her had made it easy to disguise her fear of crowds. She had relished the role of looking after him. It had given her life a purpose, a focus. She had mostly avoided meeting people when they came to the *castello* to visit her father. She stayed in the background until they left. But barely anyone but her father's doctor and physical therapists had come during the last year or two of his life. Compassion fatigue had worn out his so-called friends. And now that the money had run dry, she could see why they had drifted away, one by one. There wasn't anyone she could turn to. Having been home schooled since her mid-teens, she had lost contact with her school friends. Friends wanted you to socialise with them and that she could never do, so they, too, had drifted away.

She had no friends of her own other than Rosa, the house-keeper.

Artie took a deep breath and blinked to clear her clouded vision. The words in front of her confirmed her worst fears. Her home was mortgaged to the hilt. There was no way a bank would lend her enough funds to get the *castello* out of Luca Ferrantelli's hands. The only job she had ever had was as her father's carer. From fifteen to twenty-five she had taken care of his every need. She had no formal qualifications, no skills other than her embroidery hobby.

She swallowed and pushed the papers back across the desk.

'What about my mother's trust fund? Isn't there enough left for me to pay off the mortgage?'

'There's enough for you to live on for the short-term but not enough to cover the money owed.'

Artie's heart began to beat like a wounded frog. 'How long have I got?' It sounded like a terminal diagnosis, which in some ways it was. She couldn't imagine her life without Castello Mireille. It was her home. Her base. Her anchor.

Her entire world.

Bruno Rossi shuffled the papers back into a neat pile. 'A year or two. But even if you were by some chance to raise finance to keep the estate, the place needs considerable maintenance. Costly maintenance. The storm damage last year showed how vulnerable the *castello* is. The north wing's roof still needs some work, not to mention the conservatory. It will cost millions of euros to—'

'Yes, yes, I know.' Artie pushed back her chair and smoothed her damp palms down her thighs. The *castello* was crumbling around her—she saw evidence of it every single day. But moving out of her home was unthinkable. Impossible.

She literally *couldn't* do it.

Panic tiptoed over her skin like thousands of tiny ants wearing stilettoes. Pressure built in her chest—a crushing weight pushing against her lungs so she couldn't take another breath. She wrapped her arms around her middle, fighting to hold off a full-blown panic attack. She hadn't had one for a while but the threat was always lurking in the murky shadows of her consciousness. It had followed her like a malevolent ghost ever since she came home from hospital from the accident that killed her mother and left her father in a wheelchair.

An accident that wouldn't have occurred if it hadn't been for *her*.

The lawyer cleared his throat. 'There's something else...' The formal quality of his tone changed and another shiver skittered down Artie's spine.

She straightened her shoulders and cupped her elbows with her hands, hoping for a cool and dignified stance but falling way too short. 'W-what?'

'Signor Ferrantelli has proposed a plan for you to repay him. If you fulfil his terms, you will regain full ownership of the *castello* within six months.'

Artie's eyebrows shot up along with her heart rate. And her anxiety grew razorblade wings and flapped frantically against her stomach lining like frenzied bats. How could she ever repay those mortgage payments in such a short space of time? What on earth did he require her to do? 'A plan? What sort of plan?' Her voice came out high and strained like an overused squeaky toy.

'He didn't authorise me to discuss it with you. He insists on speaking to you in person first.' Bruno pushed back his chair, further demonstrating his unwillingness to reveal anything else. 'Signor Ferrantelli has requested a meeting with you in his Milan office nine a.m. sharp, on Monday, to discuss your options.'

Options? What possible options could there be? None she wanted to think about in any detail. Ice-cold dread slithered into her belly. What nefarious motives could Luca Ferrantelli have towards her? A woman he had never met? And what was with his drill sergeant commands?

Nine a.m. Sharp. In his office. In Milan.

Luca Ferrantelli sounded like a man who issued orders and expected them to be obeyed without question. But there was no way she could go to Milan. Not on Monday. Not any day. She couldn't get as far as the front gate without triggering crippling, stomach-emptying, mind-scattering panic.

Artie released her arms from around her body and gripped the back of the nearest chair. Her heart was racing like it was preparing for the Olympics. 'Tell him to meet me here. It's not convenient for me to go to Milan. I don't drive and, from what you've just told me, I can't afford a taxi or even an Uber.'

'Signor Ferrantelli is a busy man. He expressly told me to tell you he—'

Artie stiffened her spine and raised her chin and ground her teeth behind her cool smile. 'Tell him to meet me here, nine a.m. sharp, on Monday. Or not meet with me at all.'

Luca Ferrantelli drove his Maserati through the rusty entrance gates of Castello Mireille on Monday morning. The *castello* was like something out of a Grimm brothers' fairy tale. The centuries-old ivy-clad stone building was surrounded by gardens that looked like they hadn't been tended for years, with overgrown hedges, unpruned roses, weed-covered pathways and ancient trees that stood like gnarly sentries. The *castello* had loads of potential—years of running his late father's property development company had taught him how to spot a diamond in the rough.

And speaking of diamonds...

He glanced at the velvet box on the seat next to him containing his late grandmother's engagement ring, and inwardly smiled. Artemisia Bellante would make the perfect temporary bride. Her father, Franco, had emailed Luca a photo of his daughter shortly before he died, asking Luca to make sure she was looked after once he was gone. The photo had planted a seed in Luca's mind—a seed that had taken root and sprouted and blossomed until all he could think about was meeting her— to offer her a way out of her present circumstances. Young, innocent, sheltered—she was exactly the sort of young woman his conservative grandfather would deem suitable as a Ferrantelli bride.

Time was rapidly running out on convincing his grandfather to accept the chemo he so desperately needed. Luca had a small window of opportunity to get Nonno to change his mind. Luca would do anything—even marry a poverty-stricken heiress— to make sure his elderly and frail *nonno* could live a few more precious years. After all, it was his fault his grandfather had lost the will to live. Didn't he owe Nonno some measure of comfort, given how Luca had torn apart the Ferrantelli family?

A vision of Luca's father, Flavio, and older brother, Angelo, drifted into his mind. Their lifeless bodies pulled from the surf due to his reckless behaviour as a teenager. His reckless behaviour and their love for him—a lethal, deadly combination. Two lives cut short because of him. Two lives and their potential wasted, and his mother and grandparents' happiness permanently, irrevocably destroyed. No one had been the same since that terrible day. No one.

Luca blinked to clear away the vision and gripped the steering wheel with white-knuckled force. He couldn't bring his father and brother back. He couldn't undo the damage he had caused to his mother and Nonna and Nonno. His grandmother had died a year ago and since then, his grandfather had lost the will to live. Nonno was refusing treatment for his very treatable cancer, and if he didn't receive chemotherapy soon he would die. So far, no amount of talking, lecturing, cajoling or bribing or begging on Luca's part had helped changed his grandfather's mind.

But Luca had a plan and he intended to carry it out no matter what. He would bring home a fresh-faced young bride to give hope to his grandfather that the Ferrantelli family line would continue well into the future.

Even if that was nothing but a fairy tale.

Artie watched Luca Ferrantelli's showroom-perfect deep blue Maserati come through the *castello* gates like a prowling lion. The low purr of the engine was audible even here in the formal sitting room. The car's tinted windows made it impossible for her to get a proper glimpse of his face, but the car's sleek profile and throaty growls seemed like a representation of his forthright personality.

Didn't they say a person's choice of car told you a lot about them?

Artie already knew as much as she wanted to know. *More*

than she wanted to know. That would teach her for spending the weekend trawling over the internet for any mention of him. Her research had revealed him as a flagrant playboy who brokered property deals and broke female hearts all over the globe. Barely a week went past without a gossip page featuring Luca Ferrantelli with a star-struck sylph-like blonde draped on his arm.

The powerful sports car came to a halt at the front of the *castello*. Artie sucked in a breath as the driver's door opened, her heart giving a sudden kick, her eyes widening as a vision of potent, athletic maleness unfolded from behind the wheel. The internet photos hadn't done him justice. How could it be possible to be so spectacularly attractive? Her pulse fluttered as if someone had injected her veins with thousands of butterflies.

The good-looks fairy godmother had certainly excelled herself when it came to Luca Ferrantelli. Six foot four, lean and athletic, with wavy black hair that was casually styled in a just-out-of-bed or just-combed-with-his-fingers manner, he was the epitome of heart-stopping handsome. Even though she was looking at him from a distance, Artie's heart was stopping and starting like a spluttering engine. How was she going to be when he was in the same room as her? Breathing the same air? Within touching distance?

As if Luca Ferrantelli sensed her gaze on him, he took off his aviator-style sunglasses and locked gazes with her. Something sprang open in her chest and she suddenly couldn't breathe. She quickly stepped away from the window and leaned back against the adjacent wall, clutching a hand to her pulsing throat, heat pouring into her cheeks. She had to get a grip. And fast. The last thing she wanted to do was appear gauche and unsophisticated, but, given she had been out of society for so long, she was at a distinct disadvantage. He was the poster boy for living in the fast lane. She was a wallflower who hadn't been seen in public for a decade.

It was some minutes before the housekeeper, Rosa, led Luca Ferrantelli to where Artie was waiting to receive him, but even so, her pulse was still leaping when the sitting room door opened. What if she became tongue-tied? What if she blushed? What if she broke out in a sweat and couldn't breathe? What if—?

'Signor Ferrantelli to see you,' Rosa announced with a formal nod in Luca's direction, before going out of the room and closing the door behind her with a click.

The first thing Artie noticed was his hair wasn't completely black. There were several strands of steel-grey sprinkled around his temples, which gave him a distinguished, wise-beyond-his-years air. His eyes were framed by prominent eyebrows and were an unusual hazel—a mix of brown and green flecks, fringed by thick, ink-black lashes. His amazing eyes were a kaleidoscope of colours one would normally find in a deeply shadowed forest. His jaw was cleanly shaven but the faint shadow of regrowth around his nose and mouth hinted at the potent male hormones working vigorously behind the scenes.

The atmosphere of the room changed with his presence, as if every stick of furniture, every fibre of carpet and curtains, every portrait frame and the faces of her ancestors contained within them took a collective breath. Stunned by his looks, his commanding presence, his take-charge energy.

'*Buongiorno*, Signorina Bellante.' Luca Ferrante's voice was like the sound of his car—low and deep, with a sexy rumble that did something strange to the base of her spine. So, too, did seeing his lips move when shaping and pronouncing her name. His lower lip was full and sensual, the top lip only marginally less so, and he had a well-defined philtrum ridge beneath his nose and a shallow cleft in his chin.

Artie slipped her hand into his outstretched one and a zap of electricity shot from her fingers to her core like a lightning bolt. His grip was strong and yet strangely gentle, his fingers long and tanned with a light dusting of dark masculine hair that ran over the backs of his hands and disappeared beneath the cuffs of his business shirt and jacket. Armani, at a guess. And his aftershave an equally intoxicating blend of citrus and spice and sophistication that teased her senses into a stupor.

'*Buongiorno*, Signor Ferrantelli.'

Artie aimed for cool politeness but sounded more like a star-struck teen in front of a Hollywood celebrity. She could feel warm colour blooming in her cheeks. Could feel her heart thumping like it was having some sort of medical crisis. Could feel her female hormones responding to his male ones with little tingles and pulses deep within her body.

Let go of his hand!

Her brain gave the command but her hand was trapped in some kind of weird stasis. It was as if her hand had a mind of its own and was enjoying being held by his warm, dry one, thank you very much. Enjoying it so much, she could feel every whorl of his skin as if it were being engraved, branded into hers.

Luca removed his hand from hers but his gaze kept hers tethered. She couldn't look away if she tried. Magnetic. Enthralling. Mesmerising. His eyes seemed to draw secrets from within her while concealing his own.

'Firstly, allow me to offer my condolences on the recent passing of your father.'

'*Grazie.*'

She stepped back and waved her still-tingling hand in the direction of the sofa. 'Would you like to sit down? I'll call Rosa to bring in coffee. How do you take it?'

'Black and strong.'

Of course you do.

Artie pressed the intercom pad and summoned Rosa, surreptitiously eyeing him while she requested coffee from the housekeeper. Everything about Luca Ferrantelli was strong. Strong, determined jaw. Strong, intelligent eyes. A strong and muscled body that hinted at a man who wasn't afraid of pushing himself to the limits of endurance. A man who set goals and didn't let anyone or anything stop him from achieving them.

Artie ended the intercom conversation with Rosa and sat on

the nearest sofa, and only then did Luca take the seat opposite. He laid one arm along the back of the sofa in a casually relaxed pose she privately envied. She had to place her hands on the tops of her thighs to stop her knees from trembling. Not from fear but from a strange sense of fizzing excitement. She tried not to stare at his powerfully muscled thighs, his well-formed biceps, the flat plane of his stomach, but her gaze kept drifting over him of its own volition. Drinking in the planes and contours of his face, wondering what was going on behind the screen of his gaze, wondering if his firm lips would soften when he kissed…

Artie blinked and sat up straighter on the sofa, crossing her legs to try and control the wayward urges going on in her lower body. What was wrong with her? He had barely exchanged more than half a dozen words with her and she was undressing him with her eyes. She curled her hands into balls on her lap and fixed a smile on her lips. 'So, how was your drive from Milan? I hope it didn't inconvenience you too much to come here?' Who said she couldn't do small talk?

Luca's half-smile and his glittering forest floor eyes made something slip sideways in her stomach. 'It didn't inconvenience me at all. But we both know that was your intention, was it not?'

Artie forced herself to hold his penetrating gaze. 'Signor Ferrantelli, I am not the sort of woman to jump when a man says jump.'

The dark gleam in his eyes intensified and a hot trickle of something liquid spilled deep in her core. 'You may have no choice, given I now own nine tenths of Castello Mireille, unless you can buy me out within the next twenty-four hours.' There was a don't-mess-with-me warning in his tone that made her want to mess with him to see what would happen.

Artie disguised a swallow, her heart picking up its pace. 'My father's lawyer informed me of the unusual financial arrangement you made with my father. One wonders why you didn't buy all of it off him while you had the chance.'

His gaze was unwavering. 'He was a dying man who deserved some dignity in the last months of his life.'

Artie gave a cynical smile while her blood boiled in her veins and roaring anger bubbled in her chest. 'Do you expect me to believe you felt some measure of compassion for him? Even while you were systematically taking his home away from him ancient stone by ancient stone?'

Luca didn't change his casual posture on the sofa but a ripple of tension passed across his features, tightening his jaw, flaring his nose, hardening his eyes. 'Your father approached me late last year for help. I gave it to him. It was a straightforward business deal. And now I have come to collect on my investment.'

Artie shot up from the sofa as if someone had pressed an ejector switch. She glared at him with the full force of her fury, chest heaving like she had just completed a marathon without training first. 'You can't take my home off me. I won't allow it.'

Luca Ferrantelli's gaze was diamond-hard. 'My intention is to give the *castello* back to you—after a time. And for a price.'

Something heavy landed on the floor of her belly. 'What price? You must know I can't possibly raise the necessary funds to pay out the mortgage?'

He held her gaze in a lock that made the backs of her knees tingle. 'I will erase the debt and give the deeds of the *castello* back if you agree to be my wife for six months.'

CHAPTER TWO

ARTIE STARED AT him in open-mouthed shock, her heart pounding like it was going to punch its way out of her chest. Had she heard him correctly? Was her imagination playing tricks on her? Putting words in his mouth he couldn't possibly have said? Had he said *wife?* W.I.F.E? The woman a man chose to spend the rest of his life with in a contract of love and commitment?

'Your...*what?*'

He hooked one ankle over his bent knee, his finger idly flicking the zipper toggle on his Italian leather boot. *Flick. Flick. Flick.* So relaxed. So casual. So confident and in control it was maddening.

'You heard—I need a wife for six months. On paper.' The note of self-assurance in his voice made her dislike of him go up another notch.

On paper? Her eyes widened while her feminine ego shrank. She might not be a social butterfly or model material, but as far as she knew she hadn't broken any mirrors lately. 'You mean a marriage of convenience?'

'But of course.'

Why 'but of course'? It was ridiculous to be affronted by his unusual proposal, but what woman wanted to be dismissed outright as a potential lover?

But why would he want you? the voice of her conscience sneered. *Who would want you? You killed your mother, you maimed your father—all for the sake of going to a stupid party.*

Rosa, the housekeeper, came in at that moment carrying a tray with cups and saucers and a steaming percolator of freshly brewed coffee. Rosa handed Luca a cup before turning to give one to Artie. But as soon as Rosa left the room Artie put her coffee on a side table, not trusting her shaking hands to bring the cup safely to her tombstone-dry mouth. Her conscience was right. Why would he want to marry *her?* Why would anyone?

Luca lowered his crossed ankle to the floor and, reaching for his cup, took a sip of his coffee as if this was a regular old coffee morning. Not one in which he had delivered a bombshell proposal to a virtual stranger.

'May I ask, why me?' Artie inserted into the silence. 'You surely have no shortage of far more suitable candidates for the role.' Socialites. Supermodels. Not a shut-in like her.

Luca put his cup back in its saucer with unnerving and methodical precision. It hinted at the man he was—self-assured, focused, confident he could get anything he set his mind to. 'Your father was the one who planted the idea in my—'

'My *father?*' Artie choked over the words.

'He was concerned about your future, given how badly his financial situation had become and how it would impact on you long-term. He wanted you well provided for, so I devised a plan to make sure we both got what we wanted. You get to keep the *castello.* I get a temporary wife.'

Artie clasped her hands together, trying to keep control of her galloping pulse. Her legs were threatening to give way beneath her but she was reluctant to sit back down, because it would bring her closer to him than she wanted to be. 'But why would you want me to be your...your wife?' Saying the word felt strange on her lips and yet her mind ran with the image it evoked. Images popped into her head of her wearing a white dress and standing next to Luca at an altar. His arms going around her, drawing him closer to his muscled body. His mouth slowly coming down to seal hers in a kiss...

'You're exactly the sort of woman my grandfather would approve of as my bride,' Luca said, his gaze drifting to her mouth as if he was having the same thoughts as her. About kissing, touching, needing, wanting.

Artie arched her eyebrows. 'Oh, really? Why is that?'

His lips curved in a satirical smile. 'You're the sweet, homespun type—or so your father led me to believe.'

What else had her father told him about her? She had made him promise not to tell anyone about her social anxiety. Had he broken that promise? She was pretty sure he hadn't told Bruno Rossi, the lawyer, otherwise he would have mentioned it yesterday. It was her shameful little secret. Her father's dependence on her since the accident had made it easy for her to hide it from others, but with him no longer here...

Artie kept her expression neutral but on the inside, she was seething. How dared her father set her up for auction to this incorrigible man? It was positively feudal. And why did Luca Ferrantelli want to please his grandfather? What was at stake if he didn't? 'Look, Signor Ferrantelli, I think there's been some sort of misunderstanding between you and my father. I can't think of a single set of circumstances in which I would ever consider marrying you.'

Luca's mocking smile broadened. 'Perhaps not as sweet and biddable as your father said.' His tone was musing, the lazy sweep of his gaze assessing. 'But, no matter. You will do.'

She straightened her shoulders and sent him a look so frosty icicles could have formed on her eyelashes. 'Please leave. We have nothing left to discuss.'

Luca remained seated on the sofa, still in that annoyingly relaxed pose. But his eyes contained a glint of intractability that made her wonder if she was wise to lock horns with him. She had no experience in dealing with powerful men. She had no experience, period. Any fight between them would be like Tinkerbell trying to take down a Titan.

'The way I see it, you don't have any choice. You will lose the *castello* if you don't agree to marry me.'

Artie ground her teeth and clenched her fists, anger flicking along her nerve endings like a power surge of electricity. It was all she could do not to slap him. She pictured herself doing it—landing her palm against his lean and chiselled jaw with a resounding slap. Imagining how his rougher skin would feel under the soft skin of her palm. Imagining how he might grasp her by the wrist and haul her closer and slam his mouth down on hers in a passionate kiss...

Eek! She shouldn't have watched *Gone with the Wind* so many times.

She stretched out one arm and pointed her index finger towards the door. 'Get. Out.'

Luca raised his long, lean, athletic frame from the sofa with leonine grace and came to stand in front of her. She fought not to step back, determined to show he didn't intimidate her with his commanding, disturbing presence. Even though he did. Big time. She had to crane her neck to maintain eye-contact, and give her traitorous body a stern talking-to for reacting to his closeness with a hitch of her breath and an excited leap of her pulse.

'I'll give you twenty-four hours to consider my proposal.'

Artie raised her chin to a defiant height. 'I've already considered it and flatly turned it down. I'll give you the same answer tomorrow, so don't waste your time or mine by coming back.'

His lazy smile ignited a light behind his eyes as if her refusal had thrilled rather than disappointed him. 'You have a lot to lose, Signorina Bellante.' He swung his gaze around the room before bringing it back to meet hers. 'Are you sure you want to throw all this away for the sake of your pride?'

'Pride has nothing to do with my decision. If and when I marry, it will be for love.'

The loud cackling of her conscience rang in Artie's ears like clanging bells.

Marry for love? You? Who's going to love you?

His eyes flicked to her mouth and lingered there for a heart-stopping moment. 'You love this place, do you not? Your family's home for how many centuries? If that's not marrying for love, I don't know what is.' The deep, mellifluous tone of his voice had a mesmerising effect on her. She had to fight to stay focused on resisting him. It would be so easy to say yes. To have all her problems solved by agreeing to his plan—even if by doing so it threw up new ones. Dangerous ones. Exciting ones.

Artie pressed her lips together. 'Of course I love it. It's the only home I've ever known.'

The only home I can ever know.

His eyes meshed with hers. Dark, mysterious, unknowable. 'If you don't marry me, you will lose it. And I won't lose a wink of sleep about taking it off you. Business is business. I don't let emotions cloud the issue. Think about it, hmm?'

She tried to ignore the cynical gleam in his eyes. Tried to ignore the slippery eels of panic writhing in her belly. Tried not to think about her home being lost for ever. Of it being made into a plush hotel with strangers walking through every room, occupying every private space, every special corner made into a flashy showpiece instead of a private sanctuary where her most precious memories were housed. 'You can't force me out of my home. I have some rights, surely?'

'Your father signed those over to me when he begged for my help.'

Artie raised her chin, summoning every bit of willpower she possessed to stand up to his monumental ego. 'You came here expecting me to say yes, didn't you? Does anyone ever say no to you?'

'Not often.' He reached inside his jacket pocket and took a velvet box and held it out to her in the middle of his palm. 'This might help you come to a decision.'

Artie reared back from the box like it was a cockroach. 'You think you can bribe me with diamonds?'

'Not just diamonds.' He flicked open the velvet box with his thumb and a glittering sapphire and diamond engagement ring winked at her. 'Take it. Try it on for size.'

Artie brought her gaze back to his, her mouth tightly compressed. 'No, thank you.'

There was a beat or two of silence.

Luca snapped the lid of the ring box closed and placed it on the coffee table. If she had offended him with her point-blank refusal then he didn't show it in his expression.

'I'll be back for your decision tomorrow. *Ciao.*'

He gave a mock bow, and without another word he walked out of the salon, closing the door on his exit.

Artie let out a scalding breath, her body sagging with the aftershocks of too much cortisol racing through her system. She sat back on the sofa before she fell down, her legs shaking, her hands trembling, her mind whirling.

How could this be happening? It was like something out of a period drama. She was being blackmailed into marrying a man she didn't know in order to save her home. What had her father been thinking to plant such a ridiculous idea in Luca Ferrantelli's head? This was nothing but a business deal to Luca but it was her home that was on the line. And not just her home— her security. Her future. She would have nothing to fall back on if she didn't have the *castello*.

It was her heritage.

Her birthright.

Her safety.

How dared Luca Ferrantelli dangle it before her like a plump, juicy carrot in front of a dumb donkey?

She was *not* going to be a pawn in his game. If he thought she was so desperate for a husband she would say yes to the first man who asked her, then he had better think again.

Rosa came back into the salon to collect the coffee cups.

'Your guest left, then. What did he want?' Her eyes went to the ring box on the coffee table. 'Ooh, what's this?'

Artie got up from the sofa and speared her fingers through her hair. 'You wouldn't believe me if I told you. *Grr.* I don't know how I stopped myself from slapping him. He's the most detestable man I've ever met.'

Rosa's look was wry. 'Like you've met heaps of men. Just saying…' She prised open the lid of the ring box and whistled through her teeth. '*Mamma mia.* That is what I call an engagement ring.'

Artie snatched the box off her and snapped it shut and clutched it tightly in her hand. 'If he's representative of the men outside the *castello* walls, then I'm glad I haven't met heaps of them. Do you know what he said? He wants to marry me. For six months. A paper marriage or some such nonsense. And do you know what's worse? Papa put the idea in his head. Luca Ferrantelli will only give me back the *castello*, debt-free, if I marry him.'

'And you said?'

Artie frowned. 'What do you think I said? I said an emphatic, don't-ask-me-again *no.*'

Rosa loaded the coffee percolator onto the tray with implacable calm. 'Would you say yes if the marriage wasn't on paper?'

'No, of course not.'

'Then what's the problem? Don't you trust him to keep his word?'

Artie put her hands on her hips. She could feel the ring box digging into the soft skin of her palm but did her best to ignore it. She would *not* look at it again. She would not look at those sparkling diamonds and that impossibly blue sapphire and imagine a life free of financial stress.

She would not think of being Luca Ferrantelli's bride.

She. Would. Not.

'Are you seriously telling me I should accept his crazy proposal? Are you out of your mind?' Artie narrowed her gaze and added, 'Wait—do you know something about this? Did Papa talk to you about his scheme to marry me off to a stranger to settle his debts?'

Rosa picked up the coffee tray and held it in front of her body, her expression set in her customary pragmatic lines. 'Your father was worried about you in the weeks before he died— about what would happen to you once he was gone. You gave up your life for him these last few years. He shouldn't have asked it of you and nor should he have run the estate the way he did, but he was never the same after the accident. But you have a chance now to turn things around. To reclaim your life and your inheritance. And Luca Ferrantelli can't be much of a stranger to your father, otherwise he wouldn't have gone to him for help. Why would he have asked Luca if he didn't trust him to do the right thing by you? Six months isn't long. And as long as everything is legally sound, you've got nothing to lose and everything to gain.'

Artie tossed the ring box on the sofa. 'I can't believe you think I should marry that odious man.'

'You can't stay locked away here for ever, Artie. It's not healthy. Your father desperately wanted you to move on with your—'

Artie blew out a breath of exasperation. 'I *can't* leave. I thought you of all people understood. You've seen me at my worst. I feel paralysed with anxiety as soon as I get to the front gates. It's not as if I want to be like this. I can't help it.'

Nothing had helped. Medication. Home visits by a psychologist. Meditation and mindfulness. Nothing had freed her from the curse of her phobia. She had resigned herself to a lifetime of living in isolation.

What else could she do but accept her lot in life?

Rosa shifted her lips from side to side, her dark brown eyes serious. 'You'll have no choice but to leave if the *castello* is sold out from under you.'

The thought of leaving her home, having it taken it away

from her by force, made her skin pepper with goosebumps and her heart pound with dread. She had tried so many times to imagine a life outside of Castello Mireille. But it was like a pipedream that never could be realised. It was completely and utterly out of her reach.

Artie glanced at the ring box on the sofa, her heart giving a funny little hopscotch. 'Luca Ferrantelli is an international playboy. He changes lovers every week. What sort of husband is he going to be?'

'You'll never know if you don't marry him, *si*?' Rosa said. 'Convince him to marry you here at the *castello*—you won't have to leave at all. It's a marriage in name only so there won't be a honeymoon. In six months, you'll have full ownership again. Plus, a gorgeous ring to keep. Problem solved.'

Eek! She hadn't even thought about a honeymoon. Luca wanted a bride but not *that* sort of bride...or did he? Her lower body tingled at the thought of his hands touching her. His mouth pressing against hers. His body doing things to hers she had only fantasised about and never experienced.

Artie pressed her fingers against her temples once Rosa had left the room. What crazy parallel universe had she stumbled into that even the housekeeper thought she should marry Luca Ferrantelli? She let out a ragged breath and looked around the salon. The black velvet ring box on the white sofa seemed to signify the either/or choice she had to make. The sofa cushions still contained the impression of Luca's tall athletic body. The air still smelt faintly of his citrus and spice aftershave. Her heartrate was still not quite back to normal.

Would it ever be again?

Meeting Luca Ferrantelli had jolted her into an intense awareness of her femininity. Her body felt alive—tinglingly alive in a way it never had before. Her mind might have decided Luca was the most obnoxious man she'd ever met but her body hadn't got the memo. It was operating off script, responding to him in ways she had never thought possible. Every appraising look he cast her way, every smouldering twinkle in his hazel eyes, every lazy smile, had heated her blood and upped her pulse and fried her brain until even *she* was thinking about accepting his proposal.

Artie walked back to the sofa and picked up the ring box. She curled her fingers around it, telling herself she would put it in the safe until Luca came back tomorrow. But suddenly her fingers were prising open the lid. The ring glinted at her as if to say, *Put me on.*

It was the most beautiful ring she had ever seen. She might not be able to window shop like other people but she did plenty of shopping and browsing online. She ran her fingertip over the top of the arabesque setting, stunned by the ring's exquisite design and breathtaking quality. Money was no object to filthy rich men like Luca Ferrantelli. He thought he could dangle a ridiculously expensive diamond in front of her nose and she would accept his stupid proposal without question.

She stared at the ring some more, turning the box this way so she could see how the diamonds picked up the light coming in from the windows. It was probably too big for her anyway. Artie pulled her lower lip inside her mouth. What would it hurt to try it on just the once? No one had to know. She hadn't been in a bricks-and-mortar jewellery shop since she was a teenager, when her mother bought her a pair of earrings. This was her chance to do what others took for granted.

She took the ring out of the box and set the box down on the table again. She slipped the ring on her left ring finger, pushing it past her second knuckle. It was kind of weird that it was a perfect fit. She couldn't stop staring at it. The sheer brilliance of the diamonds and the deep blue of the sapphire stole her breath clean away.

'Don't get too comfortable there,' Artie addressed the ring. 'I'm not keeping you.'

The ring glinted back at her as if to say, *Are you sure about that?*

Artie took off the ring, placed it back in its velvet box and closed the lid with a definitive snap. She held the box in the middle of her palm, glaring at it like it contained a lethal insect. 'I'm not looking at you again, do you hear me?' She left the box on the coffee table and went to where Rosa was working in the kitchen.

Rosa looked up from where she was preparing vegetables for soup. 'Did the ring fit?'

Artie pursed her lips. 'What makes you think I tried it on?'

Rosa gave a knowing smile. 'It's not every day a girl gets to try on a ring as stunning as that.'

Artie frowned. 'I thought you'd be on my side. Aren't you the least bit concerned about my situation?'

'I'm deeply concerned you're going to lose everything if you don't do what Luca Ferrantelli says,' Rosa said. 'You could do a lot worse than him for a husband. He's handsome and rich and will no doubt spoil you, if that ring is any indication.'

'What if I don't want to be spoilt?'

Rosa picked up an onion and held it in her palm. 'See this? Men like Luca Ferrantelli are like this onion. You're only looking at the surface of him—the façade he shows the world. Peel back the layers and you'll see the man behind the mask. You never know—you might be pleasantly surprised at what you find.'

'And how will I know if peeling back his layers reduces me to tears like that onion will?'

'That's a risk we all take when we get close to someone.' Rosa sliced into the onion with a knife. 'And God knows, you're never going to get close to anyone living on your own here. This is a lifeline and you'd be a fool not to take it.'

Maybe Rosa was right, because, if Artie didn't marry Luca Ferrantelli she would have to leave the *castello*. Permanently.

She couldn't allow that to happen.

No matter what.

But how could she work this to her advantage? What could Luca do for her in return? Apart from buying her a stunningly beautiful engagement ring that just begged to come out of that box and sit proudly on her finger. Artie went back to the salon and picked up the velvet box. She told herself she was going to put it in the safe until Luca returned the following day. But before she could stop herself, she opened the box and took the ring out and placed it back on her finger. She promised herself she would only wear it for a couple of hours, just for the heck of it. Then, once she got tired of it, she would put it back in the box and hand it back to Luca tomorrow with a firm, *Thanks, but no, thanks.*

She couldn't possibly marry him...*could she?*

Later that evening, Artie was doing her embroidery when she suddenly realised the ring wasn't on her finger. She jumped off the sofa and searched around the scatter cushions, her heart racing. Where was it? Had it fallen off somewhere? Oh, God. Oh, God. Oh, God. The ring was worth a fortune. Luca would be furious if she lost his blasted ring. He had no right to buy her such an expensive ring. Her stomach pitched. Would he want her to replace it? Yes, he would.

Rosa came in at that point. 'Look, I know things are bad financially but surely you don't have to search the back of the sofa for loose change?'

Artie swung around to face her, eyes wide in panic. 'I can't find Luca's wretched engagement ring!'

Rosa frowned. 'Didn't you put it in the safe?'

'No, I stupidly put it on for a couple of hours.' Artie tossed all the scatter cushions on the floor and began lifting off the sofa cushions to no avail. 'What am I going to do?'

Rosa joined in the search. 'You'll have to retrace your steps. Where have you been in the last few hours? Did you go outside to the garden?'

'No, I've only been indoors.'

Artie emptied her embroidery basket onto the floor—thimbles, reels of thread, needles going everywhere. The disorder on the floor in front of her was the same as inside her mind. Chaos. Tangled thoughts. Prickling conscience.

'It must be here somewhere. Oh, God, how could I lose it?'

She stuffed the embroidery items haphazardly back in the basket, pricking her finger with one of her needles.

'Ouch.' She stuck her finger in her mouth and sucked up the droplets of blood. She removed her finger from her mouth and gave Rosa a baleful look. 'He had no right to give me such an expensive ring. I'll have to marry him now.'

But deep down you want to, don't you? Marriage to Luca Ferrantelli just might give you some control over your life. The control you've been seeking for a long time. Money. Freedom. Not to mention a wickedly handsome 'paper' husband...

Rosa bent down and carefully sorted through Artie's basket for a moment. 'Ah, here it is.' She handed Artie the engagement ring. 'You'd better put it back on and leave it on until you give it back to Signor Ferrantelli.'

Give it back?

Lose her one chance of taking back control of her life?

Lose her home?

Artie slipped the ring back on her finger, her thoughts finally untangling. 'I'm not giving it back. Maybe you're right. This is my chance—maybe my only chance—to take control of my life. I'm going to make this work for me. On my terms. It's only for six months—what have I got to lose?'

Rosa raised one brow. 'Your heart?'

Artie set her mouth in a determined line. 'Not going to happen. This is a business deal. If Luca Ferrantelli can keep his emotions out of this, then so can I.'

Luca could not remember looking forward to a meeting more than returning to the Castello Mireille the following day to see Artemisia Bellante. Something about her intrigued him in a way few people did. He'd expected her to be biddable and submissive and instead found her spirited defiance a refreshing change from all the sycophants who surrounded him, pandering to his every whim. He'd found it so hard to take his eyes off her—slim, but with generous curves in all the right places, flashing brown eyes, wild, curly dark brown hair and a ski-slope nose, a stubborn chin and a cherry-red mouth—he'd almost offered her a real marriage. Only joking. No real marriages for him. Ever. He neither wanted nor needed love from a partner. Love was a reckless emotion that had the potential to cause immeasurable harm. He'd had a ringside seat to see just how much harm.

But a six-month hands-off arrangement to give his grandfather the motivation to get chemo was definitely doable. He hadn't been able to save his father or brother but he could save his grandfather. And marrying Artemisia Bellante was the way to do it. The only way.

In all their phone and email conversations, Franco Bellante had told him Artemisia was shy around men. Luca hadn't seen too much shyness. He'd seen sass and spirit and a damped down sensuality that was irresistibly attractive. He'd seen her surreptitious glances at his mouth and felt the supercharged energy in the air when their gazes collided. Did that mean she would be interested in tweaking the terms of their paper marriage?

Don't even think about it.

Luca knew how to control his impulses. He had learned the hard way not to rush into things without careful consideration first. Artemisia Bellante might be the most alluring young woman he'd met in a long time but a deal was a deal and his word was his word. Their paper marriage would last six months and no longer. Nonno's doctors had given him no more than a year to live if he didn't start treatment soon. The clock was ticking on the old man's life and Luca was determined to present him with the perfect choice of bride.

The housekeeper led him to the same salon as yesterday, where Artemisia was waiting for him standing by the windows. Her hands were clasped behind her back, her posture guarded. She looked regal and elegant even though she was wearing casual clothes—blue jeans and a white shirt with a patterned scarf draped artfully around her neck. The jeans highlighted the shapely curves of her hips and the white shirt brought out the creamy tone of her skin. Her chin was at a proud height, her deep brown eyes shining with unmistakable dislike.

Hot and heavy desire tingled in his groin. Her dislike of him was a bigger turn-on than he'd expected. Dating had become a little too easy for him lately—a little too boring and predictable. But nothing about Artemisia Bellante was boring or predictable.

Rein it in, buddy. You're not going there, remember?

Luca gave a sweeping bow. '*Buongiorno*, Artemisia. Have you made your decision?'

Her indrawn breath was like the hiss of a cornered cat. 'I have.'

'And?' Luca was only conscious of holding his breath when his lungs began to tighten. He wanted her as his bride. No one else was going to do. He *had* to have *her*. He couldn't explain his intractable stance other than that something about her ticked all the boxes.

She held his gaze with her icy one, her jaw set, her colour high. 'I will marry you.'

The relief that swept through him momentarily caught him off guard. It wasn't that he'd expected her to say no but somehow he hadn't realised until now how *much* he'd wanted her to say yes. 'Good. I'm glad you see the sense in doing so.'

Her eyebrows rose ever so slightly above her glittering eyes. 'However, I have some conditions on my acceptance of your offer.'

Luca was not one to allow people to push him around but something about her expression made him make an exception. She stirred him in a way he had never been stirred before. His blood heated with a backbeat of desire, his nostrils flaring to take in the flowery scent of her perfume. 'Go on.'

She unfolded her arms and smoothed her hands down the front of her thighs. He ran his gaze down the slim length of her legs and her neat calves. She was wearing light brown suede ankle boots that gave her an inch or two more height. But even with the benefit of heels, she still wouldn't make it to the top of his shoulder. But that wasn't the only thing she was wearing—his grandmother's engagement ring winked proudly, almost defiantly, on her left hand. The arabesque design chosen so lovingly by his *nonno* to give to the love of his life—Luca's grandmother—suited Artemisia's hand as if designed especially for her. A faint alarm bell sounded at the back of his mind. He would have to be extra careful to keep his emotions out of this arrangement. Their relationship was a business deal and nothing more. There was no point feeling a little sentimental about seeing his grandmother's ring on Artie's hand. There was nothing sentimental about his choice of engagement ring. Sure, he could have bought any other ring but he had deliberately used his *nonna*'s ring knowing it would add authenticity to his committed relationship status in the eyes of his grandfather.

It was his grandfather who was sentimental.

Not him.

'Won't you sit down?' Artie's tone was all cool politeness but her eyes were hard with bitterness.

Luca gestured to the sofa nearest her. 'Ladies first.'

Artie drew in another sharp breath and sat on the sofa, her hands clasped around her crossed knee, her plump mouth tightly set. 'So, I've decided to accept your offer on the proviso we're married here at the *castello*. A quiet wedding, minimal guests.'

It intrigued him why she wanted a low-key wedding. Didn't most young women want to be a princess for the day? He could think of at least half a dozen of his ex-lovers who had dropped enormous hints about their dream wedding. It had killed his interest in them stone-dead. 'Is there any particular reason why you want to be married here and not at one of the local churches?'

Her gaze didn't quite meet his but aimed for the top of his

left shoulder. 'My father's funeral was held here, so too was my mother's. It's where many of my ancestors are buried.'

'*Sì*, but a funeral is a little different from a wedding, is it not?'

Her clear brown gaze collided with his. 'Not from my perspective. This isn't a real marriage. I would be uncomfortable desecrating a church by saying vows neither of us intends to keep. It would be disrespectful. Nor do I want a big, flashy wedding with people I don't know and have nothing in common with attending. It would be a waste of money and effort.'

Luca didn't care where they were married as long as they were married. He only hoped Nonno would be well enough to be able to travel from his home in Tuscany, but, since Umbria was a neighbouring region, it wasn't a long journey—just over two hours' drive.

'Fine. We'll marry here. Leave the arrangements to me. I've already applied for a licence so we don't have to wait the six weeks normally required. Your father sent me a copy of your birth certificate and passport before he died. I took the liberty of getting things on the move.'

Her eyes widened and her mouth fell open. 'You were so sure I would accept? But you hadn't even met me in person until yesterday.'

He shrugged one shoulder. 'Your father showed me a photo and he talked about you a lot. I was satisfied you would be suitable.'

She uncrossed her legs and sprang off the sofa, moving some distance away. 'I would have thought a man in your position wouldn't have to resort to finding a mail-order bride.' Scorn underlined every word she spoke. 'What if I'd said no?'

Luca gave a slow smile. 'I would have found some way to change your mind.'

Her chin came up and her eyes flashed. 'I can't believe my father encouraged you in this ridiculous mission to acquire a wife. When did you meet with him? I've never seen you come here before yesterday and I barely left my father's side.'

'I visited your father when he was in hospital with pneumonia late last year. He talked you up so much it intrigued me. I was disappointed not to see you on one of my visits but he said you weren't keen on hospitals since the accident. We emailed or phoned after that.'

She bit her lip and looked away. 'Did he say anything else about me?'

'Just that you were shy and not much of a party girl.'

She gave a snort of humourless laughter. 'Yes, well, that's certainly true.'

Luca rose from the sofa and walked over to a row of picture frames on a sideboard. He picked up a photo taken when Artie was a child, sitting on her mother's knee. 'Your mother was very beautiful. She was English, *si*?'

'Y-yes…' There was a slight catch in her voice.

Luca put the photo back on the sideboard and turned to face her. 'It's hard to lose a parent in your teens, especially the same sex parent.' Harder still when you were the cause of their death. And the death of your only brother. The guilt never left him. It sat on his shoulder. It followed him. It prodded him. It never let him forget. It kept him awake at night. His own personal stalker, torturing him with the what-ifs and the if-onlys.

Her brown eyes met his. 'You lost your father and older brother when you were a teenager, didn't you?'

Luca knew there was still stuff about his father and brother's death online. Not so easy to come across these days but it was still there if you did a thorough enough search. It had been a big news story at the time due to his father's high profile in business circles.

He could still see the headlines now—*Property developer CEO and son and heir lost in heavy surf in Argentina.*

There had been nothing about Luca's role in their drowning and he only found out years later it was because his *nonno* had pulled some strings in order to protect him.

Another reason his marriage to Artie had to go ahead and soon. He owed his *nonno* peace in this last stage of his life.

'Yes. When I was thirteen.' He stripped his voice of all emotion—he could have been discussing the stock exchange instead of the worst day of his life.

'I'm sorry.' Artie waited a beat and added, 'Is your mother still alive?'

'Yes. She lives in New York now.'

'Has she remarried?'

'No.'

There was a silence.

Luca could have filled it with all the reasons why his mother no longer lived in Italy. Her unrelenting grief. His strained relationship with her that nothing he said or did could fix. The constant triggers being around him caused her. The empty hole in her life that nothing could fill. The hole he had created by his actions on that fateful day. He hadn't just lost his father and brother on that day—he'd lost his entire family as he'd known it. Even his grandparents—as caring and supportive as they tried to be—had been sideswiped by grief and became shadows of their former selves. His extended family—aunts, uncles, cousins—all of them had been affected by his actions that day.

'So, what changed your mind about marrying me?' Luca decided it was safer to stay on the topic of their upcoming marriage rather than drift into territory he wanted left well alone. 'Let me guess. Was it the engagement ring?'

She swallowed, her cheeks blooming with colour. 'In a way, yes.'

Luca hadn't taken her for a gold-digger but it was a damn fine ring. His eyes flicked to her left hand. 'It looks good on you. But I hope you don't mind it being second hand. It belonged to my grandmother. She left it to me in her will.'

Her eyes widened to the size of dinner plates. 'Your grandmother's? Oh, my goodness. Just as well I—' She bit her lip and shifted her gaze a fraction, the colour in her cheeks deepening.

'Just as well you...?' Luca prompted, intrigued by her cagey expression.

Her slim throat rose and fell over a swallow and her gaze slipped out of reach of his. 'I—I misplaced it for a couple of hours. But it's your fault for giving me such a ridiculously valuable ring. A priceless heirloom, for pity's sake. What on earth were you thinking? Of course, I'll give it back to you once the six months is up.'

'I don't want it back. It's a gift.'

Her gaze flicked back to his, shock written all over her features. 'I couldn't possibly keep it. It's worth a small fortune, not to mention the sentimental value.'

Luca shrugged. 'It's no skin off my nose what you do with it once our marriage is over. It's just a ring. I will have no further use for it after this. It means nothing to me.'

Her mouth tightened. 'Is there anything that means something to you other than making disgusting amounts of money?'

Luca slanted his mouth into a cynical smile. 'There isn't a law against being successful in business. Money opens a lot of doors.'

'I would imagine it closes others. How would you know if people liked you for you or for your wealth?'

'I'm a good judge of character. I soon weed out the timewasters and hangers-on.'

Her top lip curled and her eyes shone with loathing. 'Well, bully for you.'

CHAPTER THREE

ARTIE WOULDN'T HAVE admitted it even under torture, but she was getting off on sparring with Luca Ferrantelli. Every time they exchanged words, little bubbles of excitement trickled into her bloodstream. He was intelligent and quick-witted and charming and she had to keep on her toes to keep up with him.

She couldn't understand why he had given her his grandmother's engagement ring. *Eek!* Just as well she hadn't lost it. But he didn't seem all that attached to the stunning piece of jewellery, and yet she had fallen in love with it at first sight. Surely he had at least one sentimental bone in his body, or was everything just another business deal?

Luca's brief mention of his father and brother intrigued her. Mostly because he seemed reluctant to dwell on the subject. His expression had given little away, his flat, emotionless tone even less. But still, she sensed there was pain beneath the surface—deep pain that made him distance himself from it whenever he could.

Maybe Rosa was right—Luca Ferrantelli had more than a few layers to his personality that begged to be explored.

But Artie knew all too well about deep emotional pain. Talking about her mother, thinking about the accident and its aftermath sent her into a spiral of despair. Guilt was her constant companion. Wasn't it her fault her father had lost control of his finances? He hadn't been the same after the accident. Losing Artie's mother, and losing the use of his legs as well as an acquired brain injury, had meant he was not the same man—nor ever could be—and she was entirely to blame. Nothing Artie could do would ever change that. It was only fitting that she wed Luca Ferrantelli and reclaim her family's heritage.

It was her penance. The price she must pay. But she would make the best out of the situation by owning her choice to marry Luca rather than feel he had forced her hand.

'We need to discuss the honeymoon.' Luca's expression was inscrutable. 'Do you have somewhere you'd like to go?'

Honeymoon?

Artie widened her eyes so far she thought they might pop right out of her head. She clasped her hand to her throat where her heart now seemed to be lodged. 'A…a honeymoon? Whatever for? You said it's going to be a marriage in name only. Why would we need to go on a honeymoon?' Even saying the word 'honeymoon' made her body go all tingly and her heart race and her blood heat. Heat that stormed into her cheeks and simmered in other more secret places.

One of his dark eyebrows lifted at her stuttering protest, a satirical glint shining in his gaze. 'I'm fine with a quiet wedding here at the *castello* but I insist on a honeymoon. It will give our marriage more credibility if we are seen to go away together for a short break.'

Seen? In public? Be in wide open spaces? Rushing crowds. Traffic. Noise. Busyness. Artie stumbled backwards, her arms wrapping around her body, her breathing tight and laboured. 'No. I can't do that. I don't want to go. There's no need. It's not a proper marriage and it's wrong of you to insist on it.'

Breathe. Breathe. Breathe.

Luca frowned. 'Are you worried I'll take advantage of you? Please be assured that is not going to happen. I gave you my word.'

'I don't want to go anywhere with you,' Artie said. 'How could you think I would? I don't even like you.'

His eyes dipped to her mouth then back to her gaze. 'Artemisia, we need to be seen together in public. It's not going to work unless we present as a normal couple. We'll have to live together most, if not all, of the time.'

Her stomach turned over. 'L-live together?'

'But of course. Isn't that what husbands and wives do?'

Artie gulped. Her skin prickled, her legs trembled, her mind raced. Live with Luca Ferrantelli? What would that entail? She couldn't even leave her own home. How on earth would she move into his? Should she tell him about her social phobia? Would he understand? No. Not likely. Few people did. Even the professionals who had visited her at the *castello* had more or less given up on her.

Her gaze moved out of reach of his and she fiddled with the sleeve of her shirt for something to do with her hands. 'I'm sorry, but couldn't you move in here? I mean, this place is huge and you can have your own suite of rooms and we'd hardly have to see each other and no one would ever know we're not—'

'No.' His tone was so adamant the word could have been underlined in thick black ink.

Artie swung away from him, trying to get her breathing back under control. She was light-headed and nauseous, her stomach churning fast enough to make butter. She was going to faint… No, she wasn't. She was going to fight it. Fight *him*. She took a deep breath and turned around to face him. 'I will *not* leave my home. Not for you. A marriage of convenience is supposed to be convenient for both parties. It's not convenient for me to move right now. I've only just buried my father. I'd like more time to…to spend grieving out of the view of the public.' It wasn't completely a lie. She missed her father, not because they were particularly close but because looking after him had given structure and purpose to her life.

Luca studied her for a long moment, his expression giving

nothing away. She tried not to squirm under his unnerving scrutiny but it was a mammoth effort and only added to her lightheadedness. 'All right. We'll delay the honeymoon.'

Relief swept through her and she brushed back her hair from her face, her hand not quite as steady as she would have liked. 'Thank you.'

She hadn't been in a car since coming home from hospital after the accident. She hadn't been in a plane or train or bus since she was fifteen. She hadn't been around more than two or three people in a decade. Her life was contained within these four ancient stone walls and she couldn't see it changing any time soon.

Luca closed the distance between them and held her gaze for another beat or two. 'I realise your father's financial situation has come as a shock to you. And I understand how resistant you are to my plan to turn things to your advantage. But I want my grandfather to see us married and living as a couple.'

'Why is that so important to you?'

'He's got cancer but he won't agree to treatment.'

'Oh… I'm sorry.'

Luca ran a hand down his face, the sound of his palm scraping over his regrowth loud in the silence. 'Unless he has treatment soon, he will die within a year. His dream has always been to see me settled down with a nice young woman. He disapproves of my casual approach to relationships and has been at pains to let me know at every opportunity. I want him to find a reason to live, knowing I've found a suitable bride.'

A suitable bride.

If only Luca knew how unsuitable she really was. Would he still want to marry her if he knew the truth about her? 'Will your grandfather be well enough to come here for the wedding?'

'I hope so.'

Artie bit her lip. She was conflicted about keeping her social anxiety from Luca but neither could she risk losing her home if he decided to withdraw his offer of marriage. She didn't know him well enough to trust he would make allowances for her. He'd already told her he was a ruthless businessman who didn't allow emotion to cloud his judgement. How could she hope he might be understanding and compassionate about her mental health issues? 'But you only know me as my father presented me. I might be the worst person in the world.'

A lazy smile tilted his mouth and his eyes darkened. 'I like what I've seen so far.'

Artie could feel colour pouring into her cheeks. Could feel a faint hollow ache building, beating between her thighs. Could feel a light tingling in her breasts. His gaze went to her mouth and she couldn't stop herself from sweeping them with the tip of her tongue. His eyes followed the movement of her tongue and liquid warmth spread through her core like warmed treacle. What invisible chemistry was doing this to her? What potent force did Luca Ferrantelli have over her? She had never been so aware of another person. Never so aware of her own body. Her senses were on high alert, her pulse racing.

Suddenly he wasn't standing a metre away but was close enough for her to smell the sharp, clean citrus notes of his aftershave. Had he moved or had she?

She looked into the depths of his gaze and her heart skipped a beat. And another. And another, until it felt like tiny racing footsteps were pounding against the membrane surrounding her heart.

He lifted his hand to her face, trailing his index finger down the slope of her cheek from just above her ear down to the base of her chin. Every nerve in her skin exploded with sensation. Every pore acutely sensitive to his faintest touch.

'You are much more beautiful in person than in the photo your father showed me.' Luca's tone was a bone-melting blend of rough and smooth. Honey and gravel. Temptation and danger.

Artie couldn't take her eyes off his mouth, drawn by a force as old as time. Male and female desire meeting. Wanting. Needing. Tempting. 'I don't get called Artemisia...most people call me Artie.'

Oh, for pity's sake. Couldn't you think of something a little more sophisticated to say?

Luca gave a crooked smile and something warm spread through her chest. 'Artie. It's cute. I like it. Artemisia, Queen of Halicarnassus. She was an ally of the Persian King Xerces in 430 BCE and reputedly brave in battle.'

That's me—brave. Not.

'My mother chose it. She loved Greek history.'

His gaze became hooded and he glanced at her mouth again. 'There will be times when we'll be expected to show affection towards one another. Are you going to be okay with that?'

'W-what sort of affection?'

'Kissing. Holding hands. Touching.'

Her lower body began to throb with a strange kind of ache. She couldn't stop herself thinking about places he might touch her—places that were already tingling in anticipation. How would she cope with a casual brush of his hand? His strong arm around her waist? His mouth pressed to hers? No one had ever touched her with a lover's touch. No one had ever kissed her. The desire to be touched by him was overwhelming. Her body craved it like a drug.

'Okay.'

Okay? Are you out of your mind?

Artie *was* out of her mind—with lust. She had never felt so out of control of her body. It was acting of its own volition, responding to him in ways she had never expected. She didn't even like him. He was arrogant and confident in a way she found irritating. It was as if he expected her to throw herself at him just like any other woman he had encountered. How was she going to resist him if he kissed her? How would it feel to have that firm mouth moving against hers?

Luca continued to look at her with a heart-stopping intensity. 'If you don't want me to kiss you then you need to tell me, because right now I can think of nothing I want to do more.' His voice lowered to a deep bass that sent another wave of heat coursing through her body.

'What makes you think I want you to kiss me now? What would be the point? There's no one here but us.' Artie was proud of her calm and collected tone when inside her body was steaming, simmering, smouldering.

His thumb pressed lightly on the middle of her bottom lip, sending tingles down the length of her spine. 'The way you're looking at me.'

'How am I looking at you?'

Eek. Was that her voice? She had to do something about her voice. None of that whispery, husky rubbish. She had to be brusque and matter-of-fact.

'You must be imagining it.'

He cupped one side of her face with his hand, the slight roughness of his palm making her insides coil and tighten with lust. 'Maybe.' He gave a quick on-off smile and dropped his hand from her face. 'So, the wedding. How does this weekend sound?'

Artie only just managed to suppress a gasp. '*This* weekend? What's the rush?'

'I'm not a fan of long engagements.'

'Funny. But how am I going to find a dress in time? Or are you expecting me to turn up naked?'

Argh. Why did you say that?

A dark glint came into his eyes. 'Now, there's an idea.'

Artie pursed her lips, hoping her cheeks were not glowing as hot as they felt. 'I can safely say I will never, ever be naked in front of you.'

He glided a lazy finger down her burning cheek, a smile in his eyes. 'Have you been naked in front of anyone?'

Artie stepped back, annoyed with herself for not doing so earlier. She *had* to keep her distance. It was dangerous to stand so close to him. She had so little immunity to his sensual power.

She had to remember he was a powerful magnet and she was a tiny iron filing.

'I'm not going to discuss my private life with you. It's none of your damn business.'

'We have to know a few things about each other otherwise no one will accept our marriage as the real thing.'

Artie frowned. 'What? Are you going to pretend you're in love with me or something? Who's going to believe it? We're total opposites.'

'Ah, but don't they say opposites attract?' His smile melted her bones—she could feel her legs trembling to keep her upright.

Artie compressed her lips and iced her gaze. 'This may come as a surprise to a man with an ego the size of yours but I'm not attracted to you.'

He gave a deep chuckle. 'Then you're going to have to call on every bit of acting power you possess to convince my grandfather otherwise. Think you can do that, *cara mia*?'

The Italian endearment almost made her swoon. She hoisted her chin. 'Do you, Mr Hardened Cynical Playboy, think *you* can act like a man passionately in love with his bride?'

His gaze held hers in a smouldering lock that made the backs of her knees tingle. 'That will be the easy part.'

CHAPTER FOUR

ARTIE STOOD IN FRONT of the cheval mirror in her bedroom and checked her appearance. She had decided against wearing her mother's wedding dress and chosen a cream satin ballgown of her mother's instead. It was a classic design with a tulle underskirt that emphasised her neat waist, and a close-fitting bodice that hinted at the shape of her breasts without revealing too much cleavage. She hadn't wanted to taint her mother's beautiful wedding gown with her charade of a marriage. Her parents had married for love and lived happily together until Artie insisted on going to a birthday party against their wishes when she was fifteen.

She bit down on her lip until it hurt. Why had she been so adamant about going to that stupid party? Where were those supposed friends of hers now? Only a handful came to visit her in hospital. None had come to the *castello* once she had been released. None had come to her mother's funeral. She had stood beside her father's wheelchair as her mother was lowered into the family plot at the *castello* with her heart in pieces, guilt raining down on her heavier than what was coming from the dismal sky above. How could one teenage decision have so many unforeseen consequences?

Artie plucked at the skirt of her dress, her stomach an ants' nest of nerves. Today was her wedding day. The day she married Luca Ferrantelli in a paper marriage to save her family home. Would this be another decision she would later regret? Or would the consolation of getting the *castello* back into her possession wipe out any misgivings? She glanced at the engagement ring on her hand. The longer she wore it, the more she loved it. She felt strangely connected to Luca's grandmother by wearing her ring. But would the old lady spin in her grave to know Artie was entering into a loveless union with her grandson?

Rosa came in carrying a bouquet of flowers she had picked from the garden. 'You look beautiful, Artie.' She handed her the simple but fragrant bouquet. 'You're not wearing a veil?'

Artie brought the flowers up to her nose and breathed in the heady scent of roses and orange blossom. 'This isn't a proper wedding.'

Rosa frowned. 'But it's still a legal one. You might as well look like a proper bride. And make that handsome groom of yours sit up and take notice.' She went to the large wardrobe and pulled out the long cardboard box where Artie's mother's wedding dress and veil were stored on the top shelf. She placed the box on the bed and lifted the lid and removed the tissue-wrapped heirloom hand-embroidered veil that had been worn by both Artie's mother and grandmother. Rosa shook out the veil and then brought it over to Artie. 'Come on. Indulge me.'

Artie rolled her eyes but gave in, allowing Rosa to fasten the veil on her head, securing it with hair pins. Rosa draped the veil over Artie's face and then stepped back to inspect her handiwork. 'You will knock Luca Ferrantelli's socks off, *si*?'

Artie turned back to look at her reflection. She did indeed look like a proper bride. She glanced at Rosa. 'Tell me I'm not making the biggest mistake of my life. My second biggest, I mean.'

Rosa grasped one of Artie's hands, her eyes shimmering with tears. 'You have already lost so much. You can't lose the *castello* as well. Sometimes we have to do whatever it takes to make the best of things.' She released Artie's hand and brushed at her eyes and gave a rueful smile. 'Weddings always make me emotional. Just as well I didn't get married myself.'

'Would you have liked to?' Artie was surprised she hadn't thought to ask before now. Rosa was in her sixties and had been a part of the *castello* household for as long as Artie could remember. They had talked about many things over the years but not about the housekeeper's love life or lack thereof.

Rosa made a business of fussing over the arrangement of the skirt of Artie's gown. 'I fell in love once a long time ago. It didn't work out.'

'What happened?'

Rosa bent down lower to pick a fallen rose petal off the floor. She scrunched it in her hand and gave a thin-lipped smile. 'He married someone else. I never found anyone else who measured up.'

'Oh, that's so sad.'

Rosa laughed but it sounded tinny. 'I saved myself a lot of heartache. Apparently, he's been divorced three times since then.' Her expression suddenly sobered. 'Your parents were lucky to have found each other. I know they didn't have as long together as they would have liked but it's better to have five years with the right one than fifty with the wrong one.'

But what about six months with a man who had only met her a matter of days ago? A man who was so dangerously attractive, her blood raced every time he looked at her?

Luca stood in the *castello*'s chapel, waiting for Artie to appear. His grandfather had been too unwell to travel, but Luca planned to take his new bride to meet him as soon as their marriage was official. Luca had organised for a priest to officiate rather than a celebrant, because he knew it would please his grandfather, who was a deeply religious man—hence his disapproval of Luca's life in the fast lane.

As much as he wanted his grandfather to meet Artie as soon

as possible, he was quite glad he would have her to himself for a day or two. They would hardly be convincing as a newly married couple if they didn't look comfortable and at ease with each other.

She was a challenge he was tempted to take on. Her resistance to his charm was potently attractive. Not because he didn't respect and honour the word no when a woman said it. He could take rejection and take it well. He was never so emotionally invested in a relationship that he was particularly cut up when it ended.

But he sensed Artie's interest in him. Sensed the chemistry that swirled in the atmosphere when they were together. Would it be risky to explore that chemistry? She was young and unworldly. What if she didn't accept the terms of the deal and wanted more than he was prepared to give? He couldn't allow that to happen. If she fell in love with him it would change everything.

And if he fell in love with her...

He sidestepped the thought like someone avoiding a sinkhole. Loving her would indeed be a pitfall. For her and for him. Love was a dangerous emotion. Whenever he thought of the possibility of loving someone, his heart would shy away like a horse refusing a jump. Too dangerous. Too risky. Too painful.

The back of Luca's neck started to tingle and he turned to see Artie standing in the portal. He suppressed a gasp, his eyes drinking in the vision of her dressed in a stunning cream ballgown and off-white heirloom veil. The bright golden sunlight backlit her slim frame, making her look like an angel. As she walked towards him carrying a small bouquet of flowers he had to remind himself to breathe. The closer she got, the more his heart pounded, the more his blood thundered. And a strange sensation flowed into his chest. Warmth spreading over something hard and frozen, melting, reshaping, softening.

He gave himself a mental slap. No emotions allowed. This was a business deal. Nothing else. So what if she looked as beautiful as an angel? So what if his body roared with lust at the thought of touching her? This wasn't about him—it was about his grandfather. Giving him the will to live long enough to have treatment that could cure him or at least give him a few more precious years of life.

Artie came to stand beside him, her face behind the veil composed, and yet twin circles of pink glowed in her cheeks. Her make-up highlighted the flawless, creamy texture of her skin, the deep brown of her eyes and the thick ink-black lashes that surrounded them. Her lips shone with a hint of lip gloss, making him ache to press his mouth to hers to see if it tasted as sweet and luscious as it looked. He could smell her perfume, an intoxicating blend of fresh flowers that reminded him of the sweet hope of spring after a long, bleak winter.

'You look breathtaking,' Luca said, taking her hands in his. Her small fingers moved within the embrace of his and a lightning rod of lust almost knocked him off his feet. Maybe he shouldn't have suggested a paper marriage. Maybe he should have insisted on the real deal. The thought of consummating their marriage sent a wave of heat through his body. But his conscience slammed on the brakes. No. No. No. It wouldn't be fair. He wasn't the settling-down type and she had fairy-tale romance written all over her. Which, ironically, was why she was perfect for the role of his temporary bride. No one else would satisfy his grandfather. It *had* to be her.

'I—I'm nervous...' Her voice trembled and her teeth sank into the plush softness of her bottom lip.

Luca gently squeezed her fingers. 'Don't be.' His voice was so deep and rough it sounded like it had come from the centre of the earth. He didn't like admitting it, but he was nervous too. Not about repeating the vows and signing the register—those were formalities he could easily compartmentalise in his brain. He was worried his promise to keep their relationship on paper was going to be the real kicker. He gave her hand another light squeeze and smiled. 'Let's do this.'

And they turned to face the priest and the service began...

* * *

'I, Artemisia Elisabetta, take you, Luca Benedetto, to be my husband...' Artie repeated her vows with a slight quaver in her voice. 'I promise to be true to you in good times and bad, in sickness and in health.' She swallowed and continued, conscious of Luca's dark gaze holding hers, 'I will love and honour you all the days of my life.'

She wasn't a particularly religious person but saying words she didn't mean made her wonder if she was in danger of a lightning strike. The only lightning strike she had suffered so far had been the tingling zap coursing through her body when Luca first took her hand. Every cell of her body was aware of him. Dressed in a mid-blue morning suit, he looked like he had just stepped off a billboard advertisement for designer menswear. She could smell the lemon and lime of his aftershave—it teased her nostrils, sending her senses into a tailspin. How could a man smell so damn delicious?

Eek! How could a man look so damn attractive?

Double eek! How could she be marrying him?

Luca's hand took her left one and slipped on the wedding ring as he repeated his vows. 'I, Luca Benedetto, take you, Artemisia Elisabetta, to be my wife. I promise to be true to you in good times and bad, in sickness and in health.' He paused for a beat and continued with a rough edge to his voice, 'I will love and honour you all the days of my life.'

Artie blinked back moisture gathering in her eyes. He sounded so convincing. He even looked convincing with his gaze so focused on her, his mouth smiling at her as if she was the most amazing woman who had ever walked upon the face of the earth.

It's an act. Don't be fooled by it. None of this means anything to him and neither should it mean anything to you.

'You may kiss the bride.'

The priest's words startled Artie out of her reverie and she only had time to snatch in a breath before Luca's hands settled on her hips and drew her closer, his mouth descending inexorably towards hers. The first warm, firm press of his lips sent a jolt of electricity through her body. A jolt that travelled all the way down her spine and fizzed like a sparkler deep in her core. He lifted his lips off hers for an infinitesimal moment as if time had suddenly paused. Then he brought his mouth back to hers and sensations rippled through her as his lips moved against hers with increasing pressure, his hands on her hips bringing her even closer to the hard heat of his stirring body.

One of his hands left her hip to cradle one side of her face, his touch gentle, almost reverent, and yet his mouth was pure sin. Tempting, teasing, tantalising. She opened to him and his tongue touched hers and her insides quaked and throbbed with longing. She pressed closer, her arms going around his neck, her senses reeling as his tongue invited hers in an erotic dance. Every nerve in her lips and mouth awakened to his kiss, flowering open like soft petals to strong sunshine. She became aware of her body in a way she never had before—its needs, urges, flagrantly responding to the dark primal call of his.

Luca angled his head to change position, his tongue stroking against hers, a low, deep groan sounding in his throat. It thrilled her to know he was as undone by their kiss as she was. Thrilled and excited her to realise her own sensual power. Power she hadn't known she possessed until now.

The priest cleared his throat and Luca pulled back from her with a dazed look on his face. Artie suspected she was looking just as shell-shocked as him. Her mouth felt swollen, her feminine core agitated with a roaring hunger he alone had awakened.

Luca blinked a couple of times as if to reset his equilibrium. 'Well, hello there, Signora Ferrantelli.' His voice was rusty, his gaze drifting to her mouth as if he couldn't quite believe what had happened between them moments before.

Artie licked her lips and tasted the salty sexiness of his. 'Hello…'

Luca spoke briefly to the priest, thanking him for his services, and then led Artie to where Rosa had set up refreshments in the garden. She sensed him pulling up a drawbridge, a pulling back into himself. He stood without touching her, his expression inscrutable.

'Right. Time to celebrate. And then tomorrow we'll go and visit my grandfather.'

A wave of ice-cold dread washed over her. 'But can't we leave it a while? I mean, wouldn't he expect us to be on our honeymoon and—?'

'I can't afford to leave it too long before I introduce you to him,' Luca said, frowning. 'He's in a vulnerable state of health.'

Artie chewed at her lip and lowered her gaze. 'I understand all that but I need more time to get used to being your...wife. I'm worried I'll do or say something that will make your grandfather suspicious.'

Luca gave her a smouldering look. 'If you kiss me like you did just then, any doubts he has will disappear.'

Artie could feel her cheeks firing up. 'I was only following your lead. I haven't been kissed before, so—'

'Really?' His eyebrows shot up in surprise.

She pulled away from him and hugged her arms around her body. 'Go on, mock me for being a twenty-five-year-old virgin. I must seem like a pariah to someone like you who changes lovers daily.'

Her conscience rolled its eyes. *I can't believe you just told him you're a virgin.*

He scraped a hand through his hair, making it tousled. 'Look, I kind of figured from your father that you were lacking in experience but I didn't realise you've never had a boyfriend, even as a teenager. Did your father forbid you from going out or something?'

Artie averted her gaze. 'No. I was busy looking after him after the accident that killed my mother and seriously injured him. There wasn't time for dating.'

His deep frown brought his dark eyebrows together. 'Why

were you the one looking after him? Why didn't he employ a nurse or carer?'

Artie turned slightly so she was facing the view over the estate. Luca's penetrating gaze was too unsettling, too unnerving. How could she explain her reasons for taking care of her father? How could she explain the guilt that had chained her to his side? The guilt that still plagued her and had led her to marry Luca in order to save her family's home? The home that was the only thing she had left of her family. 'It was my choice to look after him. I was happy to do it.'

Luca came up behind her and placed his hands on the tops of her shoulders and turned her to face him. He expression was still etched in a frown, his hazel eyes gentle with concern. 'You were just a child when the accident occurred. It was unfair of your father to allow you to sacrifice yourself in such a way. But what about school? Surely you would have had plenty of opportunity to mix with people your own age?'

Artie pressed her lips together for a moment. 'I finished my education online. I was given special permission. I didn't want to leave my father to the care of strangers. He was stricken with grief after losing my mother. We both were. It was my choice to take care of him—no one forced me to do it.'

His hands began a gentle massaging movement that made the tense muscles in her neck and shoulders melt like snow under warm sunshine. 'I think what you did for your father was admirable and yet I can't help feeling he exploited you. You should've had more time to yourself doing all the things teenagers and young adults do.'

Artie stepped out of his hold and interlaced her fingers in front of her body. She glanced to where Rosa was hovering with a bottle of champagne. 'Shouldn't we be mingling with Father Pasquale and our two other guests?' She didn't wait for him to answer and turned and walked towards the housekeeper standing with the priest and the other witness, who worked part-time on the Castello Mireille estate.

* * *

Luca watched Artie pick up a glass of champagne from the silver tray the housekeeper was holding. Her expression was now coolly composed but he sensed he had pressed on a nerve when discussing her role of caring for her father. He'd already suspected she was a virgin——her father had intimated as such—— but no way had he suspected she had zero experience when it came to dating.

No one had kissed her before him.

She had never had a boyfriend, not even during her teens. How had her father allowed that to happen? Surely he must have realised his daughter was missing out on socialising with people her age?

Luca ran his tongue over his lips and tasted the sweet, fruity residue of her lip gloss. He could still feel the soft imprint of her lips on his, could still feel the throb of desire kissing her had evoked in his body, the deep pulses in his groin, the tingles in his thighs and lower spine.

He had kissed many women, too many to recall in any detail, but he knew he would never forget his first kiss with Artie. It was embedded in his memory. He could recall every contour of her soft mouth, every brush and glide of her tongue, her sweet vanilla and wild-strawberry taste.

But he would have to find some way to forget, for theirs was to be a paper marriage. A six-month time frame to achieve his goal of setting his grandfather's mind at peace. Knowing Artie had so little experience was an even bigger reason to stick to his plan of a hands-off arrangement. It wouldn't be fair to explore the physical chemistry between them, because it might raise her expectations on their relationship.

He didn't *do* relationships. And certainly not *that* type of relationship.

Long-term relationships required commitment and responsibility for the health and safety of your partner. His track record on keeping those he loved safe was appalling. It was easier not to love. Easier to keep his emotions in check, to freeze them so deep inside himself they could never be thawed. To imagine oneself falling in love just because of a bit of scorching hot chemistry was a foolish and reckless thing to do. He no longer did anything reckless and foolish.

Luca glanced at Artie and something pinched in his chest. She was standing next to the ancient stone fountain, the tinkling of water and the sound of birds chirping in the shrubbery a perfect backdrop for her old-world beauty. The sunlight brought out the glossy sheen of her dark brown hair, the light breeze playing with a curl that had worked its way loose from her elegant up-do. She was looking into the distance, a small frown on her forehead, and every now and again the tip of her tongue came out and swept across her lips where his had recently pressed. She turned her head and caught him staring at her, and her cheeks pooled with a delicate shade of pink.

Had he made a mistake in choosing her to be his temporary bride? She was so innocent, so untouched and other-worldly, like she had been transported from another time in history or straight out of a classic fairy tale. And yet he'd felt a connection with her from the moment he met her. A powerful connection that no amount of logic and rationality could dismiss. His brain said *Don't go there* and yet his body roared with primal hunger.

But he would have to get his self-control back in shape, and fast, because falling for his sweet and innocent bride would be the most reckless and foolish thing of all.

CHAPTER FIVE

ARTIE WAS AWARE of Luca's gaze resting on her every time she glanced his way. Aware of the way her body responded to his lightest touch. The merest brush of his fingers set off spot fires in her flesh, sending heat travelling to every secret place in her body. Smouldering there like hot coals just waiting for a breath of oxygen to fan them into vibrant life.

His kiss...

Best not to think too much about his kiss. They were supposed to be keeping their relationship platonic, but nothing about Luca's kiss was platonic. It was sensory overload and she wondered if she would ever recover. Or stop wanting him to kiss her again. And why stop at kisses? He had woken something in her, something hungry and needy that begged to be assuaged. The idea of asking Luca to tweak the rules of their marriage slipped into her mind like an uninvited guest. It would be an ideal opportunity for her to get some experience on board. A six-month marriage where she could indulge in the delights of the flesh. What was there to lose other than her virginity?

Your pride? her conscience piped up. *He can have anyone. You're not even his type. How do you think you could ever satisfy him for six minutes, let alone six months?*

Luca took a glass of champagne off Rosa and came over to

where Artie was standing near the fountain. He glanced towards the priest and then back to her. 'Father Pasquale is having a good time indulging in Rosa's food. How long has she been working here?'

'Since I was a baby,' Artie said. 'This is her home as much as it is mine.'

'So, what would she do if you were to sell up and move away?'

Artie raised her chin. 'I would never sell the *castello*. And I don't want to live anywhere but here.'

I can't live anywhere but here.

Luca held her gaze for a long moment. 'How will you maintain the estate? It needs a lot of work, and sooner rather than later.'

She drained her champagne glass and sent him a narrowed glance. 'Is this the right time to discuss this? It's our wedding day.'

His brows drew together in a frown. 'Do I have to remind you of the terms of our marriage?'

'No.' She flashed him a pointed look. 'Do *you* need reminding? That kiss was a little enthusiastic for someone who insisted on keeping things on paper.'

His gaze went to her mouth, and the atmosphere throbbed with heightened intensity. 'Maybe, but it wasn't a one-way kiss, was it, *cara*? You were with me all the way.' His tone was so deep and rough it sent a tingle down her spine. And his eyes contained a glint that made something warm and liquid spill between her thighs.

Artie went to swing away from him but his hand came down on her arm. A shiver coursed through her body at the feel of his long, strong, tanned fingers encircling her wrist. She looked down at his hand on her flesh and the warm, liquid sensation in her lower body spread like fire throughout her pelvis. She lifted her gaze to his and raised her eyebrows in a haughty manner. 'W-what are you doing?' Her tone was breathless rather than offended.

His broad thumb began a slow caress over the pulse point on her wrist, the fast-paced throb of her blood betraying her even further. She breathed in the scent of him—the exotic mix of citrus and clean, warm male, her senses reeling from his closeness.

'We're married, *cara*. People will expect us to touch each other.'

Her heart skipped like it was trying to break some sort of record. 'I'm not used to people touching me.'

Luca brushed his bent knuckles against the curve of her cheek, his gaze holding hers in a sensual lock that made her insides quake with desire. 'But you like it when I touch you, *si*?' His thumb moved from her pulse point and stroked along her lower lip. 'You like it very much.'

Artie wanted to deny it but she had hardly helped her case by kissing him back the way she had earlier. Nor was she helping it now by not pulling away from his loose hold. Her willpower had completely deserted her—she wanted his touch, craved it like an addict craved a forbidden substance. She couldn't take her eyes off his mouth, couldn't stop thinking about the warm, sensual pleasure of it moving against hers. Couldn't stop thinking about the stroke and glide of his tongue and how it had sent torrents of need racing through her body.

She drew in a ragged breath and forced her gaze back to his. 'I'm sorry if I keep giving you mixed messages. It wasn't my intention at all.'

He brought her hand up to his mouth and pressed a barely-there kiss to her bent knuckles, his gaze unwavering on hers. 'You're not the only one sending mixed messages.' He dropped her hand and gave a rueful smile. 'I'm not going to change the terms of our marriage. It wouldn't be fair to you.'

Not fair? What was fair about denying her body the fulfilment it craved? 'Are you worried I might fall in love with you?' The question popped out before she could stop it.

His dark eyes dipped to her mouth for a moment, his forehead creasing in a frown as if he was quietly considering the possibility of her developing feelings for him. When his gaze came back to hers it was shuttered. Screened with secret thoughts. 'It would be very foolish of you to do so.' His voice contained a note of gravity that made the hairs on the back of her neck tingle.

'Have you ever been in love with anyone?'

'No.' His answer was fast and flat.

Artie twirled the empty champagne glass in her hand. 'I didn't realise it was possible to prevent oneself from falling in love. From what I've heard it just happens and there's nothing you can do to stop it. Maybe you haven't met the right person yet.'

'I have no doubt such feelings exist between other people but I have no interest in feeling that way about someone.'

'Why?'

Luca shrugged one broad shoulder, his gaze still inscrutable. 'It seems to me an impossible task to be someone's soulmate. To be everything they need and want you to be. I know I can't be that person. I'm too selfish.'

Artie wondered if that was entirely true. He was prepared to marry a virtual stranger to keep his grandfather alive for a few more years. How was that selfish? And he was prepared to hand her back the *castello* at the end of six months instead of keeping his nine-tenths ownership. Hardly the actions of a self-serving man, surely?

Rosa approached at that moment carrying a tray with fresh glasses of champagne. 'Another quick one before the official photos are taken?' she asked with a smile. 'The photographer is setting up near the rose garden.'

Artie put her used glass on the tray and took a new one. *'Grazie.'*

'And you, Signor Ferrantelli?' Rosa turned to Luca, offering him a fresh glass off the tray.

He shook his head. 'Not for me, thanks. One is enough. And please call me Luca.' He took Artie's free hand and nodded in the direction of the photographer. 'Shall we?'

Once a small set of photos were taken, Artie helped Rosa tidy away the refreshments after the priest and photographer had left. But when the housekeeper announced she was going to have an early night, Artie was left at a loose end. She hadn't seen Luca since the photo session—he'd said he wanted to check a few things out on the estate and hadn't yet returned. She'd thought about what he'd said back at the fountain and his reasons for saying it. The more she got to know him, the more she wanted to know. Why was he so adamant about keeping his emotions in check? What was so threatening about loving someone that made him so unwilling to experience it for himself? She might not have any experience when it came to falling in love, but she knew enough from her parents and books and movies it was a real and powerful emotion that was impossible to block once it happened. But since the accident, she had given up on the hope of one day finding true love. Any love she felt would be one-sided, for how could anyone return her love once they knew the destruction she had caused?

Luca had warned her about falling in love with him—*'It would be very foolish of you to do so.'* But how could she stop something that was so beyond her control? She was already aware of her vulnerability where he was concerned. He was so suave and sophisticated, and occupied a world she hadn't been party to her entire adult life. Hadn't his passionate, heart-stopping kiss shown her how at risk she was to developing feelings towards him?

Artie circled her wrist where his fingers had held her. A shiver shimmied down her spine as she recalled the tensile strength in his hand, the springy black masculine hairs that peppered his skin, the way his touch spoke to her flesh, awakening it, enlivening it, enticing it. He was temptation personified and she would be a fool indeed to allow her feelings to get the better of her. He had been clear about the terms of their relationship. Why, then, did she ache for more of his touch? Why, then, did she want to feel his mouth on hers again?

Artie sat in the main salon with her embroidery on her lap, when Luca came in. His hair looked tousled from the wind or the passage of his fingers or both. And he had changed out of his morning suit into jeans and a white cotton shirt, the sleeves rolled back to reveal his strong wrists and forearms. The white shirt highlighted his olive-toned tan, the blue jeans the muscled length of his legs. He brought in with him the fresh smell of outdoors and something else…something that made her female hormones sit up straighter and her senses to go on high alert.

She put the sampler she was working on to one side and crossed one leg over the other, working hard to keep her features neutral. 'I wasn't sure of your plans, so I got Rosa to make up one of the guest rooms for you. It's on the second floor—the green suite overlooking the vineyard.'

His gaze held hers with a watchful intensity. 'So, she knows our marriage is a hands-off affair?'

Artie moistened her lips, conscious of the slow crawl of heat in her cheeks. 'Yes, well, I thought it best. I'm not the best actor when it comes to playing charades, and she's known me a long time and would sense any hint of inauthenticity.'

'I would prefer you not to tell anyone else about the terms of our relationship.' His tone was firm. 'I don't want any idle gossip getting back to my grandfather.'

'Rosa is the soul of discretion. She would never betray a confidence.' It was the one thing Artie could rely on—the housekeeper was loyal and trustworthy to a fault. Rosa had never revealed Artie's struggles to anyone and had always been as supportive as possible.

Luca came over to the sofa where she was sitting and leaned down and picked up the sampler she'd been working on. He ran his fingers over the tiny flower buds and leaves she had embroidered. 'This is exquisite work. Have you been doing it long?' he asked.

Artie shrugged off the compliment but inside she was glowing from his praise. No one apart from her father and Rosa had ever seen her work. 'It's just a hobby. I started doing embroidery after I got out of hospital. I'm self-taught, which you can probably tell.'

He turned the sampler over and inspected the other side, where the stitches were almost as neat and precise as on the front. 'You undersell yourself, *cara*. You could start a small business doing this sort of thing. Bespoke embroidery. There's a big swing away from factory-produced or sweatshop items. What people want these days is the personal touch.'

'Yes, well, I'm not sure I'm ready for that.' Artie took the sampler out of his hand and folded it and put it inside her embroidery basket, then closed the lid with a definitive movement.

'What's stopping you?'

I'm stopping me.

Her fear of the big, wide world outside the *castello* was stopping her from reaching her potential. She knew it but didn't know how she could do anything to change it. How could she run a business locked away here? She met his probing gaze for a moment before looking away again. The thought of revealing her phobia to him made her blood run cold. What would he think of her? She had effectively married him under false pretences. 'I'm happy leaving it as a hobby, that's all. I don't want to put myself under pressure of deadlines.'

'Speaking of deadlines...' Luca rubbed a hand down his face, the raspy sound of his palm against his light stubble making her recall how it had felt against her skin when he'd kissed her. 'I'd like to make an early start in the morning. My grandfather gets tired easily, so the first part of the day is better for him to receive visitors.'

Artie blinked. Blinked again. Her pulse began to quicken. Her breathing to shorten. Her skin to tighten. She rose from the sofa on unsteady legs and moved to the bank of windows on the other side of the room. She turned her back to the room and grasped the windowsill with white-knuckled force. 'Maybe you should go alone. I need more time before I—'

'There isn't time to waste.' The intransigent edge to his tone was a chilling reminder of his forceful, goal-directed personality.

Artie swallowed a tight lump in her throat and gripped the windowsill even harder. 'I... I can't go with you.'

There was a beat or two of intense silence. A silence so thick it seemed to be pressing in on her from all four walls and even the ceiling. A silence that echoed in her head and roared in her ears and reminded her she was way out of her depth.

'What do you mean, you can't? We made an agreement, Artie. I expect you to adhere to it.' His voice throbbed with frustration. 'Be ready at seven thirty. I'm not taking no for an answer.'

Artie released her grip on the windowsill and turned to face him. Her stomach was roiling, her skin damp with perspiration, her mind reeling at the thought of going beyond the *castello* gates. 'Luca, please don't do this.' Her voice came out sandpaper-hoarse.

He gave a savage frown. 'Don't do what? All I'm asking is for you to uphold your side of our agreement. Which, I might remind you, is a legal one. You signed the papers my lawyer prepared—remember?'

Artie steepled her hands against her nose and mouth, trying to control her breathing. Her heart was doing cartwheels and star jumps and back flips and her pulse was off the charts. 'It's not that I don't want to go...'

'Then what is it?'

She lowered her hands from her face and pressed her lips together to stop them from trembling. She clasped her hands in front of her body, her fingers tightly interlaced to the point of discomfort. She couldn't bring her gaze up to meet his, so instead aimed it at the carpet near his feet. 'There's something I haven't told you…something important.'

Luca crossed the room until he was standing in front of her. He lifted her chin with the end of his finger and meshed his gaze with hers. His frown was still in place but was more concerned now than angry. 'What?' His tone was disarmingly gentle and his touch on her chin light but strangely soothing. 'Tell me what's going on. I want the truth, *cara*.'

Artie bit the inside of her mouth, trying to find the words to describe her condition. Her weakness. Her shame. 'I… I haven't been outside the *castello* grounds since I was fifteen years old. It's not that I don't want to leave it—I can't.'

His hand fell away from her face, his forehead creased in lines of puzzlement. 'Why can't you? What's stopping you?'

She gave a hollow, self-deprecating laugh and pointed a finger at her chest. '*I'm* stopping me.' She stepped back from him and wrapped her arms around her body. 'I have crippling social anxiety. I can't cope with crowds and busy, bustling places. I literally freeze or have a meltdown—a full-blown panic attack.'

He opened and closed his mouth as if trying to think of something to say.

'I'm sorry,' Artie said. 'I should have told you before now but I was too embarrassed and—'

'Please. Don't apologise.' His voice was husky, his expression etched with concern. He shook his head like he was trying to get his muddled thoughts in some sort of order. 'Why didn't your father say something to me? He led me to believe you were—'

'Normal?' She raised her brows in an arch manner. 'Is that the word you were looking for? I'm hardly that, am I?'

Luca made a rough sound at the back of his throat. '*Cara*, please don't run yourself down like that. Have you seen a health professional about it?'

'Four.'

'And?'

Artie spread her hands outwards. 'And nothing. I couldn't

cope with the side effects of medication. Meditation and mindfulness helped initially but not enough to get me outside the *castello* grounds. Talk therapy helped too at first but it was expensive and I didn't have the time with my caring responsibilities with Papa to keep going with it.' She gave a sigh and added, 'I found it exhausting, to be honest. Talking about stuff I didn't really want to talk about.'

'The accident?'

Artie nodded, her gaze slipping out of reach of his. 'So, there you have it. My life in a nutshell—no pun intended.'

Luca brushed a finger down her cheek. 'Look at me, *cara*.' It was a command but so gently delivered it made something move inside her chest like the slow flow of warm honey.

Artie raised her eyes back to his, the tip of her tongue sneaking out to sweep over her lips. 'I'm sorry for misleading you. You probably wouldn't have married me if you'd known. But I was so desperate to keep the *castello*. I don't know what I'd do without it. It's the only home I've ever known and if I'm forced to leave...' She bit her lip until she winced. 'I can't leave. I just can't.'

He touched her lip with the pad of his thumb. 'Stop doing that. You'll make it bleed.' His tone was gruff and gently reproving, his gaze surprisingly tender. 'We'll find a way to manage this.'

'How? If your grandfather is too ill to travel, then how will I ever get to meet him?'

'Technology to the rescue.' He gave a quick smile and patted his jeans pocket, where his phone was housed. 'We can set up a video call. Nonno's eyesight isn't great and he's not keen on mobile phones but it will be better than nothing.'

Artie moved a step or two away, her arms crossing over her body, her hands rubbing up and down her upper arms as if warding off a chill. 'You're being very understanding about this... I wouldn't blame you if you tore up the agreement and took full possession of the *castello*.'

Please God, don't let him do that. Please. Please. Please.

Luca came up behind her and placed his hands on her shoulders. 'That's not going to happen.' She suppressed a shiver as the movement of air when he spoke disturbed the loose strands of her hair around her neck. 'We'll work together to solve this.'

Artie turned to face him with a frown. 'Why are you being so generous? You said earlier today you're a selfish man, but I'm not seeing it.'

His smile was lopsided and his hands gently squeezed the tops of her shoulders. 'I can be extremely selfish when it comes to getting what I want.' His gaze drifted to her mouth and her heart skipped a beat. After a moment, his eyes came back to hers. Dark. Lustrous. Intense. The air suddenly vibrating with crackling energy as if all the oxygen particles had been disturbed.

'Luca?' Her voice was barely audible, whisper-soft. Her hand crept up to touch his lean jaw, her fingers trailing over the light prickle of his stubble. She sent her index finger around the firm contours of his mouth, the top lip and then the slightly fuller lower one. He drew in a sharp breath as if her touch excited him, thrilled him, tempted him.

His hand came up and his fingers wrapped around her slim wrist as if to pull her hand from his face. But then he made a low, deep sound at the back of his throat and his head came down and his mouth set fire to hers.

CHAPTER SIX

LUCA KNEW HE should stop the kiss before it got out of control. Knew he shouldn't draw her closer to his body where his blood was swelling him fit to burst. Knew he was forty times a fool to be tempted to change the rules on their paper marriage. But right then, all he could do was explore her soft mouth and let his senses run wild with the sweet, tempting taste of her lips. She opened to him on a breathless sigh and the base of his spine tingled when her tongue met his—shy and yet playful, innocent and yet daring. Need drove him to kiss her more deeply, to hold her more closely, to forget about the restrictions he'd placed on their relationship. Call him reckless, call him foolish, but right now he would die without the sweet temptation of her mouth responding to his.

Artie pressed herself against him, her arms winding around his neck, her young, slim body fitting against him as if fashioned specially for him. He ached to explore the soft perfection of her breasts, to glide his hands over her skin, to breathe in the scent of her, to taste her in the most intimate way possible.

His hands settled on her hips, holding her to the aching throb in his pelvis, his conscience at war with his body. He finally managed to find the willpower to drag his mouth off hers, but he couldn't quite bring himself to let her go.

'You know this can't happen.' His voice was so rough it sounded like he'd swallowed ground glass.

She looked up at him with eyes bright and shining with arousal. 'Why can't it? We're both consenting adults.'

Luca placed his hands around her wrists and pulled her arms from around his neck, but he still didn't release her. His fingers circled her wrists in a loose hold, his desire for her chomping at the bit like a bolting thoroughbred stallion. 'You know why.'

Her mouth tightened, her cheeks pooling with twin circles of pink. 'Because I'm a virgin? Is that it?'

Luca released her wrists and stepped away, dragging a hand through his hair in an effort to get his pulse rate to go back to somewhere near normal. 'It's not just about that.'

'Are you saying you don't find me attractive? Not desirable?' Self-doubt quavered in her tone.

Luca let out a gusty sigh. 'I find you extremely attractive and desirable but that's not why I married you. It's not part of the deal. It will make things too complicated when we end it.'

'How do you know that? People have flings all the time without falling in love with each other. Why not us?'

Luca put some distance between their bodies, but even a metre or so away he could still feel the magnetic pull of hers. 'You're young, Artie. Not just in chronological years but in experience. You said it yourself—you haven't been outside the *castello* for ten years. Those were ten valuable growing-up years.'

Her expression soured and hurt coloured her tone. 'You think I'm immature. A child in an adult's body? Is that what you're saying?'

Luca pressed his lips together, fighting to keep his self-control in check. Her adult body was temptation personified but he had to keep his hands off her. It wouldn't be fair to take things to another level, not now he knew how limited her experience. He was the first man to kiss her, to touch her, to expose her to male desire. She was like a teenager experiencing her first crush. A physical crush that had to stop before it got started. 'I'm saying I'm not the right man for you.'

'Consider my offer withdrawn.' She folded her arms around her body and sent him a sideways glance. 'Sorry if I offended you by being so brazen. Believe me, I surprised myself. I don't know what came over me.'

Luca fought back a wry smile. 'We should keep kissing to the absolute minimum.'

Artie gave an indifferent shrug but her eyes displayed her disappointment. 'Fine by me.'

The silence throbbed with a dangerous energy. An energy Luca could feel in every cell of his body. Humming, thrumming sensual energy, awakened, stirred, unsatisfied.

It would be so easy to take back everything he had said and gather her in his arms, to assuage the longing that burned in his body with hot, flicking tongues of flame, to teach her the wonder of sexual compatibility—for he was sure they would be compatible.

He had not felt such electrifying chemistry from kissing someone before. He had not felt such a rush of lust from holding someone close to his body. He had not felt so dangerously tempted to throw caution to the wind and sink his body into the soft silk of another's.

Artie released her arms from around her middle and absently toyed with her wedding ring. 'If you don't mind, I think I'll go to bed.' Her cheeks reddened and she hastily added, 'Alone, I mean. I wasn't suggesting you join—'

'Goodnight, *cara*.'

Artie bolted up the stairs as if she were being chased by a ghost. *Eek.* How could she have been so gauche as to practically beg Luca to make love to her? She couldn't understand why she had been so wanton in her behaviour. Was there something wrong with her? Had her lack of socialising with people her own age affected her development? Her body had woken from a long sleep the moment he kissed her at the wedding. His mouth had sent shivers of longing to every pore of her skin, made her aware of her female needs and desires, made her hungry for a deeper, more powerful connection. A physical connection that would ease the tight, dragging ache in her core.

She closed her bedroom door behind her, letting out a ragged breath. *Fool. Fool. Fool.* He had laid down the rules—a paper marriage with no emotional attachment. A business contract that was convenient and for both parties. But what was convenient about the way she felt about Luca? The heat and fire of his touch made her greedy for more. She had felt his physical response to her, so why was he denying them both the pleasure they both craved?

Because he doesn't want you to fall in love with him.

Artie walked over to her bed and sank onto the mattress with another sigh. Luca thought her too young and innocent for him, too inexperienced in the ways of the world for their relationship to be on an equal footing. But the way her body responded to him made her feel more than his equal. It made her feel alive and feminine and powerful in a way she had never imagined she could feel.

She looked down at the engagement and wedding rings on her left hand, the symbol of their union as a married couple. She was tied to him by law but not by love. And she was fine with that. Mostly. What she wanted was to be tied to him in desire, to explore the electrifying chemistry between them, to indulge herself in the world of heady sensuality.

Artie bounced off the bed and went to her bathroom, staring at her reflection in the mirror above the marble basin. Her eyes were overly bright, her lips still pink and swollen from Luca's passionate kiss. She touched her lower lip with her fingers, amazed at how sensitive it was, as if his kiss had released every one of her nerve endings from a deep freeze.

Artie touched a hand to the ache in the middle of her chest.

So, this was what rejection felt like. The humiliation of wanting someone who didn't want you back.

Why am I so unlucky in the lottery of life?

Luca wasn't a drinker, but right then he wanted to down a bottle of Scotch and throw the empty bottle at the wall. He wanted to stride upstairs to Artie's bedroom and take her in his arms and show her how much he wanted her. He wanted to breathe in the scent of her skin, taste the sweet nectar of her lips, glide his hands over her beautiful body and take them both to paradise. But the hard lessons learned from his father's and brother's death had made him super-cautious when it came to doing things that couldn't be undone.

Making love with Artie would change everything about their relationship. It would change the dynamic between them, pitching them into new territory, dangerous territory that clashed with his six-month time limit.

He had thought himself a good judge of character, someone who didn't miss important details. And yet he hadn't picked up on Artie's social phobia, but it all made perfect sense now. Why she hadn't been at the hospital when he'd visited her father. Why she'd insisted on the wedding being held at the *castello* instead of at one of the local churches. Why she had such a guarded air about her, closed off almost, as if she was uncomfortable around people she didn't know. He still couldn't get his head around the fact that she had spent ten years living almost in isolation. Ten years! It was unthinkable to someone like him, who was rarely in the same city two nights in a row. He lived out of hotels rather than at his villa in Tuscany. He lived in the fast lane because slowing down made him think too much, ruminate too much, hurt too much.

It was easier to block it out with work.

Work was his panacea for all ills. He had built his father's business into a behemoth of success. He had brokered deals all over the world and cashed in on every one of them. Big time.

He had more money than he knew what to do with. It didn't buy him happiness but it did buy him freedom. Freedom from the ties that bound others into dead-end jobs, going-nowhere relationships and the drudgery of duty-bound responsibilities.

Luca walked over to the windows of his suite at the *castello*. The moon was full and cast the *castello* grounds in an ethereal light. The centuries-old trees, the gnarled vines, the rambling roses were testament to how many generations of Artie's family had lived and loved here.

Love. The trickiest of emotions. The one he avoided, because loving people and then letting them down was soul destroying. The stuff of nightmares, a living torture he could do without.

Luca watched as a barn owl flew past the window on silent wings. Nature going about its business under the cloak of moonlight. The *castello* could be restored into a showcase of antiquity. The gardens tended to and nurtured back into their former glory, the ancient vines grafted and replanted to produce award-winning wine. It would cost money…lots of money—money Artie clearly didn't have. But it would be his gift to her for the time she had given up to be married to him.

Six months, and day one was just about over. A day when he had discovered his bride was an introverted social phobic who had never been kissed until his mouth touched hers. A young woman who had not socialised with her peers outside the walls of the *castello*. A young woman who was still a virgin at the age of twenty-five. A modern-day Sleeping Beauty who had yet to be woken to the pleasures of sex.

Stop thinking about sex.

But how could he when the taste of her mouth was still on his lips? The feel of her body pressed against him was branded on his flesh. The ache of desire still hot and tight and heavy in his groin.

The *castello* was huge, and Artie's bedroom was a long, wide corridor away from his, but his awareness of her had never been more heightened and his self-control never more tested. What was it about her that made him so tempted to throw his rules to one side? Her unworldly youth? Her innocence? Her sensual allure? It was all those things and more besides. Things he couldn't quite name but he was aware of them all the same. He felt it in his body when he kissed her. A sense of rightness, as if every kiss he'd experienced before had been erased from his memory so that her mouth could be the new benchmark of what a kiss should be. He felt it when he touched her face and the creamy perfection of her skin made his fingers tingle in a way they had never done when touching anyone else. He felt it when he held her close to his body, the sense that her body was a perfect match for his.

Luca turned away from the window with a sigh of frustration. He needed his laptop so he could immerse himself in work but he'd left it in the car. He knew there wouldn't be too many bridegrooms tapping away on their laptops on their wedding night, but he was not a normal bridegroom.

And he needed to keep reminding his body of that too.

When Artie came downstairs the following morning, Rosa was laying out breakfast in the morning room, but not with her usual energy and vigour. Her face was pale and there were lines of tiredness around her eyes.

'Are you okay?' Artie asked, going to her.

Rosa put a hand to her forehead and winced. 'I have the most dreadful headache.'

'Then you must go straight back to bed. I'll call the doctor and—'

'No, I'll be fine. It's just a headache. I've had them before.'

Artie frowned at the housekeeper's pallor and bloodshot eyes. 'You don't look at all well. I insist you go upstairs to bed. I'll manage things down here. It's about time you had some time to yourself. You've been going non-stop since Papa died. And well before that too.' Artie didn't like admitting how dependent she had become on the housekeeper but she wouldn't have been able to cope without Rosa running errands for her.

Rosa began to untie her apron, her expression etched with uncertainty. 'Are you sure?'

Artie took the apron from the housekeeper and tossed it to one side. 'Upstairs. Now. I'll check on you in a couple of hours. And if you're not feeling better by then, I'm calling the doctor.'

'*Sì, sì*, Signora Ferrantelli.' Rosa mock-saluted Artie and then she left the room.

Artie released a sigh and pulled out a chair to sit down at the breakfast table but her appetite had completely deserted her. What *would* she do without Rosa? The housekeeper was her link to the outside world. Her only true friend. If anything happened to Rosa she would be even more isolated.

Stranded.

But you have a husband now...

The sound of firm footsteps approaching sent a tingle down Artie's spine. She swivelled in her chair to see Luca enter the breakfast room. His hair was still damp from a shower, his face cleanly shaven, the sharp tang of his citrus-based aftershave teasing her nostrils. He was wearing blue jeans and a white T-shirt that lovingly hugged his muscular chest and ridged abdomen.

'Good morning.' Her tone was betrayingly breathless and her cheeks grew warm. 'Did you sleep well?'

'Morning.' He pulled out the chair opposite, sat down and spread his napkin over his lap. 'I ran into Rosa when I was coming down. She didn't look well.'

Artie picked up the jug of fresh orange juice and poured some into her glass. 'I've sent her back to bed. She's got a bad headache. She gets them occasionally.' She offered him the juice but he shook his head and reached for the coffee pot. The rich aroma of freshly brewed coffee filled the air.

Luca picked up his cup, glancing at her over the rim. 'Has

she got plans to retire? This is a big place to take care of. Does anyone come in to help her?'

Artie chewed at the side of her mouth. 'They used to but we had to cut back the staff a while back. I help her. I enjoy it, actually. It's a way of thanking her for helping me all these years.'

'And how does she help you?' His gaze was unwavering, almost interrogating in its intensity.

Artie lowered her gaze and stared at the beads of condensation on her glass of orange juice. 'Rosa runs errands for me. She picks up shopping for me, the stuff I can't get online, I mean. She's been with my family for a long time. This is her home. Here, with me.'

Luca put down his cup with a clatter on the saucer. 'She can't stay here for ever, Artie. And neither can you.' His tone was gentle but firm, speaking a truth she recognised but didn't want to face.

She pushed back her chair and tossed her napkin on the table. 'Will you excuse me? I want to check on Rosa.'

'Sit down, *cara*.' There was a thread of steel underlining each word. The same steel glinting in his eyes and in the uncompromising line of his jaw.

Artie toyed with the idea of defying him, a secret thrill shooting through her at the thought of what he might do to stop her flouncing out of the room. Grasp her by the wrists? Hold her to his tempting body? Bring that firm mouth down on hers in another toe-curlingly passionate kiss? She held his gaze for a heart-stopping moment, her pulse picking up its pace, the backs of her knees fizzing. But then she sat heavily in the chair, whipped her napkin across her lap and threw him a look so sour it could have curdled the milk in the jug. 'I hope you're not going to make a habit of ordering me about like I'm some sort of submissive slave.'

His eyes continued to hold hers in a battle of wills. 'I want to talk to you about your relationship with Rosa. I get that she's been supportive for a long time and you see her as a friend you can rely on, but what if she's actually holding you back from developing more autonomy?'

Artie curled her lip. 'I didn't know you had a psychology degree amongst your other impressive achievements.'

'I don't need a psychology degree to see what's happening here.' He picked up a teaspoon and stirred his coffee even though he didn't take sugar or milk. He put the teaspoon down again and continued. 'I know it's hard for you but—'

'How do you know anything of what it's like for me?' She banged her hand on the table, rattling the cups and saucers. 'You're not me. You don't live in my mind, in my body. I'm the only one who knows what this is like for me.' Her chest was tightening, her breathing becoming laboured, her skin breaking out in a sweat. She could feel the pressure building. The fear climbing up her spine. The dread roiling in her stomach. The hammering of her heart. The panic spreading, growing, expanding, threatening to explode inside her head.

Luca rose from his seat and came around to her side of the table and crouched down beside her chair. He took one of her hands in his, enclosing it within the warm shelter of his. 'Breathe, *cara*. Take a slow, deep breath and let it out on the count of three. One. Two. Three. And again. That's it. Nice and slow.'

Artie concentrated on her breathing, holding tightly to the solid anchor of his hand, drawing comfort from his deep and calming tone. The panic gradually subsided, retreating like a wild beast that had been temporarily subdued by a much bigger, stronger opponent. After a long moment, she let out a rattling sigh. 'I'm okay now... I think...' She tried to remove her hand but he kept a firm but gentle hold on her, stroking the back of her hand with his thumb in slow, soothing strokes that made every overwrought cell in her body quieten.

'Take your time, *mia piccola*.'

Artie chanced a glance at his concerned gaze. 'I suppose

you think I'm crazy. A mad person who can't walk out of her own front gate.'

Luca placed his other hand beneath her chin and locked her gaze on his. His eyes were darkened by his wide pupils, the green and brown flecks in his irises reminding her of a nature-themed mosaic. 'I don't think any such thing.' He gave a rueful twist of his mouth and continued. 'When my father and brother drowned, I didn't leave the house for a month after their funeral.' A shadow passed across his face like scudding grey clouds. 'I couldn't face the real world without them in it. It was a terrible time.' His tone was weighted with gravitas, his expression drawn in lines of deep sadness.

Artie squeezed his hand. 'It must have been so tragic for you and your mother. How did you survive such awful loss?'

One side of his mouth came up in a smile that wasn't quite a smile. 'There are different types of survival, *si*? I chose to concentrate on forging my way through the morass of grief by studying hard, acing my exams and taking over my father's company. I taught myself not to think about my father and brother. Nothing could bring them back, but I figured I could make my father proud by taking up the reins of his business even though it was never my aspiration to do so. That was my brother's dream.' His half-smile faded and the shadow was back in his gaze.

Artie ached for what he had been through, knowing first-hand how such tragic loss impacted on a person. The way it hit you at odd moments like a sudden stab, doubling you over with unbearable pain. The ongoing reminders—birthdays, anniversaries, Christmas, Mother's Day. So many days of the year when it was impossible to forget. And then there was the guilt that never went away. It hovered over her every single day of her life. 'How did your mother cope with her grief?'

Luca released her hand and straightened to his full height. Artie could sense him withdrawing into himself as if the mention of his mother pained him more than he wanted to admit.

'Enough miserable talk for now. Finish your breakfast, *cara*. And after that, we will call my grandfather and I'll introduce you to him.'

Her stomach fluttered with nerves. 'What if he doesn't accept me? What if he doesn't like me or think I'm suitable?'

Luca stroked his hand over the top of her head, his expression inscrutable. 'Don't worry. He will adore you the minute he meets you.'

CHAPTER SEVEN

LUCA CALLED HIS GRANDFATHER on his phone a short time later and selected the video-call option. He sat with Artie on the sofa in the salon and draped an arm around her waist to keep her in the range of the camera. The fragrance of her perfume wafted around his nostrils, her curly hair tickling his jaw when she leaned closer. His grandfather's image came up on the screen and Luca felt Artie tense beside him. He gave her a gentle squeeze and smiled at her before turning back to face his grandfather.

'Nonno, allow me to introduce you to my beautiful wife Artemisia—Artie for short. We were married yesterday.'

The old man frowned. 'Your wife? *Pah!* You think I'm a doddering old fool or something? You said you were never getting married and now you present me with a wife? Why didn't you bring her here to meet me in person?'

'We're on our honeymoon, Nonno,' Luca said, wishing, not for the first time, it was true. 'But soon, *sì*?'

'*Buongiorno*, Signor Ferrantelli,' Artie said. 'I'm sorry you've been ill. It must be so frustrating for you.'

'I'll tell you what's frustrating—having my only grandson gadding about all these years as a freedom-loving playboy, when all I want is to see a great-grandchild before I leave this world.

name by producing a new generation.'

Luca gave a light laugh. 'We've only just got married, Nonno. Give us time.' He suddenly realised he didn't want to share Artie with anyone. He wanted to spend time alone with her, getting to know her better. He wanted her with an ache that wouldn't go away. Ever since he'd kissed her it had smouldered like hot coals inside him. The need to explore her body, to awaken her to the explosive pleasure he knew they would experience together. But he refused to even think about the cosy domestic future his grandfather hoped for him. Babies? A new generation of Ferrantellis? Not going to happen.

'You've wasted so much time already,' Nonno said, scowling. 'Your father was married to your mother and had Angelo and you well before your age.'

'*Sì*, I know.' Luca tried to ignore the dart of pain in his chest at the mention of his father and brother. And his mother, of course. He could barely think of his mother without feeling a tsunami of guilt for how his actions had destroyed her life. Grandchildren might soften the blow for his mother, but how could he allow himself to think about providing them? Family life was something he had never envisaged for himself. How could he when he had effectively destroyed his own family of origin?

'Luca is everything I ever dreamed of in a husband,' Artie piped up in a proud little voice that made something in his chest ping. 'He's definitely worth waiting for.'

Nonno gave a grunt, his frown still in place. 'Did you give her your grandmother's engagement ring?' he asked Luca.

'*Sì*,' Luca said.

Artie lifted her hand to the camera. 'I love it. It's the most gorgeous ring I've ever seen. I feel incredibly honoured to be wearing it. I wish I could have met your wife. You must miss her terribly.'

'Every day.' Nonno shifted his mouth from side to side, his

frown softening its grip on his weathered features. 'Don't leave it too long before you come and see me in person, Artie. I haven't got all the time in the world.'

'You'd have more time if you follow your doctor's advice,' Luca said.

'I'd love to meet you,' Artie said. 'Luca's told me so much about you.'

'Yes, well, he's told me virtually nothing about you,' Nonno said, disapproval ripe in his tone. 'How did you meet?'

'I met Artie through her father,' Luca said. 'I knew she was the one for me as soon as I laid eyes on her.' It wasn't a lie. He had known straight up that Artie was the only young woman his grandfather would approve of as his bride.

Nonno gave another grunt. 'Let's hope you can handle him, Artie. He's a Ferrantelli. We are not easy to live with but if you love him it will certainly help.'

'I think he's the most amazing man I've ever met,' Artie said, softly. 'Take care of yourself, Signor Ferrantelli. I hope to meet you in person soon.'

The most amazing man she'd ever met? Luca mentally laughed off the compliment. Artie had met so few men it wasn't hard to impress her. What he wanted to do was help her get over her phobia. Not just because he wanted her to meet his grandfather but because he knew it would open up opportunities and experiences for her that had been denied her for way too long. But would she trust him enough to guide her through what would no doubt be a difficult and frightening journey for her?

Artie turned to face Luca once the call had ended. His arm was still around her waist and every nerve beneath her skin was acutely aware of its solid warm presence. 'I'm not so sure we convinced him. Are you?'

Luca's expression was etched in frowning lines. 'Who knows?' His features relaxed slightly and he added, 'You did well. That was a nice touch about me being your dream husband.

It's kind of scary how convincing you sounded.' He brushed a stray strand of hair away from her face, his gaze darkening.

Artie disguised a swallow, her heart giving a little kick when his eyes drifted to her mouth. 'Yes, well, I surprised myself, actually.' She frowned and glanced down at the engagement and wedding rings on her hand and then lifted her gaze back to his. 'I feel like I'm letting you down by not being able to leave the *castello*. If we'd gone in person to see him, or even better, married somewhere closer so your grandfather could have attended...'

'You're not letting me down at all,' Luca said. 'But what if I tried to help you? We could start small and see how it goes— baby steps.'

'I've had help before and it hasn't worked.'

'But you haven't had my help.' He smiled and took her hand, running his thumb over the back of it in gentle strokes. 'It's worth a try, surely?'

Panic crawled up her spine and sent icicles tiptoeing across her scalp. 'What, now?'

'No time like the present.'

Artie compressed her lips, trying to control her breathing. 'I don't know...'

He raised her chin with the end of his finger. 'Trust me, *cara*. I won't push you further than you can manage. We will take it one step at a time.'

Artie swallowed and then let out a long, ragged breath. 'Okay. I'll try but don't be mad at me if I don't get very far.'

He leaned down and pressed a light kiss to the middle of her forehead. 'I won't get mad at you, *mia piccola*. I'm a very patient man.'

A few minutes later, Artie stood with Luca on the front steps of the *castello*, her gaze focussed on the long walk to the brass gates in the distance. Her heart was beating so fast she could feel its echo in her ears. Her skin was already damp with perspiration, and her legs trembling like a newborn foal's. She desperately wanted to conquer her fear, now more than ever. She wanted to meet Luca's grandfather, to uphold her side of their marriage deal but what if she failed yet again? She had failed every single time she had tried to leave the *castello*. It was like a thick glass wall was blocking her exit. She could see the other side to freedom but couldn't bring herself to step over the boundary lines. The *castello* was safe. She was safe here. Other people on the outside were safe from *her*.

What would happen if she went past her self-imposed boundary?

Luca took her hand and smiled down at her. 'Ready? One step at a time. Take all the time you need.'

Artie sucked in a deep breath and went down the steps to the footpath. So far, so good. 'I've done this before, heaps of times, and I always fail.'

'Don't talk yourself into failure, *cara*.' His tone was gently reproving. 'Believe you can do something and you'll do it.'

'Easy for you to say.' Artie flicked him a glance. 'You're confident and run a successful business. You've got runs on the board. What do I have? A big fat nothing.'

Luca stopped and turned her so she was facing him, his hands holding her by the upper arms. 'You have cared for your father for a decade. You quite likely extended his life by doing so. Plus, you're a gifted embroiderer. I have never seen such detailed and beautiful work. You have to start believing in yourself, *cara*. I believe in you.'

Artie glanced past his broad shoulder to the front gates, fear curdling her insides. She let out another stuttering breath and met his gaze once more. 'Okay, let's keep going. I have to do this. I *can* do this.'

'That's my girl,' Luca said, smiling and taking her by the hand again. 'I'm with you every step of the way.'

Artie took two steps, then three, four, five until she lost count. The gates loomed closer and closer, the outside world and freedom beckoning. But just as she got to about two-thirds of the way down the path a bird suddenly flew up out of the nearby shrubbery and Artie was so startled she lost her footing and would have tripped if Luca hadn't been holding her hand. 'Oh!' she gasped.

'You're okay, it was just a bird.'

Artie glanced at the front gates, her heart still banging against her breastbone. 'I think I'm done for one day.'

He frowned. 'You don't want to try a little more? We're almost there. Just a few more steps.'

She turned back to face the safety of the *castello*, breathing hard. 'I'm sorry but I can't do any more. I'll try again tomorrow.' *And I'll fail just like every other time.*

Luca stroked his hand over the back of her head. 'You did well, *mia piccola*.'

Artie gave him a rueful look. 'I failed.'

He stroked her cheek with a lazy finger, his gaze unwavering. 'Failure is when you give up trying.' He took her hand again with another smile. 'Come on. It's thirsty work wrestling demons, *sì*?'

Once they were back inside the *castello* in the salon, Artie let out a sigh. 'It's not that I don't want to go outside…'

He handed her a glass of mineral water. 'What are you most frightened of?'

She took the glass from him and set it on the table next to her, carefully avoiding his gaze. 'I'm frightened of hurting people.'

'Why do you think you'll hurt someone?'

Artie lifted her eyes to his. 'It was my fault we had the accident.'

Luca frowned and came over to sit beside her, taking her hands in his. 'But you weren't driving, surely? You were only fifteen, *sì*?'

She looked down at their joined hands, her chest feeling so leaden it was almost impossible to take in another breath. 'I wanted to go to a party. My parents didn't want me to go but like teenagers do, I wouldn't take no for an answer. They relented and I went to the party, which wasn't as much fun as I'd hoped. And when my parents picked me up that night...well, my father was tired because it was late and he didn't see the car drifting into his lane in time to take evasive action. I woke up in hospital after being in a coma for a month to find my mother had died instantly and my father was in a wheelchair.'

Luca put his arms around Artie and held her close. 'I'm sorry. I know there are no words to take away the guilt and sadness but you were just a kid.'

Artie eased back to look up at him through blurry vision. 'I haven't ever met anyone else who truly understood.' She twisted her mouth wryly, 'Not that I've met a lot of people in the last ten years.' She lifted her hand to his face and stroked his lean jaw and added. 'But I think you do understand.'

A shadow passed through his gaze and he pulled her hand down from his face. 'You don't know me, *cara*. You don't know what I'm capable of.' His voice contained a note of self-loathing that made the back of her neck prickle.

'Why do you say that?'

He sprang off the sofa in an agitated fashion. 'I haven't told you everything about the day my father and brother died.'

She swallowed tightly. 'Do you want to tell me now?' Her voice came out whisper-soft.

Luca pulled at one side of his mouth with his straight white teeth, his hands planted on his slim hips. Then he released a ragged breath. 'It was my fault they drowned. We were on holiday in Argentina. We had gone to an isolated beach because I'd heard the waves were best there. I wanted to go back in for another surf even though the conditions had changed. I didn't listen to my father. I just raced back in and soon got into trouble.' He winced as if recalling that day caused him immeasurable pain. 'My father came in after me and then my brother. The rip took them both out to sea. I somehow survived. I can never forgive myself for my role in their deaths. I was selfish and reckless, and in trying to save me, they both lost their lives.'

Artie went to him and grasped him by both hands. 'Oh, Luca, you were only a child. Kids do stuff like that all the time, especially teenage boys. You mustn't blame yourself. But I understand how you do...you see, I blame myself for my mother's death and my dad's disability.'

'I do understand.' His eyes were full of pain. 'There were times when I wished I had been the one to die. I'm sure you wished the same. But that doesn't help anyone, does it?'

'No...' She leaned her head against the solid wall of his chest, slipping her arms back around his waist. 'Thank you.'

'For?' The deep, low rumble of his voice reverberated next to her ear.

Artie looked back up at him. 'For listening. For understanding. For not judging.' She took a little hitching breath and added, 'For wanting me when I thought no one ever could.'

Luca brushed his thumb over the fullness of her lower lip, setting off a firestorm in her flesh. 'I want you. I've tried ignoring it, denying it, resisting it, but it won't go away.' His voice dropped to a lower pitch, tortured almost, as if he was fighting a battle within himself between what he should do and what he shouldn't.

Artie licked her lips and encountered the saltiness of his thumb. 'I want you too.' She touched his firm jaw with her hand. 'I don't see why we have to stick to the rules. We are attracted to each other physically. Why not enjoy the opportunity? How else am I going to gain experience? I'm hardly going to meet anyone whilst living here, and we're married anyway, so why not?' She could hardly believe how brave she was being, speaking her needs out loud. But something about Luca made her feel brave and courageous. His desire for her spoke to her on a cellular level, making her aware of her body and its needs in a way she hadn't thought possible.

Luca cupped one side of her face in his hand, his thumb stroking over her cheek in slow, measured strokes. A frown settled between his brows, his eyes darker than she had ever seen them. 'Is that really want you want? A physical relationship, knowing it will end after six months?'

Maybe it won't end.

Artie didn't say it out loud—she was shocked enough at hearing it inside her head.

Since the accident, she had denied herself any dreams of one day finding love, of marrying and having a family. She had destroyed her family, so why should she have one of her own? But now she had met Luca, she realised what she was missing out on. The thrill of being attracted to someone and knowing they desired you back. The perfectly normal needs within her body she had ignored for so long were fully awake and wanting, begging to be assuaged. 'I want to know what it is like to make love with a man,' Artie said. 'I want that man to be you. I trust you to take care of me. To treat me with respect.'

He stroked her hair back from her forehead, his eyes dark and lustrous. 'I can't think of a time when I wanted someone more. But I told myself I wasn't going to take advantage of the situation—of you. I don't think it would be fair to give you false hope that this could lead to anything…more permanent.'

She leaned closer, winding her arms around his neck. 'Stop overthinking it. Do what your heart is telling you, not your head. Make love to me, Luca.'

Luca placed his hands on her hips and bent his head down so their lips were within touching distance. 'Are you sure? There's still time to change your mind.'

Artie pressed her lips against his, once, twice, three times. 'I'm not changing my mind. I want this. I want you.'

He stood and drew her to her feet, dropping a warm, firm kiss to her lips. 'Not here. Upstairs. I want everything to be perfect for you.'

A short time later, they were in Luca's bedroom. He closed the door softly behind them and ran his gaze over Artie. She had expected to feel shy, self-conscious about her body, but as soon as he began to undo the buttons on her top, she shivered with longing, desperate to be naked with him, to feel his skin against her own.

He kissed her lingeringly, taking his time nudging and nibbling her lips, teasing her with his tongue, tantalising her senses with his taste and his touch. His mouth moved down to just below her ear and she shivered as his lips touched her sensitive skin. One of his hands slipped beneath her unbuttoned top, gliding along the skin of her ribcage to cup one of her breasts. His touch was gentle and yet it created a tumultuous storm in her flesh. Her nipple tightened, her breast tingled, her legs weakened as desire shot through her like a missile strike.

'I want to touch you all over.' His tone had a sexy rough edge that made her senses whirl.

'I want to touch you too.' Artie tugged his T-shirt out of his jeans and slid her hands under the fabric to stroke his muscular chest. His warm, hard flesh felt foreign, exotically foreign, unlike anything she had touched before. She explored the hard planes and ridged contours of his hair-roughened chest, marvelling at the difference between their bodies. A difference that excited her, made her crazy with longing, eager to discover more.

Luca unclipped her bra and gazed at her breasts for a long moment, his eyes dark and shining with unmistakable desire. 'So beautiful.' His thumbs rolled over each of her nipples, his gaze intent, as if he found her breasts the most fascinating things he'd ever seen. Before this moment Artie had more or less ignored her breasts other than to do her monthly breast check. But now she was aware of the thousands of nerve-endings that were responding to Luca's touch. Aware of the way her tender flesh tingled and tautened under his touch. Aware of the primal need it triggered in her feminine core—of the ache that longed to feel the hard male presence of his body.

Artie gasped as Luca brought his mouth to her breasts, her hands gripping him by the waist, not trusting her legs to keep her upright as the sensations washed through her. His tongue teased her nipple into a tight point, and then he circled it with a slow sweep of his tongue.

The slight roughness of his tongue against her softer skin evoked another breathless and shuddering gasp from her. 'Oh… *Oh…*'

Luca lifted his mouth off her breast and smiled a bone-melting smile. 'You like that?'

Artie leaned closer, the feel of her naked breasts pressing against his muscular chest sending another riot of tingling sensations through her body. 'I love it when you touch me. I can't get enough of it.'

He slid his hands down to the waistband of her jeans, his fingers warm against her belly as he undid the snap button. Who knew such an action could cause such a torrent of heat in her body? Artie could barely stop her legs from shaking in anticipation. He held her gaze in a sensual lock that made her heart skip and trip. He slid his hand beneath the loosened waistband, cupping her mound through the thin, lacy barrier of her knickers. Her body responded with humid heat, slickening, moistening with the dew of desire.

'I can't seem to get enough of you either,' he said. 'But I don't want to rush you. I want to go slowly to make it good for you.'

Artie placed her hands on the waistband of his jeans. 'Can I?'

His eyes gleamed. 'Go for it.'

She held her breath and undid the fastening and slid down the zipper. She peeled back his underwear and drank in the potent sight of him engorged with blood, thickened with longing. Longing for *her*.

Luca drew in a sharp breath as her fingers skated over his erection. He removed her hand and returned his mouth to hers in a spine-tingling kiss that spoke of the primal need pulsing through his body. The flicker of his tongue against hers, the increasing urgency and pressure of his mouth drew from her a fevered response she hadn't thought possible.

Within a few breathless moments they were both naked and

lying on the bed together, Luca's eyes roving over her body in glinting hunger. He placed a hand on her hip, turning her towards him, his expression becoming sober. 'There's something we need to discuss. Protection. We can't let any accidents happen, especially given the terms of our relationship.'

Artie knew he was being reasonable and responsible but a secret part of her flinched at his adamant stance on the six-month time frame. An accidental pregnancy would change everything. It would tie them together for the next eighteen years…possibly for ever. 'I understand. I wouldn't want any…accidents either.' She had not allowed herself to think of one day having a baby but now a vision popped into her head of a gorgeous, dark-haired baby… Luca's baby.

Don't get any ideas. You know the terms. Six months and six months only.

Her conscience had an annoying habit of reminding her of the deal she had made with Luca. A deal she hoped she wouldn't end up regretting in the end.

Luca stroked his hand down the flank of her thigh, his gaze centred on hers. 'It's important to me that you enjoy our lovemaking. I want you to feel comfortable, so please tell me if something isn't working for you or you want to stop at any point.'

Artie traced the shape of his lower lip with her finger. 'I've liked everything so far. I thought I'd be nervous about being naked with someone but this feels completely natural, as if we've done this before in another lifetime. Does that make sense?'

He smiled and captured her hand and pressed a kiss to each of her fingertips, his eyes holding hers. 'In a strange way, yes, although I have to say I've never made love to a virgin before.'

'Are *you* nervous?'

His mouth twisted into a rueful grimace. 'A bit.'

'Don't be.' She pressed her lips to his in a soft kiss. 'I want you to make love to me. I feel like I've been waiting all my life for this moment.'

Luca brought his mouth back to hers in a kiss that drugged her senses and ramped up her desire for him until she was arching her back and whimpering. His hands explored her breasts in soft strokes, his lips and tongue caressing her until she was breathless with longing. The ache between her legs intensified, a hot, throbbing ache that travelled through her pelvis like the spread of fire.

He moved down her body with a series of kisses from her breasts to her belly and then to the heart of her femininity. Artie drew in a breath, tense with excitement as his fingers spread her, his lips and tongue exploring her, teasing a response from her that shook her body into a cataclysmic orgasm. It swept her up in its rolling waves, the pulsations carrying her into a place beyond the reach of thought or even full consciousness. Blissful sensations washed over her, peace flooding her being—the quiet after the storm.

'I had no idea it could be like…like *that*…' Artie could barely get her voice to work and a sudden shyness swept over her.

Luca moved back up her body to plant a kiss to her lips. She could taste herself on his lips and it added a whole new layer of disturbing but delightful intimacy. 'It will only get better.' He brushed his knuckles over her warm cheeks. 'Don't be shy, *cara*.'

Artie bit her lip. 'Easy for you to say. You've probably done this a hundred times, possibly more. I'm a complete novice.'

He smoothed her hair back from her face, his expression suddenly serious. 'The press makes a big thing out of my lifestyle but I haven't been as profligate as they make out. Unfortunately, my grandfather believes what he reads in the press.' His mouth twisted ruefully. 'I've had relationships—fleeting ones that were entirely transactional. And I've always tried not to deliberately hurt anyone. But of course, it still does happen occasionally.'

I hope I don't get hurt.

The potential to get hurt once their relationship came to its inevitable end was a real and present worry, but even so, Artie couldn't bring herself to stop things before they got any more complicated. He had revealed things about himself that made her hungry to learn more about him. His workaholism, his carefully guarded heart, his history of short-term, going-nowhere relationships. He was imprisoned by his lifestyle in the same way she was imprisoned by the *castello*. Would he go back to his playboy existence once they parted?

Artie lifted her hand and stroked his stubbly jaw. 'I want you to make love to me. I want you to experience pleasure too.'

Luca's eyes were dark and hooded as he gazed at her mouth. 'Everything about you brings me pleasure, *cara*. Absolutely everything.' And his mouth came down and sealed hers.

The kiss was long and intense and Artie could feel the tension rising in his body as well as her own. His legs were entangled with hers, his aroused body pressing urgently against her, his breathing as ragged as hers. His mouth moved down to her breasts, subjecting them to a passionate exploration that left her squirming and whimpering with need. She slid her hand down from his chest to his taut abdomen, desperate to explore the hard contours of his body. He drew in a quick breath when her hand encountered his erection and it made her all the bolder in her caresses. He was velvet-wrapped steel, so exotically, erotically different from her, and she couldn't wait to experience those differences inside her body.

Luca eased back and reached for a condom, swiftly applying it before coming back to her, his gaze meshing with hers. 'I'll go slowly but please tell me if you want to stop at any point. I don't want to hurt you.'

Artie brushed his hair back from his forehead, her lower body so aware of his thick male presence at her entrance. 'You won't hurt me.' Her tone was breathless with anticipation, her body aching for his possession.

He gently nudged apart her feminine folds, allowing her time to get used to him as he progressed. Slow, shallow, sensual. Her body welcomed him, wrapping around him without pain, without resistance.

'Are you okay?' he asked, pausing in his movements.

'More than okay.' Artie sighed with pure pleasure, her hands going to his taut buttocks to hold him to her.

He thrust a little deeper, still keeping his movements slow and measured. She arched her hips to take more of him in, her body tingling with darts and arrows of pleasure as his body moved within hers. His breathing rate changed, becoming more laboured as his pace increased. She was swept up into his rhythm, her senses reeling as the tension built to an exquisite crescendo. She was almost at the pinnacle, hovering in the infinitesimal moment before total fulfilment. Wanting, aching, needing to fly but not sure how to do it.

Luca reached down between their bodies and coaxed her swollen feminine flesh into an earth-shattering orgasm. Spirals of intense pleasure burst through her body, ripples and waves and darts of bliss, throwing her senses into a tailspin and her mind into disarray.

Luca reached his release soon after, an agonised groan escaping his lips as his body convulsed and spilled. Artie held him close, breathing in the scent of their lovemaking, thrilled to have brought him to a place of blissful satiation.

Artie lay with him in the peaceful aftermath, her thoughts drifting... The boundaries between the physical and the emotional were becoming increasingly blurred. She knew she would always remember this moment as a pivotal one in her life as a woman.

Luca Ferrantelli. Her husband. Her first lover.

The presence of his body, the desire that drew them together bonded her to him in a way that was beyond the physical. The chemistry between her and Luca was so powerful, so magical it had produced a cataclysmic reaction. An explosion of pleasure she could still feel reverberating throughout her body.

How could she have thought he was arrogant and unyield-ing? He had taken such respectful care of her every step of the way. He had held back his own release in order to make sure she was satisfied first. She couldn't have asked for a more con-siderate and generous lover.

But it didn't mean she was falling in love with him.

Artie knew the rules and had accepted them. She could be modern and hip about their arrangement. Sure she could. This was about a physical connection so intense, so rapturous she wanted to make the most of it.

Luca leaned up on one elbow and slowly withdrew from her body, carefully disposing of the condom. He rolled back to cra-dle one side of her face with his hand, his eyes searching hers. 'How do you feel?' His voice had a husky edge, his expression tender in a way she hadn't been expecting. Had he too been af-fected by her first time and their first time together?

'I'm fine.'

A frown pulled at his brow. 'I didn't hurt you?'

'Not at all.' She smoothed away his frown with her finger-tip. 'Thanks for being so gentle with me.'

His hand brushed back the hair from her face in the tender-est of movements. 'Your enjoyment is top priority for me. I don't want you to feel you ever have to service my needs above your own.'

Artie ran her fingertip over the fullness of his bottom lip, not quite able to meet his gaze. 'Was it good for you too?'

He tipped up her chin and smiled, and her chest felt like it was cracking open. 'Off the charts.' He leaned down to press a soft, lingering kiss to her lips. He lifted off again, his expression becoming thoughtful. 'I've never been a virgin trophy hunter. A woman's virginity is not something I consider a prize to be claimed or a conquest to be sought.' He captured a loose strand of her hair and tucked it back behind her ear. 'But I have to say I feel privileged to have made love with you.'

Artie wrapped her arms around his waist and leaned her

cheek against the wall of his chest. 'I feel privileged too. You made it so special.'

There was a moment or two of silence.

Luca stroked his hand down between Artie's shoulder blades to the base of her spine. 'I should let you get up and get dressed.'

Artie lifted her head off his chest to smile at him. 'Is that what you really want me to do right now?'

He grinned and pressed her back down on the bed with his weight playfully pinning her. 'Not right now.' And he brought his mouth back down to hers.

CHAPTER EIGHT

LATER THAT MORNING, Luca had to convince himself to get out of bed with Artie. He couldn't remember a time when he had spent a morning more pleasurably. Making love with her for the first time had affected him in a way he hadn't been expecting. The mutual passion they had shared had been beyond anything he had experienced before. And that was deeply troubling.

Why was it so special? Because she was innocent and he so worldly and jaded that making love with her was something completely different from the shallow hook-ups he preferred? Or was it the exquisite feel of her skin next to his? Her mouth beneath his? Her touch, her sighs, her gasps and cries that made him feel more of a man than he ever had before?

The trust she had shown in him had touched him deeply. And he had honoured that trust by making sure she was completely satisfied, and yet his own satisfaction had risen to a whole new level of experience. It was as if his body had been asleep before now. Operating on a lower setting that didn't fully register all the nuances of mind-blowing sex. The glide of soft hands on his body, the velvet-soft press of lips on his heated skin, the delicious friction of female flesh against him. Every moment was imprinted on his brain, every kiss, every touch branded on his body.

And he wanted it to continue, which was the most troubling thought of all. He, who never stayed with a lover longer than a week or two. He, who never envisaged a future with anyone. He, who had locked down his emotions so long ago he didn't think he had the capacity to feel anything for anyone any more.

And yet...

Every time Artie looked at him with those big brown eyes, something tugged in his chest. Every time her pillow-soft lips met his, fire spread through his body, a raging fire of lust and longing unlike any he had felt before. Every time she smiled it was like encountering sunshine after a lifetime of darkness.

Luca swung his legs over the side of the bed before he was tempted to make love to her for the third time. He turned and held out a hand to her. 'Come on. Time for some more exposure therapy.'

Artie unfolded her limbs and stood in front of him, her hands going to his hips, sending his blood racing. Her eyes were bright and sparkling, her lips swollen from his kisses. 'Let's stay here instead. It'll be more fun.'

Luca gave her a stern look. Exposure therapy was well known to be the pits the first few times but it still had to be endured for results. '*Cara*, you're procrastinating. It's classic avoidance behaviour and it will only make things worse.'

Her gaze lost its playful spark and her mouth tightened. Her hands fell away from his hips and she turned and snatched up a loose bed sheet and covered her nakedness, as if she was suddenly ashamed of her body. 'Last time I looked, you were my temporary husband and lover, not my therapist. I don't appreciate you trying to fix me.'

Luca suppressed a frustrated sigh. 'I'm not trying to fix you, *cara*. I'm trying to help you gain the courage to go a little further each day. I'll be with you all the time and I won't push you into doing anything you don't want to do. You can trust me, okay?'

Her teeth chewed at her lower lip, her gaze still guarded. 'Look, I know you mean well, but we tried it before and I failed.'

'That doesn't mean you'll fail today.'

There was a long moment of silence.

Artie released a long, shuddering breath. 'Okay... I'll give it another try.' She swallowed and glanced at him, her cheeks tinged with pink. 'Do you mind if I have a quick shower first?'

Luca waved his hand towards the bathroom. 'Go right ahead. I'll meet you downstairs in half an hour.' He needed to put some space between them before he was tempted to join her in the shower.

She walked to the door of the bathroom, then stopped and turned to look back at him with a frown between her eyes. 'Did you only make love to me to make me more amenable to going outside the *castello* grounds with you?'

'I made love with you because I wanted you and you wanted me.'

And I still want you. Badly.

Her teeth did another nibble of her lip, uncertainty etched on her features. 'I hope I don't disappoint you this time...'

Luca came over to her and tipped up her chin and planted a soft kiss to her lips. 'You could never disappoint me.'

Artie showered and changed with her mind reeling at what Luca wanted her to do. She had failed so many times. Why should this time be any different? Panic flapped its wings in her brain and her belly, fear chilled her skin and sent a tremble through her legs. But she took comfort in the fact he promised to stay with her, to support her as she confronted her fear—a fear she had lived with so long it was a part of her identity. She literally didn't know who she was now without it. But making love with Luca had given her the confidence to step outside her comfort zone. Her skin still sang with the magic of his touch, the slightly tender muscles in her core reminding her of the power and potency of his body.

Luca was waiting for her downstairs and took her hand at the front door. 'Ready? Our goal is to go farther than we went yesterday—even if we don't make it outside the gates it will still be an improvement. That's the way to approach difficult tasks—break them up into smaller, achievable segments.'

Artie drew in a shaky breath, her chest feeling as if a flock of frightened finches were trapped inside. 'Sounds like a sensible plan. Okay, let's give it a go.'

The sun was shining and white fluffy clouds were scudding across the sky. A light breeze scented with old-world roses danced past Artie's face. Luca's fingers wrapped around hers, strong, warm, supportive, and she glanced up at him and gave a wobbly smile. 'Thanks for being so patient.'

He looped her arm through his, holding her close as they walked slowly but surely down the cobbled footpath to the wrought-iron front gates. 'I probably made you go too fast the first time. Let's slow it down a bit. We've got plenty of time to stop and smell the roses.'

Artie walked beside him and tried to concentrate on the spicy fragrance of the roses rather than the fear crawling over her skin. She was conscious of Luca's muscular arm linked with hers and the way he matched his stride to hers. She flicked him another self-conscious glance. 'You must think this is completely ridiculous. That *I'm* completely ridiculous.'

He gave her a light squeeze. 'I don't think that at all. Fear is a very powerful emotion. It can be paralysing. Fear of failure, fear of success, fear of—'

'Commitment,' Artie offered.

There was a slight pause before he answered. 'That too.'

'Fear of love.' She was on a roll, hardly noticing how many cobblestones there were to go to the front gate.

There was another silence, longer this time, punctured only by the sound of the whispering breeze and twittering birds in the overgrown shrubbery.

'Fear of not being capable of loving.' His tone contained a rueful note.

Artie stopped walking to look up at his mask-like expression. 'Why do you think you're not capable of loving someone? You love your grandfather, don't you?'

Luca gave a twisted smile that didn't quite reach his eyes. 'Familial love is an entirely different sort of love. However, choosing to love someone for the rest of my life is not something I feel capable of doing. I would only end up hurting them by letting them down in the end.'

'But is loving someone a choice?' Artie asked. 'I mean, I haven't fallen in love myself but I've always understood it to be outside of one's control. It just happens.'

He captured a loose tendril of her hair and tucked it back behind her ear. His touch was light and yet electrifying, his gaze dark and inscrutable. 'A lucky few find love for a lifetime. But some lives are tragically cut short and then that same love becomes a torture for the one left behind.'

'Is that what happened to your mother?'

Luca's gaze drifted into the distance, his expression becoming shadowed. 'I will never forget the look of utter devastation on my mother's face when she was told my father and brother had drowned. She didn't come with us that day and when only I came home...' He swallowed tightly and continued in a tone rough and husky with banked-down emotion. 'For months, years, she couldn't look at me without crying. I found it easier to keep my distance. I hated seeing her like that, knowing I was responsible for what happened.'

Artie wrapped her arms around his waist and hugged him. 'Oh, Luca, you have to learn to forgive yourself. I'm sure your mother doesn't blame you. You were a young teenager. She was probably relieved you hadn't been taken as well. It could have happened. You could have all been drowned.'

He eased out of her hug and gave her a grim look. 'There were times in the early days when I wished I had been taken with them. But then I realised I owed it to my father and brother to live the best life I could to honour them.'

A life of hard work. A life with no love. No commitment. No emotional vulnerability. A life of isolation...not unlike her own.

A life of isolation she would go back to once their marriage was over.

Artie glanced at the front gates of the *castello* and drew in a shuddering breath. The verdigris-covered gates blurred in front of her into a grotesque vision of blue and green twisted metal. The sun disappeared behind a cloud and the birds suddenly went quiet as if disturbed by a menacing predator lurking in the shadows.

'Luca, I don't think I can go any further...'

He took her hand and looped her arm through his once more. 'You'll be fine. We're almost there. We've gone farther than yesterday. Just a few more steps and we'll be—'

'No.' Artie pulled out of his hold and took a few stumbling steps back towards the *castello*. 'I can't.'

Luca captured her by the wrist and brought her back to face him, his expression concerned. 'Whoa there. Slow down or you'll trip and twist your ankle.'

Her chest was so restricted she couldn't take a breath. Her stomach was churning, her knees shaking, her skin breaking out in a clammy sweat. She closed her eyes and a school of silverfish swam behind her eyelids. She opened her eyes but she couldn't see past the sting of tears. She tried to gulp in a breath but her throat wouldn't open enough for it to get through.

I'm going to die. I'm going to die. I'm going to die.

The words raced through her mind as if they were being chased by the formless fear that consumed her.

Luca gathered her close to his chest and stroked her stiff back and shoulders with slow, soothing strokes. 'Breathe, *cara*. Take a deep breath and let it out on the count of three. One. Two. Three. And again. One. Two. Three. Keep going, *mia piccola*. One. Two. Three.'

His gently chanted words and the stroke of his hands began to quieten the storm inside her body. The fog in Artie's brain slowly lifted, the fear gradually subsiding as the oxygen returned to her bloodstream.

She was aware of every point of contact with his body—her breasts pressed against his chest, the weight of his arm around her back, his other hand moving up and down between her shoulder blades in those wonderfully soothing strokes, his pelvis warm and unmistakably male against hers, his chin resting on the top of her head. She was aware of the steady *thud, thud, thud* of his heart against her chest, the intoxicating smell of his skin, the need awakening anew in her body. Pulses, contractions, flickers and tingles deep in her core.

Luca lifted his chin off her head and held her slightly aloft, his gaze tender. 'You did well—it's only our second try. Don't feel bad you didn't make it all the way. We'll try again tomorrow.'

Artie chewed her lip, ashamed she hadn't gone further. 'What if I'm never able to do it? What if I—?'

His finger pressed softly down on her lips to silence her self-destruction beliefs. 'Don't talk yourself into failure, *cara*. I know you can do it. You want to get better and that's half the battle, is it not?'

Artie gave a tremulous smile, heartened by his belief in her. Comforted by his commitment to helping her. Touched by his concern and patience and support. 'I do want to get better. I'm tired of living like this. I want to experience life outside the walls of the *castello*.'

He cupped one side of her face in his hand. 'And I can't wait to show you life outside these walls. There are so many things we can do together—dinner, dancing, sightseeing, skiing, trekking. I will enjoy showing you all my favourite places.'

Artie gave a self-deprecating smile. 'I have a lot of catching up to do. And only six months in which to do it.'

Luca's hand fell away from her face, his expression tightening as if her mentioning the time limit on their relationship was jarring to him. 'Of course, the most important thing we need to do is introduce you to my grandfather. I can't use the excuse of being on honeymoon for weeks or months on end.'

'Maybe he'll be well enough to come here soon.' It was a lame hope but she articulated it anyway.

His hand scraped back his hair in a distracted manner. 'There's no guarantee that's going to happen. Besides, I have work to see to. I can't stay here indefinitely.'

'I'm not stopping you from doing your work,' Artie said. 'You can leave any time you like.'

His gaze met hers. Strong. Determined. Intractable. 'I want you with me.'

A frisson scooted down her spine at the dark glint in his eyes. The glint that spoke of the desire still smouldering inside him—the same desire smouldering inside her. She could feel the crackle of their chemistry in the air. Invisible currents of electricity that zapped and fizzed each time their eyes met and each time they touched. He stepped closer and slid his hand beneath the curtain of her hair, making her skin tingle and her blood race. His gaze lowered to her mouth, the sound of his breath hitching sending another shiver cascading down her spine.

'I didn't think it was possible that I could want someone so much.' His tone was rough around the edges.

Artie moved closer, her hands resting on the hard wall of his chest, her hips clamped to his, heat pooling in her core. 'I want you too.'

He rested his forehead on hers, their breath mingling in the space between their mouths. 'It's too soon for you. You'll be sore.' His voice was low, his hands resting on her hips.

Artie brought her mouth closer to his, pressing a soft kiss to his lips. 'I'm not sore at all. You were so gentle with me.'

He groaned and drew her closer, his mouth coming down on hers in a kiss that spoke of banked-down longing. She opened to the commanding thrust of his tongue, her senses whirling as he called her tongue into sensual play. Need fired through her body, hot streaks of need that left no part of her unaffected. Tingles shot down her spine and through her pelvis, heating her to boiling point. Her intimate muscles responded with flickers and fizzes of delight, her bones all but melting. One of his hands moved from her hip to cup her breast through her clothes, sending another fiery tingle through her body.

He deepened the kiss even further, his hand going beneath her top and bra to cup her skin on skin. The warmth of his palm and the possessive weight of his fingers sent her pulse soaring. He stroked her nipple into a tight bud of exquisite sensations, powerful sensations for such a small area of her body. He lifted his mouth off hers and lowered his lips to her breast, his tongue swirling over her engorged nipple, his teeth gently tugging and releasing in a passionate onslaught that made her gasp with delight.

The sound of Luca's phone ringing from inside his trouser pocket evoked a curt swear word from him as he lifted his mouth off her breast. 'I'd better get this. It's the ringtone I set up for Nonno's carer.' He pulled out his phone and took the call, a frown pulling at his forehead.

Artie rearranged her clothes and tried not to eavesdrop but it was impossible not to get the gist of the conversation. His grandfather had suffered a fall and was being taken to hospital with a suspected broken hip. Luca ended the call after reassuring his grandfather's carer he would leave for the hospital straight away.

He slipped the phone back in his pocket and gave Artie a grave look. 'You heard most of that?'

Artie placed her hand on his forearm. 'I'm so sorry. Is he going to be okay?'

He shrugged one shoulder, the almost casual action at odds with the dark shadows in his eyes. 'Who knows? Nonno is eighty-three. A broken hip is a big deal for someone of that age.' He released a breath and continued. 'I'm going to the hospital now. I want to speak to the orthopaedic surgeon. I want to make sure Nonno gets the very best of care.' He held her gaze for a moment. 'This might be your only chance to meet him.' His voice was husky with carefully contained emotion but she could sense the effort it took. His jaw was locked tight, his nostrils flaring as he fought to control his breathing.

Artie's throat tightened. 'I wish I could go with you, Luca. I really do.'

He gave a movement of his lips that wasn't quite a smile. He reached for her hand and gave it a gentle press. 'I'll be back as soon as I can.'

'Please send my best wishes for a speedy recovery.' Artie knew the words were little more than useless platitudes when all Luca wanted was her by his side. She was never more aware of letting down her side of the bargain. Letting *him* down. It pained her she was unable to harness her fear for his sake.

She watched as he drove away, her heart feeling as if it was torn in two. It felt wrong not to be with him—wrong in a way she hadn't expected to feel. As if part of her was missing now he was gone. The *castello* had never been more of a prison, her fear never more of a burden. Why couldn't she feel the fear and do it anyway? Was she to be imprisoned within these walls for the rest of her life? Luca needed her and she wasn't able to be with him, and yet she wanted nothing more than to be by his side.

She wanted to be with him because she loved him.

Artie could no longer suppress or deny her feelings about him. She had fallen in love with him in spite of his rules, in spite of her own efforts to keep her heart out of their arrangement. But her heart had been in it from the moment Luca kissed her. He had awoken her out of a psychological coma, inspiring her to live life in a full and vibrant way. How could she let him down now when he needed her? How could she not fight through her fears for him?

Rosa came out to join her, shading her eyes from the blinding sunshine. 'Do you know when he'll be back?'

Artie gave a despondent sigh. 'No. I feel so bad I wasn't able to go with him. What sort of wife am I that I can't even be by my husband's side when he needs me most?'

Rosa gave her a thoughtful look. 'I guess you have to measure up which thing is bigger—your fear of leaving here or your fear of not being there for him.'

Artie bit her lip, struggling to hold back a tumult of negative emotion. Her sense of failure, her lack of courage, her inability to overcome her phobia.

You're hopeless. A failure. An embarrassment.

Her harsh internal critic rained down abuse until she wanted to curl up into a tiny ball and hide away. But hiding never solved anything, did it? She had hidden here for ten years and nothing had changed.

And yet...something *had* changed. Luca had changed her. Awakening her to feelings and sensations she hadn't thought possible a few days ago. Feelings she could no longer hide from—feelings that were not part of Luca's rules but she felt them anyway. How could she not? He was the light to her darkness, the healing salve to her psychological wound, the promise of a life outside these cold stone walls. He was her gateway to the outside world, the world that had frightened and terrified her so much because she didn't trust it to keep her safe.

But she trusted Luca.

She had trusted him with her body, giving herself to him, responding to him with a powerful passion she could still feel in her most intimate flesh. Her love for him was bigger than her fear. Much bigger. That was what she would cling to as she stared down her demons. She had the will, she had the motivation, she had her love for him to empower her in a way nothing had been able to before. Luca was outside her prison walls, and the only way she could be with him in his hour of need was to leave the *castello*, propelled, empowered, galvanised by the love she felt for him.

Love was supposed to conquer all.

She would damn well prove it.

CHAPTER NINE

LUCA GOT TO the hospital in time to speak to his grandfather before he was taken for surgery. Nonno looked ashen and there was a large purple and black bruise on his face as well as his wrist and elbow where he had tried to break his fall. Luca took the old man's papery hand and tried to reassure him. 'I'll be here when you come out of theatre. Try not to worry.'

Nonno grimaced in pain and his eyes watered. 'When am I going to meet this new wife of yours? You'd better hurry up and bring her to me before I fall off my perch.'

'Soon,' Luca said, hoping it was true. 'When you're feeling better. You don't want to scare her off with all those bruises, do you?'

A wry smile played with the corners of Nonno's mouth. 'It's good that you've settled down, Luca. I've been worried about you since…well, for a long time now.'

'I know you have.' Luca patted his grandfather's hand, his chest tightening as if it were in a vice. 'I was waiting for the right one to come along. Just like you did with Nonna.'

The strange thing was, Artie did feel right. Right in so many ways. He couldn't imagine making love to anyone else, which was kind of weird, given there was a time limit on their relationship. A six-month time limit he insisted on because no way was he interested in being in for the long haul. Not with his track record of destroying people's lives.

'Your grandmother was a wonderful woman,' Nonno said, with a wistful look on his weathered features. 'I miss her every day.'

'I know you do, Nonno. I miss Nonna too.'

Another good reason not to love someone—the pain of losing them wrecked your life, leaving you alone and heartsore for years on end. If that wasn't a form of torture, what was? None Luca wanted any part of, not if he could help it.

He was already missing Artie, and he'd only been away from her the couple of hours it took to drive to the hospital. He'd wanted her to come with him to meet his grandfather but that wasn't the only reason. He genuinely enjoyed being with her, which was another new experience for him. The women he'd dated in the past were nice enough people, but no one had made him feel the way Artie did.

Making love with her had been like making love for the first time, discovering things about his body as well as hers. Being tuned in to his body in a totally different way, as if his response settings had been changed, ramped up, intensified, so he would want no one other than her. No one else could trigger the same need and drive. No one else would satisfy him the way she did. He ached for her now. What he would give to see her smile, to feel her hand slide into his and her body nestle against him.

His grandfather turned his head to lock gazes with Luca. 'I've been hard on you, Luca, over the years. I see it now when it's too late to do anything about it. I've expected a lot of you. You had to grow up too fast after your father and Angelo died.' He sighed and continued. 'You've worked hard, too hard really, but I know your father would be proud of your achievements. You've carried on his legacy and turned Ferrantelli Enterprises into a massive success.' He gave a tired smile. 'I've only ever wanted you to be happy. Success is good, but personal fulfilment is what life is really about.'

The hospital orderly arrived at that point to take Nonno down to the operating theatre.

Luca grasped his grandfather's hand and gave it a gentle squeeze. 'Try and get well again, Nonno. I'll be waiting here for you when you come back.'

Once his grandfather had been wheeled out of the room, Luca leaned back in the visitors' chair in his grandfather's private room and stretched out his legs and closed his eyes. Hospitals stirred emotions in him he didn't want to feel. It was a trigger response to tragedy. Being surrounded by death and disease and uncertainty caused an existential crisis in even the most level-headed of people. Being reminded of a loved one's mortality and your own. It would be a long wait until Nonno came out of theatre and then recovery but he wanted to be here when his grandfather came back. His gut churned and his heart squeezed and his breath caught.

If he came back…

Artie put her small overnight case in the back of Rosa's car and pressed the button to close the boot. She took a deep breath and mentally counted to three on releasing it. She came around to the passenger side and took another breath. 'Okay. I can do this.'

I have to do this. For Luca. For myself. For his grandfather.

She got in the car and pulled the seatbelt into place, her heart pounding, her skin prickling with beads of perspiration.

Rosa started the engine and shifted the gearstick into 'drive'. 'Are you sure about this?'

Artie nodded with grim determination. 'I'm sure. It won't be easy but I want to be with Luca. I need to be with him.'

Rosa drove towards the bronze gates, which opened automatically because of the sensors set on either side of the crushed limestone driveway. Artie concentrated on her breathing, trying to ignore the fear that was like thousands of sticky-footed ants crawling over her skin. Her chest was tight, her heart hammering like some sort of malfunctioning construction machinery, but she was okay...well, a little bit okay.

Rosa flicked a worried glance her way. 'How are you doing?'

Artie gripped the strap of the seatbelt that crossed her chest. Her stomach had ditched the butterflies and recruited bats instead. Frantically flapping bats. 'So far, so good. Keep going. We're nearly outside.'

They drove the rest of the way out of the gates and Artie held her breath, anticipating a crippling flood of panic. But instead of the silent screams of terror inside her head, she heard Luca's calm, deep voice, coaching her through the waves of dread.

'Breathe, cara. One. Two. Three.'

It wasn't the first time someone had taught her breath control—two of the therapists had done so with minimal results. But for some reason Luca's voice was the one she listened to now. It gave her the courage to go further than she had gone in over a decade. Out through the *castello* gates and into the outside world.

Artie looked at Rosa and laughed. 'I did it! I'm out!'

Rosa blinked away tears. '*Sì*, you're out.'

Artie wished she could say the rest of the journey was easy. It was not. They had to stop so many times for her to get control of her panic. The nausea at one stage was so bad she thought she was going to vomit. She distracted herself with the sights and sounds along the way. Looking at views she never thought she would see again—the rolling, verdant fields, the lush forests and the mountains, the vineyards and orchards and olive groves of Umbria. Scenes from her childhood, places she had travelled past with her parents. The memories were happy and sad, poignant and painful, and yet also gave her a sense of closure. It was time to move on. Luca had given her the tools and the motivation to change her thinking, to shift her focus. And the further away from the *castello* they got, the easier it became, because she knew she was getting closer to Luca.

But then they came to the hospital.

Artie had forgotten about the hospital. Hospitals. Busyness. Crowds. People rushing about. Patients, staff, cleaners, security personnel. The dead, the dying and the injured. A vision of her mother's lifeless, bruised and broken body flashed into her brain. A vision of her father in the Critical Care Spinal Unit, his shattered spine no longer able to keep him upright.

Her fault. Her fault. Her fault.

She had destroyed her family.

Artie gripped the edges of her seat, her heart threatening to pound its way out of her chest. 'I can't go in there. I can't.'

Rosa parked the car in the visitor's parking area and turned off the engine. 'You've come this far.'

'It was a mistake.' Artie closed her eyes so she didn't have to look at the front entrance. 'I can't do this. I'm not ready.'

I will never be ready.

'What if I call Luca to come out and get you?'

Artie opened her eyes and took a deep breath and slowly released it. Luca was inside that building. She was only a few metres away from him. She had come this far, further than she had in ten years. All she had to do was get to Luca. 'No. I'm not giving up now. I want to be with Luca more than anything. But I need to do this last bit on my own. You can go home and I'll talk to you in a few days once we know what's happening with Luca's grandfather.' She released her tight grip on the car seat and smoothed her damp palms down her thighs. 'I'm ready. I'm going in. Wish me luck?'

Rosa smiled and brushed some tears away from her eyes with the back of her hand. 'You've got this.'

Luca opened his eyes when he heard the door of his grandfather's room open, but instead of seeing a nurse come in he saw Artie. For a moment he thought he was dreaming. He blinked and blinked again then sprang out of the chair, taking her by the arms to make sure she was actually real and not a figment of his imagination. '*Cara?* How did you get here? I can barely believe my eyes.'

She smiled, her eyes bright, her cheeks flushed pink. 'Rosa brought me. I wanted to be with you. I forced myself to get here. I can't say it was easy. It was awful, actually. But I kept doing the slow breathing thing and somehow I made it.'

Luca gathered her close to his chest, breathing in the flowery scent of her hair where it tickled his chin. He was overcome with emotion, thinking about the effort it must have cost her to stare down her fears.

For him?

Fears she had lived with for ten years and she had pushed through them to get to his side. To be with him while he faced the very real possibility of losing his grandfather. He wasn't sure how it made him feel...awed, honoured, touched in a way he had rarely been touched. He was used to having entirely transactional relationships with people. He took what he wanted and they did too.

But Artie had given him something no one had ever done before—her complete trust.

'You were very brave, *mia piccola*. It's so good to have you here.' He held her apart from him to smile down at her, a locked space inside his chest flaring open. 'I still can't believe it.' He brushed his bent knuckles down her cheek. 'Nonno will be so pleased to meet you.'

Her forehead creased in concern. 'How is he? Did you get to speak to him before—?'

'Yes, he's in Theatre, or maybe in Recovery by now.' Luca took both of her hands in his. 'I've missed you.'

'I've missed you too.' Her voice whisper-soft, her gaze luminous.

He released her hands and gathered her close again, lowering his mouth to hers in a kiss that sent scorching streaks of heat shooting through his body. She pressed herself closer, her mouth opening to the probe of his tongue. Tingles went down the backs of his legs, blood thundered to his groin, rampant need pounding in his system. Her lips tasted of strawberries and milk with a touch of cinnamon, her little gasps of delight sweet music to his ears and fuel for his desire. A desire that burned and boiled and blistered with incendiary heat right throughout his body in pummelling waves. How could one kiss do so much damage? Light such a fire in his flesh?

Because it was *her* kiss.

Her mouth.

Her.

Luca lifted his mouth off hers to look down at her flushed features and shimmering eyes. 'If we weren't in my grandfather's hospital room, I would show you just how much I've missed you right here and now.'

Her cheeks went a delightful shade of pink. 'I've sent Rosa back home. It's okay for me to stay with you, isn't it?'

Luca smiled. 'I can think of nothing I'd like more. My villa is only half an hour from here.'

She stroked his face with her fingers, sending darts of pleasure through his body. 'Thank you for helping me move past my fear. I know it's still early days, and I know I'll probably have lots of setbacks, but I feel like I'm finally moving in the right direction.'

Luca tucked a loose strand of her hair back behind her ear, feeling like someone had spilled warm honey into his chest cavity. 'I'm so proud of you right now. The first steps are always the hardest in any difficult journey.'

Artie toyed with the open collar of his shirt, her eyes not quite meeting his. 'I found it helped to shift my focus off myself and put it on you instead. I knew you wanted me with you and I wanted to be with you too. So, so much. That had to be a bigger driver than my fear of leaving the *castello*. And thankfully, it was.'

Luca framed her face in his hands, meshing his gaze with

hers. 'Once Nonno is out of danger, I am going to introduce you to everything you've only dreamed of until now.'

She wound her arms around his neck and stepped up on tip-toe to plant a soft kiss to his mouth. 'I can hardly wait.'

A short time later, Luca's grandfather was wheeled back into the room. Artie held on to Luca's hand, feeling nervous at meeting the old man for the first time. She had met so few people over the last decade and had lost the art of making small talk. But she drew strength from having Luca by her side and basked in his pride in her for making it to the hospital. Something had shifted in their relationship, a subtle shift that gave her more confidence around him. He might not love her but he wanted her with him and that was more than enough for now.

It *had* to be enough.

Her love for him might seem sudden, but wasn't that how it happened for some people? An instant attraction, a chemistry that couldn't be denied, an unstoppable force. Luca didn't believe himself capable of loving someone, but then, she hadn't believed herself capable of being able to leave the *castello*. But she had left. She had found the courage within to do so. Would it not be the same for him? He would need to find the courage to love without fear.

Nonno groaned and cranked one eye open. 'Luca?'

Luca moved forward, taking Artie with him. He took his grandfather's hand in his. 'I'm here, Nonno. And so is Artie.'

The old man turned his head on the pillow and his sleepy gaze brightened. 'Ah, my dear girl. I'm so glad to meet you in person. I hope you'll be as happy with Luca as I was with my Marietta.'

Artie stepped closer. '*Buongiorno*, Signor Ferrantelli. It is so lovely to meet you face to face.'

The old man grasped her hand. 'Call me Nonno. You're family now, *si*?'

Family. If only Nonno knew how short a time she would be

a part of the Ferrantelli family. Artie smiled and squeezed his hand back in a gesture of warm affection. 'Yes, Nonno. I'm family now.'

An hour or so later, Luca drove Artie to his sprawling estate in Tuscany a few kilometres from the town of San Gimignano, where fourteen of the once seventy-two medieval towers created an ancient skyline. The countryside outside the medieval town was filled with sloping hills and lush valleys interspersed with slopes of grapevines and olive groves and fields of bright red poppies. Tall pines stood like sentries overlooking the verdant fields and the lowering sun cast a golden glow over the landscape, the angle of light catching the edges of the cumulous clouds and sending shafts and bolts of gold down to the earth in a spectacular fashion.

Artie drank in the view, feeling overawed by the beauty to the point of tears. She brushed at her eyes and swallowed a lump in her throat. 'It's so beautiful…the colours, the light—everything. I can't believe I'm seeing it in real time instead of through a screen or the pages of a book or magazine.' She turned to him. 'Do you mind if we stop for a minute? I want to stand by the roadside and smell the air and listen to the sounds of nature.'

'Sure.' Luca stopped the car and came around to open her door. He took her hand and helped her out of the car, a smile playing at the corners of his mouth, creating attractive crinkles near his eyes. 'It's an amazing part of the country, isn't it?'

'It sure is.' Artie stood beside him on the roadside and lifted her face to feel the dance of the evening breeze. She breathed in the scent of wild grasses and sun-warmed pine trees. Listened to the twittering of birds, watched an osprey ride the warm currents of air as it searched for prey below. A swell of emotion filled Artie's chest that Luca had helped her leave the prison of her past. 'I never thought I'd be able to do things like this again.'

Luca put an arm around her waist and gathered her closer

against his side. 'I'm proud of you. It can't have been easy, but look at you now.'

She glanced up at him and smiled. 'I don't know how to thank you.'

'I can think of a way.' His eyes darkened and his mouth came down to press a lingering kiss to hers. After a few breathless moments, he lifted his mouth from hers and smiled. 'We'd better get going before it gets dark.'

Once they were back in the car and on their way again, he placed her hand on the top of his thigh and her fingers tingled at the hard warmth of his toned muscles beneath her palm. 'Thank you for being so sweet to Nonno,' he went on. 'He already loves you. You remind him of my grandmother.'

Artie basked in the glow of his compliment. 'What was she like? Were you close to her?'

His expression was like the sky outside—shifting shadows as the light gradually faded. 'I was close to her in the early days, before my father and brother drowned. Their deaths hit her hard and she lost her spark and never quite got it back.' His hands tightened on the steering wheel, making his knuckles bulge to white knobs of tension. 'Like my mother, being around me reminded her too much of what she'd lost. I was always relieved when it was time to go back to boarding school and even more so when I moved away for university.'

Artie stroked his thigh in a comforting fashion, her heart contracting for the way he had suffered as a young teenager. She was all too familiar with how grief and guilt were a deadly combination. Destroying hope, suffocating any sense of happiness or fulfilment. 'I can only imagine how hard it was for all of you, navigating your way through so much grief. But what about your mother? You said she lives in New York now. Do you ever see her?'

'Occasionally, when I'm there for work.' His mouth twisted. 'It's…difficult being with her, as it is for her to be with me.'

'I don't find it hard to be with you.' The words were out of her mouth before she could stop them. She bit her lip and mentally cringed as heat flooded her cheeks. Next she would be blurting out how much she loved him. Words he clearly didn't want to hear. Love wasn't part of their six-month arrangement. Romantic love wasn't part of his life, period.

Luca glanced her way, a smile tilting the edges of his mouth and his eyes dark and warm. 'I don't find it hard to be with you either.' His voice was low and deep and husky and made her long to be back in his arms. To feel the sensual power of his body, the physical expression of his need, even if love wasn't part of why he desired her. But she realised now her desire was a physical manifestation of her love for him. A love that had awakened the first time his lips touched hers, waking her from a psychological coma. A coma where she had denied herself the right to fully engage in life and relationships. Locking herself away out of fear. But she was free now, freed by Luca's passion for her and hers for him.

'Will I get to meet your mother? I mean, is that something you'd like me to do?' Artie asked.

A frown formed a double crease between his eyes. 'I'm not sure it will achieve much.'

'But what if I'd like to?'

He flicked her a brief unreadable glance. 'Why do you want to?'

Artie sighed. 'I lost my mother when I was fifteen. It left such a hole in my life. I can barely watch a television show or commercials or movies with mothers in them because it makes me miss my mother all the more.'

'You have no need to be envious of my relationship with my mother,' Luca said in a weighted tone.

'At least you still have her.'

There was a protracted silence.

Luca released a heavy breath. 'Look, I know you are only trying to help but some family dynamics are best left alone. Nothing can be changed now.'

'But that's what I thought about my fear of leaving the *castello*,' Artie said. 'I lost years of my life by giving in to my fears, allowing them to control me instead of me controlling them. I never thought I could do it, but you helped me see that I could. Maybe it's the same with your relationship with your mother. You shouldn't give up on trying to improve the relationship just because it's been a little difficult so far. What you went through as a family was horrendously tragic. But you still have a family, Luca. You have your mother and your grandfather. I have no one now.'

Luca reached for her hand and brought it up to his mouth, pressing a soft kiss to her fingers. 'You have me, *cara*.' His voice had a note of tenderness that made her heart contract.

But for how long? Six months and no longer.

And then she would be alone again.

A short time later, Luca drove through the gates of his estate and pulled up in front of the imposing medieval villa.

Built like a fortress with four storeys, a central dome and several turrets, it was surrounded by landscaped gardens with a tinkling fountain at the front. 'Don't be put off by the grim façade,' he said, turning off the engine. 'I've done extensive renovations inside.'

'I try never to judge a book or a person by their cover,' Artie said. 'Not that I've met a lot of people lately, but still. Hopefully that's going to change.'

Luca's eyes glinted. 'I'm not sure I want to share you with anyone just yet. This is our honeymoon, *si*?'

A shiver coursed down Artie's spine and a pool of liquid fire simmered in her core. She sent him a shy smile. 'So, we'll be alone here? Just you and me?'

He leaned closer across the gear shaft and, putting a hand to the back of her head, brought her closer to his descending mouth. 'Just you and me.'

CHAPTER TEN

ARTIE WOKE THE next morning to find her head tucked against Luca's chest and his arms around her and her legs tangled with his. One of his hands was moving up and down her spine in a slow stroking motion that made her pelvis start to tingle. His hand went lower, to the curve of her bottom, and every nerve in her skin did a happy dance. Her inner muscles woke to his touch, instantly recalling the magic of the night before and wanting more. Would she ever tire of feeling his hands on her body? His touch was gentle and yet created a storm in her flesh. A tumult of sensations that made her ache for closer, deeper, more intimate contact.

Luca turned her onto her back and leaned on one elbow to gaze down at her. He brushed some wayward strands of her hair back from her face, his eyes darkly hooded, a lazy smile tipping up one side of his mouth. 'Well, look who's been sleeping in my bed.' His voice had a sexy early-morning rasp to it that made something in her belly turn over.

Artie traced a straight line down his strong nose, a playful smile tilting her own mouth. 'I don't know that I did much sleeping.' Her finger began to circle his stubble-surrounded mouth and chin. 'Unless I was dreaming about you making love to me...how many times was it?'

His eyes darkened. 'Three.' He stroked her bottom lip with his thumb, a small frown settling between his brows. 'I would have gone for four or even five but I didn't want to make you sore. This is all so new to you and...'

Artie smoothed his frown away with her finger. 'New, but wonderful.' She looked deep into his eyes, holding her hand against his prickly jaw. 'I didn't think it would be so...so wonderful. Is it always like this?'

Luca held her gaze for a long moment, his eyes moving between each of hers before lowering to her mouth. He released a soft gust of air, his lopsided smile returning. 'No. It's not always as good as this.'

'Really? Are you just saying that to make me feel good?'

He picked up one of her hands and turned it over to plant a kiss to the middle of her palm, his eyes holding hers. 'I'm saying it because it's true. It feels...different with you.'

'In what way?'

He interlaced his fingers with hers, a contemplative frown interrupting his features. 'I can't explain it. It just feels different.'

Artie aimed her gaze at his mouth rather than meet his eyes. 'Is it because of my lack of experience? I must seem a bit of a novelty to someone like you who's had so many lovers.'

He tipped up her chin and his eyes met hers, and something shifted in the atmosphere. A new, electric energy, a background hum, as if each and every oxygen particle had paused to take a breath.

'I'm not going to dismiss any of my past lovers to faceless bodies who didn't leave a single impression on me, because it's simply not true.'

He stroked his thumb over her lower lip again—a slow-motion stroke that set her mouth buzzing.

'But with you...it feels like I'm discovering sex for the first time. Feeling things on a different level. A more intense level.'

Artie toyed with the hair at the back of his neck, her lower body tinglingly aware of the growing ridge of his erection.

Aware of the potent energy that pulsed and throbbed between them. 'I couldn't have asked for a better first lover.'

His mouth came down and sealed hers in a mind-altering kiss that set her pulse racing. His fingers splayed through her hair, his tongue meeting hers in a playful dance with distinctive erotic overtones. Her lower body quaked with longing, her flesh recognising the primal call to connect in the most physically intimate way of all. Her legs tangled with his rougher ones, her breasts crushed against the firm wall of his chest, her nipples already tightening into pert buds.

One of Luca's hands cradled one of her breasts, his touch light, and yet it sent shockwaves of need coursing through her body. Molten heat was licking along her flesh…lightning-fast zaps and tingles that made her groan in pleasure. She moved closer, pressing her mound to his erection, opening her legs for him, desperate to have him inside her.

'Not so impatient, *cara*.' He gave a light laugh and reached for protection, deftly applying it before coming back to her, his eyes gleaming with the fiery desire she could feel roaring through her own body.

Artie framed his head in her hands, her breathing erratic. 'I want you so much it's like pain.'

'I want you too. Badly.' He kissed her mouth in a kiss that spoke of his own thrumming desire, his lips firm, insistent, hungry.

He moved down her body, kissing her breasts, her belly, and to the secret heart of her womanhood. He separated her and anointed her with his lips and tongue, making her writhe and gasp with bone-melting pleasure. The wave broke over her in a rush, sending her spinning into a place of sheer physical bliss. The storm in her flesh slowly abated but then he created another one by moving up her body again, entering her with a slow, deep thrust that made every hair on her head tingle and tighten at the roots. Her back arched, her thighs trembled, her breath stalled and then came out in a rush of rapturous delight. Delicious sensations rippled through her as he continued to thrust, his breathing rate increasing along with his pace, his touch like fire where his hand was holding her hip, tilting her to him. The pressure built in her body, the primal need a drumbeat working its way up to a powerful crescendo. Blood pounded through her veins, a hot rush fuelled by the intense sensations activated by the erotic friction of his hard male body.

Artie lifted her hips to get him where she most wanted him but it was still not quite the pressure she needed. 'I'm so close... so damn close...'

'Relax, *mia piccola*. Don't fight it.' Luca slipped a hand between their bodies and stroked the swollen heart of her flesh, sending her over the edge into a cataclysmic orgasm that surpassed everything she had enjoyed so far. Starlight burst behind her eyelids, fireworks exploded in her body, heat pouring like liquid flames all through her pelvis and down her legs to curl her toes.

'Oh, God. Oh, God. Oh, God,' she panted, like she had run a marathon, her heart pounding, her flesh tinglingly alive with mind-smashing ecstasy.

Luca's release followed hers and swept her up in its power and intensity. His entire body seemed to tighten as if he were poised on the edge of a vertiginous cliff. And then he gave an agonised groan and shuddered as if consumed with a rabid fever, his essence spilling, his body finally relaxing against hers.

Artie stroked her hands down his back where his firm flesh was still peppered with goosebumps. The in and out of his breath tickled the side of her neck but she didn't want to move in case it broke the magical spell washing over her, binding her to him in a way no words could possibly describe. There was a rightness about their union—a sense of belonging together for all time.

But you've only got six months, remember?

The prod of her conscience froze her breath and stopped her heart for a moment. It wasn't long enough. Six months was a joke. She wanted for ever. She wanted to be in his arms like this for the rest of her life. How could she ever move on from her relationship with him? Who would ever measure up? How could she love anyone else when he had stolen her heart from the first time he kissed her?

She didn't want to love anyone else. Her heart belonged to him and only him.

Luca must have sensed the subtle change in her mood, and quickly disposed of the condom, and then leaned up on one elbow to look at her, his hand idly brushing her wild hair out of her face. 'What's wrong?' His tone and gaze were gently probing.

Artie painted a smile on her lips. 'Nothing.'

His eyes moved between each of hers like a powerful search-light looking for something hidden in the shadows. His thumb began to stroke the pillow of her lower lip in slow movements that sent hot tingles through every corridor of her flesh. 'I've been around long enough to know that "nothing" usually means "something". Talk to me, *cara*. Tell me what's worrying you.'

She aimed her gaze at his Adam's apple, her heart skipping rope in her chest. How could she be honest with him without relaying how she felt? He might call an end to their physical relationship and go back to the paper marriage he'd first insisted on. 'I'm just wondering how I will ever find another lover who makes me feel the way you do. I mean, in the future, when we're done.'

There was a beat or two of thick silence.

Then Luca's hand fell away from her face and he released a heavy sigh and rolled onto his back, one arm flung over the edge of the bed, the other coming up to cover his eyes. 'The last thing I want to think about right now is you with someone else.' There was a rough quality to his voice that hinted at a fine thread of anger running under the surface.

'But it's going to happen one day,' Artie said. 'We're both

going to move on with our lives. Isn't that what you planned? What you insisted on?'

He removed his arm from across his face and sat upright, the muscles of his abdomen rippling like coils of steel. He swung his legs over the edge of the bed, his hands resting on either side of his thighs, his back towards her, his head and shoulders hunched forward as if he was fighting to control his emotions.

There was another tight silence.

Artie swallowed, wondering if she had pushed him too far. 'Luca?' She reached out and stroked her hand down between his tense shoulder blades, and he flinched as if her touch burned him. 'What's wrong?'

'Nothing.' The word was bitten out. Hard. Blunt. *Keep-away* curt.

She had a strange desire to smile—her lips twitched as she tried to control it. What was sauce for the goose and all that. 'You know, someone told me recently that "nothing" usually means "something".'

Luca let out a gush of air and gave a deep, self-deprecating chuckle. He turned back to face her. 'Touché.' He took her nearest hand and brought it up to his mouth, locking his gaze with hers. He bit down gently on the end of her index finger and then drew it into his mouth, sucking on it erotically. She shivered and a wave of heat passed through her body, simmering, smouldering like hot coals in her core.

He released her finger from his mouth and returned to holding her hand in his. 'Sometimes I wonder if I need my head read for allowing this to go this far between us.' His thumb stroked over the fleshy part of her thumb, the back-and-forth motion making her stomach do a flip turn. 'But I can't seem to stop myself from wanting you.'

Artie leaned closer, placing her free hand on the rock-hard wall of his chest, her mouth just below his. 'Want me all you like.' She pressed her lips to his in a barely-there kiss, pulling back to gaze into his eyes. 'We've got six months.'

She kept her tone light. *I'm-totally-cool-with-having-a-time-limit-on-our-relationship* light.

He held her gaze for a long moment, shadows shifting in his eyes like filtered sunlight moving across a forest floor. Then his eyes lowered to her mouth, a muscle in his cheek pulsing as if something wasn't quite at peace within him. 'Then let's make the most of it,' he said and covered her mouth with his.

The following evening, after spending some time visiting Nonno, Luca took Artie out for dinner at a restaurant in San Gimignano with a spectacular view over the region. She sat opposite him at a table at the window at the front of the restaurant, feeling both nervous and excited about her first meal out at a restaurant since she was a teenager.

Artie took a sip of the crisp white wine Luca had ordered, and then surveyed the menu. 'So much to choose from...'

'Take your time.' His tone was indulgent, as if he sensed how overawed she was feeling.

Once their orders were taken by the waiter, Artie glanced up at Luca with a rueful expression. 'I'm frightened I might use the wrong cutlery or something. It's been so long since I've eaten in public. I'm glad the restaurant isn't busy tonight.'

He reached for her hand across the table, holding it gently in the cradle of his. 'I made sure it wasn't busy. I know the owner. I asked him to keep this part of the restaurant clear for us.'

Artie blinked at him in surprise. 'Really? But wouldn't that have incurred a considerable loss of income for him?'

Luca shrugged one broad shoulder. 'Don't worry. I've more than compensated him.'

She chewed at the side of her mouth, touched that Luca had gone to so much trouble and expense for her comfort. 'I guess I can hardly call myself a cheap date, now, can I?'

His fingers squeezed hers, a smile playing about his mouth. 'You're worth more than you realise, *cara*. My grandfather certainly thinks so—he was in much better spirits today. Meeting you has done him the power of good. He told me when you were using the bathroom earlier today that he's decided to go ahead with the chemo for his cancer. I have you to thank for his change in attitude. He wants to live now. You've given him a reason to.'

'I'm so glad,' Artie said. 'But I hope the chemo won't be too gruelling. He's not a young man.'

'No, but he's a tough old guy.' Luca stroked his thumb over the back of her hand and added in a heavy tone, 'It's something I've been dreading—losing him. He's the last link to my father and brother, apart from my mother, of course.'

Artie could sense the deep love he had for his grandfather and it gave her hope that he might one day learn to embrace other forms of love—romantic love. Love-for-a-lifetime love. *Her* love.

'Has your mother been to see Nonno recently?'

His mouth twisted, a shadow passing through his gaze. 'They talk on the phone now and again. My mother hates flying back to Italy. It reminds her too much of our flight back from Argentina with my father's and brother's bodies.' He released her hand and picked up his wine glass, staring at the golden liquid with a frowning expression.

Artie placed her hand on his other forearm where it was resting on the table. 'I can only imagine how devastated you both were on that trip home. I can relate to it with my own journey home from hospital after the accident. It felt surreal, like I was having a nightmare or something. I kept expecting my mother to be there when I got home, but of course she wasn't. And my father was a shell of himself. A broken shell. I blamed myself, just as you did and still do.'

Luca leaned forward and took both of her hands in his. 'We've both suffered terrible tragedies. Nothing is going to change the past. It's done and can't be undone. But it's important to live your own life.'

Artie looked down at their joined hands. 'At least I'm living my life now, thanks to you. I think I was asleep to myself for the last ten years.' She raised her gaze to his and continued, 'I didn't realise how much I'd let my fear control me. It kind of crept up on me until I was completely imprisoned by it. But somehow you got me to change my focus, to shift my thinking. How can I ever thank you for that?'

'You don't have to thank me. You did it all by yourself.' Luca idly stroked her hands with his thumbs. 'You're doing so well now. I can't tell you how shocked and delighted I was to see you appear at the hospital the other day. I thought I was dreaming.'

'I was sick with nerves,' Artie confessed. 'But knowing you were there at the end of my journey really helped. It gave me a clear goal to aim for.'

Luca smiled and released one of her hands, then took a flat rectangular jewellery box out of his jacket pocket. 'I have something for you.' He placed the box on the table between them. 'Open it.'

Artie prised open the lid to find a beautiful diamond and sapphire pendant and matching earrings. 'Oh, Luca, they're absolutely gorgeous!' She picked up one of the dangling earrings. 'But they're the same design as your grandmother's engagement ring. Does that mean they're—?'

'*Sì*, they were Nonna's. I want you to have the whole collection.'

'But they're priceless heirlooms. Why are you giving them to me?'

'Don't you think you're worth it?'

She put the earring back in the box, and ran her fingertip over the fine gold chain of the pendant. 'It's not that so much...' She glanced up at him. 'It's more that I feel uncomfortable with you being so generous to me when we're only going to be together for six months. I mean, I seem to be the biggest winner in this arrangement of ours. I get to keep the *castello* and all this amazing jewellery, and what do you get?'

His eyes held hers in a strange little lock that made the hairs on the back of her neck tingle. 'I get some wonderful memories of our time together. Plus, my grandfather will hopefully recover now he's agreed to go ahead with the treatment.'

Artie frowned. 'But don't you want more than that?'

A screen came up in his gaze. 'What more could I want?'

Me. You could want me, for ever.

Artie couldn't bring herself to say it out loud but she wondered if he could hear her hopes in the ringing silence. 'Don't you want to keep your grandmother's jewellery in case one day you change your mind about marrying someone else?'

'Not going to happen.' He sat back in his chair, lifted his wine glass from the table and took a measured sip. 'I have no plans of that nature.'

Not going to happen.

The words taunted her for the rest of the meal.

Not going to happen.

He was so adamant about never falling in love.

Not going to happen.

How could he be so confident it wouldn't happen?

And how could she be so hopeful it would? That he would fall in love with her?

CHAPTER ELEVEN

ONCE DINNER WAS OVER, Luca led the way back to his car past a wine bar where live music was being played. The sweet strains of a well-known Italian love song filled the night air. He glanced down at Artie's wistful expression, and stopped in front of the entrance. 'Do you fancy going in for a bit?'

She shifted from foot to foot, looking like she was torn between running away and going in and letting her hair down. 'I haven't heard live music before. And I've never been to a wine bar. Or danced with anyone before.'

He took her hand and looped it through his arm. 'Come on, then. Let's dance.'

A short time later, Luca held Artie in his arms as they slow-waltzed to another old love song. Her head was resting against his chest, her hair tickling his chin, her flowery fragrance teasing his nostrils. Her body moved in perfect time with his, as if they had been dancing together for ever. The naturalness of their motion reminded him of the natural rhythm of their lovemaking. It was as if their bodies were in tune with each other, recognising the other as the perfect partner.

Perfect partner? You're hardly that.

The sharp prod of his conscience made him miss a step and he had to gather Artie closer to stop her from bumping into another couple on the small dance floor. 'Sorry,' he said. 'I lost my concentration.' Or maybe he'd momentarily lost his mind, thinking about the possibility of a future with her.

A future he couldn't offer her.

When he'd first offered her a six-month marriage it had seemed an inordinately long time to be tied to someone, and yet now it didn't seem long enough. He avoided thinking about their inevitable divorce. Avoided thinking about a time when she wouldn't be in his life. Avoided thinking about her with someone else. He felt sick to his guts at the thought of her making love with some other man. He'd never considered himself the jealous type but he couldn't stomach the thought of her with someone else. What if they didn't treat her with respect? What if they weren't patient with her struggles in public? What if they didn't understand how sensitive and caring she was?

Artie looked up at him with luminous eyes, her face wreathed in smiles. 'This is so much fun. Can we do this another night soon?'

Luca smiled and bent his head to kiss her. 'I can think of nothing I'd like more.'

The next couple of weeks passed in a whirlwind of activity where Artie's feet barely touched the ground. There were visits to the hospital to see Luca's grandfather, who was making good progress after his hip surgery. Then there were trips to various sightseeing spots, and picnics in the countryside overlooking the hills and valleys of the region. Luca taught her about the skill of wine-making and olive production and showed her the vines and groves on his estate. He took her for romantic dinners in award-winning restaurants as well as less famous ones, where the food was just as fabulous and the atmosphere intimate and cosy. Luca took her shopping and spoilt her with a completely new wardrobe of clothes, including a collection of swimsuits and gorgeous lingerie.

But it was the nights at home she enjoyed the most. Just being

with him, sitting in the salon chatting, watching a movie or listening to music together, her head resting on his chest and his
arms around her. It gave her a glimpse of what life could be like
if they stayed together longer than the six months he'd stipu-
lated. He was still driven by work and was often on the phone
or answering emails, but she noticed he was more relaxed than
before and seemed to smile and laugh more. Was it because his
grandfather was on the mend and had decided to go ahead with
his cancer treatment? Or was it because she had helped Luca to
see there was more to life than work? That being in a romantic
relationship could be positive rather than negative?

Artie had to bite her tongue so many times to stop herself
from confessing how she felt about him but she let her actions do
the talking instead. Every time she kissed him, she let her lips
communicate her love. Every touch of her hands, every stroke
of her fingers, every press of her body on his, love poured out
of her. But she wanted to say it out loud. She needed to say it
out loud. She needed him to hear the words—I love you.

They were sitting on the sofa watching the moon rise through
the salon windows after a day of sightseeing. The moonlight
cast a silver light over the surface of the infinity pool outside
on the terrace overlooking the vineyard. Luca's arm was around
her shoulders, her head resting on his shoulder, and soft music
was playing through the sound system—cellos, violins and the
sweetly lilting tones of a flute. A romantic ballad that tugged
at her heartstrings and made her wish there wasn't a limit on
their time together.

'Luca?'

'Mmm?' One of his hands began to play with her hair, sending shivers coursing down her spine.

Artie tilted her head to look at him. 'Luca, I want to talk to
you about something. Something important.'

He brushed an imaginary hair away from her face, his eyes
dark and serious. 'Go on.' His tone held a note of caution, unease, guardedness, but she refused to let it daunt her.

She swallowed a tight knot in her throat. 'There's so much I enjoy about being with you. You've spoilt me like a princess. You've treated me with so much patience and kindness and helped me build my confidence.'

He gave a half-smile, some of the wariness in his gaze fading. 'I like seeing you blossom, *cara*. You're a beautiful person who's been hiding away for too long.'

Artie touched his face with her fingers, her love for him taking up all the room in her chest so she could barely take a breath. 'I never thought I'd meet someone like you. And not just because I was locked away in the *castello*. But because I didn't think people as wonderful as you existed.'

Luca took her by the upper arms in a firm grip, his expression clouding. 'Look, don't go making me out to be a hero, Artie. I'm hardly that. You're confusing good chemistry with...other feelings.' Even the way he hesitated over the rest of his sentence showed how reluctant he was to the notion of love, but Artie pressed on regardless.

'Luca...' She took a deep breath and plunged in. 'I don't want our relationship to be temporary. I want more, and deep down I think you do too.'

His hands fell away from her arms and he sprang off the sofa to put some distance between them. 'You're wrong, Artie. That's not what I want. I've never wanted that. We made an agreement—'

Artie jumped off the sofa as well and stood in front of him. 'We made an agreement and then we changed it to what it is now—a physical relationship that works on every level but the one that means the most to me. I can't make love with you and keep my feelings to one side. They *are* the reason I want to make love with you. The only reason. I love you.'

Luca drew in a harsh-sounding breath and released it in a stuttered stream. He placed his hands on his hips, his shoulders hunched forward. 'You're young and inexperienced, of course, you're going to think the first person who makes love to you is the love of your life. But believe me, I am not that person.' His expression was like a walled fortress. Closed. Locked.

Keep out or face the consequences.

'You are that person.' Artie choked over the words as emotion welled in her throat. 'You've been that person from the moment we kissed at our wedding. Something happened that day—I knew it on a cellular level. And—'

'Will you listen to yourself?' His tone had a cutting edge that sliced at her self-esteem like a switchblade. 'You're spouting forth a fairy-tale fantasy. It's not real, Artie. You've fashioned me into some sort of romantic hero who ticks all the boxes for you. You need more life experience. You need to date other men so you can gain more perspective. You'll thank me in the end. Tying yourself to me indefinitely would be a mistake. A mistake you'll regret for the rest of your life.' He turned away from her, drawing in another ragged breath, his tone softening. 'Let's leave this for now. I don't want to upset you.'

Artie swallowed a tight restriction in her throat, tears stinging at the backs of her eyes. 'But you've already upset me by not accepting that I love you. You've dismissed it as if I don't know my own mind. I know what I feel.' She banged her fist against her chest for emphasis. 'I can't deny my feelings or ignore them as you seem to do. They're here with me all the time.'

Luca turned back around and opened and closed his eyes in a slow, *God-give-me-strength* blink. 'Look, you're one of the nicest people I've ever met, *cara*. You have so much to offer and I want you to be happy. I really do. But I'm not the person to make you happy. It's not in my skill set. I don't want the same things as you.'

Artie pressed her lips together for a moment to stop them from trembling. 'I think you do want the same things but you don't feel you deserve them because of what happened to your father and brother. I understand that more than most people, because I've experienced the same guilt for the last ten years. It completely imprisoned me, kept me from having a life of my own. But meeting you changed that. You freed me from my prison of fear and showed me I could have more than I ever thought possible.' She came up to him and placed her hand on his forearm. 'I know you have deep feelings locked away inside you. I feel it every time you kiss me. I feel it every time you make love to me.'

Luca brushed off her arm as if it was soiling his sleeve, his gaze hard, his mouth tight, his firewall still up. 'You're mistaking good sex for something else. It's an easy mistake to make, especially when you're not very experienced. But in time, you'll gain experience and realise this is just a crush, an infatuation that can't last.'

'I don't have to be experienced to know how I feel,' Artie said. 'They're *my* feelings. I feel them. I own them.'

'And I know how I feel and it doesn't include the sort of love you're talking about.' He ran a hand over his face and continued, 'I care about you, of course. I enjoy being with you but that's all it is—companionship and mutual desire that has an end point, as per our agreement.'

Artie's heart gave a painful spasm, and for a moment she couldn't locate her voice. He cared about her and enjoyed being with her but that was all it was? How could she have got it so wrong? She was sure he was developing feelings for her—sure enough to reveal her own. He thought her young and gauche, a girl in the throes of her first crush. How could she get through to him? How could she prove she loved him? Or was it pointless? Was she fooling herself that he would one day change? Didn't so many deluded women fall for that fantasy? The vain hope that in time, enough love would change their difficult men to the man of their dreams?

But what if Luca never changed?

What if he was incapable of it?

'Luca, I took a huge risk in leaving the *castello* for you,' Artie said. 'Why can't you take a risk and allow yourself to feel what I know is in your heart? I know it's scary to admit how much you care about someone. And I know the last thing you want to do is be reckless and spontaneous but we've connected in a way people rarely do. Surely you can't deny it? We have so much in common, can't you see that? We're perfect for each other.'

Luca turned his back, drawing in a deep breath, his hands on his hips in a braced position. 'Stop it, Artie. This is a pointless discussion. You're making me out to be someone I can never be.'

Artie ran her tongue over her dry lips, tasting the metallic bitterness of disappointment. She clasped her hands together in front of her body, trying to contain the emotions rioting through her. 'You'll never be free of the prison of the past unless you learn to let go of control. To allow yourself to be reckless with your heart, to open it to the feelings I know you've buried there. I've let go of control. I've opened my heart to you. Why can't you do it for me? If you won't do it for me, then it wouldn't be fair to either of us to continue in a relationship that is so out of balance.'

'It's not out of balance.' Luca swung back around to face her. 'I made it so we both get what we want. At the end of six months, you get to keep the *castello* and Nonno completes his chemo. It's a win-win.'

She shook her head at him. 'It's a lose-lose but you can't see it. I would choose love over a run-down old castle any day. And how are you going to explain the end of our marriage to your grandfather?'

He gave a dismissive shrug. 'Marriages break up all the time. It won't matter by then because he'll have finished the course of treatment. As I said—win-win.' His tone had a businesslike ring to it. No emotions. Ticking a box. Deal done.

Artie steepled her fingers around her nose and mouth, concentrating on keeping calm even though inside she was crumbling, the very foundations of her under assault as self-doubts rained down on her. She wasn't worthy of his love. She wasn't good enough. She was defective, damaged. He didn't love her. He would *never* love her. He had only married her as a means to an end, and yet she had fooled herself he was developing feelings for her. She was a fool for thinking he felt more for her than companionship and care.

Her old friend panic crept up behind her...lurking in the background.

You can't survive on your own. Stay with him. Put up and shut up.

Her skin prickled, fear slid into her stomach and coiled around her intestines, squeezing, tightening.

You'll lose the castello if you leave him now.

But Artie knew she couldn't lock herself in another prison. Staying with Luca in a loveless marriage for the next few months would be the same as locking herself in the *castello*. Shutting herself away from her hopes and dreams. From her potential.

From love.

She couldn't go back to being that frightened person now. She had to forge her way through with the strength and courage Luca had inspired in her. He had awakened her to what she most wanted in life and it would be wrong to go backwards, to silence the hopes and dreams she harboured. She owed it to herself to embrace life. To live life fully instead of living in negative solitude.

Artie lowered her hands from her face and straightened her shoulders, meeting his cold gaze with a sinking feeling in her stomach. 'I don't think there's any point in waiting out the six months. It will only make it harder for me. It's best if I leave now.'

A ripple of tension whipped over his face and his hands clenched into fists by his sides. 'Now? Are you crazy? You can't leave. We made an agreement.' There was a restricted quality to his voice. 'You'll lose everything if you leave now.'

Artie sighed. 'I can't be with you if you don't love me. It wouldn't be healthy for me. It would only reinforce the negative feelings I've had about myself in the past. That I'm not worthy, that I'm somehow the cause of everything bad that happens to

me and those I care about. I need to leave that part of my life
behind now. I need to embrace life as a fully awakened adult
woman who knows what she wants and isn't afraid to ask for it.'

His hand scraped through his hair, leaving tracks in the thick
black strands. He muttered a curse word in Italian, his mouth
pulled so tight there were white tips at the corners. 'I can't stop
you leaving but I should warn you there will be consequences.
I'm not going to hand over a property with the potential of Castello Mireille just because you've pulled the plug on our agreement. I will keep it. I will develop it into a hotel and then I'll
sell it.' His eyes flashed with green and brown sparks of anger.
An anger so palpable it crackled in the air.

Artie ground her teeth, fighting to keep control of her own
anger. 'Do what you need to do, Luca. I won't stand in your way.
And I don't expect you to stand in mine.' She moved across to
where she had left her phone. 'I'm going to call Rosa to come
and get me.'

'Don't be ridiculous,' Luca said. 'It'll take her hours to get
here.'

Artie faced him, phone in hand, eyebrows arched. 'Will you
drive me?'

His top lip curled and his eyes turned to flint. 'You must
be joking.'

Her chin came up. 'I'm not.'

He released a savage breath and muttered another curse. 'I'll
organise a driver.' He took out his own phone and selected a
number from his contacts.

Artie turned away as he told his employee to come and collect her for the journey back to Umbria. There was nothing in
his tone to suggest he was shattered by her decision to leave
him. He was angry, yes, but not devastated. Not as devastated
as she was feeling. But how could he be? He didn't love her, so
why would he feel anything but anger that she was pulling out
of their agreement? His plans had been disrupted. His heart
was unaffected.

Luca slipped the phone back in his pocket, his expression set in cold, emotionless lines. 'Done. Emilio will be here in five minutes.'

Artie moistened her parchment-dry lips again. Was this really happening? He was letting her go without a fight? It validated her decision to leave now, before she got even more invested in their relationship. But how much more invested could she be than what she was now? She loved him with her entire being and yet he felt nothing more for her than he would for a pet or a pot plant. He *cared* about her. That wasn't enough for her. It would never be enough. 'Thank you. I'd better go and pack a few things.' She turned for the door, waiting, hoping for him to call her back. She even slowed her steps, giving him plenty of time to do so. One step. Two steps. Three steps. Four...

'Artie.'

Her heart lifted like a helium balloon and she spun around. Had he changed his mind? Would he beg her to rethink her decision?

Oh, please, beg me to stay. Tell me you love me.

'Yes?'

His expression was mask-like but his throat rose and fell over a tight swallow. 'Keep safe.' His tone was gruff.

An ache pressed down on her chest, an avalanche of emotion that made it impossible for her to take a breath. Her eyes burned with unshed tears. She. Would. Not. Cry. Not now. She would not make herself look any more gauche and desperate. She would take a dignified stance. She would take a leaf from his relationship playbook—she would be cool and calm and collected, detached. Their business deal was over and she would move on. End of story. 'You too. And thanks for...everything.' She pulled the heirloom engagement ring off her finger as well as the wedding band and held them out to him. 'You'd better take the rings back. The earrings and pendant are upstairs. I'll leave them on the dressing table.'

'Keep them.'

'But they're family heirlooms—'

'I said, keep them.' The words were bitten out through a paper-thin slit between his lips, a savage frown pleating his brow.

Artie put the rings on one of the side tables and then turned and walked out of the room, closing the door softly but firmly behind her.

CHAPTER TWELVE

As soon as the car carrying her away disappeared from sight Luca sucked in a breath that tore at his throat like wolf claws. What did she expect him to do? Run after her and beg her to stay? He had told her the terms from the outset. He had made it clear where his boundaries were.

But you shifted the boundaries. You slept with her.

He dragged a hand down his face, his gut clenching with self-disgust. Yes, he had shifted the boundaries and he should have known better. Artie was so young and inexperienced, and sleeping with him had made things so much worse. It had fuelled her romantic fantasies about him, fantasies he could never live up to. But he hadn't been able to help himself. He'd wanted her the moment he met her, maybe even before that.

She was light and he was darkness.

She was naïve and trusting and he was ruthless and cynical.

She was in touch with her emotions and he had none…well, none that he wanted to acknowledge. Emotions were not his currency. It was a language he didn't speak and nor did he want any fluency in it.

Luca picked up the engagement and wedding rings from the side table, curling his fingers around them so he didn't have to look at the mocking, accusing eyes of the diamonds. He rattled them in his hand like dice and tossed them back on the table, turning away with an expletive.

He was not going to go after her. He. Was. Not. He was *not* going after her. His old self would have run up the stairs even before she packed and got down on bended knee and begged her to stay.

But he was not that reckless teenage boy any more. He was able to regulate his reactions, to think logically and carefully about his actions. He was able to weigh the checks and balances and act accordingly...except when it came to making love with her. That had been reckless and ill-advised and yet he had done it anyway. Done it and enjoyed every pulse-racing second of it. Artie had got to him in a way no one else ever had.

He *felt* different.

Something inside him had changed and he wasn't sure he could dial it back. But he was damn well going to try.

Artie spent the first month back at Castello Mireille vainly waiting for the phone to ring. She longed to hear Luca's voice, she longed to feel his touch, to be in his arms again. She was suffering terrible withdrawal symptoms, missing the stroke and glide of his body within hers, the passionate press of his lips on her mouth, her breasts and her body. She reached for him in the middle of the night, her heart sinking when she found the other side of the bed cold and empty.

She realised with a sickening jolt that this was what her father had gone through after the accident. He had grieved both physically and emotionally for her mother. The loss of an intimate partner was felt on so many levels, little stabs and arrows every time you were reminded of the person, every time a memory was triggered by sight, sound, taste, touch or hearing.

Losing Luca was like a death. He was gone from her life and she couldn't get him back, not unless she compromised herself in the process. And hadn't she compromised herself enough for the last decade? Denying herself any sort of life, any sort of enjoyment and happiness out of guilt?

She was no longer the girl in a psychological coma. She was awake to her potential, awake to what she wanted and no longer afraid to aim for it, even if it meant suffering heartbreak along the way. Luca was everything she wanted in a husband, but if he didn't love her, then how could she ever be happy settling for anything less than his whole heart?

Artie was working in the morning room on a christening gown for one of the villager's baby, waiting for Rosa to bring in morning tea. There was a certain sadness in working on babies' clothes when it was highly likely she would never have a baby now. How could she without Luca, the only man she wanted to have children with? The only man she could ever love? She placed another neat stitch in the christening gown, wondering what he was doing now. Working, no doubt. Visiting his grandfather. Taking a new lover to replace her... Her insides revolted at the thought of him making love to someone else. Artie forced herself to concentrate on her embroidery rather than torturing herself. The weeks since coming home, she had decided to pour her energy into her craft and had even set up a social media page and website. To take it from a hobby to a business. She had orders coming in so quickly she could barely keep up. But it gave her the distraction she needed to take her mind off Luca and their broken marriage.

Rosa came in carrying a tray with their refreshments. She set it on the table in front of Artie and then sat down beside her, taking a cup of tea for herself off the tray. 'I'm thinking about taking a little holiday. I know my timing isn't good, given the situation with you and Luca, but I thought it was time I saw a bit of the world outside these walls now you're a little more independent.'

Artie put the christening gown to one side, wrapping it in the white muslin cloth she used to protect it. 'Oh, Rosa, I feel bad you've been stuck here with me for so long. But you don't have to worry about me now. I've been to the village several times this week on my own and even had coffee at the café a couple of times. I can't say it's easy, but I do it and feel better for it.'

'I'm so glad you're able to do more.' Rosa sighed and continued, 'While you were staying with Luca, I realised I might have been holding you back. Don't get me wrong—I wanted to help you, but I think my reasons were not as altruistic as you think.'

Artie frowned. 'What do you mean?'

Rosa looked a little shamefaced. 'When I got my heart broken all those years ago, I locked myself away here working for your family. It was my way of avoiding being hurt again. But I worry that I might have inadvertently held you back by allowing you to become dependent on me.'

'You haven't done any such thing,' Artie said. 'I held myself back and now I'm moving forward. But I can't thank you enough for being there when I needed you.'

Rosa's expression was tender with concern. 'Have you heard from Luca?'

Artie sighed and shook her head. 'No. Nothing.'

'Have you called or texted him?'

Artie leaned forward to reach for a teacup. 'What would be the point? I told him how I feel and he didn't feel the same, so end of story. I have to move on with my life. Without him.'

Rosa toyed with the hem of her flowered dress in an abstracted manner. 'What will you do if or when he sells the *castello*?'

'I'll find somewhere else to live. I can't live in a place this big. It's not practical.' Artie's shoulders went down on a sigh. 'I'll always have wonderful memories of being here with Mama and Papa before the accident but it's well and truly time to move on. Someone else can live here and make their own memories.'

Rosa straightened the folds of her dress over her knees. 'The holiday I was telling you about…? I'm going with a…a friend.'

Artie's interest was piqued by the housekeeper's sheepish

tone. She put the teacup back down on the table in front of her. 'Who is the friend?'

Twin spots of colour appeared in Rosa's cheeks. 'Remember I told you about the love of my life who got away? Well, Sergio and I met up while you were staying with Luca. We've been seeing each other now and again since. He's asked me to go away with him for a short holiday. I won't go if you need me here, though.'

Artie leaned over to give Rosa a hug. 'I'm so happy for you.' She leaned back to look at her. 'I will always need you, Rosa, but as a friend, not as a babysitter.'

Rosa grimaced. 'You don't think I'm too old to be galivanting off with a man?'

Artie smiled. 'Not if you love him and he loves you.'

If only I should be so lucky.

Luca put off telling his grandfather about Artie leaving him for as long as he could because he didn't want to say the words out loud. *She left me.* But when Nonno was released from hospital and transferred into a cancer therapy unit, Luca had to explain why Artie wasn't with him. *She left me.* Those three words were like bullet wounds in his chest, raw, seeping, deep.

Nonno's distress at hearing Luca's news about his marriage was almost as bad as his own. 'But why? She's perfect for you, Luca. Why haven't you gone after her and brought her back?'

'Nonno, gone are the days when a man can carry a woman back to his cave,' Luca said. 'I can't force her to stay with me. She made the choice to leave.'

Nonno scowled. 'If you loved Artie like I loved your grandmother, nothing would stop you from doing everything in your power to get her back. A man in love is a force to be reckoned with.'

The silence was telling.

Luca loosened the collar of his shirt and leaned forward to

rest his forearms on his thighs. 'Enough about my dramas. Is there anything I can get you?'

Nonno shook his head and closed his eyes. 'No. I just need to sleep.'

Luca stood from the bedside and laid a gentle hand on his grandfather's weathered arm. 'I'll be in again tomorrow.'

He was on his way out of the hospital when his phone rang with his mother's ring tone and his chest seized with the all too familiar dread. But instead of letting his phone go to message service as he often did, this time he answered it. 'Mama.'

'Luca, how is Nonno? I tried calling him but he must have his phone off. His carer rang to tell me he had a fall a week or two ago. She also told me you're married. Is that true? Why didn't you invite me to your wedding?'

Guilt gnawed at his conscience. 'Nonno's doing okay. As to my marriage—it's a long story and I hate to tell you it hasn't got a happy ending.'

'Oh, Luca.' His mother's sigh only intensified the pain riddling his chest. 'What's happened to us that you didn't want me to be there on your special day?'

Luca cleared his suddenly blocked throat and stepped out of the way of visitors coming through the hospital entrance. He pinched the bridge of his nose, scrunching his eyes closed briefly. 'It's not you. It's me. It's always been me that's the problem.'

'You're too hard on yourself,' his mother said. 'You're so like your father it's uncanny.' She sighed again and went on, 'It's why I found it increasingly difficult to be around you as you grew into a man. I couldn't look at you without seeing him. It reminded me of my role in what happened.'

Luca frowned, his hand going back to his side. 'Your role? What are you talking about? I was the one who entered the surf that day. You weren't even at the beach.'

'No.' Her voice was ragged. 'I wasn't there. I went shopping instead of spending the day with my family as your father wanted. Do you know how much I regret that now? It's tortured me for years. What if I had gone along? I could've called for help instead of you trying to do it on your own. I can't bear to think of you running along that deserted beach, half drowned yourself, trying to find someone to help.' She began to sob. 'Whenever I've looked at you since, I've seen that traumatised, terrified young boy and felt how I let you and your papa and Angelo down.'

Luca blinked away stinging moisture from his eyes. He swallowed deeply against the boulder-sized lump in his throat. 'Mama, please don't cry. Please don't blame yourself. I'm sorry I haven't called you. I'm sorry I've let you suffer like this without being there for you. It was selfish of me.'

'You haven't got a selfish bone in your body,' his mother said. 'Your father was the same. Too generous for words, always hard-working, trying to make the world a better place. But tell me, what's going on with your marriage? It breaks my heart to think of you missing out on finding the love of your life. I'm so grateful I had those precious years with your father. They have sustained me through the long years since. I live off the memories.'

Luca gave a serrated sigh and pushed his hair back off his forehead. 'I'd rather not talk about it now, but next time I'm in New York do you want to catch up over dinner?'

'I would love that.' His mother's voice was thick with emotion. 'Give Nonno my best wishes.'

'Sì,' Luca said. 'I will.'

Luca tried not to think about Artie in the next couple of weeks and he mostly succeeded. Mostly. He blocked his memories of her smile, her touch and her kiss with a punishing regime of work that left him feeling ragged at the end of each day. One would think he would stumble into bed and fall instantly asleep out of sheer exhaustion, but no, that was when the real torture got going. The sense of emptiness could be staved off during the day but at night it taunted him with a vengeance. He tossed, he turned, he paced, he swore, he thumped the pillows and doggedly ignored the vacant side of the bed where Artie had once lain. He did his best to ignore the fragrance of her perfume that stubbornly lingered in the air at his villa as if to taunt him. He did his best to ignore the pain that sat low and heavy in his chest, dragging on his organs like a tow rope.

She left you.

But then more words joined in the mocking chorus.

You let her go.

He allowed them some traction occasionally, using them as a rationalisation exercise. Of course he'd let her go. It was the right thing to do. She wanted more than he could give, so it was only fair that he set her free.

But you're not free.

What was it with his conscience lately? Reminding him of things he didn't want reminding about. No, he didn't feel free and—even more worrying—he didn't *want* to feel free. He wanted to feel connected, bonded to Artie, because when he was with her, he felt like a fully functioning human being. He felt things he hadn't felt before. Things he didn't think he was capable of feeling. Things that were terrifying because they made him vulnerable in a way he had avoided feeling for most of his adult life.

He had shut down his emotional centre.

Bludgeoned it into a coma.

But since his conversation with his mother there were tiny flickers of life deep in his chest like the faint trace of a heartbeat on an electrocardiograph. A pulse of something he had thought long dead. A need he had denied for so long he had fooled himself he wasn't capable of feeling it.

The need to love and be loved.

Three more words popped into his head like a blinding flash of light.

You love her.

Luca let them sit for a moment, for once not rushing to block them or erase them or deny them.

You love her.

And then he tweaked them, substituting the 'you' for 'I'.

I love her.

Bringing himself inexorably closer to the truth, step by step.

I. Love. Her.

He embraced the truth of those words like someone sucking in oxygen after near strangulation.

I love her.

His chest ballooned with hope, positive energy zapping round his body.

I love her.

Luca snatched up his car keys and the wedding and engagement rings from the bedside table. He'd placed them there as a form of self-torture but now he couldn't wait to see them back on Artie's finger where they belonged. Nonno was right. Luca's love for Artie was a force to be reckoned with—nothing would stop him from bringing her home.

Artie heard a car roaring through the *castello* gates and her heart turned over. She peered through the window in the sitting room and saw Luca unfold his tall, athletic figure from his car. Her pulse picked up its pace, her heart slamming into her breastbone, her skin tingling all over.

He's here.

She walked as calmly as she could to open the front door, schooling her features into a mask of cool politeness. After all, there was no point setting her hopes too high—he hadn't made a single effort to contact her over the past month. 'Luca. What brings you here?' She was proud of her impersonal tone. It belied the tumult of emotions in her chest.

He stepped through the open doorway with brisk efficiency, closing it with a click behind him. 'You bring me here, *cara*. You and only you.' He stood there with his hands by his sides and his expression set in grave lines. He looked tired around the eyes and his face hadn't seen a razor in a couple of days. 'I need to talk to you.'

Artie took a step back, her arms folding across her chest, her chin lifting. 'To say what?'

He unpeeled her arms from around her body, taking her hands in his. 'I've been such a fool. It's taken me the best part of a month to realise what's been there all the time.' He squeezed her hands. 'I love you, *mia piccola*. I love you so damn much it hurts. I can't believe I let you go. Can you ever forgive me?' He blinked a couple of times and she was surprised to see moisture in his eyes. 'I made a terrible mistake in not telling you sooner. But I wasn't able to recognise it until it was too late.' He drew her closer, holding her hands against his chest. 'Tell me it's not too late. I love you and want to spend the rest of my life with you. Please say yes. Please say you'll come back to me. Please give me another chance to prove how much I adore you.'

Artie brought one of her hands up to his prickly jaw, stroking it lovingly. 'I never thought I'd hear you say those words to me. I had given up hope, especially over the last few weeks.'

He grimaced and hugged her tightly to his chest. 'Don't remind me what a stubborn fool I've been. I can never forgive myself for that. I was in such denial that I couldn't even bring up your name on my phone. I knew it would hurt too much, so I didn't do it. Classic avoidance behaviour.'

Artie eased back to smile up at him. 'You're here now, so that's the main thing. I've missed you so much. I felt only half alive without you.'

He framed her face with his hands. 'You're everything I could ever want in a life partner. You complete me, complement me and challenge me to be the best man I can be. I can barely find the words to describe how much you mean to me.'

'I love you too, more than I can say.'

Luca lowered his mouth to hers and happiness exploded through her being. He was here. He loved her. He wanted to spend the rest of his life with her. His kiss communicated it all, passionately, fervently, devotedly. Even the steady thud of his heartbeat under her hand seemed to say the same. *I love you. I love you. I love you.*

After a moment, Luca lifted his mouth off hers and took something out of his trouser pocket. He held the wedding and engagement rings between his fingers. 'I think it's time these were put back where they belong, don't you?'

'Yes, please.' Artie held out her hand for him to slip them back on her ring finger. 'I'm never taking those rings off again.'

Luca smiled. 'I want you to meet my mother. Will you come to New York with me as soon as possible?'

Artie raised her eyebrows in delight. 'You've spoken to her?'

His face lit up with happiness. 'We had a chat about things and I realised how blinkered I'd been all these years, reading things into her behaviour that weren't accurate at all. You've taught me so much about myself, *cara*. I can never thank you enough for that. I hope you won't mind sharing my mother with me? I should warn you that she'll very likely shower you with love.'

'I won't mind sharing her at all. I can't wait to meet her.' Artie lifted her face for his kiss, her heart swelling with love. Her sad, closed-off life had somehow turned into a fairy tale. She was free from her self-imposed prison, and Luca, the man of her dreams, her Prince Charming, had claimed her as the love of his life.

Luca finally lifted his head and looked down at her with heart-stopping tenderness. 'Will you come away for a honeymoon with me after we visit my mother?'

'Just try and stop me.'

He stroked the curve of her cheek with his finger. 'I wasn't going to sell Castello Mireille.'

Artie smiled and gave him a fierce hug. 'I think on some level I knew that.' She eased back to look at him again. 'But I don't need it any more. What I need is you. It doesn't matter where I live as long as you're there with me.'

His eyes shimmered with emotion and her heart swelled with love to see how in touch with his feelings he was now. 'I've spent most of my life avoiding feeling like this—loving someone so much it hurts to think of ever losing them. I was in denial of my feelings from the moment I met you. You woke me to the needs I'd shut down inside myself. The need to love and be loved by an intimate partner. I can't believe how lucky I am to have found you.'

Artie pressed a soft kiss to his mouth. 'I'm lucky to have been found by *you*. If it hadn't been for you, I might still be locked away from all that life has to offer.'

Luca smiled, his eyes twinkling. 'I know it's early days, but maybe we can think about having those bambinos Nonno was talking about?'

She beamed with unfettered joy. 'Really? You want to have children?'

'Why not?' He kissed the tip of her nose. 'Building a family with you will be a wonderful experience. You'll be the best mother in the world.'

'I think you'll be an amazing father,' Artie said. 'I can't wait to hold our baby in my arms. I never thought I wanted to have a family until I met you. I didn't allow myself to think about it. But now it's like a dream come true.'

Luca gazed down at her with love shining in his eyes. 'Thank you for being you. Adorable, sweet, amazing you.'

Artie gave him a teasing smile. 'So, you don't think I'm too naïve and innocent for you now?'

'You're perfect for me.' He planted a smacking kiss on her lips. 'And as to remaining innocent, well, I'll soon take care of that.'

Artie laughed and flung her arms around his neck. 'Bring it on.'

* * * * *

The Uncompromising Italian

Cathy Williams

All about the author...
Cathy Williams

CATHY WILLIAMS was born in the West Indies and has been writing Harlequin® romances for some fifteen years. She is a great believer in the power of perseverance, as she had never written anything before (apart from school essays a lifetime ago!), and from the starting point of zero has now fulfilled her ambition to pursue this most enjoyable of careers. She would encourage any would-be writer to have faith and go for it! She lives in the beautiful Warwickshire countryside with her husband and three children, Charlotte, Olivia and Emma. When not writing she is hard-pressed to find a moment's free time in between the millions of household chores, not to mention being a one-woman taxi service for her daughters' never-ending social lives. She derives inspiration from the hot, lazy, tropical island of Trinidad (where she was born), from the peaceful countryside of middle England and, of course, from her many friends, who are a rich source of plots and are particularly garrulous when it comes to describing Harlequin Presents® heroes. It would seem, from their complaints, that tall, dark and charismatic men are way too few and far between. Her hope is to continue writing romance fiction, providing those eternal tales of love for which, she feels, we all strive.

Other titles by Cathy Williams available in ebook:

To my wonderful daughters.

CHAPTER ONE

LESLEY FOX SLOWLY drew to a stop in front of the most imposing house she had ever seen.

The journey out of London had taken barely any time at all. It was Monday, it was the middle of August and she had been heading against the traffic. In all it had taken her under an hour to leave her flat in crowded Ladbroke Grove and arrive at a place that looked as though it should be plastered on the cover of a *House Beautiful* magazine.

The wrought-iron gates announced its splendour, as had the tree-lined avenue and acres of manicured lawns through which she had driven.

The guy was beyond wealthy. Of course, she had known that. The first thing she had done when she had been asked to do this job had been to look him up online.

Alessio Baldini—Italian, but resident in the UK for a long time. The list of his various companies was vast and she had skipped over all of that. What he did for a living was none of her business. She had just wanted to make sure that the man existed and was who Stan said he was.

Commissions via friends of friends were not always to be recommended, least of all in her niche sideline business. A girl couldn't be too careful, as her father liked to say.

She stepped out of her little Mini, which was dwarfed in the vast courtyard, and took a few minutes to look around her.

The brilliance of a perfect summer's day made the sprawling green lawns, the dense copse to one side lush with lavender and the clambering roses against the stone of the mansion facing her seem almost too breathtakingly beautiful to be entirely real.

This country estate was in a league of its own.

There had been a bit of information on the Internet about where the man lived, but no pictures, and she had been ill-prepared for this concrete display of wealth.

A gentle breeze ruffled her short brown hair and for once she felt a little awkward in her routine garb of lightweight combat trousers, espadrilles and one of her less faded tee-shirts advertising the rock band she had gone to see five years ago.

This didn't seem the sort of place where dressing down would be tolerated.

For the first time, she wished she had paid a little more attention to the details of the guy she was going to see.

There had been long articles about him but few pictures and she had skimmed over those, barely noting which one he was amidst the groups of boring men in business suits who'd all seemed to wear the identical smug smiles of people who had made far too much money for their own good.

She grabbed her laptop from the passenger seat and slammed the door shut.

If it weren't for Stan, she wouldn't be here now. She didn't need the money. She could afford the mortgage on her one-bedroom flat, had little interest in buying pointless girly clothes for a figure she didn't possess to attract men in whom she had scant interest—or who, she amended with scrupulous honesty to herself, had scant interest in *her*—and she wasn't into expensive, long-haul holidays.

With that in mind, she had more than enough to be going on with. Her full-time job as a website designer paid well and, as far as she was concerned, she lacked for nothing.

But Stan was her dad's long-time friend from Ireland. They had grown up together. He had taken her under his wing when she had moved down to London after university and she owed him.

With any luck, she would be in and out of the man's place in no time at all.

She breathed in deeply and stared at the mansion in front of her.

It seemed a never-ending edifice of elegant cream stone, a dream of a house, with ivy climbing in all the right places and windows that looked as though they dated back to the turn of the century.

This was just the sort of ostentatious wealth that should have held little appeal, but in fact she was reluctantly charmed by its beauty.

Of course, the man would be a lot less charming than his house. It was always the way. Rich guys always thought they were God's gift to women even when they obviously weren't. She had met one or two in her line of work and it had been a struggle to keep a smile pinned to her face.

There was no doorbell but an impressive knocker. She could hear it reverberating through the bowels of the house as she banged it hard on the front door and then stood back to wait for however long it would take for the man's butler or servant, or whoever he employed to answer doors for him, to arrive on the scene and let her in.

She wondered what he would look like. Rich and Italian, so probably dark-haired with a heavy accent. Possibly short, which would be a bit embarrassing, because she was five-eleven and a half and likely to tower over him—never a good thing. She knew from experience that men hated women who towered over them. He would probably be quite dapper, kitted out in expensive Italian gear and wearing expensive Italian footwear. She had no idea what either might look like but it was safe to say that trainers and old clothes would not feature on the sartorial menu.

She was fully occupied amusing herself with a variety of mental pictures when the door was pulled open without warning.

For a few seconds, Lesley Fox lost the ability to speak. Her lips parted and she stared. Stared in a way she had never stared at any man in her life before.

The guy standing in front of her was, quite simply, beautiful. Taller than her by a few inches, and wearing faded jeans and a navy-blue polo shirt, he was barefoot. Raven-black hair was combed back from a sinfully sexy face. His eyes were as black as his hair and lazily returned her stare, until she felt the blood rush to her face and she returned to Planet Earth with a feeling of sickening embarrassment.

'Who are you?'

His cool, rich, velvety voice galvanised her senses back into working order and she cleared her throat and reminded herself that she wasn't the type of girl who had ever been daunted by a guy, however good-looking he was. She came from a family of six and she was the only girl. She had been brought up going to rugby matches, watching the football on television, climbing trees and exploring the glorious countryside of wild Ireland with brothers who hadn't always appreciated their younger sister tagging along.

She had always been able to handle the opposite sex. She had lived her life being one of the lads, for God's sake!

'I'm here about your... Er...my name's Lesley Fox.' As an afterthought, she stuck out her hand and then dropped it when he failed to respond with a return gesture.

'I wasn't expecting a girl.' Alessio looked at her narrowly. That, he thought, had to be the understatement of the year. He had been expecting a Les Fox—Les, as in a man. Les, as in a man who was a contemporary of Rob Dawson, his IT guy. Rob Dawson was in his forties and resembled a beach ball. He had been expecting a forty-something-year-old man of similar build.

Instead, he was looking at a girl with cropped dark hair,

eyes the colour of milk chocolate and a lanky, boyish physique, wearing...

Alessio took in the baggy sludge-green trousers with awkward pockets and the faded tee-shirt.

He couldn't quite recall the last time he had seen a woman dressed with such obvious, scathing disregard for fashion.

Women always tried their very hardest when around him to show their best side. Their hair was always perfect, make-up always flawless, clothes always the height of fashion and shoes always high and sexy.

His eyes drifted down to her feet. She was wearing cloth shoes.

'I'm so sorry to have disappointed you, Mr Baldini. I take it you *are* Mr Baldini and not his manservant, sent to chase away callers by being rude to them?'

'I didn't think anyone used that term any more...'

'What term?'

'*Manservant.* When I asked Dawson to provide me with the name of someone who could help me with my current little... problem, I assumed he would have recommended someone a bit older. More experienced.'

'I happen to be very good at what I do.'

'As this isn't a job interview, I can't very well ask for references.' He stood aside, inviting her to enter. 'But, considering you look as though you're barely out of school, I'll want to know a little bit about you before I explain the situation.'

Lesley held on to her temper. She didn't need the money. Even though the hourly rate that she had been told about was staggering, she really didn't have to stand here and listen to this perfect stranger quiz her about her experience for a job she hadn't applied for. But then she thought of Stan and all he had done for her and she gritted back the temptation to turn on her heel, climb back into her car and head down to London without a backward glance.

'Come on in,' Alessio threw over his shoulder as she remained hovering on the doorstep and, after a few seconds, Lesley took a step into the house.

She was surrounded by pale marble only broken by the richness of a Persian rug. The walls were adorned with the sort of modern masterpieces that should have looked out of place in a house of this age but somehow didn't. The vast hall was dominated by a staircase that swept upwards before branching out in opposite directions, and doors indicated that there was a multitude of rooms winging on either side, not that she wouldn't have guessed.

More than ever, she felt inappropriately dressed. He might be casual, but he was casual in the sort of elegant, expensive way of the very wealthy.

'Big place for one person,' she said, staring around her, openly impressed.

'How do you know I haven't got a sprawling family lurking somewhere out of sight?'

'Because I looked you up,' Lesley answered truthfully. Her eyes finally returned to him and once again she was struck by his dark, saturnine good looks. And once again she had to drag her eyes away reluctantly, desperate to return her gaze to him, to drink him in. 'I don't usually travel into unknown territory when I do my freelance jobs. Usually the computer comes to me, I don't go to the computer.'

'Always illuminating to get out of one's comfort zone,' Alessio drawled. He watched as she ran her fingers through her short hair, spiking it up. She had very dark eyebrows, as dark as her hair, which emphasised the peculiar shade of brown of her eyes. And she was pale, with satiny skin that should have been freckled but wasn't. 'Follow me. We can sit out in the garden and I'll get Violet to bring us something to drink... Have you had lunch?'

Lesley frowned. Had she? She was careless with her eating habits, something she daily promised herself to rectify. If she ate more, she knew she'd stand a fighting chance of not looking like a gawky runner bean. 'A sandwich before I left,' she returned politely. 'But a cup of tea would be wonderful.'

'It never fails to amuse me that on a hot summer's day you English will still opt for a cup of tea instead of something cold.'

'I'm not English. I'm Irish.'

Alessio cocked his head to one side and looked at her, consideringly. 'Now that you mention it, I do detect a certain twang...'

'But I'm still partial to a cup of tea.'

He smiled and she was knocked sideways. The man oozed sex appeal. He'd had it when he'd been unsmiling, but now... it was enough to throw her into a state of confusion and she blinked, driving away the unaccustomed sensation.

'This isn't my preferred place of residence,' he took up easily as he led the way out of the magnificent hall and towards sprawling doors that led towards the back of the house. 'I come here to give it an airing every so often but most of my time is spent either in London or abroad on business.'

'And who looks after this place when you're not in it?'

'I have people who do that for me.'

'Bit of a waste, isn't it?'

Alessio spun round and looked at her with a mixture of irritation and amusement. 'From whose point of view?' he asked politely and Lesley shrugged and folded her arms.

'There are such extreme housing problems in this country that it seems crazy for one person to have a place of this size.'

'You mean, when I could subdivide the whole house and turn it into a million rabbit hutches to cater for down and outs?' He laughed drily. 'Did my guy explain to you what the situation was?'

Lesley frowned. She had thought he might have been offended by her remark, but she was here on business of sorts, and her opinions were of little consequence.

'Your guy got in touch with Stan who's a friend of my dad and he... Well, he just said that you had a sensitive situation that needed sorting. No details.'

'None were given. I was just curious to find out whether idle speculation had entered the equation.' He pushed open some doors and they emerged into a magnificent back garden.

Tall trees bordered pristine, sprawling lawns. To one side was a tennis court and beyond that she could see a swimming pool with a low, modern outbuilding which she assumed was changing rooms. The patio on which they were standing was as broad as the entire little communal garden she shared with the other residents in her block of flats and stretched the length of the house. If a hundred people were to stand side by side, they wouldn't be jostling for space.

Low wooden chairs were arranged around a glass-topped table and as she sat down a middle-aged woman bustled into her line of vision, as though summoned by some kind of whistle audible only to her.

Tea, Alessio instructed; something cold for him, a few things to eat.

Orders given, he sat down on one of the chairs facing her and leaned forward with his elbows resting on his knees.

'So the man my guy went to is a friend of your father's?'

'That's right. Stan grew up with my dad and when I moved down to London after university… Well, he and his wife took me under their wing. Made room for me in their house until I was settled—even paid the three months' deposit on my first rental property because they knew that it would be a struggle for my dad to afford it. So, yeah, I owe Stan a lot and it's why I took this job, Mr Baldini.'

'Alessio, please. And you work as…?'

'I design websites but occasionally I work as a freelance hacker. Companies employ me to see if their firewalls are intact and secure. If something can be hacked, then I can do it.'

'Not a job I immediately associate with a woman,' he murmured and raised his eyebrows as she bristled. 'That's not meant as an insult. It's purely a statement of fact. There are a couple of women in my IT department, but largely they're guys.'

'Why didn't you get one of your own employees to sort out your problem?'

'Because it's a sensitive issue and, the less my private life is discussed within the walls of my offices, the better. So you design websites. You freelance and you claim you can get into anything.'

'That's right. Despite not being a man.'

Alessio heard the defensive edge to her voice and his curiosity was piqued. His life had settled into a predictable routine when it came to members of the opposite sex. His one mistake, made when he was eighteen, had been enough for him to develop a very healthy scepticism when it came to women. The fairer sex, he had concluded, was a misconception of stunning magnitude.

'So if you could explain the situation...' Lesley looked at him levelly, her mind already flying ahead to the thrill of solving whatever problem lay in store for her. She barely noticed his housekeeper placing a pot of tea in front of her and a plate crammed with pastries, produced from heaven only knew where.

'I've been getting anonymous emails.' Alessio flushed as he grappled with the unaccustomed sensation of admitting to having his hands tied when it came to sorting out his own dilemma. 'They started a few weeks ago.'

'At regular intervals?'

'No.' He raked his fingers through his hair and looked at her earnest face tilted to one side... A small crease indented her forehead and he could almost hear her thinking, her mind working as methodically as one of the computers she dealt with. 'I ignored them to start with but the last couple have been... how shall I describe them?...a little *forceful*.' He reached for the pitcher of homemade lemonade to pour himself a glass. 'If you looked me up, you probably know that I own several IT companies. Despite that, I confess that my knowledge of the ins and outs of computers is scant.'

'Actually, I have no idea what companies you own or don't own. I looked you up because I wanted to make sure that there was nothing dodgy about you. I've done this sort of thing before. I'm not looking for background detail, I'm generally looking for any articles that might point a suspicious finger.'

'Dodgy? You thought I might be *dodgy*?'

He looked so genuinely shocked and insulted that she couldn't help laughing. 'You might have had newspaper cuttings about suspect dealings, mafia connections...you know the sort of thing. I'd have been able to find even the most obscure article within minutes if there had been anything untoward about you. You came up clean.'

Alessio nearly choked on his lemonade. 'Mafia dealings... because I'm Italian? That's the most ridiculous thing I've ever heard.'

Lesley shrugged sheepishly. 'I don't like taking chances.'

'I've never done a crooked thing in my entire life.' He flung his arms wide in a gesture that was peculiarly foreign. 'I even buck the trend of the super-rich and am a fully paid-up member of the honest, no-offshore-scams, tax-paying club! To suggest that I might be linked to the Mafia because I happen to be Italian...'

He sat forward and stared at her and she had to fight off the very feminine and girlish response to wonder what he thought of her, as a woman, as opposed to a talented computer whizz-kid there at his bidding. Suddenly flustered, she gulped back a mouthful of hot tea and grimaced.

Wondering what men thought of her wasn't her style. She pretty much *knew* what they thought of her. She had lived her whole life knowing that she was one of the lads. Even her job helped to advance that conclusion.

No, she was too tall, too angular and too mouthy to hold any appeal when it came to the whole sexual attraction thing. Least of all when the guy in question looked like Alessio Baldini. She cringed just thinking about it.

'No, you've been watching too many gangster movies. Surely you must have heard of me?' He was always in the newspapers. Usually in connection with big business deals—occasionally in the gossip columns with a woman hanging onto his arm.

He wasn't sure why he had inserted that irrelevant question but, now that he had, he found that he was awaiting her answer with keen curiosity.

'Nope.'

'No?'

'I guess you probably think that everyone's heard of you, but in actual fact I don't read the newspapers.'

'You don't read the newspapers…not even the gossip columns?'

'Especially not the gossip columns,' she said scathingly. 'Not all girls are interested in what celebs get up to.' She tried to reconnect with the familiar feeling of satisfaction that she wasn't one of those simpering females who became embroiled in silly gossip about the rich and famous, but for once the feeling eluded her.

For once, she longed to be one of those giggly, coy girls who knew how to bat their eyelashes and attract the cute guys; she wanted to be part of the prom set instead of the clever, boyish one lurking on the sidelines; she wanted to be a member of that invisible club from which she had always been excluded because she just never seemed to have the right code words to get in.

She fought back a surge of dissatisfaction with herself and had to stifle a sense of anger that the man sitting opposite her had been the one to have generated the emotion. She had conquered whatever insecurities she had about her looks a long time ago and was perfectly content with her appearance. She might not be to everyone's taste, and she certainly wouldn't be to *his,* but her time would come and she would find someone. At the age of twenty-seven, she was hardly over the hill and, besides, her career was taking off. The last thing she needed or wanted was to be side-tracked by a guy.

She wondered how they had ended up talking about something that had nothing at all to do with the job for which she had been hired.

Was this part of his 'getting to know her' exercise? Was he quietly vetting her the way she had vetted him, when she had skimmed over all that information about him on the computer, making sure that there was nothing worrying about him?

'You were telling me about the emails you received...' She brought the conversation back to the business in hand.

Alessio sighed heavily and gave her a long, considering look from under his lashes.

'The first few were innocuous enough—a couple of one-liners hinting that they had information I might be interested in. Nothing worrying.'

'You get emails like that all the time?'

'I'm a rich man. I get a lot of emails that have little or nothing to do with work.' He smiled wryly and Lesley felt that odd tingling feeling in her body once again. 'I have several email accounts and my secretary is excellent when it comes to weeding out the dross.'

'But these managed to slip through?'

'These went to my personal email address. Very few people have that.'

'Okay.' She frowned and stared off into the distance. 'So you say that the first few were innocuous enough and then the tenor of the emails changed?'

'A few days ago, the first request for money came. Don't get me wrong, I get a lot of requests for money, but they usually take a more straightforward route. Someone wants a sponsor for something; charities asking for hand-outs; small businesses angling for investment...and then the usual assortment of nut cases who need money for dying relatives or to pay lawyers before they can claim their inheritance, which they would happily share with me.'

'And your secretary deals with all of that?'

'She does. It's usually called pressing the delete button on the computer. Some get through to me but, in general, we have established charities to which we give healthy sums of money, and all requests for business investment are automatically referred to my corporate finance division.'

'But this slipped through the net because it came to your personal address. Any idea how he or she could have accessed that information?' She was beginning to think that this sounded a little out of her area of expertise. Hackers usually went for information or, in some cases tried to attack the accounts, but this was clearly...personal. 'And don't you think that this might be better referred to the police?' she inserted, before he could answer.

Alessio laughed drily. He took a long mouthful of his drink and looked at her over the rim of the glass as he drank.

'If you read the papers,' he drawled, 'you might discover that the police have been having a few off-months when it comes to safeguarding the privacy of the rich and famous. I'm a very private man. The less of my life is splashed across the news, the better.'

'So my job is to find out who is behind these emails.'

'Correct.'

'At which point you'll...?'

'Deal with the matter myself.'

He was still smiling, with that suggestion of amusement on his lips, but she could see the steel behind the lazy, watchful dark eyes. 'I should tell you from the offset that I cannot accept this commission if there's any suggestion that you might turn...err...*violent* when it comes to sorting out whoever is behind this.'

Alessio laughed and relaxed back in his chair, stretching out his long legs to cross them at the ankle and loosely linking his fingers on his stomach. 'You have my word that I won't turn, as you say, violent.'

'I hope you're not making fun of me, Mr Baldini,' Lesley said stiffly. 'I'm being perfectly serious.'

'Alessio. The name's Alessio. And you aren't still under the impression that I'm a member of the Mafia, are you? With a stash of guns under the bed and henchmen to do my bidding?'

Lesley flushed. Where had her easy, sassy manner gone? She was seldom lost for words but she was now, especially when those dark, dark eyes were lingering on her flushed cheeks, making her feel even more uncomfortable than she already felt. A burst of shameful heat exploded somewhere deep inside her, her body's acknowledgment of his sexual magnetism, chemistry that was wrapping itself around her like a web, confusing her thoughts and making her pulses race.

'Do I strike you as a violent man, Lesley?'

'I never said that. I'm just being…cautious.'

'Have you had awkward situations before?' The soft pink of her cheeks when she blushed was curiously appealing, maybe because she was at such pains to project herself as a tough woman with no time for frivolity.

'What do you mean?'

'You intimated that you checked me out to make sure that I wasn't *dodgy*…and I think I'm quoting you here. So are you cautious in situations like these… when the computer doesn't go to you but you're forced to go to the computer…because of bad experiences?'

'I'm a careful person.' Why did that make her sound like such a bore, when she wasn't? Once again weirdly conscious of the image she must present to a guy like him, Lesley inhaled deeply and ploughed on. 'And yes,' she asserted matter-of-factly, 'I *have* had a number of poor experiences in the past. A few months ago, I was asked to do a favour for a friend's friend only to find that what he wanted was for me to hack into his ex-wife's bank account and see where her money was being spent. When I refused, he turned ugly.'

'Turned ugly?'

'He'd had a bit too much to drink. He thought that if he pushed me around a bit I'd do what he wanted.' And just in case her awkward responses had been letting her down, maybe giving him the mistaken impression that she was anything but one hundred per cent professional, she concluded crisply, 'Of course, it's annoying, but nothing I can't handle.'

'You can handle men who turn ugly.' Fascinating. He was in the company of someone from another planet. She might have the creamiest complexion he had ever seen, and a heart-shaped face that insisted on looking ridiculously feminine despite the aggressive get-up, but she was certainly nothing like any woman he had ever met. 'Tell me how you do that,' he said with genuine curiosity.

Absently, he noticed that she had depleted the plate of pastries by half its contents. A hearty appetite; his eyes flicked to her body which, despite being well hidden beneath her anti-fashion-statement clothing, was long and slender.

On some subliminal level, Lesley was aware of the shift in his attention, away from her face and onto her body. Her instinct was to squirm. Instead, she clasped her hands tightly together on her lap and tried to force her uncooperative body into a position of relaxed ease.

'I have a black belt in karate.'

Alessio was stunned into silence. 'You do?'

'I do.' She shrugged and held his confounded gaze. 'And it's not that shocking,' she continued into the lengthening silence. 'There were loads of girls in my class when I did it. 'Course, a few of them fell by the wayside when we began moving up the levels.'

'And you did these classes...when, exactly?'

In passing, Lesley wondered what this had to do with her qualifications for doing the job she had come to do. On the other hand, it never hurt to let someone know that you weren't the sort of woman to be messed with.

'I started when I was ten and the classes continued into my teens with a couple of breaks in between.'

'So, when other girls were experimenting with make-up, you were learning the valuable art of self-defence.'

Lesley felt the sharp jab of discomfort as he yet again unwittingly hit the soft spot inside her, the place where her insecurities lay, neatly parcelled up but always ready to be unwrapped at a moment's notice.

'I think every woman should know how to physically defend herself.'

'That's an extremely laudable ambition,' Alessio murmured. He noticed that his long, cold drink was finished. 'Let's go inside. I'll show you to my office and we can continue our conversation there. It's getting a little oppressive out here.' He stood up, squinted towards his gardens and half-smiled when he saw her automatically reach for the plate of pastries and whatever else she could manage to take in with her.

'No need.' He briefly rested one finger on her outstretched hand and Lesley shot back as though she had been scalded. 'Violet will tidy all this away.'

Lesley bit back an automatic retort that it was illuminating to see how the other half lived. She was no inverted snob, even though she might have no time for outward trappings and the importance other people sometimes placed on them, but he made her feel defensive. Worse, he made her feel gauche and awkward, sixteen all over again, cringing at the prospect of having to wear a frock to go to the school leaving dance, knowing that she just couldn't pull it off.

'I'm thinking that your mother must be a strong woman to instil such priorities in her daughter,' he said neutrally.

'My mother died when I was three—a hit-and-run accident when she was cycling back from doing the shopping.'

Alessio stopped in his tracks and stared down at her until she was forced uncomfortably to return his stare.

'Please don't say something trite like *I'm sorry to hear that.*'

She tilted her chin and looked at him unblinkingly. 'It happened a long time ago.'

'No. I wasn't going to say that,' Alessio said in a low, musing voice that made her skin tingle.

'My father was the strong influence in my life,' she pressed on in a high voice. 'My father and my five brothers. They all gave me the confidence to know that I could do whatever I chose to do, that my gender did not have to stand in the way of my ambition. I got my degree in maths—the world was my oyster.'

Heart beating as fast as if she had run a marathon, she stared up at him, their eyes tangling until her defensiveness subsided and gave way to something else, something she could barely comprehend, something that made her say quickly, with a tight smile, 'But I don't see how any of this is relevant. If you lead the way to your computer, it shouldn't take long for me to figure out who your problem pest is.'

CHAPTER TWO

THE OFFICE TO which she was led allowed her a good opportunity to really take in the splendour of her surroundings.

Really big country estates devoured money and consequently were rarely in the finest of conditions. Imposing exteriors were often let down by run-down, sad interiors in want of attention.

This house was as magnificent inside as it was out. The pristine gardens, the splendid ivy-clad walls, were replicated inside by a glorious attention to detail. From the cool elegance of the hall, she bypassed a series of rooms, each magnificently decorated. Of course, she could only peek through slightly open doors, because she had to half-run to keep up with him, but she saw enough to convince her that serious money had been thrown at the place—which was incredible, considering it was not used on a regular basis.

Eventually they ended up in an office with book-lined walls and a massive antique desk housing a computer, a lap-top and a small stack of legal tomes. She looked around at the rich burgundy drapes pooling to the ground, the pin-striped sober wallpaper, the deep sofa and chairs.

It was a decor she would not have associated with him and, as though reading her mind, he said wryly, 'It makes a change from what I'm used to in London. I'm more of a modern man myself but I find there's something soothing about working in a turn-of-the-century gentleman's den.' He moved smoothly round to the chair at the desk and powered up his computer. 'When I bought this house several years ago, it was practically derelict. I paid over the odds for it because of its history and because I wanted to make sure the owner and her daughter could be rehoused in the manner to which they had clearly once been accustomed. Before, that is, the money ran out. They were immensely grateful and only suggested one thing—that I try and keep a couple of the rooms as close as possible to the original format. This was one.'

'It's beautiful.' Lesley hovered by the door and looked around her. Through the French doors, the lawns outside stretched away to an impossibly distant horizon. The sun turned everything into dazzling technicolour. The greens of the grass and the trees seemed greener than possible and the sky was blindingly turquoise. Inside the office, though, the dark colours threw everything into muted relief. He was right; the space was soothing.

She looked at him frowning in front of the computer, sitting forward slightly, his long, powerful body still managing to emanate force even though he wasn't moving.

'There's no need to remain by the door,' he said without looking at her. 'You'll actually need to venture into the room and sit next to me if you're to work on this problem. Ah. Right. Here we go.' He stood up, vacating the chair for her.

The leather was warm from where he had been sitting, and the heat seemed to infiltrate her entire body as she took his place in front of the computer screen. When he leaned over to tap on the keyboard, she felt her breathing become rapid and shallow and she had to stop herself from gasping out loud.

His forearm was inches away from her breasts and never had the proximity of one person's body proved so rattling. She willed herself to focus on what he was calling up on the screen in front of her and to remember that she was here in a professional capacity.

Why was he getting to her? Perhaps she had been too long without a guy in her life. Friends and family were all very good, but maybe her life of pleasant celibacy had made her unexpectedly vulnerable to a spot of swarthy good looks and a wicked smile.

'So…'

Lesley blinked herself back into the present to find herself staring directly into dark, dark eyes that were far too close to her for comfort.

'So?'

'Email one—a little too familiar, a little too chatty, but nothing that couldn't be easily ignored.'

Lesley looked thoughtfully at the computer screen and read through the email. Her surroundings faded away as she began studying the series of emails posted to him, looking for clues, asking him questions, her fingers moving swiftly and confidently across the key board.

She could understand why he had decided to farm out this little problem to an outside source.

If he valued his privacy, then he would not want his IT division to have access to what appeared to be vaguely menacing threats, suggestions of something that could harm his business or ruin his reputation. It would be fodder for any over-imaginative employee, of which there were always a few in any office environment.

Alessio pushed himself away from the desk and strolled towards one of the comfortable, deep chairs facing her.

She was utterly absorbed in what she was doing. He took time out to study her and he was amused and a little surprised to discover that he enjoyed the view.

It wasn't simply the arrangement of her features that he found curiously captivating.

There was a lively intelligence to her that made a refreshing change from the beautiful but intellectually challenged women he dated. He looked at the way her short chocolate-brown hair spiked up, as though too feisty and too wilful to be controlled. Her eyelashes were long and thick; her mouth, as he now saw, was full and, yes, sexy.

A sexy mouth, especially just at this very moment, when her lips were slightly parted.

She frowned and ran her tongue thoughtfully along her upper lip and, on cue, Alessio's body jerked into startling life. His libido, which had been unusually quiet since he'd ended his relationship with a blonde with a penchant for diamonds two months ago, fired up.

It was so unexpected a reaction that he nearly groaned in shock.

Instead, he shifted on the chair and smiled politely as her eyes briefly skittered across to him before resuming their intent concentration on the computer screen.

'Whoever's sent this knows what they're doing.'

'Come again?' Alessio crossed his legs, trying to maintain the illusion that he was in complete control of himself.

'They've been careful to make themselves as untraceable as possible.' Lesley stretched, then slumped back into the chair and swivelled it round so that she was facing him.

She stuck out her legs and gazed at her espadrilles. 'That first email may have been chatty and friendly but he or she knew that they didn't want to be traced. Why didn't you delete them, at least the earlier ones?'

'I had an instinct that they might be worth hanging onto.' He stood up and strolled towards the French doors. He had intended this meeting to be brief and functional, a blip that needed sorting out in his hectic life. Now, he found that his mind was stubbornly refusing to return to the matter in hand. Instead, it was relentlessly pulled back to the image he had of her sitting in front of his computer concentrating ferociously. He wondered what she would look like out of the unappealing ensemble. He wondered whether she would be any different from all the other naked women who had lain across his bed in readiness for him.

He knew she would—instinct again. Somehow he couldn't envisage her lying provocatively for him to take her, passive and willing to please.

No. That wasn't what girls with black belts in karate and a sideline in computer hacking did.

He played with the suddenly tempting notion of prolonging her task. Who knew what might happen between them if she were to be around longer than originally envisaged?

'What would you suggest my next step should be? Because I'm taking from the expression on your face that it's not going to be as straightforward as you first thought.'

'Usually it's pretty easy to sort something like this out,' Lesley confessed, linking her hands on her stomach and staring off at nothing in particular. The weird, edgy tension she had felt earlier on had dissipated. Work had that effect on her. It occupied her whole mind and left no room for anything else. 'People are predictable when it comes to leaving tracks behind them, but obviously whoever is behind this hasn't used his own computer. He's gone to an Internet café. In fact, I wouldn't be surprised if he goes to a variety of Internet cafés, because we certainly would be able to trace the café he uses if he sticks there. And it wouldn't be too much of a headache finding out which terminal is his and then it would be a short step to identifying the person... I keep saying *he* but it might very well be a *she*.'

'How so? No, we'll get to that over something to drink—and I insist you forfeit the tea in favour of something a little more exciting. My housekeeper makes a very good Pimm's.'

'I couldn't,' Lesley said awkwardly. 'I'm not much of a drinker and I'm...err...driving anyway.'

'Fresh lemonade, in that case.' Alessio strolled towards her and held out his hand to tug her up from the chair to which she seemed to be glued.

For a few seconds, Lesley froze. When she grasped his hand—because frankly she couldn't think of what else to do without appearing ridiculous and childish—she felt a spurt of red-hot electricity zap through her body until every inch of her was galvanised into shrieking, heightened awareness of the dangerously sexy man standing in front of her.

'That would be nice,' she said a little breathlessly. As soon as she could she retrieved her scorching hand and resisted the urge to rub it against her trousers.

Alessio didn't miss a thing. She was a different person when she was concentrating on a computer. Looking at a screen, analysing what was in front of her, working out how to solve the problem he had presented, she oozed self-confidence. He idly wondered what her websites looked like.

But without a computer to absorb her attention she was prickly and defensive, a weird, intriguing mix of independent and vulnerable.

He smiled, turning her insides to liquid, and stood aside to allow her to pass by him out of the office.

'So we have a he or a she who goes to a certain Internet café, or more likely a variety of Internet cafés, for the sole reason of emailing me to, well, purpose as yet slightly unclear, but if I'm any reader of human motivation I'm smelling a lead-up to asking for money for information he or she may or may not know. There seem to be a lot of imponderables in this case.'

They had arrived at the kitchen without her being aware of having padded through the house at all, and she found a glass of fresh lemonade in her hands while he helped himself to a bottle of mineral water.

He motioned to the kitchen table and they sat facing one another on opposite sides.

'Generally,' Lesley said, sipping the lemonade, 'This should be a straightforward case of sourcing the computer in question, paying a visit to the Internet café—and usually these places have CCTV cameras. You would be able to find the culprit without too much bother.'

'But if he's clever enough to hop from café to café...'

'Then it'll take a bit longer but I'll get there. Of course, if you have no skeletons in the cupboard, Mr Baldini, then you could just walk away from this situation.'

'Is there such a thing as an adult without one or two skeletons in the cupboard?'

'Well, then.'

'Although,' Alessio continued thoughtfully, 'Skeletons imply something…wrong, in need of concealment. I can't think of any dark secrets I have under lock or key but there are certain things I would rather not have revealed.'

'Do you honestly care what the public thinks of you? Or maybe it's to do with your company? Sorry, but I don't really know how the big, bad world of business operates, but I'm just assuming that if something gets out that could affect your share prices then you mightn't be too happy.'

'I have a daughter.'

'You *have a daughter*?'

'Surely you got that from your search of me on the Internet?' Alessio said drily.

'I told you, I just skimmed through the stuff. There's an awful lot written up about you and I honestly just wanted to cut to the chase—any articles that could have suggested that I needed to be careful about getting involved. Like I said, I've fine-tuned my search engine when it comes to picking out relevant stuff or else I'd be swamped underneath useless speculation.' *A daughter?*

'Yes. I forgot—the "bodies under the motorway" scenario.' He raised his eyebrows and once again Lesley felt herself in danger of losing touch with common sense.

'I never imagined anything so dramatic, at least not really,' she returned truthfully, which had the effect of making that sexy smile on his face even broader. Flustered, she continued, 'But you were telling me that you have a daughter.'

'You still can't erase the incredulity from your voice,' he remarked, amused. 'Surely you've bumped into people who have had kids?'

'Yes! Of course! But...'

'But?'

Lesley stared at him. 'Why do I get the feeling that you're making fun of me?' she asked, ruffled and red-faced.

'My apologies.' But there was the echo of a smile still lingering in his voice, even though his expression was serious and contrite. 'But you blush so prettily.'

'That's the most ridiculous thing I've ever heard in my life!' And it was. Ridiculous. 'Pretty' was something she most definitely was *not*. Nor was she going to let this guy, this *sex God* of a man—who could have any woman he wanted, if you happened to like that kind of thing—get under her skin.

'Why is it ridiculous?' Alessio allowed himself to be temporarily side-tracked.

'I know you're probably one of these guys who slips into flattery mode with any woman you happen to find yourself confined with, but I'm afraid that I don't go into meltdown at empty compliments.' *What on earth was she going on about?* Why was she jumping into heated self-defence over nonsense like this?

When it came to business, Alessio rarely lost sight of the goal. Right now, not only had he lost sight of it, but he didn't mind. 'Do you go into meltdown at compliments you think are genuine?'

'I... I...'

'You're stammering,' he needlessly pointed out. 'I don't mean to make you feel uncomfortable.'

'I don't...err...feel uncomfortable.'

'Well, that's good.'

Lesley stared helplessly at him. He wasn't just sinfully sexy. The man was beautiful. He hadn't looked beautiful in those pictures, but then she had barely taken them in—a couple of grainy black-and-white shots of a load of businessmen had barely registered on her consciousness. Now, she wished she had paid attention so that she at least could have been prepared for the sort of effect he might have had on her.

Except, she admitted truthfully to herself, she would still have considered herself above and beyond being affected by any man, however good-looking he might happen to be. When it came to matters of the heart, she had always prided herself on her practicality. She knew her limitations and had accepted them. When and if the time came that she wanted a relationship, then she had always known that the man for her would not be the sort who was into looks but the sort who enjoyed intelligence, personality—a meeting of minds as much as anything else.

'You were telling me about your daughter...'

'My daughter.' Alessio sighed heavily and raked his fingers through his dark hair.

It was a gesture of hesitancy that seemed so at odds with his forceful personality that Lesley sat up and stared at him with narrowed eyes.

'Where is she?' Lesley looked past him, as though half-expecting this unexpected addition to his life suddenly to materialise out of nowhere. 'I thought you mentioned that you had no family. Where is your wife?'

'No *sprawling* family,' Alessio amended. 'And no wife. My wife died two years ago.'

'I'm so sorry.'

'There's no need for tears and sympathy.' He waved aside her interruption, although he was startled at how easily a softer nature shone through. 'When I say *wife,* it might be more accurate to say *ex-wife*. Bianca and I were divorced a long time ago.'

'How old is your daughter?'

'Sixteen. And, to save you the hassle of doing the maths, she was, shall we say, an unexpected arrival when I was eighteen.'

'You were a *father* at eighteen?'

'Bianca and I had been seeing each other in a fairly loose fashion for a matter of three months when she announced that her contraceptive pill had failed and I was going to be a father.' His lips thinned. The past was rarely raked up and when it was, as now, it still brought a sour taste to his mouth.

Unfortunately, he could see no way around a certain amount of confidential information exchanging hands because he had a gut feeling that, whatever his uninvited email correspondent wanted, it involved his daughter.

'And you weren't happy about that.' Lesley groped her way to understanding the darkening of his expression.

'A family was not something high on my agenda at the time,' Alessio imparted grimly. 'In fact, I would go so far as to say that it hadn't even crossed my radar. But, naturally, I did the honourable thing and married her. It was a match approved by both sides of the family until, that is, it became apparent that her family's wealth was an illusion. Her parents were up to their eyes in debt and I was a convenient match because of the financial rewards I brought with me.'

'She married you for your *money*?'

'It occurred to no one to do a background check.' He shrugged elegantly. 'You're looking at me as though I've suddenly landed from another planet.'

His slow smile knocked her sideways and she cleared her throat nervously. 'I'm not familiar with people marrying for no better reason than money,' she answered honestly.

Alessio raised his eyebrows. 'In that case, we really *do* come from different planets. My family is extremely wealthy, as am I. Believe me, I am extremely well versed in the tactics women will employ to gain entry to my bank balance.' He crossed his legs, relaxing. 'But you might say that, once bitten, twice shy.'

She made an exceptionally good listener. Was this why he had expanded on the skeleton brief he could have given her? Had gone into details that were irrelevant in the grand scheme of things? He hadn't been lying when he had told her that his unfortunate experience with his ex had left him jaded about women and the lengths they would go to in order to secure themselves a piece of the pie. He was rich and women liked money. It was therefore a given that he employed a healthy amount of caution in his dealings with the opposite sex.

But the woman sitting in front of him couldn't have been less interested in his earnings.

His little problem intrigued her far more than *he* did. It was a situation that Alessio had never encountered in his life before and there was something sexy and challenging about that.

'You mean you don't intend to marry again? I can understand that. And I guess you have your daughter. She must mean the world to you.'

'Naturally.' Alessio's voice cooled. 'Although I'll be the first to admit that things have not been easy between us. I had relatively little contact with Rachel when she was growing up, thanks to my ex-wife's talent for vindictiveness. She lived in Italy but travelled extensively, and usually when she knew that I had arranged a visit. She was quite happy to whip our daughter out of school at a moment's notice if only to make sure that my trip to Italy to visit would be a waste of time.'

'How awful.'

'At any rate, when Bianca died Rachel naturally came to me, but at the age of fourteen she was virtually a stranger and a fairly hostile one. Frankly, a nightmare.'

'She would have been grieving for her mother.' Lesley could barely remember her own mother and yet *she* still grieved at the lack of one in her life. How much more traumatic to have lost one at the age of fourteen, a time in life when a maternal, guiding hand could not have been more needed.

'She was behind in her schoolwork thanks to my ex-wife's antics, and refused to speak English in the classroom, so the whole business of teaching her was practically impossible. In the end, boarding school seemed the only option and, thankfully, she appears to have settled in there with somewhat more success. At least, there have been no phone calls threatening expulsion.'

'Boarding school...'

Alessio frowned. 'You say that as though it ranks alongside "prison cell".'

'I can't imagine the horror of being separated from my family. My brothers could be little devils when I was growing up but we were a family. Dad, the boys and me.'

Alessio tilted his head and looked at her, considering, tempted to ask her if that was why she had opted for a male-dominated profession, and why she wore clothes better suited to a boy. But the conversation had already drifted too far from the matter at hand. When he glanced down at his watch, it was to find that more time had passed than he might have expected.

'My gut feeling tells me that these emails are in some way connected to my daughter,' Alessio admitted. 'Reason should dictate that they're to do with work but I can't imagine why anyone wouldn't approach me directly about anything to do with my business concerns.'

'No. And if you're as above board as you say you are…'

'You doubt my word?'

Lesley shrugged. 'I don't think that's really my business; the only reason I mention it is because it might be pertinent to finding out who is behind this. 'Course, I shall continue working at the problem, but if it's established that the threat is to do with your work then you might actually be able to pinpoint the culprit yourself.'

'How many people do you imagine work for me?' Alessio asked curiously, and Lesley shrugged and gave the matter some thought.

'No idea.' The company she worked for was small, although prominent in its field, employing only a handful of people on the creative side and slightly fewer on the admin side. 'A hundred or so?'

'You really skimmed through those articles you called up on your computer, didn't you?'

'Big business doesn't interest me,' she informed him airily. 'I may have a talent for numbers, and can do the maths without any trouble at all, but those numbers only matter when it comes to my work. I can work things out precisely but it's really the artistic side of my job that I love. In fact, I only did maths at university because Shane, one of my brothers, told me that it was a man's subject.'

'Thousands.'

Lesley looked at him blankly for a few seconds. 'What are you talking about?'

'Thousands. In various countries. I own several companies and I employ thousands, not hundreds. But that's by the by. This isn't to do with work. This is to do with my daughter. The only problem is that we don't have a great relationship and if I approach her with my suspicions, if I quiz her about her friends, about whether anyone's been acting strangely, asking too many questions…well, I don't anticipate a good outcome to any such conversation. So what would you have done if you hadn't done maths?'

Time had slipped past and they were no nearer to solving the problem, yet he was drawn to asking her yet more questions about herself.

Lesley—following his lead and envisaging the sort of awkward, maybe even downright incendiary conversation that might ensue in the face of Alessio's concerns, should he confront a hostile teenager with them—was taken aback by his abrupt change of topic.

'You said that you only did maths because your brother told you that you couldn't.'

'He never said that I *couldn't*.' She smiled, remembering their war of words. Shane was two years older than her and she always swore that his main purpose in life was to annoy her. He was now a barrister working in Dublin but he still teased her as though they were still kids in primary school. 'He said that it was a man's field, which immediately made me decide to do it.'

'Because, growing up as the only girl in a family of all males, it would have been taken as a given that, whatever your brothers could do, you could as well.'

'I'm wondering what this has to do with the reason I've come here.' She pulled out her mobile phone, checked the time on it and was surprised to discover how much of the day had flown by. 'I'm sorry I haven't been able to sort things out for you immediately. I'd understand perfectly if you want to take the matter to someone else, someone who can devote concentrated time to working on it. It shouldn't take too long, but longer than an hour or two.'

'Would you have done art?' He overrode her interjection as though he hadn't heard any of it and she flung him an exasperated look.

'I did, actually—courses in the town once a week. It was a good decision. It may have clinched me my job.'

'I have no interest in farming out this problem to someone else.'

'I can't give it my full-time attention.'

'Why not?'

'Because,' she said patiently, 'I have a nine-to-five job. And I live in London. And by the time I get back to my place— usually after seven, what with working overtime and then the travel—I'm exhausted. The last thing I need is to start trying to sort your problem out remotely.'

'Who said anything about doing it remotely? Take time off and come here.'

'I beg your pardon?'

'A week. You must be able to take some holiday time? Take it off and come here instead. Trying to sort this out remotely isn't the answer. You won't have sufficient time to do it consistently and also, while this may be to do with unearthing something about my own past, it may also have to do with something in my daughter's life. Something this person thinks poses a risk, should it be exposed. Have you considered that?'

'It had crossed my mind,' Lesley admitted.

'In which case, there could be a double-pronged attack on this problem if you moved in here.'

'What do you mean?'

'My daughter occupies several rooms in the house, by which I mean she has spread herself thin. She has a million books, items of clothing, at least one desk-top computer, tablets... If this has to do with anything Rachel has got up to, then you could be on hand to go through her stuff.'

'You want me to *invade her privacy* by searching through her private things?'

'It's all for the greater good.' Their eyes locked and she was suddenly seduced by the temptation to take him up on his offer, to step right out of her comfort zone.

'What's the point of having misplaced scruples? Frankly, I don't see the problem.'

In that single sentence, she glimpsed the man whose natural assumption was that the world would fall in line with what he wanted. And then he smiled, as if he had read her mind, and guessed exactly what was going through it. 'Wouldn't your company allow you a week off? Holiday?'

'That's not the point.'

'Then what is? Possessive boyfriend, perhaps? Won't let you out of his sight for longer than five minutes?'

Lesley looked at him scornfully. 'I would never get involved with anyone who wouldn't let me out of his sight for longer than five minutes! I'm not one of those pathetic, clingy females who craves protection from a big, strong man.' She had a fleeting image of the man sitting opposite her, big, strong, powerful, protecting his woman, making her feel small, fragile and delicate. She had never thought of herself as delicate—too tall, too boyish, too independent. It was ridiculous to have that squirmy sensation in the pit of her stomach now and she thanked the Lord that he really couldn't read her mind.

'So, no boyfriend,' Alessio murmured, cocking his head to one side. 'Then explain to me why you're finding reasons not to do this. I don't want to source anyone else to work on this for me. You might not have been what I expected, but you're good and I trust you, and if my daughter's possessions are to be searched it's essential they be searched by a woman.'

'It wouldn't be ethical to go through someone else's stuff.'

'What if by doing that you spared her a far worse situation? Rachel, I feel, would not be equipped to deal with unpleasant revelations that could damage the foundations of her young life. Furthermore, I won't be looking over your shoulder. You'll be able to work to your own timetable. In fact, I shall be in London most of the time, only returning here some evenings.'

Lesley opened her mouth to formulate a half-hearted protest, because this was all so sudden and so out of the ordinary, but with a slash of his hand he cut her off before any words could leave her mouth.

'She also returns in a few days' time. This is a job that has a very definite deadline; piecemeal when you get a chance isn't going to cut it. You have reservations—I see that—but I need this to be sorted out and I think you're the one to do it. So, please.'

Lesley heard the dark uncertainty in his voice and gritted her teeth with frustration. In a lot of ways, what he said made sense. Even if this job were to take a day or two, she would not be able to give it anything like her full attention if she worked on it remotely for half an hour every evening. And, if she needed to see whether his daughter had logged on to other computer devices, then she would need to be at his house where the equipment was to hand. It wasn't something she relished doing—everyone deserved their privacy—but sometimes privacy had to be invaded as a means of protection.

But moving in, sharing the same space as him? He did something disturbing to her pulse rate, so how was she supposed to live under the same roof?

But the thought drew her with the force of the forbidden.

Watching, Alessio smelled his advantage and lowered his

eyes. 'If you won't do this for me…and I realise it would be inconvenient for you…then do it for my daughter, Lesley. She's sixteen and vulnerable.'

CHAPTER THREE

'THIS IS IT...'

Alessio flung back the door to the suite of rooms and stood to one side, allowing Lesley to brush past him.

It was a mere matter of hours since he had pressed home his advantage and persuaded her to take up his offer to move into the house.

She had her misgivings, he could see that, but he wanted her there at hand and he was a man who was accustomed to getting what he wanted, whatever the cost.

As far as he was concerned, his proposition made sense. If she needed to try and hunt down clues from his daughter's possessions, then the only way she could do that would be here, in his house. There was no other way.

He hadn't anticipated this eventuality. He had thought that it would be a simple matter of following a trail of clues on his computer which would lead him straight to whoever was responsible for the emails.

Given that it was not going to be as straightforward as he first thought, it was a stroke of luck that the person working on the case was a woman. She would understand the workings of the female mind and would know where to locate whatever information she might find useful.

Added to that...

He looked at Lesley with lazy, brooding eyes as she stepped into the room.

There was something about the woman. She didn't pull her punches and, whilst a part of him was grimly disapproving of her forthright manner, another part of him was intrigued.

When was the last time he had been in the company of a woman who didn't say what she wanted him to hear?

When had he *ever* been in the company of any woman who didn't say what she wanted him to hear?

He was the product of a life of privilege. He had grown up accustomed to servants and chauffeurs and then, barely into adulthood, had found himself an expectant father. In a heart-beat, his world had changed. He'd no longer had the freedom to make youthful mistakes and to learn from them over time. Responsibility had landed on his doorstep without an invitation and then, on top of that, had come the grim realisation that he had been used for his money.

Not even out of his teens, he had discovered the bitter truth that his fortune would always be targeted. He would never be able to relax in the company of any woman without suspecting that she had her eye to the main chance. He would always have to be on his guard, always watchful, always making sure that no one got too close.

He was a generous lover, and had no problem splashing out on whatever woman happened to be sharing his bed, but he knew where to draw the line and was ruthless when it came to making sure that no woman got too close, certainly not close enough ever to harbour notions of longevity.

It was unusual to find himself in a situation such as this. It was unusual to be in close personal confines with a woman where sex wasn't on the menu.

It was even more unusual to find himself in this situation with a woman who made no effort to try and please him in any way.

'I was expecting a bedroom.' Lesley turned to look at him. 'Posters on the walls, cuddly toys, that sort of thing.'

'Rachel occupies one wing of the house. There are actually three bedrooms, along with a sitting room, a study, two bathrooms and an exercise room.' He strolled towards her and looked around him, hands shoved in the pockets of his cream trousers. 'This is the first time I've stepped foot into this section of the house since my daughter returned from boarding school for the holidays. When I saw the state it was in, I immediately got in touch with Violet, who informed me that she, along with her assistants, were barred from entry.'

Disapproval was stamped all over his face and Lesley could understand why. The place looked as though a bomb had been detonated in it. The tiled, marble floor of the small hallway was barely visible under discarded clothes and books and, through the open doors, she could see the other rooms appeared to be in a similar state of chaos.

Magazines were strewn everywhere. Shoes, kicked off, had landed randomly and then had been left there. School books lay open on various surfaces.

Going through all of this would be a full-time job.

'Teenagers can be very private creatures,' Lesley said dubiously. 'They hate having their space invaded.' She picked her way into bedroom number one and then continued to explore the various rooms, all the time conscious of Alessio lounging indolently against the wall and watching her progress.

She had the uneasy feeling of having been manipulated. How had she managed to end up here? Now she felt *involved*. She was no longer doing a quick job to help her father's pal out. She was ensconced in the middle of a family saga and wasn't quite sure where to begin.

'I will get Violet to make sure that these rooms are tidied first thing in the morning,' Alessio said as she finally walked towards him. 'At least then you will have something of a clean slate to start on.'

'Probably not such a good idea.' Lesley looked up at him. He was one of the few men with whom she could do that and, as she had quickly discovered, her breathing quickened as their eyes met. 'Adolescents are fond of writing stuff down on bits of paper. If there is anything to be found, that's probably where I'll find it, and that's just the sort of thing a cleaner would stick in the bin.' She hesitated. 'Don't you communicate with your daughter *at all*? I mean, how could she get away with keeping her room—her *rooms*—as messy as this?'

Alessio took one final glance around him and then headed for the door. 'Rachel has spent most of the summer here while I have been in London, only popping back now and again. She's clearly intimidated the cleaners into not going anywhere near her rooms and they've obeyed.'

'You've just *popped back here now and again* to see how she's doing?'

Alessio stopped in his tracks and looked at her coolly. 'You're here to try and sort out a situation involving computers and emails. You're not here to pass judgement on my parenting skills.'

Lesley sighed with obvious exasperation. She had been hustled here with unholy speed. He had even come with her to her office, on the pretext of having a look at what her company did, and had so impressed her boss that Jake had had no trouble in giving her the week off.

And now, having found herself in a situation that somehow didn't seem to be of her own choosing, she wasn't about to be lectured to in that patronising tone of voice.

'I'm not passing opinions on your parenting skills,' she said with restraint. 'I'm trying to make sense of a picture. If I can see the whole picture, then I might have an idea of how and where to proceed.' She had not yet had time since arriving to get down to the business of working her way through the emails and trying to trace the culprit responsible for them.

That was a job for the following day. Right now, she would

barely have time to have dinner, run a bath and then hit the sack. It had been a long day.

'I mean,' she said into an unresponsive silence, 'If and when I do find out who is responsible for those emails, we still won't know why he's sending them. He could clam up, refuse to say anything, and then you may still be left with a problem on your hands in connection with your daughter.'

They had reached the kitchen, which was a vast space dominated by a massive oak table big enough to seat ten. Everything in the house was larger than life, including all the furnishings.

'They may have nothing to do with Rachel. That's just another possibility.' He took a bottle of wine from the fridge and two wine glasses from one of the cupboards. There was a rich smell of food and Lesley looked around for Violet, who seemed to be an invisible but constant presence in the house.

'Where's Violet?' she asked, hovering.

'Gone for the evening. I try and not keep the hired help chained to the walls at night.' He proffered the glass of wine. 'And you can come inside, Lesley. You're not entering a lion's den.'

It felt like it, however. In ways she couldn't put her finger on, Alessio Baldini felt exciting and dangerous at the same time. Especially so at night, here, in his house with no one around.

'She's kindly prepared a casserole for us. Beef. It's in the oven. We can have it with bread, if that suits you.'

'Of course,' Lesley said faintly. 'Is that how it works when you're here? Meals are prepared for you so that all you have to do is switch the oven on?'

'One of the housekeepers tends to stick around when Rachel's here.' Alessio flushed and turned away.

In that fleeting window, she glimpsed the situation with far more clarity than if she had had it spelled out for her.

He was so awkward with his own daughter that he preferred to have a third party to dilute the atmosphere. Rachel probably

felt the same way. Two people, father and daughter, were circling one another like strangers in a ring.

He had been pushed to the background during her formative
years, had found his efforts at bonding repelled and dismantled
by a vengeful wife, and now found himself with a teenager he
didn't know. Nor was he, by nature, a people person—the sort
of man who could joke his way back into a relationship.

Into that vacuum, any number of gremlins could have entered.

'So you're *never* on your own with your daughter? Okay. In
that case you really wouldn't have a clue what was happening
in her life, especially as she spends most of the year away from
home. But you were saying that this may not have anything directly to do with Rachel. What did you mean by that?'

She watched him bring the food to the table and refill their
glasses with more wine.

Alessio gave her a long, considered look from under his
lashes.

'What I am about to tell you stays within the walls of this
house, is that clear?'

Lesley paused with her glass halfway to her mouth and
looked at him over the rim with astonishment.

'And you laugh at me for thinking that you might have links
to the Mafia?'

Alessio stared at her and then shook his head and slowly
grinned. 'Okay, maybe that sounded a little melodramatic.'

Lesley was knocked sideways by that smile. It was so full
of charm, so lacking in the controlled cool she had seen in him
before. It felt as though, the more time she spent in his company, the more intriguing and complex he became. He was not
simply a mega-rich guy employing her to do a job for him, but
a man with so many facets to his personality that it made her
head spin.

Worse than that, she could feel herself being sucked in, and
that scared her.

'I don't do melodrama,' Alessio was saying with the remnants of his smile. 'Do you?'

'Never.' Lesley licked her lips nervously. 'What are you going to tell me that has to stay here?'

His dark eyes lingered on her flushed face. 'It's unlikely that our guy would have got hold of this information but, just in case, it's information I would want to protect my daughter from knowing. I certainly would not want it in the public arena.' He swigged the remainder of his wine and did the honours by dishing food onto the plates which had already been put on the table, along with glasses and cutlery.

Mesmerised by the economic elegance of his movements, and lulled by the wine and the creeping darkness outside, Lesley cupped her chin in her hand and stared at him.

He wasn't looking at her. He was concentrating on not spilling any food. He had the expression of someone unaccustomed to doing anything of a culinary nature for themselves—focused yet awkward at the same time.

'You don't look comfortable with a serving spoon,' she remarked idly and Alessio glanced across to where she was sitting, staring at him. She wore a thin gold chain with a tiny pendant around her neck and she was playing with the pendant, rolling it between her fingers as she looked at him.

Suddenly and for no reason, his breathing thickened and heat surged through his body with unexpected force. His libido, that had not seen the light of day for the past couple of months, reared up with such urgency that he felt his sharp intake of breath.

She was not trying to be seductive but somehow he could feel her seducing him.

'I bet you don't do much cooking for yourself.'

'Come again?' Alessio did his best to get his thoughts back in order. An erection was jamming against the zipper of his trousers, rock-hard and painful, and it was a relief to sit down.

'I said, you don't look as though handling pots and pans

comes as second nature to you.' She tucked into the casserole, which was mouth-wateringly fragrant. They should be discussing work but the wine had made her feel relaxed and mellow and had allowed her curiosity about him to come out of hiding and to take centre stage.

Sober, she would have chased that curiosity away, because she could feel its danger. But pleasantly tipsy, she wanted to know more about him.

'I don't do much cooking, no.'

'I guess you can always get someone else to do it for you. Top chefs or housekeepers, or maybe just your girlfriends.' She wondered what his girlfriends looked like. He might have had a rocky marriage that had ended in divorce, but he would have lots of girlfriends.

'I don't let women near my kitchen.' Alessio was amused at her disingenuous curiosity. He swirled his wine around in the glass and swallowed a mouthful.

With a bit of alcohol in her system, she looked more relaxed, softer, less defensive.

His erection was still throbbing and his eyes dropped to her mouth, then lower to where the loose neckline of her tee-shirt allowed a glimpse of her shoulder blades and the soft hint of a cleavage. She wasn't big breasted and the little she had was never on show.

'Why? Don't you ever go out with women who like to cook?'

'I've never asked whether they like to cook or not,' he said wryly, finishing his wine, pouring himself another glass and keeping his eyes safely away from her loose-limbed body. 'I've found that, the minute a woman starts eulogising about the joys of home-cooked food, it usually marks the end of the relationship.'

'What do you mean?' Lesley looked at him, surprised.

'It means that the last thing I need is someone trying to prove that they're a domestic goddess in my kitchen. I prefer that the women I date don't get too settled.'

'In case they get ideas of permanence?'

'Which brings me neatly back to what I wanted to say.' That disturbing moment of intense sexual attraction began to ebb away and he wondered how it had arisen in the first place.

She was nothing like the women he dated. Could it be that her intelligence, the strange role she occupied as receiver of information no other woman had ever had, the sheer difference of her body, had all those things conspired against him?

There was a certain intimacy to their conversation. Had that entered the mix and worked some kind of passing, peculiar magic?

More to the point, a little voice inside him asked, what did he intend to do about it?

'I have a certain amount of correspondence locked away that could be very damaging.'

'Correspondence?'

'Of the non-silicon-chip variety,' Alessio elaborated drily. 'Correspondence of the old-fashioned sort—namely, letters.'

'To do with business?' She felt a sudden stab of intense disappointment that she had actually believed him when he had told her that he was an honest guy in all his business dealings.

'No, not to do with business, so you can stop thinking that you've opened a can of worms and you need to clear off as fast as you can. I told you I'm perfectly straight when it comes to my financial dealings and I wasn't lying.'

Lesley released a long sigh of relief. Of course, it was because she would have been in a very awkward situation had he confessed to anything shady, especially considering she was alone with him in his house.

It definitely wasn't because she would have been disappointed in him as a man had he been party to anything crooked.

'Then what? And what is the relevance to the case?'

'This could hurt my daughter. It would certainly be annoying for me should it hit the press. If I fill you in, then you might be able to join some dots and discover if this is the subject of his emails.'

'You have far too much confidence in my abilities, Mr Baldini.' She smiled. 'I may be good at what I do but I'm not a miracle worker.'

'I think we've reached the point where you can call me Alessio. It occurred to me that there may have been stray references in the course of the emails that might point in a certain direction.'

'And you feel that I need to know the direction they may point in so that I can pick them up if they're there?'

'Something like that.'

'Wouldn't you have seen them for yourself?'

'I only began paying attention to those emails the day you were hired. Before that, I had kept them, but hadn't examined them in any depth and I haven't had the opportunity to do so since. It's a slim chance but we can cover all bases.'

'And what if I do find a link?'

'Then I shall know what options to take when it comes to dealing with the perpetrator.'

Lesley sighed and fluffed her short hair up with her fingers. 'Do you know, I have never been in this sort of situation before.'

'But you've had a couple of tricky occasions.'

'Not as complicated as this. The tricky ones have usually involved friends of friends imagining that I can unearth marital affairs by bugging computers, and then I have to let them down. If I can even be bothered to see what they want in the first place.'

'And this?'

'This feels as though it's got layers.' And she wasn't sure that she wanted to peel them back to see what was lying underneath. It bothered her that he had such an effect on her that he had been able to entice her into taking time off work to help him in the first place.

And it bothered her even more that she couldn't seem to stop wanting to stare at him. Of course he was good-looking, but she was sensible when it came to guys, and this one was definitely off-limits. The gulf between them was so great that they could be living on different planets.

And yet her eyes still sought him out, and that was worrying.

'I had more than one reason for divorcing my wife,' he said heavily, after a while. He hesitated, at a loss as to where to go from there, because sharing confidences was not something he ever did. From the age of eighteen, he had learnt how to keep his opinions to himself—first through a sense of shame that he had been hoodwinked by a girl he had been seeing for a handful of months, a girl who had conned him into thinking she had been on the pill. Later, when his marriage had predictably collapsed, he had developed a forbidding ability to keep his emotions and his thoughts under tight rein. It was what he had always seen as protection against ever making another mistake when it came to the opposite sex.

But now...

Her intelligent eyes were fixed on his face. He reminded himself that this was a woman against whom he needed no protection because she had no ulterior agenda.

'Not only did Bianca lie her way into a marriage but she also managed to lie her way into making me believe that she was in love with me.'

'You were a kid,' Lesley pointed out, when he failed to elaborate on that remark. 'It happens.'

'And you know because...?'

'I don't,' she said abruptly. 'I wasn't one of those girls anyone lied to about being in love with. Carry on.'

Alessio tilted his head and looked at her enquiringly, tempted to take her up on that enigmatic statement, even though he knew he wouldn't get anywhere with it.

'We married and, very shortly after Rachel was born, my wife began fooling around. Discreetly at first, but that didn't last very long. We moved in certain circles and it became a bore to try and work out who she wanted to sleep with and when she would make a move.'

'How awful for you.'

Alessio opened his mouth to brush that show of sympathy to one side but instead stared at her for a few moments in silence. 'It wasn't great,' he admitted heavily.

'It can't have been. Not at any age, but particularly not when you were practically a child yourself and not equipped to deal with that kind of disillusionment.'

'No.' His voice was rough but he gave a little shrug, dismissing that episode in his life.

'I can understand why you would want to protect your daughter from knowing that her mother was…promiscuous.'

'There's rather more.' His voice was steady and matter-of-fact. 'When our marriage was at its lowest ebb, Bianca implied, during one of our rows, that I wasn't Rachel's father at all. Afterwards she retracted her words and said that she hadn't been thinking straight. God knows, she probably realised that Rachel was her lifeline to money, and the last thing she should do was to jeopardise that lifeline, but the words were out and as far as I was concerned couldn't be taken back.'

'No, I can understand that.' Whoever said that money could buy happiness? she thought, feeling her heart constrict for the young boy he must have been then—deceived, betrayed, cheated on; forced to become a man when he was still in his teens.

'One day when she was out shopping, I returned early from work and decided, on impulse, to go through her drawers. By this time, we were sleeping in separate rooms. I found a stash of letters, all from the same guy, someone she had known when she was sixteen. Met him on holiday somewhere in Majorca. Young love. Touching, don't you think? They kept in contact and she was seeing him when she was married to me. I gathered from reading between the lines that he was the son of a poor fisherman, someone her parents would certainly not have welcomed with open arms.'

'No.'

'The lifestyles of the rich and famous,' he mocked wryly. 'I bet you're glad you weren't one of the privileged crowd.'

'I never gave it much thought, but now that you mention it...' She smiled and he grudgingly returned the smile.

'I have no idea whether the affair ended when her behaviour became more out of control but it certainly made me wonder whether she was right about our daughter not being biologically mine. Not that it would have made a scrap of difference but...'

'You'd have to find out that sort of thing.'

'Tests proved conclusively that Rachel is my child but you can see why this information could be highly destructive if it came to light, especially considering the poor relationship I have with my daughter. It could be catastrophic. She would always doubt my love for her if she thought that I had taken a paternity test to prove she was mine in the first place. It would certainly destroy the happy memories she has of her mother and, much as Bianca appalled me, I wouldn't want to deprive Rachel of her memories.'

'But if this information was always private and historic, and only contained in letter form, then I don't see how anyone else could have got hold of it.' But there were always links to links to links; it just took one person to start delving and who knew what could come out in the wash? 'I'll see if I can spot any names or hints that this might be the basis of the threats.'

And at the same time, she would have her work cut out going through his daughter's things, a job which still didn't sit well with her, even though a part of her know that it was probably essential.

'I should be heading up to bed now,' she said, rising to her feet.

'It's not yet nine-thirty.'

'I'm an early-to-bed kind of person,' she said awkwardly, not knowing whether to leave the kitchen or remain where she was, then realising that she was behaving like an employee waiting for her boss to dismiss her. But her feet remained nailed to the spot.

'I have never talked so much about myself,' Alessio murmured, which got her attention, and she looked at him quizzically. 'It's not in my nature. I'm a very private man, hence what I've told you goes no further than this room.'

'Of course it won't,' Lesley assured him vigorously. 'Who would I tell?'

'If someone could consider blackmailing me over this information, then it might occur to you that you could do the same. You would certainly have unrivalled proof of whatever you wanted to glean about my private life in the palm of your hand.'

It was a perfectly logical argument and he was, if nothing else, an extremely logical man. But Alessio still felt an uncustomary twinge of discomfort at having spelled it out so clearly.

He noticed the patches of angry colour that flooded her cheeks and bit back the temptation to apologise for being more blunt than strictly necessary.

She worked with computers; she would know the value of logic and reason.

'You're telling me that you don't trust me.'

'I'm telling you that you keep all of this to yourself. No girly gossip in the toilets at work, or over a glass of wine with your friends, and certainly no pillow talk with whoever you end up sharing your bed with.'

'Thank you for spelling it out so clearly,' Lesley said coldly. 'But I know how to keep a confidence and I fully understand that it's important that none of this gets out. If you have a piece of paper, you can draft something up right here and I'll sign it!'

'Draft something up?' Under normal circumstances, he certainly would have had that in place before hiring her for the job, but for some reason it simply hadn't occurred to him.

Perhaps it had been the surprise of opening the front door to a girl instead of the man he had been expecting.

Perhaps there was something about her that had worked its

way past his normal defences so that he had failed to go down the predicted route.

'I'm happy to sign whatever silence clause you want. One word of what we've spoken about here, and you will have my full permission to fling me into jail and throw away the key.'

'I thought you said that you weren't melodramatic.'

'I'm insulted that you think I'd break the confidence you have in me to do my job and keep the details of it to myself.'

'You may be insulted, but are you surprised?' He rose to his feet, towering over her, and she fell back a couple of steps and held onto the back of the kitchen chair.

Alessio, on his way to make them some coffee, sensed the change in the atmosphere the way a big cat can sense the presence of prey in the shift of the wind. Their eyes met and something inside him, something that operated on an instinctual level, understood that, however scathing and derisive her tone of voice had been, she was tuned in to him in ways that matched his.

Tuned in to him in ways that were sexual.

The realisation struck him from out of nowhere and yet, as he held her gaze a few seconds longer than was necessary, he actually doubted himself because her expression was so tight, straightforward and openly annoyed.

'I am a man who is accustomed to taking precautions,' he murmured huskily.

'I get that.' Especially after everything he had told her. Of course he would want to make sure that he didn't leave himself open to exploitation of any kind. That was probably one of the rules by which he lived his life.

So he was right; why should she be surprised that he had taken her to task?

Except she had been lulled into a false sense of confidences shared, had warmed to the fact that he had opened up to her, and in the process had chosen to ignore the reality, which was that he had decided that he had no choice. He hadn't opened up to her because she was special. He had opened up to her because it was necessary to make her task a little easier.

'Do you?'

'Of course I do,' she said on a sigh. 'I'm just not used to people distrusting me. I'm one of the most reliable people I know when it comes to keeping a secret.'

'Really?' Mere inches separated them. He could feel the warmth radiating from her body out towards his and he wondered again whether his instincts had been right when they had told him that she was not as unaffected by him as she would have liked to pretend.

'Yes!' She relaxed with a laugh. 'When I was a teenager, I was the one person all the lads turned to when it came to confidences. They knew I would never breathe a word when they told me that they fancied someone, or asked me what I thought it would take to impress someone else...'

And all the while, Alessio thought to himself, you were taking lessons in self-defence.

Never one to do much prying into female motivations, he was surprised to find that he quite wanted to know more about her. 'You've won your argument,' he said with a slow smile.

'You mean, you won't be asking me to sign something?'

'No. So there will be no need for you to live in fear that you will be flung into prison and the key thrown away if the mood takes me.' His eyes dipped down to the barely visible swell of her small breasts under the baggy tee-shirt.

'I appreciate that,' Lesley told him sincerely. 'I don't know how easy I would have found it, working for someone who didn't trust me. So I shall start first thing in the morning.' She suddenly realised just how close their bodies were to one another and she shuffled a couple of discreet inches back. 'If it's all the same to you, you can point me in the direction of your computer and I'll spend the morning there, and the afternoon going through your daughter's rooms just in case I find anything of interest. And you needn't worry about asking your housekeeper to prepare any lunch for me. I usually just eat on the run. I can fill you in when you return from London or else I can call you if you decide to stay in London overnight.'

Alessio inclined his head in agreeable assent—except, maybe there would be no need for that.

Maybe he would stay here in the country—so much more restful than London and so much easier were he to be at hand.

CHAPTER FOUR

LESLEY WAS NOT finding life particularly restful. Having been under the impression that Alessio would be commuting to and from London, with a high possibility of remaining in London for at least part of the time, she'd been dismayed when, two days previously, he'd informed her that there had been a change of plan.

'I'll be staying here,' he had said the morning after she had arrived. 'Makes sense.'

Lesley had no idea how he had reached that conclusion. How did it make sense for him to be around: bothering her; getting under her skin; just *being* within her line of vision and therefore compelling her to look at him?

'You'll probably have a lot of questions and it'll be easier if I'm here to answer them.'

'I could always phone you,' she had said, staring at him with rising panic, because she'd been able to see just how the week was going to play out.

'And then,' he had continued, steamrollering over her interruption, 'I would feel guilty were I to leave you here on your own. The house is very big. My conscience wouldn't be able to live with the thought that you might find it quite unsettling being here with no one around.'

He had directed her to where she would be working and she'd been appalled to find that she would be sharing office space with him.

'Of course, if you find it uncomfortable working in such close proximity to me, then naturally I can set up camp somewhere else. The house has enough rooms to accommodate one of them being turned into a makeshift work place.'

She had closed her mouth and said nothing, because what had there been to say? That, yes, she *would* find it uncomfortable working in such close proximity to him, because she was just too *aware* of him for her own good; because he made her nervous and tense; because her skin tingled the second he got too close?

She had moved from acknowledging that the man was sexy to accepting that she was attracted to him. She had no idea how that could be the case, given that he just wasn't the sort of person she had ever envisaged herself taking an interest in, but she had given up fighting it. There was just something too demanding about his physicality for her to ignore.

So she had spent her mornings in a state of rigid, hyper-sensitive awareness. She had been conscious of his every small move as he'd peered at his computer screen, reached across his desk to get something or swivelled his chair so that he could find a more comfortable position for his long legs.

She had not been able to block out the timbre of his deep voice whenever he was on the phone. She wouldn't have been able to recall any of the conversations he had had, but she could recall exactly what that voice did to her.

The range of unwanted physical sensations he evoked in her was frankly exhausting.

So she had contrived to have a simple routine of disappearing outside to communicate with her office on the pretext that she didn't want to disturb him.

Besides, she had added, making sure to forestall any objections, she never got the chance to leave London. She had never been to stay at a country estate in her life before. It would be marvellous if she could take advantage of the wonderful opportunity he had given her by working outdoors so that she could enjoy being in the countryside, especially given that the weather was so brilliant.

He had acquiesced although when he had looked at her she had been sure that she could detect a certain amount of amusement.

Now, in a break with this routine, Lesley had decided to start on Rachel's rooms.

She had gone over all of the emails with a fine toothcomb and had found no evidence that the mystery writer was aware of Bianca's past.

She looked around room number one and wondered where to begin.

As per specific instructions, Violet had left everything as it was and Lesley, by no means a neat freak, was not looking forward to going through the stacks of dispersed clothes, books, magazines and random bits of paper that littered the ground.

But she dug in, working her way steadily through the chaos, flinging clothes in the stainless-steel hamper she had dragged from the massive bathroom and marvelling that a child of sixteen could possess so much designer clothing.

This was what money bought: expensive clothes and jewellery. But no amount of expensive clothes and jewellery could fix a broken relationship and, over the past two days, she had seen for herself just how broken the relationship between father and daughter was.

He kept his emotions under tight control but every so often there were glimpses of the man underneath who was confused at his inability to communicate with his daughter and despairing of what the future held for them.

And yet, he wanted to protect her, and would do anything to that end.

She began rifling through the pockets of a pair of jeans, her mind playing with the memory of just how weirdly close the past couple of days had brought them.

Or, at least, *her*.

But then, she thought ruefully, she was handicapped by the fact that she found him attractive. She was therefore primed to analyse everything he said, to be super-attentive to every stray remark, to hang onto his every word with breathless intensity.

Thank God he didn't know what was going through her head.

It took her a couple of seconds before the piece of paper she extracted from the jeans pocket made sense and then a couple more seconds before the links she had begun to see in the emails began to tie up in front of her.

More carefully now, she began feeling her way through the mess, inspecting everything in her path. She went over the clothes she had carelessly chucked into the hamper just in case she had missed something.

Had she expected to find anything at all like this, searching through a few rooms? No; maybe when she got to the computer or the tablet, or whatever other computer gadgets might be lying around.

But scribbles on a bit of paper? No. She thought that teenagers were way beyond using pens and paper by way of communication.

What else might she find?

She had lost that initial feeling of intruding in someone else's space. Something about the messiness made her search more acceptable.

No attempts had been made to hide anything and nothing was under lock and key.

Did that make a difference? In a strange way it did, as did the little things lying about that showed Rachel for the child she still was, even if she had entered the teenage battleground of rebellion and disobedience.

Her art book was wonderful. There were cute little doodles in the margins of her exercise books. Her stationery was very cute, with lots of puppy motifs on the pencil cases and folders. It was at odds with the rest of what was to be found in the room.

An hour and a half into the search, Lesley opened the first of the wardrobes and gasped at the racks of clothes confronting her.

You didn't need to be a connoisseur of fine clothing to know that these were the finest money could buy. She ran her hands through the dresses, skirts and tops and felt silk, cashmere and pure cotton. Some of them were youthful and brightly coloured, others looked far too grown-up for a sixteen-year-old child. Quite a few things still had tags attached because they had yet to be used.

As she pushed the clothes at the front aside, she came across some dresses at the back that were clearly too old for a sixteen-year-old; they must have belonged to Rachel's mother. Lesley gently pulled a demure black dress from the selection and admired the fine material and elegant cut of the design. She knew that it was wrong to try on someone else's clothes but she lost her head for a moment and suddenly found herself slipping into the gorgeous creation. As she turned to look at herself in the mirror, she gasped.

Usually she was awkward, one of the lads, at her most comfortable when she was exchanging banter; yet the creature staring back at her wasn't that person at all. The creature staring back at her was a leggy, attractive young woman with a good figure, good legs and a long neck.

She spun away from the mirror suddenly as she heard the door open and saw Alessio look at her in shock.

'What are you doing here?' She felt naked as his eyes slowly raked over her, from the top of her head, along her body and then all the way back again.

Alessio couldn't stop looking at her. He had left the office to stretch his legs and had decided to check on how Lesley's search was coming along. He hadn't expected to find her in a stunning cocktail dress, her legs seeming to go on for ever.

'Well?' Lesley folded her arms defensively, although what she really wanted to do was somehow reach down and cover her exposed thighs. The skirt should have been a couple of inches above the knee but, because she was obviously taller than Rachel's mother had been, it was obscenely short on her.

'I've interrupted a catwalk session,' he murmured, walking slowly towards her. 'My apologies.'

'I was… I thought…'

'It suits you, just in case you're interested in what I think. The dress, I mean. You should reveal your legs more often.'

'If you would please just go, I'll get changed. I apologise for having tried on the dress. It was totally out of order, and if you want to give me my marching orders then I would completely understand.' She had never felt so mortified in her entire life. What must he be thinking? She had taken something that didn't belong to her and put it on, an especially unforgivable offence, considering she was under his roof in the capacity of a paid employee.

His 'catwalk' comment struck her as an offensive insult but there was no way she was going to call him out on that. She just wanted him to leave the room but he showed no signs of going.

'Why would I give you your marching orders?' She was bright red and as stiff as a plank of wood.

Any other woman would have been overjoyed to be the centre of his attention, as she now was, but instead she was staring straight ahead, unblinking, doing her utmost to shut him out of her line of vision.

He had never wanted a woman as much as he wanted this one right now. Mind and body fused. This wasn't just another of his glamorous, sex-kitten women. This thinking, questioning, irreverent creature was in a different league.

The attraction he had felt for her, which had been there from the second they had met, clarified into the absolute certainty that he wanted her in his bed. It was a thought he had flirted with, dwelled on; rejected because she'd challenged him on too many levels and he liked his women unchallenging.

But, hell…

'Please leave.'

'You don't have to take off the dress,' he said in a lazy drawl. 'I'd quite like to see you working in that outfit.'

'You're making fun of me and I don't like it.' She had managed to blank him out, so that she was just aware of him on the periphery of her vision, but she could still feel his power radiating outwards, wrapping around her like something thick, suffocating and tangible.

She felt like something small and helpless being circled by a beautiful, dangerous predator.

Except he would never hurt her. No; his capacity for destruction lay in his ability to make her hurt herself by believing what he was saying, by allowing her feelings for him get the better of her. She had never realised that lust could be so overwhelming. Nothing had prepared her for the crazy, inappropriate emotions that rode roughshod over her prized and treasured common sense.

'I'll pretend I didn't hear that,' Alessio said softly. Then he reached out and ran his hand along her arm, feeling its soft, silky smoothness. She was so slender. For a few seconds, Lesley didn't react, then the feel of his warm hand on her skin made her stumble backwards with a yelp.

His instincts had been right. How could he have doubted himself? The electricity between them flowed both ways. He stepped back and looked at her lazily. Her eyes were huge and she looked very young and very vulnerable. And she was still wobbling in the high stilettos; that was how uncomfortable she was in a pair of heels. He was struck with a pressing desire to see her dolled up to the nines and, with an even more contradictory one, to have her naked in his arms.

'I'll leave you to get back into your clothes,' he said with the gentleness of someone trying to calm a panicked, highly strung thoroughbred. 'And, to answer your question as to what I'm doing here, I thought I would just pop in and see if your search up here was being fruitful.'

Relieved to have the focus off her and onto work, Lesley allowed some of the tension to ooze out of her body.

'I *have* found one or two things you might be interested in,' she said with staccato jerkiness. 'And I'll come right down to the office.'

'Better still, meet me outside. I'll get Violet to bring us out some tea.' He smiled, encouraging her to relax further. It was all he could do not to let his eyes wander over her, drink her in. He lowered his eyes and reluctantly spun round, walking towards the door and knowing that she wouldn't move a muscle until he was well and truly out of the suite of rooms and heading down the staircase.

Once outside, he couldn't wait for her to join him. He was oblivious to his surroundings as he stared off into the distance, thinking of how she had looked in that outfit. She had incredible legs, an incredible body and it was all the more enhanced by the fact that she was so unaware of her charms.

Five brothers; no mother; karate lessons when the rest of her friends were practising the feminine skills that would serve them well in later life. Was that why she was so skittish around him? Was she skittish around *all* men, or was it just him? Was that why she chose to dress the way she did, why she projected such a capable image, why she deliberately seemed to spurn feminine clothes?

He found himself idly trying to work out what made her tick and he was enjoying the game when he saw her walking towards him with a sheaf of papers in her hand, all business as usual.

'Thank you.' Lesley sat down, taking the glass that was offered to her. She had been so hot and bothered after he had left that she had taken time out to wash her face in cold water and gather herself. 'First of all—and I'm almost one-hundred-percent sure about this—our emailing friend has no idea about your wife or the sort of person she was.'

Alessio leant closer, forearms resting on his thighs. 'And you've reached that conclusion because…?'

'Because I've been through each and every email very carefully, looking for clues. I've also found a couple of earlier emails which arrived in your junk box and for some reason weren't deleted. They weren't significant. Perhaps our friend was just having a bit of fun.'

'So you think this isn't about a blackmail plot to do with revelations about Bianca?'

'Yes, partly from reading through the emails and partly common sense. I think if they involved your ex-wife there would have been some sort of guarded reference made that would have warned you of what was to come. And, whilst he or she knew what they were doing and were careful to leave as few tracks behind them as they could, some of those emails are definitely more rushed than others.'

'Woman's intuition?' There was genuine curiosity in his voice and Lesley nodded slowly.

'I think so. What's really significant, though, is that the Internet cafés used were all in roughly the same area, within a radius of a dozen miles or so, and they are all in the general vicinity of where Rachel goes to school. Which leads me to think that she is at the centre of this in some way, shape or form because the person responsible probably knows her or knows of her.'

Alessio sat back and rubbed his eyes wearily. Lesley could see the strain visible beneath the cool, collected exterior when he next looked at her. He might have approached this problem with pragmatism and detachment, as a job to be done—but his daughter was involved and that showed on his face now, in the worry and the stress.

'Any idea of what could be going on? It could still be that our friend, as you call him, has information on Bianca and wants me to pay him for not sharing that information with Rachel.'

'Does Rachel know anything about what her mother was like as…err…a young girl? I mean, when she was still married to you? I know your daughter would have been a toddler with no memories of that time, but you know how it is: overheard conversations between adults, bits and pieces of gossip from friends or family or whatever.'

Alessio leaned back in the chair and closed his eyes.

'As far as I am aware, Rachel is completely in the dark about Bianca, but who knows? We haven't talked about it. We've barely got past the stage of polite pleasantries.'

Lesley stared at his averted profile. Seeing them in repose, as now, she felt the full impact of his devastating good looks. His sensual mouth lost its stern contours; she could appreciate the length and thickness of his eyelashes, the strong angle of his jaw, the tousled blackness of his slightly too-long hair. His fingers were linked loosely on his stomach; she took in the dark hair on his forearms and then burned when she wondered where that dark hair was replicated.

She wondered whether she should tell him about those random scribbles she had found and decided against it. They formed part of the jigsaw puzzle but she would hang on until more of the pieces came together. It was only fair. He was a desperately concerned father, worried about a daughter he barely knew; to add yet more stress to his situation, when she wasn't even one-hundred per cent sure whether what she had found would prove significant in the end, seemed downright selfish.

The lingering embarrassment she had brought with her after the mini-skirt-wearing episode faded as the silence lengthened between them, a telling indication of his state of mind.

It would have cost him dearly to confide the personal details of his situation with his ex-wife. No matter that he had been practically a child at the time. No one enjoyed being used and Alessio, in particular, was a proud man today and would have been a proud boy all those years ago.

Her heart softened and she resisted the temptation to reach out and stroke the side of his cheek.

'I'm making you feel awkward,' Alessio murmured, breaking the silence, but not opening his eyes or turning in her direction.

Lesley buried the wickedly tantalising thought of touching his cheek. 'Of course not!'

'I don't suppose you banked on this sort of situation when you agreed to the job.'

'I don't suppose you banked on it either when you decided to hire me.'

'True,' he admitted with a ghost of a smile. 'So, where do you suggest we go from here? Quiz Rachel when she gets home day after tomorrow? Try and find out if she has any idea what's going on?' He listened as she ran through some options. He liked hearing her talk. He liked the soft but decisive tone of her voice. He liked the way she could talk to him like this, on his level, with no coy intonations and no irritating indications that she wanted the conversation to take any personal detours.

Mind you, she had so much information about him that personal detours were pretty much an irrelevance: there really weren't that many nooks and crannies left to discover.

His mind swung back to when he had caught her wearing that dress and his body began to stir into life.

'Talk to me about something else,' he ordered huskily when there was a pause in the conversation. This was as close to relaxation he had come in a long time, despite the grim nature of what was going on. He had his eyes closed, the sun was on his face and his body felt lazy and nicely lethargic.

'What do you want me to talk about?' She could understand why he might not want to dwell ad infinitum on a painful subject, even one that needed to be discussed.

'You. I want you to talk about you.'

Even though he wasn't looking at her, Lesley still reddened. That voice of his; had he any idea how sexy it was? No, of course not.

'I'm a very boring person,' she half-laughed with embarrassment. 'Besides, you know all the basic stuff: my brothers; my dad bringing us all up on his own.'

'So let's skip the basics. Tell me what drove you to try on that dress.'

'I don't want to talk about that.' Lesley's skin prickled with acute discomfort. The mortification she had felt assailed her all over again and she clenched her fists on her lap. 'I've already apologised and I'd really rather we drop the subject and pretend it never happened. It was a mistake.'

'You're embarrassed.'

'Of course I am.'

'No need to be, and I'm not prying. I'm really just trying to grasp anything that might take my mind off what's happening right now with Rachel.'

Suddenly Lesley felt herself deflate. While she was on her high horse, defending her position and beating back his very natural curiosity, he was in the unenviable position of having had to open the door to his past and let her in.

Was it any wonder that he was desperate to take his mind off his situation? Talking relentlessly about something worrying only magnified the worry and anxiety.

'I—I don't know why I tried it,' Lesley offered haltingly. 'Actually, I do know why I tried it on. I was never one for dresses and frocks when I was a teenager. That was stuff meant for other girls but not for me.'

'Because you lacked a mother's guiding hand,' Alessio contributed astutely. 'And even more influential was the fact that you had five brothers.' He grinned and some of the worry that had been etched on his face lifted. 'I remember what I was like and what my friends were like when we were fourteen—not sensitive. I bet they gave you a hard time.'

Lesley laughed. 'And the rest of it. At any rate, I had one embarrassing encounter with a mini-skirt and I decided after that that I was probably better off not going down that road.

Besides, at the age of fourteen I was already taller than all the other girls in my class. Downplaying my height didn't involve wearing dresses and short skirts.'

Alessio slowly opened his eyes and then inclined his head so that he was looking directly at her.

Her skin was like satin. As far as he knew, she had yet to make use of the swimming pool, but sitting outside for the past couple of afternoons in the blazing sun had lent a golden tint to her complexion. It suited her.

'But you're not fourteen any longer,' he said huskily.

Lesley was lost for words. Drowning in his eyes, her throat suddenly went dry and her body turned to lead. She couldn't move a muscle. She could just watch him, watching her.

He would physically have to get out of his chair if he were to come any closer, and he made no move to do anything of the sort, but she still overwhelmed by the feeling that he was going to kiss her. It was written in the dark depths of his eyes, a certain intent that made her quiver and tremble inside.

'No, I don't suppose I am,' she choked out.

'But you still don't wear short skirts...'

'Old habits die hard.' She gave up trying to look away. She didn't care what he thought—not at this moment in time, at any rate. 'I... There's no need to dress up for the sort of job that I do. Jeans and jumpers are what we all wear.'

'You don't do justice to your body.' He glanced at his watch. He had broken off working in part, as he had said, to check on Lesley and see whether she had managed to find anything in Rachel's quarters; but also in part because he was due in London for a meeting.

The time had run away. It was much later than he had imagined...something about the sun, the slight breeze, the company of the woman sitting next to him, the way she had frozen to the spot... He wondered whether any man had ever complimented her about the way she looked or whether she had spent a lifetime assuming that no one would, therefore making sure that she carved her own niche through her intelligence and ambition.

He wondered what she would do if he touched her, kissed her.

More than ever, he wanted to have her. In fact, he was tempted to abandon the meeting in London and spend the rest of this lazy afternoon playing the game of seduction.

Already she was standing up, all of a fluster, telling him that she was feeling a little hot and wanted to get back into the shade. With an inward, rueful sigh of resignation, he followed suit.

'You're doing a brilliant job, trying to unravel what the hell is going on with these emails,' he said, uncomfortably aware of his body demanding a certain type of attention that was probably going to make his drive down to London a bit uncomfortable.

Lesley put some much-needed physical distance between them.

What had happened just then? He seemed normal enough now. Had it been her imagination playing tricks on her, making her think that he was going to kiss her? Or was it her own forbidden attraction trying to find a way to become a reality?

It absolutely terrified her that she might encourage him to think that she was attracted to him. It was even more terrifying that she might be reading all sorts of nonsense into his throwaway remarks. The guy was the last word in eligible. He was charming, highly intelligent and sophisticated, and he probably had that sexy, ever so slightly flirty manner with every woman he spoke to. It was just the kind of person he was and misinterpreting anything he said in her favour would be something she did at her own peril.

'Thank you. You're paying me handsomely to do just that.'

Alessio frowned. He didn't like money being brought into the conversation. It lowered the tone.

'Well, carry on the good work,' he said with equal politeness. 'And you'll have the house all to yourself until tomorrow to do it. I have an important meeting in London and I'll be spending the night there in my apartment.' He scowled at her immediate look of relief. Hell, she was attracted to him, but she was determined to fight it, despite the clear signals he had sent that the feeling was reciprocated. Didn't she know that for a man like him, a man who could snap his fingers and have any woman he wanted, her reticence was a challenge?

And yet, was he the type to set off in pursuit of someone who was reluctant—even though she might be as hot for him as he was for her?

A night away might cool him down a bit.

He left her dithering in the hall, seeing him off, but with a look of impatience on her face for him to be gone.

She needed this. Her nerves were getting progressively more shot by the minute; she couldn't wait for him to leave. She went to see him off, half-expecting him suddenly to decide that he wasn't going anywhere after all, and sagged with relief when the front door slammed behind him and she heard the roar of his car diminishing as he cleared the courtyard and disappeared down the long drive.

She couldn't stay. Certainly, she wanted to be out by the time his daughter arrived. She just couldn't bear the tension of being around him: she couldn't bear the loss of self-control, the way her eyes wanted to seek him out, the constant roller-coaster ride of her emotions. She felt vulnerable and confused.

Well, she had found rather more searching through Rachel's room than she had told him. Not quite enough, but just a little bit more information and she would have sufficient to present to him and leave with the case closed.

She had seen the desk-top computer and was sure that there would be a certain amount of helpful information there.

She had an afternoon, a night and hopefully part of the day tomorrow, and during that time she would make sure that everything was sorted, because she desperately needed to return to the safety of her comfort zone...

CHAPTER FIVE

LESLEY FLEXED HER FINGERS, which were stiff from working solidly on Rachel's desk-top for the past two and a half hours.

Alessio had given her the green light to look through anything and everything in his daughter's room and she knew that he was right to allow her to do so. If Rachel was under some sort of threat, whatever that threat was, then everything had to be done to neutralise the situation, even if it meant an invasion of her privacy.

However, Lesley had still felt guilty and nervous when she had sat down in front of the computer to begin opening files.

She had expected to find lots of personal teenage stuff. She had never been one of those girls who had sat around giggling and pouring her heart out to all her friends. She and her friends had mostly belonged to the sporting set, and the sporting set had only occasionally crossed over into the cheerleader set, which was where most of the giggling about boys and confiding had taken place.

However, the computer seemed largely to store school work. Lesley had assumed that the more personal information was probably carried on Rachel's tablet, or else her mobile phone, neither of which were in the house.

But she had found a couple of little strands that added to the building jigsaw puzzle.

Most of the really important information, however, had been gathered the old-fashioned way: pockets of jeans; scraps of paper; old exercise books; margins of text books; letters tossed carelessly in the drawer by the bed.

There had been no attempt to hide any of the stuff Lesley had gathered, and that made her feel much better.

Rachel might have given orders to a very pliant housekeeper not to go anywhere near her rooms, but had there been a little part of her that maybe wanted the information to be found? Was that why she had not destroyed notes that were definitely incriminating?

Lesley could only speculate.

By six that evening, she was exhausted. She ached all over, but she knew that she would be able to hand everything she had found over to Alessio and be on her way.

She felt a little panicky when she thought about getting into her little car and driving away from him for ever, then she told herself that it was just as well she was going to do that, because panicking at the prospect of not seeing him was a very dangerous place to be.

How had he managed to get under her skin so thoroughly and so fast?

When it came to men, she was a girl who had always taken things slowly. Friendships were built over a reasonable period of time. Generally speaking, during that protracted build-up any prospect of the friendship developing into something more serious was apt to fizzle out, which always reassured her that the relationship had not been destined.

But the speed with which Alessio had succeeded in filling her head was scary.

She found that even being alone in his house for a few hours was an unsettling business because she missed his presence!

In the space of only a couple of days, she had become accustomed to living life in the emotional fast lane; had become used to a heightened state of awareness, knowing that he was *around*. When she sat outside in the garden—working on her lap-top, enjoying the peace of the countryside, telling herself what a relief it was that she was not in the same room as him—she was still *conscious* of the fact that he was in the house. Somewhere.

With a little sigh of frustration, she decided that she would have a swim.

She hadn't been near the pool since she had arrived. She hadn't been able to deal with the prospect of him suggesting that he join her, even less with the prospect of him seeing just how angular, flat-chested and boyish her figure was.

He might have made the occasional flirty remark, but she had seen the sort of women he was attracted to. He had handed over his computer files to her and within them were photos of him with various busty, curvaceous, five-foot-two blonde bombshells. They all looked like clones of Marilyn Monroe.

But he wasn't here now, and it was still so hot and muggy, even at this hour of the evening.

When she looked at herself in the mirror, she was startled at how much it changed her appearance. However, she had seen herself in her navy-blue bikini sufficient times to be reassured that she was the same lanky Lesley she had always been.

Without bothering to glance at her reflection, she grabbed a towel from the bathroom and headed downstairs for the pool.

She should have felt wary venturing out with no one around, and just acres upon acres of fields and open land stretching away into the distance, but she didn't. In fact, she felt far more cautious in London, where she was constantly surrounded by people and where there was no such thing as complete darkness even in the dead of night in the middle of winter.

She dived cleanly into the water, gasping at the temperature, but then her body acclimatised as she began swimming.

She was a good swimmer. After being cooped up in front of a computer for several hours, it felt good to be exercising, and she swam without stopping, cutting through the water length after length after length.

She wasn't sure exactly how long she swam; maybe forty-five minutes. She could feel the beginning of that pleasant burn in her body that indicated that her muscles were being stretched to their limit.

At this point, she pulled herself up out of the pool, water sluicing down her body, her short, dark hair plastered down… and it was only then that she noticed Alessio standing to one side, half-concealed in the shadow of one of the trees fringing the side of the veranda.

It took a few seconds for her brain to register his presence there at all because she hadn't been expecting him.

And it took a few seconds more for her to realise that, not only was he standing there, but she wasn't even sure how long he had been standing there looking at her.

With an outraged yelp she walked quickly over to where she had dumped her towel on one of the chairs by the pool and, by the time she had secured it around her, he had walked lazily to where she was standing.

'I hope I didn't interrupt your workout,' he murmured without a hint of an apology in his voice.

'You're not supposed to be here!'

'There was a slight change of plan.'

'You should have warned me that you were going to be coming back!'

'I didn't think I needed to inform you that I would be returning to my own home.'

'How long have you been standing there?' She couldn't bring herself to meet those amused dark eyes. She was horribly conscious of what she must look like, with her wet hair like a cap on her head and her face completely bare of make-up—not that she ever wore much, but still.

'Long enough to realise that it's been a while since I used that pool. In fact, I can't remember the last time I stepped foot in it.' Water droplets were like tiny diamonds on her eyelashes and he wished she would look at him so that he could read the expression in her eyes. Was she genuinely annoyed that he had disturbed her, shown up unexpectedly? Or was she all of a dither because she had been caught off-guard, because he was seeing her for the first time without her armour of jeans, flats and faded tee-shirts? Clothes that neutralised her femininity.

He wondered what she would say if he told her just how delicious she looked, standing there dripping wet with only a towel that barely covered her.

He also wondered what she would say if he told her that he had been standing there for the better part of fifteen minutes, mesmerised as he'd watched her swimming, as at home in the water as a seal. He had been so wrapped up in the sight that he had completely forgotten why he had been obliged to drive back from London.

'Wait right here,' he urged suddenly. 'I'm going to join you. Give me ten minutes. It'll do me good to get rid of the London grime.'

'Join me?' Lesley was frankly horrified.

'You don't have a problem with that, do you?'

'No...err...'

'Good. I'll be back before you can get back in the water.'

Lesley was frozen to the spot as she watched him disappear back through the sprawling triple-fronted French doors that led into the conservatory.

Then, galvanised into action—because diving in while he watched was just out of the question—she hurried back into the water. What choice did she have? To have told him that she was fed up swimming and wanted to go inside, just as he was about to join her in the pool, would have been tantamount to confessing just how awkward he made her feel. The last thing she wanted was for him to know the effect he had on her. He might have some idea that she wasn't as impartial to his pres-

ence as she liked to pretend but her feelings were more confused than that and ran a lot deeper.

That was something she was desperate to keep to herself.
She could just about cope if he thought that she fancied him;
half the female population in the country between the ages of
eighteen and eighty would have fancied the man, so it would be
no big deal were he to include her in that category.

But it was more than that. Not only was she not the type to
randomly fancy guys because of the way they looked, but her
reactions to him pointed to something a lot more complex than
a simple case of lust which could easily be cured by putting
some distance between them.

She had just reached the shallow end of the pool when Alessio emerged back out in the mellow evening sunshine.

Lesley thought that she might faint. Only now did she fully
comprehend how much time she had spent daydreaming about
him, about what he might look like under those expensive, casual designer clothes he was fond of wearing.

What would his body look like?

Now she knew: lean, bronzed and utterly beautiful. His
shoulders were broad and muscled and his torso tapered to a
narrow waist and hips.

He was at home with his body, that much was evident from
the way he moved with an easy, casual grace.

Lesley sat on one of the steps at the shallow end of the pool,
so that she was levered into a half-sitting position on her elbows
while her long legs and most of her body remained under the
surface of the water. She felt safer that way.

He dived into the water, as straight as an arrow, and swam
steadily and powerfully towards her. It took every ounce of will
power not to flinch back as he reared up out of the water and
joined her on the step.

'Nice,' he said appreciatively, wiping his face with the palm
of his hand, then leaning back just as she did.

'You haven't explained what you're doing here.' Lesley eyed the proximity of his body nervously.

'And I shall do that as soon as we're inside. For the moment, I just want to enjoy being out here. I don't get much by way of time out. I don't want to spoil it by launching into the unexpected little problem that's cropped up.' He glanced across to her. 'You're a good swimmer.'

'Thank you.'

'Been swimming a long time?'

'Since I was four.' She paused and then continued, because talking seemed a bit less stressful than remaining silent and concentrating all her energies on what he was doing to her. 'My father had always been a good swimmer. All my brothers were as well. After my mother died, he got it into his head that he would channel all his energy into getting me into competitive swimming. The boys were all a bit older and had their own hobbies, but he's fond of telling me that I was fertile ground for him to work on.' Lesley laughed and relaxed a little. 'So he made sure to take me down to the local swimming baths at least twice a week. I was out of arm bands and swimming by the time I was five.'

'But you didn't end up becoming a professional swimmer.'

'I didn't,' Lesley admitted. 'Although I entered lots of competitions right up until I went to secondary school, then once I was in secondary school I began to play lots of different types of sport and the swimming was put on the back burner.'

'What sport did you play?' Alessio thought of his last girlfriend, whose only stab at anything energetic had involved the ski slope. He had once made the mistake of trying to get her to play a game of squash with him and had been irritated when she had shrieked with horror at the thought of getting too sweaty. Her hair, apparently, would not have been able to cope. He wondered whether she would have submerged herself in the pool the way Lesley had or whether she would have spent her time lying on a sun lounger and only dipping her feet in when the heat became unbearable.

Any wonder he had broken up with her after a couple of months?

'Squash, tennis, hockey, and of course in between I had my self-defence classes.'

'Energetic.'

'Very.'

'And in between all of that vigorous exercise you still had time for studying.'

Hence no time at all for what every other teenage girl would have been doing. Lesley read behind that mild observation. 'How else would I have ever been able to have a career?' Lesley responded tartly. 'Playing sport is all well and good but it doesn't get you jobs at the end of the day.' She stood up. 'I've been out here for long enough. I should really get back inside, have a shower. Please don't let me keep you from enjoying the pool. It's a shame to have this and not make use of it, especially when you think that it's so rare for the weather to be as good as it has been recently.' She didn't give him time to answer. Instead, she headed for her towel and breathed a sigh of relief when she had wrapped it around her.

When she turned around, it was to find him standing so close to her that she gave a little stumble back, almost crashing into the sun lounger behind her.

'Steady.' Alessio reached out and gripped her arms, then left his hands on her arms. 'I should really talk to you about what's brought me back here. I've got quite a bit of work to catch up on and I'll probably work through the night.'

Lesley found that she couldn't focus on anything while he was still holding her.

'Of course,' she eventually managed to croak. 'I'll go and have a shower, and then shall I meet you in the office?' She could smell him—the clean, chlorinated scent of the swimming pool combined with the heady aroma of the sun drying him as he stood there, practically naked.

'Meet me in the kitchen instead.' Alessio released her abruptly. Just then every instinct inside him wanted to pull her towards him and kiss her, taste her, see whether she would be as delectable as his imagination told him she would be. The intensity of what had shot through him was disturbing.

'I… I didn't expect you to return; I told Violet that there was no need to prepare anything for me before she left. In fact, I let her go early. I do hope you don't mind but I'm accustomed to cooking for myself. I was only going to do myself a plate of pasta.'

'Sounds good to me.'

'Right, then,' Lesley said faintly. She pushed her fingers through her hair, spiking it up.

She left him watching her and dashed upstairs for a very quick shower.

She should have found his unexpected arrival intensely annoying. It had thrown her whole evening out of sync. But there was a dark excitement swirling around inside her and she found that she was looking forward to having dinner with him, stupidly thrilled that he was back at the house.

She told herself that it was simply because she would be able to fill him in on all sorts of discoveries she had made and, the faster she filled him in, the sooner she would be able to leave and the quicker her life would return to normal. Normality seemed like a lifetime away.

He wasn't in the kitchen when she got there half an hour later, with all her paperwork in a folder, so she poured herself a glass of wine and waited for him.

She couldn't think what might have brought him back to his country estate. Something to do with his daughter, she was sure, but what? Might he have discovered something independently? Something that would make it easier for her to tell him what she thought this whole situation was about?

He strolled in when she was halfway through her glass of wine and proceeded to pour himself a whisky and soda.

'I need this,' Alessio said heavily, sinking onto the chair at the head of the table and angling it so that he could stretch his legs out whilst still facing her. 'My mother-in-law called when I was in the middle of my meetings.'

'Is that unusual?'

'Extremely. We may well be on cordial terms but not so cordial that she telephones out of the blue. There's still that ugly residue of their manipulation, although I will concede that Bianca's mother was not the one behind it. And it has to be said that, for the duration of our divorce, it was only thanks to Claudia that I ever got to see Rachel at all. I can count the number of times that happened on the fingers of one hand, but then Claudia never was a match for her daughter.' He caught himself in the act of wanting to talk more about the destructive marriage that had made him the cynical man he was today. How had that happened?

'What did she want?' Lesley eventually asked.

'Rachel has been staying with her for the past four weeks. Pretty much as soon as her school ended, she decided that she wanted to go over there. She doesn't know a great deal of people around here and only a handful in London. The down side of a boarding school out in the country, I suppose.' He sighed heavily and tipped the remainder of his drink down before resting the empty glass on the table and staring at it in brooding silence.

'Yes,' Lesley contributed vaguely. 'It must be difficult.'

'At any rate, the upshot appears to be that my daughter is refusing to return to the UK.'

Lesley's mouth fell open and Alessio smiled crookedly at her. 'She's refusing to speak to me on the telephone. She's dug her heels in and has decided to set up camp with Claudia and, Claudia being Claudia, she lacks the strength to stand up to my daughter.'

'You must be a little put out.'

'That's the understatement of the hour.' He stood up and signalled to her that they should start preparing something to eat. He needed to move around. For a small window, he had been so preoccupied with her, with arriving back and surprising her in the swimming pool, that he had actually put the gravity of the situation to the back of his mind, but now it had returned in full force.

Strangely, he was thankful that Lesley was there.

As if knowing that he would return to the topic in his own time, Lesley began preparing their meal. She had earlier piled all the ingredients she would need on the counter and now she began chopping mushrooms, tomatoes, onions and garlic.

For once, his silence didn't send her into instant meltdown. Rather, she began chatting easily and pleasantly. She told him about her lack of cooking experience. She joked that her brothers were all better cooks than she was and that two of them had even offered to show her the basics. She could sense him begin to unwind, even though she wasn't looking at him at all and he wasn't saying anything, just listening to her rabbit on aimlessly about nothing in particular.

It was soothing, Alessio thought as he watched her prepare the vegetables slowly and with the painstaking care of someone who wasn't comfortable in the arena of the kitchen.

Nor was he feeling trapped at the thought of a woman busying herself in his kitchen. He cleared as she cooked. It was a picture-perfect snapshot of just the sort of domesticity he avoided at all costs.

'So...' They were sitting at the kitchen table with bowls of pasta in front of them. She had maintained a steady flow of non-threatening conversation, and it had been surprisingly easy, considering she was always a bundle of nervous tension whenever she was in his presence. 'When you say that Rachel is digging her heels in and doesn't want to return to the UK, are you saying *for ever*, or just for the remainder of the summer holidays?'

'I'm saying that she's decided that she hates it over here and doesn't want to return at all.'

'And your mother-in-law can't talk her out of that?'

'Claudia has always been the pushover in the family. Between her bullying husband and Bianca, she was the one who got dragged into their plot and now, in this situation, well, it's probably a mixture of not wanting to hurt or offend her only grandchild and wanting to go down the path of least resistance.'

'So what are you going to do about that?'

'Well, there's simply no question of Rachel staying out there and going to school.' He pushed his empty plate to one side and sat back to look at her. 'I could have waited until tomorrow to come back here and tell you this but...'

'But...?' Lesley rested her chin in the palm of her hand and looked at him. The kitchen lights hadn't been switched on. It had still been bright when they had started preparing dinner, but the sun had suddenly faded, giving way to a violet twilight that cast shadows and angles across his face.

'I have a favour to ask of you.'

'What is it?' Lesley asked cautiously. She began standing to clear the table and he circled her wrist with his hand.

'Sit. Tidying can come later, or not at all. Violet will do it in the morning. I need to ask you something and I will need your undivided attention when I do so.'

She subsided back into the chair, heart beating madly.

'I want you to accompany me to Italy,' Alessio said heavily. 'It's a big ask, I know, but my fear is that, short of dragging Rachel to the plane and forcibly strapping her to the seat, she will simply refuse to listen to a word I have to say.'

'But I don't even know your daughter, Alessio!'

'If I cannot persuade my daughter to return to the UK, this will spell the end of any chance of a relationship I will ever have with her.' He rubbed his eyes wearily and then leaned back and stared blankly up at the ceiling.

Lesley's heart went out to him. Was that how it would be? Most likely. And yet…

'There's something you should see.' She stood up and went to the folder which she had brought down with her. This was the point at which she should now point out that she had gathered as much information as she could and it was up to him to do what needed to be done. In the end, it had been fiddly, but not impossible.

'You've found something?' Alessio was suddenly alert. He sat forward and pulled his chair towards her as she began smoothing out the various bits of paper she had found and the pages she had printed out over the past couple of days she had been at the house.

She had only given him a rough, skeleton idea of her findings before, not wanting to build any pictures that might be incorrect.

'I collated all of this and, well, okay, so I told you that I didn't think that this had anything to do with your wife…'

'Ex-wife.'

'Ex-wife. Well, I was right. I managed to trace our friend. He jumped around a bit, used a few different Internet cafés to cover his tracks, but the cafés, as I told you, were all in the vicinity of your daughter's school. It took a bit of time, but I eventually identified the one he used most frequently. Most importantly, though, in one of the very early emails—one of the emails you never identified as coming from him—he used his own computer. It was a little bit tougher than I thought but I got through to the identity of the person.'

Alessio was listening intently. 'You know who he is?'

'It would have been a bit more difficult to piece together conclusively if I hadn't discovered those very early emails when he'd obviously just been testing the ground. They were very innocuous, which is why he probably thought that they would have been deleted. I guess he didn't figure that they would still be uncovered and brought out of hiding.' She shoved the stack of printed emails across to Alessio and watched as he read them one by one. She had highlighted important bits, phrases, certain ways of saying things that pointed to the same writer behind them.

'You're brilliant.'

Lesley flushed with pleasure. 'I was only doing what you paid me to do.'

'So, build me the picture,' he said softly.

She did and, as she did so, she watched his expression darken and change.

'So now you pretty much have the complete story,' she finished. 'I gathered all this so that I could actually present it to you tomorrow when you returned. I was going to tell you that there's really nothing left for me to do now.'

'I still want you to come with me to Italy.'

'I can't,' Lesley said quickly, with a note of desperation in her voice.

'You've sorted all of this out, but there is still the problem of my daughter. Bringing her back over here with this information, it's going to be even more difficult.'

That was something Lesley had not taken into account when she had worked out her plan to present him with her findings and leave while common sense and her instinct for self-preservation were still intact.

'Yes, but it all remains the same. She's going to be—I can't imagine—certainly not warm and welcoming to the person who brought the whole thing to light.'

'But you have no personal axe to grind with her.' Would she come? It suddenly seemed very important that she was at his side. He was uneasily aware that there was an element of need there. How and why had that happened? He swept aside his discomfort.

'I also have my job, Alessio.' She was certain that she should be feeling horrified and indignant at his nerve in asking her to go way beyond the bounds of what she had been paid to do.

Especially when she had made such a big effort to wrap everything up so that she could escape the suffocating, dangerous effect he had on her.

'You can leave that to me,' he murmured.

'Leave that to you? How do you work that one out?'

'I've just concluded a deal to buy a string of luxury boutique hotels in Italy. Failing business, mismanagement, feuding amongst the board members; that's what the trip to London was all about. I needed to be there to finalise the details with lawyers.'

'How exciting,' Lesley said politely.

'More so than you might imagine. It's the first time I shall be dabbling in the leisure industry and, naturally, I will want a comprehensive website designed.'

'You have your own people to do that.'

'They're remarkably busy at the moment. This will be a job that will definitely have to be outsourced. Not only could it be worth a great deal of money to the company lucky enough to get the job, but there's no telling how many other jobs will come in its wake.'

'Are you *coercing* me?'

'I prefer to call it *persuasion*.'

'I don't believe it.'

'I usually get what I want,' Alessio said with utter truth. 'And what I want is for you to come with me to Italy and, if this proves a helpful lever, then that's all to the good. I'm sure when I explain to your boss the size and scale of the job, and the fact that it would be extremely useful to have you over there so that you can soak up the atmosphere and get a handle on how best to pitch the project...' He gave an elegant shrug and a smile of utter devastation; both relayed the message that she was more or less trapped.

Naturally she could turn down his offer but her boss might be a little miffed should he get to hear that. They were a thriving company but, with the current economic climate, potential setbacks lurked round every corner.

Whatever work came their way was not to be sniffed at, especially when the work in question could be highly lucrative and extensive.

'And if you're concerned about your pay,' he continued, 'Rest assured that you will be earning exactly the same rate as you were for the job you just so successfully completed.'

'I'm not concerned about the money!'

'Why don't you want to come? It'll be a holiday.'

'You don't need me there, not really.'

'You have no idea what I need or don't need,' Alessio murmured softly.

'You might change your mind when you see what else I have to show you.' But already she was trying to staunch the wave of anticipation at the thought of going abroad with him, having a few more days in his company, feeding her silly addiction.

She rescued papers from the bottom of the folder, pushed them across to him and watched carefully as he rifled through them.

But then, the moment felt too private, and she stood up and began getting them both a couple of cups of coffee.

What would he be thinking? she wondered as he looked at the little collection of articles about him which she had found in a scrap book in Rachel's room. Again, no attempt had been made to conceal them. Rachel had collected bits and pieces about her father over the years; there were photographs as well, which she must have taken from an album somewhere. Photos of him as a young man.

Eventually, when she could no longer pretend to be taking her time with the coffee, she handed a mug to him and sat back down.

'You found these…' Alessio cleared his throat but he couldn't look her in the eyes.

'I found them,' Lesley said gently. 'So, you see, your daughter isn't quite as indifferent to you as you might believe. Having the conversation you need to have with her might not be quite so difficult as you imagine.'

CHAPTER SIX

'THIS IS QUITE a surprise.' This was all Alessio could find to say and he knew that it was inadequate. His daughter had been collecting a scrap book about him. That reached deep down to a part of him he'd thought no longer existed. He stared down at the most recent cutting of him printed off the Internet. He had had an article written in the business section of the *Financial Times* following the acquisition of a small, independent bank in Spain. It was a poor picture but she had still printed it off and shoved it inside the scrap book.

What was he to think?

He rested his forehead against his clenched fist and drew in a long breath.

A wave of compassion washed over Lesley. Alessio Baldini was tough, cool, controlled. If he hadn't already told her, his entire manner was indicative of someone who knew that they could get what he wanted simply by snapping his fingers. It was a trait she couldn't abide in anyone.

She hated rich men who acted as though they owned the world and everything in it.

She hated men who felt that they could fling money at any problem and, lo and behold, a solution would be forthcoming.

And she hated anyone who didn't value the importance of

family life. Family was what grounded you, made you put everything into perspective; stopped you from ever taking yourself too seriously or sacrificing too much in pursuit of your goals.

Alessio acted as he if he owned the world and he certainly acted as though money was the root of solving all problems. If he was a victim of circumstances when it came to an unfortunate family life, then he definitely did not behave as though now was the time when he could begin sorting it out.

So why was she now reaching out to place her hand on his arm? Why had she pulled her chair just that little bit nearer to his so that she could feel the heat radiating from his body?

Was it because the vulnerability she had always sensed in him whenever the subject of his daughter came up was now so glaringly obvious?

Rachel was his Achilles heel; in a flash of comprehension, Lesley saw that. In every other area, Alessio was in complete control of his surroundings, of his *life*, but when it came to his daughter he floundered.

The women he had dated in the past had been kept at a distance. Once bitten, twice shy, and after his experiences with Bianca he had made sure never to let any other woman get past the steel walls that surrounded him. They would never have glimpsed the man who was at a loss when it came to his daughter. She wondered how many of them even *knew* that he had a daughter.

But here she was. She had seen him at his most naked, emotionally.

That was a good thing, she thought, and a bad thing. It was good insofar as everyone needed a sounding board when it came to dark thoughts and emotions. Those were burdens that could not be carried single-handed. He might have passed the years with his deepest thoughts locked away, but there was no way he would ever have been able to eradicate them, and letting them out could only be a good thing.

With this situation, he had been forced to reveal more about those thoughts to her than he ever had to anyone else. She was certain of that.

The down side was that, for a proud man, the necessity of having to confide thoughts normally hidden would eventually be seen as a sign of weakness.

The sympathetic, listening ear would only work for so long before it turned into a source of resentment.

But did that matter? Really? They wouldn't be around one another for much longer and right here, right now, in some weird, unspoken way, he needed her. She *felt* it, even though it was something he would never, ever articulate.

Those cuttings had moved him beyond words. He was trying hard to control his reaction in front of an audience; that was evident in the thickness of the silence.

'You'll have to return that scrap book to where you found it,' he said gruffly when the silence had been stretched to breaking point. 'Leave it with me overnight and I'll give it to you in the morning.'

Lesley nodded. Her hand was still on his arm and he hadn't shrugged it away. She allowed it to travel so that she was stroking upwards, feeling the strength of his muscles straining under the shirt and the definition of his shoulders and collarbone.

Alessio's eyes narrowed on her.

'Are you feeling sorry for me?' His voice was less cold than it should have been. 'Is that a pity caress?'

He had never confided in anyone. He certainly had never been an object of pity to anyone, any woman, ever. The thought alone was laughable. Women had always hung onto his every word, longed for some small indication that they occupied a more special role in his life than he was willing to admit to them.

Naturally, they hadn't.

Lesley, though…

She was in a different category. The pity caress did not evoke the expected feelings of contempt, impatience and anger that he would have expected.

He caught her hand in his and held on to it.

'It's not a *pity caress*.' Lesley breathed. Her skin burned where he was touching it, a blaze that was stoked by the expression in his eyes: dark, thoughtful, insightful, amused. 'But I know it must be disconcerting, looking through Rachel's scrap book, seeing pictures of yourself there, articles cut out or printed off from the Internet.' He still wasn't saying anything. He was still just staring at her, his head slightly to one side, his expression brooding and intent.

Her voice petered out and she stared right back at him, eyes wide. She could barely breathe. The moment seemed as fragile as a droplet of water balancing on the tip of a leaf, ready to fall and splinter apart.

She didn't want the moment to end. It was wrong, she knew that, but still she wanted to touch his face and smooth away those very human, very uncertain feelings she knew he would be having; feelings he would be taking great care of to conceal.

'The scrap book was just lying there,' she babbled away as she continued to get lost in his eyes. 'On the bed. I would have felt awful if I had found it hidden under the mattress or at the bottom of a drawer somewhere, but it was just there, waiting to be found.'

'Not by me. Rachel knew that I would never go into her suite of rooms.'

Lesley shrugged. 'I wanted you to see that you're important to your daughter,' she murmured shakily, 'Even if you don't think you are because of the way she acts. Teenagers can be very awkward when it comes to showing their feelings.' He still wasn't saying anything. If he thought that she felt sorry for him, then how was it that he was staying put, not angrily stalking off? 'You remember being a teenager.' She tried a smile in an attempt to lighten the screaming tension between them.

'Vaguely. When I think back to my teenage years, I inevitably end up thinking back to being a daddy before I was out of them.'

'Of course,' Lesley murmured, her voice warm with understanding. At the age of fourteen, not even knowing it, he would have been a mere four years away from becoming a father. It was incredible.

'You're doing it again,' Alessio said under his breath.

'Doing what?'

'Smothering me with your sympathy. Don't worry. Maybe I like it.' His mouth curved into a wolfish smile but underneath that, he thought with passing confusion, her sympathy was actually very welcome.

He reached out and touched her face, then ran two fingers along her cheek, circling mouth then along her slender neck, coming to rest at the base of her collarbone.

'Have you felt what I've been feeling for the past couple of days?' he asked.

Lesley wasn't sure she was physically capable of answering his question. Not with that hand on her collarbone and her brain reliving every inch of its caress as it had touched her cheek and moved sensuously over her mouth.

'Well?' Alessio prompted. He rested his other hand on her thigh and began massaging it, very gently but very thoroughly, just the one spot, but it was enough to make the breath catch in her throat.

'What do you mean? What are you talking about?' As if she didn't know. As if she wasn't constantly aware of the way he unsettled her. And was she conscious that the electricity flowed both ways? Maybe she was. Maybe that was why the situation had seemed so dangerous.

She had thought that she needed to get out because her attraction to him was getting too much, was threatening to become evident. Maybe a part of her had known that the real reason she needed to get out was because, on some level, she knew that he was attracted to her as well. That underneath the lighthearted flirting there was a very real undercurrent of mutual sexual chemistry.

And that was not good, not at all. She didn't do one-night stands, or two-day stands, or 'going nowhere so why not have a quick romp?' stands.

She did *relationships.* If there had been no guy in her life for literally years, then it was because she had never been the kind of girl who had sex just for the sake of it.

But with Alessio something told her that she could be that girl, and that scared her.

'You know exactly what I mean. You want me. I want you. I've wanted you for a while...'

'I should go up to bed.' Lesley breathed unevenly, nailed to the spot and not moving an inch despite her protestations. 'Leave you to your thoughts...'

'Maybe I'm not that keen on being alone with my thoughts,' Alessio said truthfully. 'Maybe my thoughts are a black hole into which I have no desire to fall. Maybe I want your pity and your sympathy because they can save me from that fall.'

And what happens when you've been saved from that fall? What happens to me? You're in a weird place right now and, if I rescue you now, what happens when you leave that weird place and shut the door on it once again?

But those muddled thoughts barely had time to settle before they were blown away by the fiercely exciting thought of being with the man who was leaning towards her, staring at her with such intensity that she wanted to moan.

And, before she could retreat behind more weak protestations, he was cupping the back of her neck and drawing her towards him, very slowly, so slowly that she had time to appreciate the depth of his dark eyes; the fine lines that etched his features; the slow, sexy curve of his mouth; the length of his dark eyelashes.

Lesley fell into the kiss with a soft moan, part resignation, part despair; mostly intense, long-awaited excitement. She spread her hand behind his neck in a mirror gesture to how he was holding her and, as his tongue invaded the soft contours of her mouth, she returned the kiss and let that kiss do its work— spread moisture between her legs, pinch her nipples into tight, sensitive buds, raise the hairs on her arms.

'We shouldn't be doing this,' she muttered, breaking apart for a few seconds and immediately wanting to draw him back towards her again.

'Why not?'

'Because this isn't the right reason for going to bed with someone.'

'Don't know what you're talking about.' He leaned to kiss her again but she stilled him with a hand on his chest and met his gaze with anxious eyes.

'I don't pity you, Alessio,' she said huskily. 'I'm sorry that you don't have the relationship with your daughter that you'd like, but I don't pity you. And when I showed you that scrap book it was because I felt the contents were something you needed to know about. What I feel is...understanding and compassion.'

'And what I feel is that we shouldn't get lost in words.'

'Because words are not your thing?' But she smiled and felt a rush of tenderness towards this strong, powerful man who was also capable of being so wonderfully *human*, hard though he might try to fight it.

'You know what they say about actions speaking louder...' He grinned at her. His body was on fire. She was right—words weren't his thing, at least not the words that made up long, in- volved conversations about feelings. He scooped her up and she gave a little cry of surprise, then wriggled and told him to put her down immediately; she might be slim but she was way too tall for him to start thinking he could play the caveman with her.

Alessio ignored her and carried her up the stairs to his bed- room.

'Every woman likes a caveman.' He gently kicked open his bedroom door and then deposited her on his king-sized bed.

Night had crept up without either of them realising it and, without the bedroom lights switched on, the darkness only allowed them to see one another in shadowy definition.

'I don't,' Lesley told him breathlessly as he stood in front of her and began unbuttoning his shirt.

She had already seen him barely clothed in the pool. She should know what to expect when it came to his body and yet, as he tossed his shirt carelessly on the ground, it was as if she was looking at him for the first time.

The impact he had on her was as new, as raw, as powerful.

But then, this was different, wasn't it? This wasn't a case of watching him covertly from the sidelines as he covered a few lengths in a swimming pool.

This was lying on his bed, in a darkened room, with the promise of possession flicking through her like a spreading fire.

Alessio didn't want to talk. He wanted to take her, fast and hard, until he heard her cry out with satisfaction. He wanted to pleasure her and feel her come with him inside her.

But how much sweeter to take his time, to taste every inch of her, to withstand the demands of his raging hormones and indulge in making love with her at a more leisurely pace.

'No?' he drawled, hand resting on the zipper of his trousers before he began taking those off as well, where they joined the shirt in a heap on the ground, leaving him in just his boxers. 'You think I'm a caveman because I carried you up the stairs?'

He slowly removed his boxers. He regretted not having turned some lights on because he would have liked to really appreciate the expression on her face as he watched her watching him. He strolled towards the side of the bed and stood there, then he touched himself lightly and heard her swift intake of breath.

'I just think you're a caveman in general,' Lesley feasted her eyes on his impressive erection. When he held it in his hand, she longed to do the same to herself, to touch herself down there. Her nerves were stretched to breaking point and she wished she was just a little more experienced, a little more knowing about what to do when it came to a man like him, a man who probably knew everything there was to know about the opposite sex.

She sat up, crossed her legs and reached out to touch him, replacing his hand with hers and gaining confidence as she felt him shudder with appreciation.

It was a strange turn-on to be fully clothed while he was completely naked.

'Is that right?'

As she took him into her mouth, Alessio grunted and flung his head back. He had died and gone to heaven. The wetness of her mouth on his hard erection, the way she licked, teased and tasted, his fingers curled into her short hair, made him breathe heavily, well aware that he had to come down from this peak or risk bringing this love-making session to an extremely premature conclusion, which was not something he intended to do.

With a sigh of pure regret, he eased her off him.

Then he joined her on the bed. 'Would I be a caveman if I stripped you? I wouldn't...' he slipped his fingers underneath the tee-shirt and began easing it over her head '...want to...' Then came the jeans, which she wriggled out of so that she remained in bra and pants, white, functional items of clothing that looked wonderfully wholesome on her. 'Offend your feminist sensibilities.'

For the life of her, Lesley couldn't find where she had misplaced those feminist sensibilities which he had mentioned. She reached behind to unhook her bra but he gently drew her hands away so that he could accomplish the task himself.

He half-closed his eyes and his nostrils flared with rampant appreciation of her small but perfectly formed breasts. Her nipples were big, brown, circular discs. She had propped herself up on both elbows and her breasts were small, pointed mounds offering themselves to him like sweet, delicate fruit.

In one easy movement, he straddled her, and she fell back against the pillow with a soft, excited moan.

She was wet for him. As he reached behind him to slip his

hand under the panties, she groaned and covered her eyes with one hand.

'I want to see you, my darling.' Alessio lowered himself so that he was lightly on top of her. 'Move your hand.'

'I don't usually do this sort of thing,' Lesley mumbled. 'I'm not into one-night stands. I never have been. I don't see the point.'

'Shh.' He gazed down at her until she was burning all over. Then he gently began licking her breast, moving in a concentric circle until his tongue found her nipple. The sensitised tip had peaked into an erect nub, and as he took her whole nipple into his mouth so that he could suckle on it she quivered under him, moving with feverish urgency, arching back so that not a single atom of the pleasurable sensations zinging through her was lost.

She had to get rid of her panties, they were damp and uncomfortable, but with his big body over hers she couldn't reach them. Instead she clasped her hand to the back of his head and pressed him down harder on her breasts, giving little cries and whimpers as he carried on sucking and teasing, moving between her breasts and then, when she was going crazy from it, he trailed his tongue over her rib cage and down to the indentation of her belly button.

His breath on her body was warm and she was breathing fast, hardly believing that what was happening really was happening and yet desperate for it to continue, desperate to carry on shamelessly losing herself in the moment.

He felt her sharp intake of breath as he slipped her underwear down, and then she was holding her breath as he gently parted her legs and flicked his tongue over her core.

Lesley groaned. This was an intimacy she had not experienced before. She curled her fingers into his dark hair and tugged him but her body was responding with a shocking lack of inhibition as he continued to taste her, teasing her swollen bud until she lost the ability to think clearly.

Alessio felt her every response as if their bodies had tuned into the same wavelength. In a blinding, revelatory flash, he realised that everything else that had come before with women could not compete with what was happening right now, because this woman had just seen far more of him than anyone else ever had.

This had not been a simple game of pursuit and capture. She hadn't courted this situation, nor had he anticipated it. Certainly, there had come a point when he had looked at her and liked what he had seen; had wanted what he had seen; had even vaguely *planned* on having her because, when it came to him and women, wanting and having were always the same side of the coin.

But he knew that he hadn't banked on what was happening between them now. For the first time, he had the strangest feeling that this wasn't just about sex.

But the sex was great.

He swept aside all his unravelling thoughts and lost himself in her body, in her sweet little whimpers and her broken groans as she wriggled under him, until at last, when he could feel her wanting to reach her orgasm, he broke off to fumble in the bedside cabinet for a condom.

Lesley could hardly bear that brief pause. She was alive in a way she had never been before and that terrified her. Her relationships with the opposite sex had always been guarded and imbued with a certain amount of defensiveness that stemmed from her own private insecurities.

Having been raised in an all-male family, she had developed brilliant coping skills when it came to standing her ground with the opposite sex. Her brothers had toughened her up and taught her the value of healthy competition, the benefits of never being cowed by a guy, of knowing that she could hold her own.

But no one had been able to help her during those teenage years when the lines of distinction between boys and girls were drawn. She had watched from the sidelines and decided that lipstick and mascara were not for her, that sport was far more enjoyable. It wasn't about how you looked, it was about what was inside you and what was inside her—her intelligence, her sense of humour, her capacity for compassion—did not need to be camouflaged with make-up and sexy clothes.

The only guys she had ever been attracted to were the ones who'd seen her for the person she was, the ones whose heads hadn't swivelled round when a busty blonde in a short skirt had walked past.

So what, it flashed through her head, was she doing with Alessio Baldini?

She sighed and reached up to him as he settled back on her, nudging her legs apart, then she closed her eyes and was transported to another planet as he thrust into her, deep and hard, building a rhythm that drove everything out of her mind.

She flung her head back and succumbed to loud, responsive cries as he continued to fill her.

She came on a tidal wave of intense pleasure and felt her whole body shudder and arch up towards him in a wonderful fusing of bodies.

The moment seemed to last for ever and she was only brought back down to earth when he withdrew from her and cursed fluently under his breath.

'The condom has split.'

Lesley abruptly surfaced from the pleasant, dreamy cloud on which she had been happily drifting, and the uncomfortable thoughts which had been sidelined when he had begun touching her returned with double intensity.

What on earth had she done? How could she have allowed herself to end up in bed with this man? Had she lost her mind? This was a situation that was going nowhere and would never go anywhere. She was Lesley Fox, a practical, clever, not at all sexy woman who should have known better than to be sweet talked into sleeping with a man who wouldn't have looked twice at her under normal circumstances.

On every level, he was just the sort of man she usually

wouldn't have gone near and, had he seen her passing on the street, she certainly would not have been the sort of woman he would have noticed. She would literally have been invisible to him because she just wasn't his type.

Fate had thrown them together and an attraction had built between them but she knew that she would be a complete fool not to recognise that that attraction was grounded in novelty.

'How the hell could that have happened?' Alessio said, his voice dark with barely contained anger. 'This is the last thing I need right now.'

Lesley got that. He had found himself tricked into marriage by a pregnancy he had not courted once upon a time and his entire adult life had been affected. Of course he would not want to repeat that situation.

Yet, she couldn't help but feel the sting of hurt at the simmering anger in his voice.

'It won't happen,' she said stiffly. She wriggled into a sitting position and watched as he vaulted upright and began searching around for his boxers, having disposed of the faulty condom.

'And you know that because?'

'It's the wrong time of month for that to happen.' She surreptitiously crossed her fingers and tried to calculate when she had last had her period. 'And, rest assured, the last thing I would want would be to end up pregnant, Alessio. As it stands, this was a very bad idea.'

In the process of locating a tee-shirt from a chest of drawers, he paused and strolled back to the bed. The condom had split and there was nothing he could do about that now. He could only hope that she was right, that they were safe.

But, that aside, how could she say that making love had been a very bad idea? He was oddly affronted.

'You know what. This. Us. Ending up in bed together. It shouldn't have happened.'

'Why not? We're attracted to one another. How could it have been a bad idea? I was under the impression that you had actually enjoyed the experience.' He looked down at her and felt his libido begin to rise once again.

'That's not the point.' She swung her legs over the side of the bed and stood up, conscious of her nudity, gritting her teeth against the temptation to drag the covers off the bed and shield herself from him.

'God, you're beautiful.'

Lesley flushed and looked away, stubbornly proud, and refusing to believe that he meant a word of that. Novelty was a beautiful thing but became boring very quickly.

'Well?' He caught her wrist and tilted her face so that she had no option but to look at him.

'Well what?' Lesley muttered, lowering her eyes.

'Well, let's go back to bed.'

'Didn't you hear a word I just said?'

'Every word.' He kissed her delicately on the corner of her mouth and then very gently on her lips.

In a heartbeat, and to her disgust, Lesley could feel her determination begin to melt away.

'You're not my type,' she mumbled, refusing to cave in, but his lips were so soft against her jaw that her disobedient body was responding in all sorts of stupidly predictable ways.

'Because I'm a caveman?'

'Yes!' Her hands crept up to his neck and she protested feebly as he lifted her off her feet and back towards the bed to which she had only minutes previously sworn not to return.

'So, what are you looking for in a man?' Alessio murmured.

This time, he drew the covers over them. It was very dark outside. Even with the curtains open, the night was black velvet with only a slither of moon penetrating the darkness and weakly illuminating the bedroom.

He could feel her reluctance, her mind fighting her body, and it felt imperative that her body win the battle because he wanted her, more than he had ever wanted any woman in his life before.

'Not someone like you, Alessio,' Lesley whispered, pressing her hands flat against his chest and feeling the steady beat of his heart.

'Why? Why not someone like me?'

'Because…' *Because safety was not with a man who looked like him, a man who could have anyone he wanted.* She knew her limits. She knew that she was just not the sort of girl who drew guys to her like a magnet. She never had been. She just didn't have the confidence; had never had the right preparation; had never had a mother's guiding hand to show her the way to all those little feminine wiles that went into the mix of attraction between the sexes.

But bigger than her fear of involvement with him was her fear of *not* getting involved, *not* taking the chance.

'You're just not the sort of person I ever imagined having any kind of relationship with, that's all.'

'We're not talking marriage here, Lesley, we're talking about enjoying each other.' He propped himself up on one elbow and traced his finger along her arm. 'I'm not looking for commitment any more than you probably are.'

And certainly not with someone like you; Lesley reluctantly filled in the remainder of that remark.

'And you still haven't told me the sort of man you would call "your type".' She was warm and yielding in his arms. She might make a lot of noises about this being a mistake, but she wanted him as much as he wanted her, and he knew that if he slipped his fingers into her he would feel the tell-tale proof of her arousal.

He could have her right here and right now, despite whatever she said about him not being her type. And who, in the end, cared whether he was her type or not? Hadn't he just told her that this wasn't about commitment and marriage? In other words, did it really matter if he wasn't her type?

But he was piqued at the remark. She was forthright and spoke her mind; he had become accustomed to that very quickly. But surely what she had said amounted to an unacceptable lack of tact! He thought that there was nothing wrong in asking her to explain exactly what she had meant.

His voice had dropped a few shades.

'You're offended, aren't you?' Lesley asked and Alessio was quick to deny any such thing.

Lesley could have kicked herself for asking him that question. Of course he wouldn't be offended! To be offended, he would actually have had to care about her and that was not the case here, as he had made patently clear.

'That's a relief!' she exclaimed lightly. 'My type? I guess thoughtful, caring, sensitive; someone who believes in the same things that I do, who has similar interests…maybe even someone working in the same field. You know—artistic, creative, not really bothered about the whole business of making money.'

Alessio bared his teeth in a smile. 'Sounds a lot of fun. Sure someone like that would be able to keep up with you? No, scrap that—too much talk. There are better things to do and, now that we've established that you can't resist me even though I'm the last kind of person you would want in your life, let's make love.'

'Alessio…'

He stifled any further protest with a long, lingering kiss that released in her a sigh of pure resignation. So this made no sense, so she was a complete idiot… Where had the practical, level-headed girl with no illusions about herself gone? All she seemed capable of doing was giving in.

'And,' he murmured into her ear. 'In case you think that Italy is off the agenda because I'm not a touchy-feely art director for a design company, forget it. I still want you there by my side. Trust me, I will make it worth your while.'

CHAPTER SEVEN

EVERYTHING SEEMED TO happen at the speed of light after that. Of course, there was no inconvenient hanging around for affordable flights or having to surf the Internet for places to stay. None of the usual headaches dogged Alessio's spur-of-the-moment decision to take Lesley to Italy.

Two days after he had extended his invitation, they were boarding a plane to Italy.

It was going to be a surprise visit. Armed with information, they were going to get the full story from his daughter, lay all the cards on the table and then, when they were back in the UK, Alessio would sort the other half of the equation out. He would pay an informal visit to his emailing friend and he was sure that they would reach a happy conclusion where no money changed hands.

Lessons, he had assured her, would regrettably have to be learnt.

Lesley privately wondered what his approach to his daughter would be. Would similar lessons also 'regrettably have to be learnt'? How harsh would those lessons be? He barely had a relationship with Rachel and she privately wondered how he intended ever to build on it if he went in to 'sort things out' with the diplomacy of a bull in a china shop.

That was one of the reasons she had agreed to go to Italy with him.

Without saying it in so many words, she knew that he was looking to her for some sort of invisible moral back-up, even though he had stated quite clearly that he needed her there primarily to impart the technicalities of what she had discovered should the situation demand it.

'You haven't said anything for the past half an hour.' Alessio interrupted her train of thought as they were shown into the first class cabin of the plane. 'Why?'

Lesley bristled. 'I was just thinking how fast everything's moved,' she said as they were shown to seats as big as armchairs and invited to have a glass of champagne, which she refused.

She stole a glance at his sexy face, lazy and amused at the little show of rebellion.

'I came to do a job for you, thinking that I would be in and out of your house in a matter of a few hours and now here I am, days later, boarding a plane for Italy.'

'I know. Isn't life full of adventure and surprise?' He waved aside an awe-struck air hostess and settled into the seat next to her. 'I confess that I myself am surprised at the way things unfolded. Surprised but not displeased.'

'Because you've got what you wanted,' Lesley complained. She was so accustomed to her independence that she couldn't help feeling disgruntled at the way she had been railroaded into doing exactly what he had wanted her to do.

Even though, a little voice inside her pointed out, this rollercoaster ride was the most exciting thing she had ever done in her life—even though it was scary, even though it had yanked her out of her precious comfort zone, even though she knew that it would come to nothing and the fall back to Planet Earth would be painful.

'I didn't force your hand,' Alessio said comfortably.

'You went into the office and talked to my boss.'

'I just wanted to point out the world of opportunity lying at his feet if he could see his way to releasing you for one week to accompany me to Italy.'

'I dread to think what the office grapevine is going to make of this situation.'

'Do you care what anyone thinks?' He leant against the window so that he could direct one hundred per cent of his undivided attention on her.

'Of course I do!' Lesley blushed because she knew that, whilst she might give the impression of being strong, sassy and outspoken, she still had a basic need to be liked and accepted. She just wasn't always good at showing that side of herself. In fact, she was uncomfortably aware of the fact that, whilst Alessio might have shown her more of himself than he might have liked, she had likewise done the same.

He would not know it, but against all odds she had allowed herself to walk into unchartered territory, to have a completely new experience with a man knowing that he was not the right man for her.

'Relax and enjoy the ride,' he murmured.

'I'm not going to enjoy confronting your daughter with all the information we've managed to uncover. She's going to know that I went through her belongings.'

'If Rachel had wanted to keep her private life private, then she should have destroyed all the incriminating evidence. The fact is that she's still a child and she has no vote when it comes to us doing what was necessary to protect her.'

'She may not see it quite like that.'

'She will have to make a very big effort to, in that case.'

Lesley sighed and leaned back into the seat with her eyes shut. What Alessio did with his daughter was really none of her business. Yes, she'd been involved in bringing the situation to light, but its solutions and whatever repercussions followed would be a continuing saga she would leave behind. She would return to the blessed safety of what she knew and the family story of Alessio and his daughter would remain a mystery to her for ever.

So there was no need to feel any compunction about just switching off.

Yet she had to bite back the temptation to tell him what she thought, even though she knew that he would have every right to dismiss whatever advice she had to offer about the peculiarity of their relationship, if a 'relationship' was what it could be called. She was his lover, a woman who probably knew far too much about his life for his liking. She had been paid to investigate a personal problem, yet had no right to have any discussions about that problem, even though they were sleeping together.

In a normal relationship, she should have felt free to speak her mind, but this was not a normal relationship, was it? For either of them. She had sacrificed her feminist principles for sex and she still couldn't understand herself, nor could she understand how it was that she felt no regrets.

In fact, when he looked at her the way he was looking at her right now, all she felt was a dizzying need to have him take her.

If only he could see into her mind and unravel all her doubts and uncertainties. Thank goodness he couldn't. As far as he was concerned, she was a tough career woman with as little desire for a long-term relationship as him. They had both stepped out of the box, drawn to each other by a combination of proximity and the pull of novelty.

'You're thinking,' Alessio said drily. 'Why don't you spit it out and then we can get it out of the way?'

'Get what out of the way?'

'Whatever disagreements you have about the way I intend to handle this situation.'

'You hate it when I tell you what I think,' Lesley said with asperity. Alessio shrugged and continued looking at her in the way that made her toes curl and her mouth run dry.

'And I don't like it when I can see you thinking but you're saying nothing. "Between a rock and a hard place" comes to mind.' He was amazed at how easily he had adapted to her out-spoken approach. His immediate instinct now was not to shove her back behind his boundary lines and remind her about over-stepping the mark.

'I just don't think you should confront Rachel and demand to know what the hell is going on.' She shifted in the big seat and turned so that she was completely facing him.

The plane was beginning to taxi in preparation for taking off, and she fell silent for a short while as the usual canned talk was given about safety exits, but as soon as they were airborne she looked at him worriedly once again.

'It's hard to know how to get answers if you don't ask for them,' he pointed out.

'We know the situation.'

'And I want to know how it got to where it finally got. It's one thing knowing the outcome but I don't intend to let history repeat itself.'

'You might want to try a little sympathy.'

Alessio snorted.

'You said yourself that she's just a kid,' Lesley reminded him gently.

'You *could* always spare me the horror of making a mess of things by talking to Rachel yourself,' he said.

'She's not my daughter.'

'Then allow me to work this one out myself.' But he knew that she was right. There was no tactful way of asking the questions he would have to ask, and if his daughter disliked him now then she was about to dislike him a whole lot more when he was finished talking to her.

Of course, there were those photos, cuttings of him—some indication, as Lesley had said, that she wasn't completely in-different to the fact that he was her father.

But would that be enough to take them past this little crisis? Unlikely. Especially when she discovered that the photos and cuttings had been salvaged in an undercover operation.

'Okay.'

Alessio had looked away, out through the window to the dense bank of cloud over which they were flying. Now, he turned to Lesley with a frown.

'Okay. I'll talk to Rachel if you like,' she said on a reluctant sigh.

'Why would you do that?'

Why would she? Because she couldn't bear to see him looking the way he was looking now, with the hopeless expression of someone staring defeat in the face.

And why did she care? she asked herself. But she shied away from trying to find an answer to that.

'Because I'm on the outside of this mess. If she directs all her teenage anger at me, then by the time she gets to you some of it may have diffused.'

'And the likelihood of that is...?' But he was touched at her generosity of spirit.

'Not good odds,' Lesley conceded. 'But worth a try, don't you think?' He was staring at her with an expression of intense curiosity and she continued quickly, before he could interrupt with the most obvious question: *why?* A question to which she had no answer. 'Besides, I'm good at mediating. I got a lot of practice at doing that when I was growing up. When there are six kids in a family, a dad worked off his feet, and five of those six are boys, there's always lots of opportunity to practise mediation skills.'

But just no opportunity to practise *being a girl*. And that was why she was the way she was now: hesitant in relationships; self-conscious about whether she had what it took to make any relationship last; willing not to get into the water at all rather than diving in and finding herself out of her depth and unable to cope.

Only since Alessio had appeared on the scene had she really seen the pattern in her behaviour, the way she kept guys, smiling, at arm's length.

He was so dramatically different from any man she had ever been remotely drawn to that it had been easy to pinpoint her own lack of self-confidence. She was a clever career woman with a bright life ahead of her and yet that sinfully beautiful face had reduced all those achievements to rubble.

She had looked at him and returned to her teenage years when she had simply not known how to approach a boy because she had had no idea what they were looking for.

For her, Alessio Baldini was not the obvious choice when it came to picking a guy to sleep with, yet sleep with him she had, and she was glad that she had done so. She had broken through the glass barrier that had stood between her and the opposite sex. It was strange, but he had given her confidence she hadn't really even known she had needed.

'And mediation skills are so important when one is growing up,' Alessio murmured.

Basking in her new-found revelations, Lesley smiled. 'No, they're not,' she admitted with more candour than she'd ever done to anyone in her life before. 'In fact, I can't think of any skill a teenage girl has less use for than mediation skills,' she mused. 'But I had plenty of that.' She leaned back and half-closed her eyes. When she next spoke it was almost as though she was talking with no audience listening to what was being said.

'My mum died when I was so young, I barely remember her. I mean, Dad always told us about her, what she was like and such, and there were pictures of her everywhere. But the truth is, I don't have any memories of her—of doing anything with her, if you see what I mean.'

She glanced sideways at him and he nodded. He had always fancied himself as the sort of man who would be completely at sea when it came to listening to women pour their hearts out, hence it was a tendency that he had strenuously discouraged.

Now, though, he was drawn to what she was saying and by the faraway, pensive expression on her face.

'I never thought that I missed having a mother. I never knew what it was like to have one and my dad was always good enough for me. But I can see now that growing up in a male-only family might have given me confidence with the opposite sex but only when it came to things like work and study. I was encouraged to be as good as they were, and I think I succeeded, but I wasn't taught, well...'

'How to wear make-up and shop for dresses?'

'Sounds crazy but I do think girls need to be taught stuff like that.' She looked at him gravely. 'I can see that it's easy to have bags of confidence in one area and not much in another,' she said with a rueful shake of her head. 'When it came to the whole game-playing, sexual attraction thing, I don't think I've ever had loads of confidence.'

'And now?'

'I feel I have, so I guess I should say thank you.'

'*Thank you?* What are you thanking me for?'

'For encouraging me to step out of the box,' Lesley told him with that blend of frankness and disingenuousness which he found so appealing.

Alessio was momentarily distracted from the headache awaiting him in Italy. He had no idea where she was going with this but it had all the feel of a conversation heading down a road he would rather not explore.

'Always happy to oblige,' he said vaguely. 'I hope you've packed light clothes. The heat in Italy is quite different from the heat in England.'

'If I hadn't taken on this job, there's not a chance in the world that I would ever have met you.'

'That's true enough.'

'Not only do we not move in the same circles, we have no interests in common whatsoever.'

Alessio was vaguely indignant at what he thought might be an insult in disguise. Was she comparing him to the 'soul mate' guy she had yet to meet, the touchy-feely one with the artistic side and a love of all things natural?

'And if we *had* ever met, at a social do or something like that, I would never have had the confidence to approach you.'

'I'm not sure where you're going with this.'

'Here's what I'm saying, Alessio. I feel as though I've taken huge strides in gaining self-confidence in certain areas and it's thanks in some measure to you. I could say that I'm going to be a completely different person when I get back to the UK and start dating again.'

Alessio could not believe what he was hearing. He had no idea where this conversation had come from and he was enraged that she could sit there, his lover, and talk about going back on the dating scene!

'The dating scene.'

'Is this conversation becoming a little too deep for you?' Lesley asked with a grin. 'I know you don't do deep when it comes to women and conversations.'

'And how do you know that?'

'Well, you've already told me that you don't like encouraging them to get behind a stove and start cooking a meal for you, just in case they think, I don't know, they have somehow managed to get a foot through the door. So I'm guessing that meaningful conversations are probably on the banned list as well.'

They were. It was true. He had never enjoyed long, emotional conversations which, from experience, always ended up in the same place—invitations to meet the parents, questions about commitment and where the relationship was heading.

In fact, the second that type of conversation began rearing its head, he usually felt a pressing need to end the relationship. He had been coerced into one marriage and he had made a vow never to let himself be railroaded into another similar mistake, however tempting the woman in question might be.

He looked into her astute, brown eyes and scowled. 'I may not be looking for someone to walk down the aisle with, but that doesn't mean that I'm not prepared to have meaningful discussions with women. I'm also insulted,' he was driven to continue, 'That I've been used as some kind of trial run for the real thing.'

'What do you mean?' Lesley was feeling good. The vague unease that had been plaguing her ever since she had recognised how affected she was by Alessio had been boxed away with an explanation that made sense.

Sleeping with him had opened her eyes to fears and doubts she had been harbouring for years. She felt that she had buried a lack of self-confidence in her own sexuality under the guise of academic success and then, later on, success in her career. She had dressed in ways that didn't enhance her own femininity because she had always feared that she lacked what it took.

But then she had slept with him, slept with a man who was way out of her league, had been wanted and desired by him, and made to feel proud of the way she looked.

Was it any wonder that he had such a dramatic effect on her? It was a case of lust mixed up with a hundred other things.

But the bottom line was that he was no more than a learning curve for her. When she thought about it like that, it made perfect sense. It also released her from the disturbing suspicion that she was way too deep in a non-relationship that was going nowhere, a relationship that meant far more to her than it did to him.

Learning curves provided lessons and, once those lessons had been learnt, it was always easy to move on.

Learning curves didn't result in broken hearts.

She breathed in quickly and shakily. 'Well?' she flung at him, while her mind continued to chew over the notion that her involvement with him had been fast and hard. She had been catapulted into a world far removed from hers, thrown into the company of a man who was very, very different from the sort of men she was used to, and certainly worlds apart from the sort of man she would ever have expected herself to be attracted to.

But common sense had been no match for the power of his appeal and now here she was.

When she thought about never seeing him again, she felt faintly, sickeningly panicked.

What did that mean? Her thoughts became muddled when she tried to work her way through what suddenly seemed a dangerous, uncertain quagmire.

'I mean that you used me,' Alessio said bluntly. 'I don't like being used. And I don't appreciate you talking about jumping back into the dating scene, not when we're still lovers. I expect the women I sleep with to only have eyes for me.'

The unbridled arrogance of that statement, which was so fundamentally *Alessio,* brought a reluctant smile to her lips.

She had meant it when she had told him that under normal circumstances they would never have met. Their paths simply wouldn't have crossed. He didn't mix in the same circles as she did. And, even if by some freak chance they *had* met, they would have looked at one another and quickly looked away.

She would have seen a cold, wealthy, arrogant cardboard cut-out and he would have seen, well, a woman who was nothing like the sort of women he went out with and therefore she'd have been invisible. But the circumstances that had brought them together had uniquely provided them with a different insight into one another.

She had seen beneath the veneer to the three-dimensional man and he had seen through the sassy, liberal-minded, outspoken woman in charge of her life to the uncertain, insecure girl.

She was smart enough to realise, however, that that changed nothing. He was and always would be uninterested in any relationship that demanded longevity. He was shaped by his past and his main focus now was his daughter and trying to resolve the difficult situation that had arisen there. He might have slept with her because she was so different from what he was used to and because she was there, ready and willing but, whereas he had fundamentally reached deep and changed her, she hadn't done likewise with him.

'You're smiling.' Alessio was reluctant to abandon the conversation. When, he thought, was this dive back into the dating scene going to begin? Had she put time limits on what they had? Wasn't he usually the one to do that?

'I don't want to argue with you.' Lesley kept that smile pinned to her face. 'Who will you introduce me as when we get to Italy?'

'I haven't given it any thought. Where is all this hectic dating going to take place?'

'I beg your pardon?'

'You can't start conversations you don't intend to finish. So, where will you be going to meet Mr Right? I'm taking it you intend to start hunting when we return to England, or will you be looking around Italy for any suitable candidates?'

'Are you upset because I said what I said?'

'Why would I be upset?'

'I have no idea,' Lesley said as flippantly as she could. 'Because we both know that what we have isn't going to last.' She allowed just a fraction of a second in which he could have contradicted her, but of course he said nothing, and that hurt and reinforced for her the position she held in his life. 'And of course I'm not going to be looking around Italy for suitable candidates. I haven't forgotten why I'll be there in the first place.'

'Good,' Alessio said brusquely.

But the atmosphere between them had changed, and when he flipped open his lap-top and began working Lesley took the hint and excavated her own lap-top so that she too could begin working, even though she couldn't concentrate.

What she had said had put his nose out of joint, she decided. He wanted her to be his, to belong to him for however long he deemed it suitable, until the time came when he got bored of her and decided that it was time for her to go. For her to talk to him about dating other men would have been a blow to his masculine pride, hence his reaction. He wasn't upset, nor was he jealous of these imaginary men she would soon be seeking out. If they existed.

Her thoughts drifted and meandered until the plane began its descent. Then they were touching down at the airport in Liguria and everything vanished, except the reason why they were here in the first place.

Even the bright sunshine vanished as they stepped out and were ushered into a chauffeur-driven car to begin the journey to his house on the peninsula.

'I used to come here far more frequently in the past,' he mused as he tried to work out the last time he had visited his coastal retreat.

'And then what happened?' It was her first time in Italy and she had to drag her eyes away from the lush green of the backdrop, the mountains that reared up to one side, the flora which was eye-wateringly exuberant.

'Life seemed to take over.' He shrugged. 'I woke up to the fact that Bianca had as little to do with this part of Italy as she possibly could and, of course, where she went, my daughter was dragged along. My interest died over a period of time and, anyway, work prohibited the sort of lengthy holidays that do this place justice.'

'Why didn't you just sell up?'

'I had no pressing reason to. Now I'm glad I hung onto the place. It may have been a bit uncomfortable had we been under the same roof as Rachel and Claudia, given the circumstances. I hadn't planned on saying anything to my mother-in-law about our arrival, but in all events I decided to spare her the shock of a surprise visit—although I've told her to say nothing to Rachel, for obvious reasons.'

'Those reasons being?'

'I can do without my teenage daughter scarpering.'

'You don't think she would, do you? Where would she go?'

'I should think she knows Italy a lot better than I do. She certainly would have friends in the area I know nothing about. I think it's fair to say that my knowledge of the people she hangs out with isn't exactly comprehensive.' But he smiled and then stared out of the window. 'I shudder to think of Claudia trying to keep control of my daughter on a permanent basis.'

The conversation lapsed. The sun was setting by the time they finally made it to his house, which they approached from the rear and which was perched on a hill top.

The front of the house overlooked a drop down to the sea and the broad wooden-floored veranda, with its deep rattan-framed sofas, was the perfect spot from which you could just sit and watch the changing face of the ocean.

Only when they had settled in, shown to their bedroom by a housekeeper—yet another employee keeping a vacant house going—did Alessio inform her that he intended visiting his mother-in-law later that evening.

'It won't be too late for her,' he said, prowling through the bedroom and then finally moving to the window to stare outside. He turned to look at her. In loose-fitting trousers and a small, silky vest, she looked spectacular. It unsettled him to think that, even with this pressing business to conclude, she had still managed to distract him to the point where all he could think of was her returning to London and joining the singles scene.

He wouldn't have said that his ego was so immense that it could be so easily bruised, but his teeth clamped together in grim rejection of the thought of any man touching her. Since when had he been the possessive type, let alone jealous?

'It will also allow Rachel to sleep on everything, give her time to put things into perspective and to come to terms with returning with us on the next flight over.'

'You make it sound as though we'll be leaving tomorrow.' Lesley hovered by the bed, sensing his mood and wondering whether it stemmed from parental concern at what was to come. She wanted to reach out and comfort him but knew, with unerring instinct, that that would be the last thing he wanted.

Yet hadn't he implied that they would be in the country for at least a week? She wondered why the rush was suddenly on to get out as quickly as possible. Did he really think that she had been using him? Had he decided that the sooner he was rid of her, the better, now that she had bucked the trend of all his other women and displayed a lack of suitable clinginess?

Pride stopped her from asking for any inconvenient explanations.

'Not that it matters when we leave,' she hastened to add. 'Would I have time to have a shower?'

'Of course. I have some work I need to get through anyway. I can use the time to do that and you can meet me downstairs in the sitting room. Unlike my country estate, you should be able to find your way around this villa without the use of a map.'

He smiled, and Lesley smiled back and muttered something suitable, but she was dismayed to feel a lump gathering at the back of her throat.

The sex between them was so hot that she would have expected him to have given her that wolfish grin of his, to have joined her in the shower, to have forgotten what they had come here for...just for a while.

Instead, he was vanishing through the door without a backward glance and she had to swallow back her bitter disappointment.

Once showered, and in a pair of faded jeans and a loose tee-shirt, she found him waiting for her in the sitting room, pacing while he jangled car keys in his pocket. The chauffeur had departed in the saloon car in which they had been ferried and she wondered how they were going to get to Claudia's villa, but there was a small four-wheel-drive jeep tucked away at the side of the house.

She had all the paperwork in a backpack which she had slung over her shoulder. 'I hope I'm not underdressed,' she said suddenly, looking up at him. 'I don't know how formal your mother-in-law is.'

'You're fine,' Alessio reassured her. A sudden image of her naked body flashed through his head with such sudden force that his heart seemed to skip a beat. He should have his mind one hundred per cent focused on the situation about to unravel, he told himself impatiently, instead of thinking about her and whatever life choices she decided to make. 'Your dress code isn't the issue here,' he said abruptly and Lesley nodded and turned away.

'I know that,' she returned coolly. 'I just wouldn't want to offend anyone.'

Alessio thought that that was rather shutting the door after the horse had bolted, considering she had had no trouble in offending *him*, but it was such a ridiculous thought that he swept it aside and offered a conciliatory smile.

'Don't think that I don't appreciate what you're doing,' he told her in a low voice. 'You didn't have to come here.'

'Even though you made sure I did by dangling that carrot of a fabulous new big job under my boss's nose?' She was still edgy at his dismissive attitude towards her but, when he looked at her like that, his dark eyes roving over her face, her body did its usual thing and leapt into heated response.

As if smelling that reaction, Alessio felt some of the tension leave his body and this time when he smiled it was with genuine, sexy warmth.

'I've always liked using all the tools in my box,' he murmured and Lesley shot him a fledgling grin.

His black mood had evaporated. She could sense it. Perhaps now that they were about to leave some of his anxiety about what lay ahead was filtering away, replaced by a sense of the inevitable.

At any rate, she just wanted to enjoy this return to normality between them. For that little window when there had been tension between them, she had felt awful. She knew that she had to get a grip, had to put this little escapade into perspective.

She would give herself the remainder of what time was left

in Italy and then, once they returned to the UK, whatever the outcome of what happened here, she would return to the life she had temporarily left behind. She had already laid the groundwork for a plausible excuse, one that would allow her to retreat with her dignity and pride intact.

It was time to leave this family saga behind her.

CHAPTER EIGHT

THE DRIVE TO Claudia's villa took under half an hour. He told her that he hadn't been back to Portofino for a year and a half, and then it had been a flying visit, but he still seemed to remember the narrow roads effortlessly.

They arrived at a house that was twice the size of Alessio's. 'Bianca always had a flair for the flamboyant,' he said drily as he killed the engine and they both stared at an imposing villa fronted by four Romanesque columns, the middle two standing on either side of a bank of shallow steps that led to the front door. 'When we were married and she discovered that money was no object, she made it her mission to spend. As I said, though, she ended up spending very little time here—too far from the action. A peaceful life by the sea was not her idea of fun.'

Lesley wondered what it must be like to nip out at lunchtime and buy a villa by the sea for no better reason than *you could*. 'Is your mother-in-law expecting me?'

'No,' Alessio admitted. 'As far as Claudia is concerned, I am here on a mission to take my wayward daughter in hand and bring her back with me to London. I thought it best to keep the unsavoury details of this little visit to myself.' He leaned across to flip open the passenger door. 'I didn't think,' he continued,

'That Rachel would have appreciated her grandmother know-ing the ins and outs of what has been going on. Right. Let's get this over and done with.'

Lesley felt for him. Underneath the cool, composed exterior she knew that he would be feeling a certain dread at the con-versation he would need to have with his daughter. He would be the Big, Bad Wolf and, for a sixteen-year-old, there would be no extenuating circumstances.

The ringing of the doorbell reverberated from the bowels of the villa. Just when Lesley thought that no one was in despite the abundance of lights on, she heard the sound of footsteps, and then the door was opening and there in front of them was a diminutive, timid looking woman in her mid-sixties: dark hair, dark, anxious eyes and a face that looked braced for an unpleas-ant surprise until she registered who was at the door and the harried expression broke into a beaming smile.

Lesley faded back, allowing for a rapid exchange of Italian, and only when there was a lull in the conversation did Claudia register her presence.

Despite what Alessio had said, Lesley had expected some-one harder, tougher and colder. Her daughter, after all, had not come out of Alessio's telling of the story as an exemplary char-acter, but now she could see why he had dismissed Claudia's ability to cope with Rachel.

Their arrival had been unannounced; they certainly had not been expected for supper. Alessio had been vague, Claudia told her, gripping Lesley's arm as she led them towards one of myriad rooms that comprised the ground floor of the ornately decorated house.

'I was not even sure that he would be coming at all,' she con-fided. 'Far less that he would be bringing a lady friend with him...'

Caught uncomfortably on the outside of a conversation she couldn't understand, Lesley could only smile weakly as Alessio fired off something in Italian and then they were entering the dining room where, evidently, dinner had been interrupted.

Standing a little behind both Claudia and Alessio, Lesley nervously looked around the room, feeling like an intruder in this strange family unit.

For a house by the coast, it was oddly furnished with ornate, dark wooden furniture, heavy drapes and a patterned rug that obscured most of the marble floor. Dominating one of the walls was a huge portrait of a striking woman with voluptuous dark good looks, wild hair falling over one shoulder and a haughty expression. Lesley assumed that it was Bianca and she could see why a boy of eighteen would have been instantly drawn to her.

The tension in the room was palpable. Claudia had bustled forward, but her movements were jerky and her smile was forced, while Alessio remained where he was, eyes narrowed, looking at the girl who had remained seated and was returning his stare with open insolence.

Rachel looked older than sixteen but then Lesley knew by now that she was only a few weeks away from her seventeenth birthday.

The tableau seemed to remain static for ages, even though it could only have been a matter of seconds. Claudia had launched into Italian and Rachel was pointedly ignoring her, although her gaze had shifted from Alessio, and now she was staring at Lesley with the concentration of an explorer spotting a new sub-species for the first time.

'And who are *you*?' She tossed her hair back, a mane of long, dark hair similar to the woman's in the portrait, although the resemblance ended there. Rachel had her father's aristocratic good looks. This was the gangly teenager whose leather mini-skirt Lesley had stealthily tried on. She reminded Lesley of the cool kids who had ruled the school as teenagers, except now a much older and more mature Lesley could see her for what she really was: a confused kid with a lot of attitude and a need to be defensive. She was scared of being hurt.

'Claudia.' Alessio turned to the older woman. 'If you would excuse us, I need to have a quiet word with my daughter.'

Claudia looked relieved and scuttled off, shutting the door quietly behind her.

Immediately Rachel launched into Italian and Alessio held up one commanding hand.

'English!'

It was the voice of complete and utter authority and his daughter glared at him, sullenly defiant but not quite brave enough to defy him.

'I'm Lesley.' Lesley moved forward into the simmering silence, not bothering to extend a hand in greeting because she knew it wouldn't be taken, instead sitting at the dining room table where she saw that Rachel had been playing a game on her phone.

'I helped to create that.' She pointed to the game with genuine pleasure. 'Three years ago.' She dumped the backpack onto the ground. 'I was seconded out to help design a website for a starter computer company and I got involved with the gaming side of things. It made a nice change. If I had only known how big that game would have become, I would have insisted on putting my name to it and then I would be getting royalties.'

Rachel automatically switched off the phone and turned it upside down.

Alessio had strolled towards his daughter and adopted the chair next to her so that she was now sandwiched between her father and Lesley.

'I know why you've come.' Rachel addressed her father in perfect, fluent English. 'And I'm not going back to England. I'm not going back to that stupid boarding school. I hate it there and I hate living with you. I'm staying here. Grandma Claudia said she's happy to have me.'

'I'm sure,' Alessio said in a measured voice, 'That you would love nothing more than to stay with your grandmother, running wild and doing whatever you want, but it is not going to happen.'

'You can't make me!'

Alessio sighed and raked his fingers through his hair. 'You're still a minor. I think you will find that I can.'

Looking between them, Lesley wondered if either realised just how alike they were: the proud jut of their chins, their stubbornness, even their mannerisms. Two halves of the same coin waiting to be aligned.

'I don't intend to have a protracted argument with you about this, Rachel. Returning to England is inevitable. We are both here because there is something else that needs to be discussed.'

He was the voice of stern authority and Lesley sighed as she reached down to the backpack and began extracting her folder, which she laid on the shiny table.

'What's that?' But her voice was hesitant under the defiance.

'A few weeks ago,' Alessio said impassively, 'I started getting emails. Lesley came to help me unravel them.'

Rachel was staring at the folder. Her face had paled and Lesley saw that she was gripping the arms of the chair. Impulsively she reached out and covered the thin, brown hand with hers and surprisingly it was allowed to remain there.

'It's thanks to me,' she said quietly, 'That all this stuff was uncovered. I'm afraid I looked through your bedroom. Your father, of course, would have rather I didn't, but it was the only way to compile the full picture.'

'You looked *through my things*?' Dark eyes were now focused accusingly on her, turned from Alessio. Lesley had become the target for Rachel's anger and confusion and Lesley breathed a little sigh of relief because, the less hostility directed at Alessio, the greater the chance of him eventually repairing his relationship with his daughter. It was worth it.

It was worth it because she loved him.

That realisation, springing out at her from nowhere, should have knocked her for six, but hadn't she already arrived that conclusion somewhere deep inside her? Hadn't she known that, underneath the arguments about lust and learning curves, stepping out of comfort zones and finding her sexuality, the simple truth of the matter was that she had been ambushed by the one thing she had never expected? It had struck her like a lightning bolt, penetrating straight through logic and common sense and obliterating her defences.

'You had no right,' Rachel was hissing.

Lesley let it wash over her and eventually the vitriol fizzled out and there was silence.

'So, tell me,' Alessio said in a voice that brooked no argument, 'About a certain Jack Perkins.'

Lesley left them after the initial setting out of the information. It was a sorry story of a lonely teenager, unhappy at boarding school, who had fallen in with the wrong crowd—or, rather, fallen in with the wrong boy. Piecing together the slips of paper and the stray emails, Lesley could only surmise that she had smoked a joint or two and then, vulnerable, knowing that she would be expelled from yet another school, she had become captive to a sixteen-year-old lad with a serious drug habit.

The finer details, she would leave for Alessio to discover. In the meantime, not quite knowing what to do with herself, she went outside and tried to get her thoughts in order.

Where did she go from here? She had always been in control of her life; she had always been proud of the fact that she knew where she was heading. She hadn't stopped for a minute to think that something as crazy as falling in love could ever derail her plans because she had always assumed that she would fall in love with someone who slotted into her life without causing too much of a ripple. She hadn't been lying when she had told Alessio that the kind of guy she imagined for herself would be someone very much like her.

How could she ever have guessed that the wrong person would come along and throw everything into chaos?

And what did she do now?

Still thinking, she felt rather than saw Alessio behind her and she turned around. Even in the darkness he had the bearing of a man carrying the weight of the world on his shoulders, and she instinctively walked towards him and wrapped her arms around his waist.

Alessio felt like he could hold onto her for ever. Wrong-footed by the intensity of that feeling, he pulled her closer and covered her mouth with his. His hand crept up underneath the tee-shirt and Lesley stepped back.

'Is sex the *only* thing you ever think about?' she asked sharply, and she answered the question herself, providing the affirmative she knew was the death knell to any relationship they had.

He wanted sex, she wanted more—it was as simple as that. Never had the gulf between them seemed so vast. It went far beyond the differences in their backgrounds, their life experiences or their expectations. It was the very basic difference between someone who wanted love and someone who only wanted sex.

'How is Rachel?' She folded her arms, making sure to keep some space between them.

'Shaken.'

'Is that all you have to say? That she's *shaken*?'

'Are you deliberately trying to goad me into an argument?' Alessio looked at her narrowly. 'I'm frankly not in the mood to soothe whatever feathers I've accidentally ruffled.' He shook his head, annoyed with himself for venting his stress on her, but he had picked something up—something stirring under the surface—even though, for the life of him, he couldn't understand what could possibly be bugging her. She certainly hadn't spent the past hour trying and failing to get through to a wayward teenager who had sat in semi-mute silence absorbing everything that was being said to her but responding to nothing.

He was frustrated beyond endurance and he wondered if his own frustration was making him see nuances in her behaviour that weren't there.

'And I'm frankly amazed that you could talk to your daughter, have this awkward conversation, and yet have so little to report back on the subject.'

'I didn't realise that it was my duty to *report back* to you,' Alessio grated and Lesley reddened.

'Wrong choice of words.' She sighed. Here were the cracks, she thought with a hollow sense of utter dejection. Things would go swimmingly well just so long as she could disentangle sex from love, but she was finding that she couldn't now. She spiked her fingers through her short hair and looked away from him, out towards the same black sea which his villa down the road overlooked.

She could see the way this would play out: making love would become a bittersweet experience; she would be the temporary mistress, making do, wondering when her time would be up. She suspected that that time would come very quickly once they returned to England. The refreshing, quirky novelty of bedding a woman with brains, who spoke her mind, who could navigate a computer faster than he could, would soon pall and he would begin itching to return to the unchallenging women who had been his staple diet.

Nor would he want a woman around who reminded him of the sore topic of his daughter and her misbehaviour, which had almost cost him a great deal of money.

'Would it be okay if I went to talk to her?' Lesley asked, and Alessio looked at her in surprise.

'What would you hope to achieve?'

'It might help talking to someone who isn't you.'

'Even though she sees you as the perpetrator of the "searching the bedroom" crime? I should have stepped in there and told her that that was a joint decision.'

'Why?' Lesley asked with genuine honesty. 'I guess you had enough on your plate to deal with and, besides, I will walk away from this and never see either of you again. If she pins the blame on me, then I can take it.'

Alessio's jaw hardened but he made no comment. 'She's still

in the dining room,' he said. 'At least, that's where I left her. Claudia has disappeared to bed, and frankly I don't blame her. In the morning, I shall tell her that my daughter has agreed that the best thing is to return to England with me.'

'And school?'

'As yet to be decided, but it's safe to say that she won't be returning to her old stamping ground.'

'That's good.' She fidgeted, feeling his distance and knowing that, while she had been responsible for creating it, she still didn't like it. 'I won't be long,' she promised, and backed away.

Like a magnet, his presence seemed to want to pull her back towards him but she forced herself through to the dining room, little knowing what she would find.

She half-expected Rachel to have disappeared into another part of the house, but the teenager was still sitting in the same chair, staring vacantly through the window.

'I thought we might have a chat,' Lesley said, approaching her warily and pulling a chair out to sit right next to her.

'What for? Have you decided that you want to apologise for going through my belongings when *you had no right*?'

'No.'

Rachel looked at her sullenly. She switched on her mobile phone, switched it off again and rested it on the table.

'Your dad's been worried sick.'

'I'm surprised he could take the time off to be worried,' Rachel muttered, fiddling with the phone and then eventually folding her arms and looking at Lesley with unmitigated antagonism. 'This is all your fault.'

'Actually, it's got nothing to do with me. I'm only here because of you and you're in this position because of what you did.'

'I don't have to sit here and listen to some stupid employee preach to me.' But she remained on the chair, glaring.

'And I don't have to sit here, but I want to, because I grew up without a mum and I know it can't be easy for you.'

'Oh puh…lease….' She dragged that one word out into a lengthy, disdainful, childish snort of contempt.

'Especially,' Lesley persevered, 'As Alessio—your father—isn't the easiest person in the world when it comes to touchy-feely conversations.'

'*Alessio*? Since when are you on first-name terms with my father?'

'He wants nothing more than to have a relationship with you, you know,' Lesley said quietly. She wondered if this was what love did, made you want to do your utmost to help the object of your affections, to make sure they were all right, even if you knew that they didn't return your love and would happily exit your life without much of a backward glance.

'And that's why he never bothered to get in touch when I was growing up? *Ever*?'

Lesley's heart constricted. 'Is that what you really believe?'

'It's what I was told by my mum.'

'I think you'll find that your father did his best to keep in touch, to visit… Well, you'll have to talk to him about that.'

'I'm not going to be talking to him again.'

'Why didn't you come clean with your dad, or even one of the teachers, when that boy started threatening you?' She had found a couple of crumpled notes and had quickly got the measure of a lad who had been happy to extort as much of Rachel's considerable pocket money as he could by holding it over her head that he had proof of the one joint she had smoked with him and was willing to lie to everyone that it had been more than that. When the pocket money had started running out, he must have decided to go directly to the goose that was laying the golden eggs: pay up or else he would go to the press and disclose that one of the biggest movers and shakers in the business world had a druggie teenage daughter. 'You must have been scared stiff,' she mused, half to herself.

'That's none of your business.'

Some of the aggression had left her voice. When Lesley

looked at her, she saw the teenage girl who had been bullied and threatened by someone willing to take advantage of her one small error of judgement.

'Well, you dad's going to sort all of that out. He'll make the whole thing go away.' She heard the admiring warmth in her voice and cleared her throat. 'You should give him a chance.'

'And what's it to you?'

Lesley blushed.

'Oh, right.' She gave a knowing little laugh and sniffed. 'Well, I'm not about to give anyone a chance, and I don't care if he sorts that thing out or not. So. He dumped me and I had to traipse around with my mum and all her boyfriends.'

'You *knew* your mum…err…? Well, none of my business.' She stood up. 'You should give your dad a chance and at least listen to what he has to say. He tried very hard to keep in touch with you but, well, you should let him explain how that went—and you should go get some sleep.'

She exited the room, closing the door quietly behind her. Had she got through to Rachel? Who knew? It would take more than one conversation to break down some of those teenage walls, but several things had emerged.

Aside from the fact that everything was now on the table—and, whether she admitted it or not, that would have come as a huge relief to Rachel—it was clear that the girl had had no idea just how hard her father had tried to keep in touch with her, how hard he had fought to maintain contact.

And Alessio had no idea that his daughter was aware of Bianca's wild, promiscuous temperament.

Join those two things together, throw into the mix the fact that Rachel had kept a scrapbook of photos and cuttings, and Lesley suspected that an honest conversation between father and daughter would go some distance to opening the door to a proper relationship.

And if Rachel was no longer at a boarding school, but at a

day school in London, they would both have the opportunity to start building a future and leaving the past behind.

She went outside to find Alessio still there and she quietly told him what she had learned during the conversation with his daughter.

'She thinks you abandoned her,' she reinforced bluntly. 'And she would have been devastated at the thought of that. It might explain why she's been such a rebel, but she's young. You're going to have to take the lead and lower your defences if you want to get through to her.'

Alessio listened, head tilted to one side, and when she had finished talking he nodded slowly and then told her in return what he intended to do to sort the small matter of a certain Jack Perkins. He had already contacted someone he trusted to supply him with information about the boy and he had enough at his disposal to pay a visit to his parents and make sure the matter was resolved quickly and efficiently, never again to rear its ugly head.

'When I'm through,' Alessio promised in a voice of steel, 'That boy will think twice before he goes near an Internet café again, never mind threatening anyone.'

Lesley believed him and she didn't doubt that Jack Perkins' life of crime was about to come crashing down around his head. It had transpired that his family was well-connected. Not only would they be horrified at what their son had done, and the drug problems he was experiencing, but his father would know that Alessio's power stretched far; if he were to be crossed again by a delinquent boy, then who knew what the repercussions would be?

The problem, Alessio assured her, would wait until he returned to the UK. It wasn't going anywhere and, whilst he could hand over the business of wrapping it up to a trusted advisor and friend, he would much rather do it himself.

'When I'm attacked,' he said softly, 'Then I prefer to retaliate using my own fists rather than relying on my bodyguards.'

Everything, Lesley thought, had been neatly wrapped up and she was certain that father and daughter would eventually find their way and become the family unit they deserved to be.

Which left her...the spectator whose purpose had been served and whose time had come to depart.

They drove in silence back to Alessio's villa. He planned on returning to his mother-in-law's the following morning and he would talk to his daughter once again.

He didn't say what that conversation would be, but Lesley knew that he had taken on board what she had said, and he would try and grope his way to some sort of mutual ground on which they could both converse.

Alessio knew that, generally speaking, the outcome to what could have been a disaster had been good.

Jack Perkins had revealed problems with his daughter that would now be addressed, and Lesley's mediation had been pretty damn fantastic. How could his daughter not have known that he had tried his hardest? He would set her straight on that. He could see that Rachel had been lost and therefore far too vulnerable in a school that had clearly allowed too much freedom. He might or might not take them to task on that.

'Thanks,' he suddenly said gruffly as they pulled up into the carport at the side of the villa. He killed the engine and looked at Lesley. 'You didn't just sort out who was behind this but you went the extra mile, and we both know, gentle bribe or no gentle bribe, you didn't have to do that.' Right now, all he wanted to do was get inside the villa, carry her upstairs to the bedroom and make love to her. Take all night making love to her. He had never felt as close to any woman.

No, Lesley thought with a tinge of bitterness, she really had had no need to go the extra mile, but she had, and it had had nothing to do with bribes, gentle or otherwise.

'We should talk,' she said after a while.

Alessio stilled. 'I thought we just had.'

Lesley hopped out of the car, slammed the door behind her

and waited for him. Just then, in the car, it had felt way too intimate. Give it just a few more seconds sitting there, breathing him in, hearing that lazy, sexy drawl, and all her good intentions would have gone down the drain.

'Want to tell me what this is all about?' was the first thing he asked the second they were inside his villa. He threw the car keys on the hand-carved sideboard by the front door and led the way into the kitchen where he helped himself to a long glass of water from a bottle in the fridge. Then he sat down and watched as she took the seat furthest away from him.

'How long,' she finally asked, 'Do you plan on staying here?'

'Where is that question leading?' For the first time, he could feel quicksand underneath his feet and he didn't like it. He wished he had had something stronger to drink; a whisky would have gone down far better than a glass of water. He didn't like the way she had sat a million miles across the room from him; he didn't like the mood she had been in for the past few hours; he didn't like the way she couldn't quite seem to meet his eyes. 'Oh, for God's sake,' he muttered when she didn't say anything. 'At least until the end of the week. Rachel and I have a few things to sort out, not to mention a frank discussion of where she will go to school. There are a lot of fences to be mended and they won't be mended overnight; it'll take a few days before we can even work out where the holes are. But what has that got to do with anything?'

'I won't be staying on here with you.' She cleared her throat and took a deep breath. 'I do realise that I promised I would stay the week, but I think my job here is done, and it's time for me to return to London.'

'Your job here *is done*?' Alessio could not believe what he was hearing.

'Yes, and I just want to say that there's every chance that you and your daughter will find a happy solution to the difficulties you've been experiencing in your relationship.'

'Your job here...*is done*? So you're *heading back*?'

'I don't see the point of staying on.'

'And I don't believe I'm hearing this. What do you mean you don't *see the point of staying on*?' He point-blank refused to ask *what about us?* That was not a question that would ever pass his lips. He remembered what she had said about wanting to head back out there, get into the thick of the dating scene— now that she had used him to reintroduce her to the world of sex; now that she had overcome her insecurities, thanks to him.

Pride slammed in and he looked at her coldly.

'What we have, Alessio, isn't going anywhere. We both agreed on that, didn't we?' She could have kicked herself for the plaintive request she heard in her voice, the request begging him to contradict her. 'And I'm not interested in having a fling until we both run out of steam. Actually, probably until we get back to London. I'm not in the market for a holiday romance.'

'And what are you in the market for?' Alessio asked softly.

Lesley tilted her chin and returned his cool stare. Was she about to reveal that she was in the market for a long-term, for ever, happy-ever-after, committed relationship? Would she say that so that he could naturally assume that she was talking about *him*? Wanting that relationship *with him*? It would be the first conclusion he would reach. Women, he had told her, always seemed to want more than he was prepared to give. He would assume that she had simply joined the queue.

There was no way that she would allow her dignity to be trampled into the ground.

'Right now...' her voice was steady and controlled, giving nothing away '...all I want is to further my career. The company is still growing. There are loads of opportunities to grow with it, even perhaps to be transferred to another part of the country. I want to be there to take advantage of those opportunities.' She thought she sounded like someone trying to sell themselves at an interview, but she held her ground and her eyes remained clear and focused.

'And the career opportunities are going to disappear unless you hurry back to London as fast as you can?'

'I realise you'll probably pull that big job out from under our feet.' That thought only now struck her, as did the conclusion that she wasn't going to win employee of the week if her boss found out that she had been instrumental in losing a job that would bring hundreds of thousands of pounds to the company and extend their reach far wider than they had anticipated.

Alessio wondered whether her thirst for a rewarding career would make her change her mind about not staying on, about not continuing what they had. It revolted him to think that it might. He had never had to use leverage to get any woman into his bed and he wasn't about to start now.

Nor had he ever had to beg any woman to stay in his bed once she was there, and he certainly wasn't about to start *that* now.

'You misjudge me,' he said coldly. 'I offered that job to your boss and I am not a man who would renege on a promise, least of all over an affair that goes belly up. Your company has the job and everything that goes with it.'

Lesley lowered her eyes. He was a man of honour. She had known that. He just wasn't a man in love.

'I also think that when I decide to embark on another relationship.'

'You mean after you've launched yourself back into the singles scene.'

She shrugged, allowing him to think something she knew to be way off mark. She could think of nothing less likely than painting the town red and clubbing.

'I just feel that, if I decide to get involved with anyone, then it should be with the person who is right for me. So, I think we should call it a day for us.'

'Good luck with your search,' Alessio gritted. 'And, now that you've said your piece, I shall go and do some work downstairs. Feel free to use the bedroom where your suitcase has been put; I shall sleep in one of the other bedrooms and you can book your return flight first thing in the morning. Naturally, I will cover the cost.' He stood up and walked towards the door. 'I intend to go to Claudia's by nine tomorrow. If I don't see you before I go, have a safe flight. The money I owe you will be in your bank account by the time you land.' He nodded curtly and shut the kitchen door behind him.

This is all for the best, Lesley thought, staring at the closed door and trying to come to terms with the thought that she would probably never see him again.

It was time for her to move on...

CHAPTER NINE

LESLEY PAUSED IN front of the towering glass house and stared up and up and up. Somewhere in there, occupying three floors in what was the most expensive office block in central London, Alessio would be hard at work. At least, she hoped so. She hoped he wasn't out of the country. She didn't think she could screw up her courage and make this trip to see him a second time.

A month ago, she had walked out on him and she hadn't heard from him since. Not a word. He had duly deposited a wad of money into her account, as he had promised—far too much, considering she had bailed on their trip a day in.

How had his talk with his daughter turned out? Had they made amends, begun the protracted process of repairing their relationship? Where was she at school now?

Had he found someone else? Had he found her replacement?

For the past few weeks, those questions had churned round and round in her head, buzzing like angry hornets, growing fat on her misery until... Well, until something else had come along that was so big and so overwhelming that there was no room left in her head for those questions.

She took a deep breath and propelled her reluctant feet forward until she was standing in the foyer of the building, surrounded by a constant river of people coming and going, some in snappy suits, walking with an air of purpose; others, clearly tourists, staring around them, wondering where they should go to get to the viewing gallery or to one of the many restaurants.

In front of her a long glass-and-metal counter separated a bank of receptionists from the public. They each had a snazzy, small computer screen in front of them and they were all impeccably groomed.

She had worked out what she was going to say, having decided beforehand that it wasn't going to be easy gaining access to the great Alessio Baldini—that, in fact, he might very well refuse to see her at all. She had formulated a borderline sob story, filled with innuendo and just enough of a suggestion that, should she not be allowed up to whatever floor he occupied, he would be a very angry man.

It worked. Ten minutes after she had arrived, a lift was carrying her up to one of the top floors, from which she knew he would be able to overlook all of London. She had no idea how much the rent was on a place like this and her head spun thinking about it. She had been told that she would be met at the lift, and she was, but it was only as they were approaching his office that nerves really truly kicked in and she had to fight to keep her breathing steady and even and not to hyperventilate.

She was aware of his personal assistant asking concerned questions and she knew that she was answering those questions in a reassuring enough voice, but she felt sick to the stomach.

By the time they reached his office suite, she was close to fainting.

She didn't even know if she was doing the right thing. The decision to come here had been taken and then rejected and then taken again so many times that she had lost count.

The outer office, occupied by his personal assistant, was luxurious. In one corner, a massive semi-circular desk housed several phones and a computer terminal. Against one of the walls was a long, grey bench-like sofa that looked very uncomfort-

able. Against the other wall was a smooth, walnut built-in cupboard with no handles, just a bank of smooth wood.

It was an intimidating office, but not as intimidating as the
massive door behind which Alessio would be waiting for her.

And waiting for her he most certainly was. He had been in
the middle of a conference call when he had been buzzed by
his secretary and informed that a certain Lesley Fox was downstairs in reception and should she be sent away or brought up?

Alessio had cut short his conference call without any pre-
amble. His better self had told him to refuse her entry. Why
on earth would he want to have anything further to do with a
woman who had slept with him, had not denied having slept
with him as part of her preparations for entering the world of
hectic dating and then walked out of his life without a backward glance? Why would he engage in any further conversation with someone who had made it perfectly clear that he was
not the sort of man she was looking for, even though they had
slept together? Even though there had been no complaints there!

He had made sure that the money owed to her was deposited
into her bank account, and had had no word from her confirm-
ing whether she had received it or not, despite the fact that he
had paid her over and above the agreed amount, including paying her for time she had not worked for him at all.

The time he had wasted waiting for a phone call or text from
her had infuriated him.

Not to mention the time he had wasted just *thinking* about
her. She was hardly worth thinking about and yet, in the past
few weeks, she had been on his mind like a background refrain
he just couldn't get out of his head.

And so, when he had been called on his internal line to be
told that she was there in the building, that she wanted to see
him, there had been no contest in his head.

He had no idea what she could possibly want, and underwrit-
ing his curiosity was the altogether pleasant day dream that she
had returned to beg for him back. Perhaps the wild and won-

derful world of chatting up random men in bars and clubs had not quite lived up to expectation. Maybe having fun with the wrong guy was not quite the horror story she had first thought. Maybe she missed the sex; she had certainly seemed to enjoy every second of being touched by him.

Or, more prosaically, maybe her boss had sent her along on something to do with the job he had put their way. It made sense. She knew him. Indeed, they had landed that lucrative contract without even having to tender for it because of her. If anything needed to be discussed, her boss would naturally assume that she should be the one to do it and there would be no way that she could refuse. At least, not unless she started pouring out the details of her private life, which he knew she would never do.

He frowned, not caring for that scenario, which he immediately jettisoned so that he could focus as he waited for her on more pleasurable ones.

By the time his secretary, Claire, announced her arrival, through the internal line to which she exclusively had access, Alessio had come to the conclusion that he was only mildly curious as to the nature of her surprise visit—that he didn't care a whit what she had to say to him and that the only reason he was even allowing her entry into his office was because he was gentlemanly enough not to have her chucked out from the foyer in full view of everyone.

Still, he made her wait a while, before sitting back in his leather chair and informing Claire that his visitor could be ushered in—cool, calm and screamingly forbidding.

Lesley felt the breath catch jaggedly in her throat as she heard the door close quietly behind her. Of course, she hadn't forgotten what he looked like. How could she when his image had been imprinted in her brain with the red-hot force of a branding iron?

But nothing had prepared her for the cold depths of those dark eyes or the intimidating silence that greeted her arrival in his office.

She didn't know whether to keep standing or to confidently

head for one of the leather chairs in front of his desk so that she could sit down. She certainly felt as though her legs didn't have much strength left in them.

Eventually, she only scuttled towards one of the chairs when he told her to sit, simultaneously glancing at his watch as though to remind her that, whilst she might have been offered a seat, she should make sure that she didn't get too comfortable because he didn't have a lot of time for her.

This was the guy she had fallen in love with. She knew she would have dented his pride when she had walked out on him, but still she had half-hoped that he might contact her in some way, if only to ask whether she had received the money he had deposited into her account.

Or else to fill her in on what had happened in his family drama. Surely that would have been the polite thing to do?

But not a word, and she knew that had she not arrived on his doorstep, so to speak, then she would never have seen him again. Right now, those brooding dark eyes were surveying her with all the enthusiasm of someone contemplating something the cat had inadvertently brought in.

'So,' Alessio finally drawled, tapping his rarely used fountain pen on the surface of his desk. 'To what do I owe this unexpected pleasure?' To his disgust, he couldn't help but think that she looked amazing.

He had made one half-hearted attempt to replace her with one of the women he had dated several months ago, a hot blonde with big breasts and a face that could turn heads from a mile away, but he had barely been able to stick it out for an evening in her company.

How could he when he had been too busy thinking of the woman slumped in the chair in front of him? Not in her trademark jeans this time but a neat pair of dark trousers and a snug little jacket that accentuated the long, lean lines of her body.

On cue, he felt himself begin to respond, which irritated the hell out of him.

'I'm sorry if I'm disturbing you,' Lesley managed. Now that she was here, she realised that she couldn't just drop her bombshell on him without any kind of warning.

'I'm a busy man.' He gesticulated widely and shot her a curving smile that contained no warmth. 'But never let it be said that I'm rude. An ex-lover deserves at least a few minutes of my time.'

Lesley bit her tongue and refrained from telling him that that remark in itself was the height of rudeness.

'I won't be long. How is Rachel?'

'You made this journey to talk about my daughter?'

Lesley shrugged. 'Well, I became quite involved in what was going on. I'm curious to know how things turned out in the end.'

Alessio was pretty sure that she hadn't travelled to central London and confronted him at his office just to ask one or two questions about Rachel, but he was willing to play along with the game until she revealed the true reason for showing up.

'My daughter has been...subdued since this whole business came out in the open. She returned to London without much fuss and she seems relieved that the boarding school option is now no longer on the cards. Naturally, I have had to lay down some ground rules for her—the most important of which is that I don't want to hear from anyone in the school that she's been acting up.' Except he had been far less harsh in delivering that message than it sounded.

Rachel might have been a complete idiot, led astray for reasons that were fairly understandable, but he had to accept his fair share of the blame as well. He had taken his eye off the ball.

Now, there was dialogue between them, and he had high hopes that in time that dialogue would turn into fluent conversation. Would that be asking too much?

He had certainly taken the unfortunate affair by the horns and sorted it all out, personally paying a visit to the boy's parents and outlining for them in words of one syllable what would happen if he ever had another email from the lad.

He had shied away from taking the full hard line, however, confident that the boy's parents, who had seemed decent but bewildered, would take matters in hand. They both travelled extensively and only now had it dawned on them that in their absence they had left behind a lonely young man with a drug problem that had fortunately been caught in the bud.

Rachel had not commented on the outcome, but he had been shrewd enough to see the relief on her face. She had found herself caught up in something far bigger than she had anticipated and, in the end, he had come to her rescue, although that was something he had taken care not to ram home.

'That's good.' Lesley clasped her hands together.

'So is there anything else you want? Because if that's all…' He looked at the slender column of her neck, her down-bent head, the slump of her shoulders, and wanted to ask her if she missed him.

Where the hell had *that* notion come from?

'Just one other thing.' She cleared her throat and looked at him with visible discomfort.

And, all at once, Alessio knew where she was going with this visit of hers. She wanted back in with him. She had walked away with her head held high and a load of nonsense about needing to find the right guy, wherever the hell he might be. But, having begun her search, she had obviously fast reached the conclusion that the right guy wasn't going to be as easy to pin down as she had thought and, in the absence of Mr Right, Mr Fantastic Sex would do instead.

Over his dead body.

Although, it had to be said that the thought of her begging for him was an appealing one. He turned that pleasant fantasy over in his head and very nearly smiled.

He was no longer looking at his watch. Instead, he pushed the chair away from the desk and relaxed back, his fingers lightly linked together on his flat, hard stomach.

Should he rescue her from the awkwardness of what she

wanted to say? Or should he just wait in growing silence until her eventual discomfort propelled her into speech? Both options carried their own special appeal.

Eventually, with a rueful sigh that implied that far too much of his valuable time had already been wasted, he said, shaking his head, 'Sorry. It's a little too late for you.'

Lesley looked at him in sudden confusion. She knew that this was an awkward situation. She had appeared at his office and demanded to see him, and now here she was, body as stiff as a plank of wood, sitting in mute silence while she tried to work how best to say what she had come to say. No wonder he wanted to shuffle her out as fast as he could. He must be wondering what the hell she was doing, wasting his time.

'You're—you're busy,' she stammered, roused into speech as her brain sluggishly cranked back into gear just enough to understand that he wanted her out because he had more important things to do.

Once again, she wondered whether she had been replaced. Once again, she wondered whether he had reverted to type, back to the sexy blondes with the big breasts and the big hair.

'Have you been busy?' she blurted out impulsively, almost but not quite covering her mouth with her hand in an instinctive and futile attempt to retract her words.

Alessio got her drift immediately. No matter that the question hadn't been completed. He could tell from the heightened colour in her cheeks and her startled, embarrassed eyes that she was asking him about his sex life, and he felt a groundswell of satisfaction.

'Busy? Explain.'

'Work. You know.' When she had thought about having this conversation, about seeing him again, she had underestimated the dramatic effect he would have on her senses. In her head, she had pictured herself cool, composed—a little nervous, understandably, but strong enough to say her piece and leave.

Instead, here she was, her thoughts all over the place and her body responding to him on that deep, subterranean level that was so disconcerting. The love which she had hoped might have found a more settled place—somewhere not to the forefront—pounded through her veins like a desperate virus, destroying everything in its path and making her stumble over her words.

Not to mention she'd hoped not to ask questions that should never have left her mouth, because she could tell from the knowing look in those deep, dark eyes that he knew perfectly well what she had wanted to know when she had asked him whether he had been 'busy'.

'Work's been…work. It's always busy. Outside of work…' Alessio thought of his non-date with a non-contender for a partner and felt his hackles rise that the woman staring at him with those big, almond-shaped brown eyes had driven him into seeking out someone for company simply to try and replace the images of her he had somehow ended up storing in his head. He shrugged, letting her assume that his private life was a delicate place to which she was not invited—hilarious, considering just how much she knew about him. 'What about you?' He smoothly changed the subject. 'Have you found your perfect soul-mate as yet?'

'What did you mean when you said that it was a little too late for me?' The remark had been playing at the back of her mind and she knew that she needed him to spell it out in words of one syllable.

'If you think that you can walk back into my life because you had a bit of trouble locating Mr Right, then it's not going to happen.'

Pride. But then, what the hell was wrong with pride? He certainly had no intention of telling her the truth, which was that he was finding it hard to rid his system of her, even though she should have been no more than a blurry memory by now.

He was a man who moved on when it came to women. Always had been—never mind when it came to moving on from a woman who had dumped him!

Just thinking about that made his teeth snap together in rage.

'I don't intend walking back into your life,' Lesley replied coolly. So, now she knew where she stood. Was she still happy that she had come here? Frankly, she could still turn around and walk right back through that door but, yes, she was happy she was here, whatever the outcome.

Alessio's eyes narrowed. He noticed what he had failed to notice before—the rigid way she was sitting, as though every nerve in her body was on red-hot alert; the way she was fiddling with her fingers; the determined tilt of her chin.

'Then why are you here?' His voice was brusque and dismissive. Having lingered on the pleasant scenario of her pleading to be a part of his life once again, he was irrationally annoyed that he had misread whatever signals she had been giving off.

'I'm here because I'm pregnant.'

There. She had said it. The enormous thing that had been absorbing every minute of every day of her life since she had done that home pregnancy test over three days ago was finally out in the open.

She had skipped a period. It hadn't even occurred to her that she could be pregnant; she had forgotten all about that torn condom. She had had far too much on her mind for that little detail to surface. It was only as she'd tallied the missed period with tender breasts that she remembered the very first time they had made love...and the outcome of that had been very clear to see in the bright blue line on that little plastic stick.

She hadn't bothered to buy more, to repeat the test. Why would she do that, when in her heart she knew that the result was accurate?

She had had a couple of days to get used to the idea, to move from feeling as though she was falling into a bottomless hole to gradually accepting that, whatever the landing, she would have to deal with it; that the hole wouldn't be bottomless.

She had had time to engage her brain in beginning trying to work out how her life would change, because there was no way that she would be getting rid of this baby. And, as her brain had engaged, her emotions had followed suit and a flutter of excitement and curiosity had begun to work their way into the equation.

She was going to be a mum. She hadn't banked on that happening, and she knew that it would bring a host of problems, but she couldn't snuff out that little flutter of excitement.

Boy or girl? What would it look like? A miniature Alessio? Certainly, a permanent reminder of the only man she knew she would ever love.

And should she tell him? If she loved him, would she ruin his life by telling him that he was going to be a father—again? Another unplanned and unwanted pregnancy. Would he think that she was trapping him, just like Bianca had, into marriage for all the wrong reasons?

Wouldn't the kindest thing be to keep silent, to let him carry on with his life? It was hardly as though he had made any attempt at all to contact her after she had left Italy! She had been a bit of fun and he had been happy enough to watch her walk away. Wouldn't the best solution be to let him remember her as a bit of fun rather than detonate a bomb that would have far-reaching and permanent ramifications he would not want?

In the end, she just couldn't bring herself to deny him the opportunity of knowing that he was going to be a father. The baby was half his and he had his rights, whatever the outcome might be.

But it was still a bomb she'd detonated, and she could see that in the way his expression changed from total puzzlement to dawning comprehension and then to shock and horror.

'I'm sorry,' she said in a clear, high voice. 'I know this is probably the last thing you were expecting.'

Alessio was finding it almost impossible to join his thoughts up. Pregnant. She was pregnant. For once he couldn't find the right words to deal with what was going through his head, to express himself. In fact, he actually couldn't find any words at all.

'It was that first time,' Lesley continued into the lengthening silence. 'Do you remember?'

'The condom split.'

'It was a one in a thousand chance.'

'The condom split and now you're pregnant.' He leant forward and raked his fingers through his hair, keeping his head lowered.

'It was no one's fault,' Lesley said, chewing her lower lip and looking at his reaction, the way he couldn't even look at her. Right now he hated her; that was clear. He was listening to the sound of his life being derailed and, whether down to a burst condom or not, he was somehow blaming her.

'I wasn't going to come here...'

That brought his head up, snapping to attention, and he looked at her in utter disbelief. 'What, you were just going to disappear with my baby inside you and not tell me about it?'

'Can you blame me?' Lesley muttered defensively. 'I know the story about how you were trapped into a loveless marriage by your last wife; I know what the consequences of that were.'

'Those consequences being...?' When Bianca had smiled smugly and told him that he was going to be a father, he had been utterly devastated. Now, strangely, the thought that this woman might have spared him devastation second time round didn't sit right. In fact, he was furious that the thought might even have crossed her mind although, in some rational part of himself, he could fully understand why. He also knew the answer to his own stupid question, although he waited for her to speak while his thoughts continued to spin and spin, as though they were in a washing machine with the speed turned high.

'No commitment,' Lesley said without bothering to dress it up. 'No one ever allowed to get too close. No woman ever thinking that she could get her foot through the door, because you were always ready to bang that door firmly shut the minute you smelled any unwanted advances in that direction. And please don't look at me as though I'm talking rubbish, Alessio.

We both know I'm not. So excuse me for thinking that it might have been an idea to spare you the nightmare of…of this…'

'So you would have just disappeared?' He held onto that tangible, unappealing thought and allowed his anger to build up. 'Walked away? And then what—in sixteen years' time I would have found out that I'd fathered a child when he or she came knocking on my door asking to meet me?'

'I hadn't thought that far into the future.' She shot him a mutinous look from under her lashes. 'I looked into a future a few months away and what I saw was a man who would resent finding himself trapped again.'

'You can't speculate on what my reactions might or might not have been.'

'Well, it doesn't matter. I'm here now. I've told you. And there's something else—I want you to know straight off that I'm not asking you for anything. You know the situation and that's my duty done.' She began standing up and found that she was trembling. Alessio stared at her with open-mouthed incredulity.

'Where do you think you're going?'

'I'm leaving.' She hesitated. This was the right time to leave. She had done what she had come to do. There was no way that she intended to put any pressure on him to do anything but carry on with his precious, loveless existence, free from the responsibility of a clinging woman and an unwanted baby.

Yet his presence continued to pull her towards him like a powerful magnet.

'You're kidding!' Alessio's voice cracked with the harshness of a whip. 'You breeze in here, tell me that you're carrying my child, and then announce that you're on your way!'

'I told you, I don't want anything from you.'

'What you want is by the by.'

'I beg your pardon?'

'It's impossible having this sort of conversation here. We need to get out, go somewhere else. My place.'

Lesley stared at him in utter horror. Was he mad? The last

thing she wanted was to be cooped up with him on his turf. It was bad enough that she was in his office. Besides, where else was the conversation going to go?

Financial contributions; of course. He was a wealthy man and in possession of a muddy conscience; he would salve it by flinging money at it.

'I realise you might want to help out on the money front,' she said stiltedly. 'But, believe it or not, that's not why I came here. I can manage perfectly well on my own. I can take maternity leave and anyway, with what I do, I should be able to work from home.'

'You don't seem to be hearing me.' He stood up and noticed how she fell back.

She might want him out of her life but it wasn't going to happen. Too bad if her joyful hunt for the right guy had crashed and burned; she was having his baby and he was going to be part of her life whether she liked it or not.

The thought was not as unwelcome as he might have expected. In fact, he was proud of how easily he was beginning to take the whole thing on board.

It made sense, of course. He was older and wiser. He had mellowed over time. Now that sick feeling of having an abyss yawn open at his feet was absent.

'If you want to discuss the financial side of things, then we can do that at a later date. Right now, I'll give you time to digest everything.'

'I've digested it. Now, sit back down.' This was not where he wanted to be. An office couldn't contain him. He felt restless, in need of moving. He wanted the space of his apartment. But there was no way she would go there with him; he was astute enough to decipher that from her dismayed reaction to the suggestion. And he wasn't going to push it.

It crossed his mind that this might have come as a bolt from the blue for him, turning his life on its axis and sending it spiralling off in directions he could never have predicted, but it would likewise have been the same for her. Yet here she was, apparently in full control. But then, hadn't he always known that there was a thread of absolute bravery and determination running through her?

And when she said that she didn't want anything from him, he knew that she meant it. This situation could not have been more different from the one in which he had found himself all those years ago.

Not that that made any difference. He was still going to be a presence in her life now whether she liked it or not.

Lesley had reluctantly sat back down and was now looking at him with a sullen lack of enthusiasm. She had expected more of an explosion of rage, in the middle of which she could have sneaked off, leaving him to calm down. He seemed to be handling the whole thing a great deal more calmly than she had expected.

'This isn't just about me contributing to the mother and baby fund,' he said, in case she had got it into her head that it might be. 'You're having my baby and I intend to be involved in this every single step of the way.'

'What are you talking about?'

'Do you really take me for a man who walks away from responsibility?'

'I'm not your ex-wife!' Lesley said tightly, fists clenched on her lap. 'I haven't come here looking for anything and you certainly don't owe me or this baby anything!'

'I'm not going to be a part-time father,' Alessio gritted. 'I was a part-time father once, not of my own choosing, and it won't happen again.'

Not once had Lesley seen the situation from that angle. Not once had she considered that he would want actual, active involvement, yet it made perfect sense. 'What are you suggesting?' she asked, bewildered and on the back foot.

'What else is there to suggest but marriage?'

For a few frozen seconds, Lesley thought that she might

have misheard him, but when she looked at him his face was set, composed and unyielding.

She released a hysterical laugh that fizzled out very quickly. 'I don't believe I'm hearing this. Are you mad? Get married?'

'Why so shocked?'

'Because...' *Because you don't love me. You probably don't even like me very much right now.* 'Because having a baby isn't the right reason for two people to get married,' she said in as controlled a voice as she could muster. 'You of all people should know that! Your marriage ended in tears because you went into it for all the wrong reasons.'

'Any marriage involving my ex-wife would have ended in tears.' Alessio was finding it hard to grapple with the notion that she had laughed at his suggestion of marriage. Was she *that* intent on finding Mr Right that she couldn't bear the thought of being hitched to him? It was downright offensive! 'You're not Bianca, and you need to look at the bigger picture.' Was that overly aggressive? He didn't think so but he saw the way she stiffened and he tempered what he was going to say with a milder, more conciliatory voice. 'By which I mean that this isn't about us as individuals but about a child that didn't ask to be brought into the world. To do the best for him or her is to provide a united family.'

'To do the best for him or her is to provide two loving parents who live separately instead of two resentful ones joined in a union where there's no love lost.' Just saying those words out loud made her feel ill because what she should really have said was that there was no worse union than one in which love was given but not returned. What she could have told him was that she could predict any future where they were married, and what she could see was him eventually loathing her for being the other half of a marriage he might have initiated but which had eventually become his prison cell.

There was a lot she could have told him but instead all she said was, 'There's no way I would ever marry you.'

CHAPTER TEN

THE PAIN STARTED just after midnight. Five months before her due date. Lesley awoke, at first disorientated, then terrified when, on inspection, she realised that she was bleeding.

What did that mean? She had read something about that in one of the many books Alessio had bought for her. Right now, however, her brain had ceased to function normally. All she could think of doing was getting on her mobile phone and calling him.

She had knocked him back, had told him repeatedly that she wasn't going to marry him, yet he had continued to defy her low expectations by stealthily becoming a rock she could lean on. He was with her most evenings, totally disregarding what she had said to him about pregnancy not being an illness. He had attended the antenatal appointments with her. He had cunningly incorporated Rachel into the picture, bringing his daughter along with him many of the times he'd visited her, talking as though the future held the prospect of them all being a family, even though Lesley had been careful to steer clear of agreeing to any such sweeping statements.

What was he hoping to achieve? She didn't know. He didn't love her and not once had he claimed to.

But, bit by bit, she knew that she was beginning to rely on him—and it was never so strongly proved as now, when the sound of his deep voice over the end of the phone had the immediate effect of calming her panicked nerves.

'I should have stayed the night,' was the first thing he told her, having made it over to her house in record time.

'It wasn't necessary.' Lesley leaned back and closed her eyes. The pain had diminished but she was still in a state of shock at thinking that something might be wrong. That she might lose the baby. Tears threatened close to the surface but she pushed them away, focusing on a good outcome, despite the fact that she knew she was still bleeding.

And then something else occurred to her, a wayward thought that needled its way into her brain and took root, refusing to budge. 'I shouldn't have called you,' she said more sharply than she had intended. 'I wouldn't have if I'd thought that you were going to fret and worry.' But she hadn't thought of doing anything *but* picking up that phone to him. To a man who had suddenly become indispensable despite the fact that she was not the love of his life; despite the fact that he wouldn't be in this car here with her now if she had never visited him in his office.

She had never foreseen the way he had managed to become so ingrained into the fabric of her daily life. He brought food for her. He stocked her up with pregnancy books. He insisted they eat in when he was around because it was less hassle than going out. He had taken care of that persistent leak in the bathroom which had suddenly decided to act up.

And not once had she sat back and thought of where all this was leading.

'Of course you should have called me,' Alessio said softly. 'Why wouldn't you? This baby is mine as well. I share all the responsibilities with you.'

And share them he had, backing away from trying to foist his marriage solution onto her, even though he had been baffled at her stubborn persistence that there was no way that she was going to marry him.

Why not? He just didn't get it. They were good together. They were having a baby. Hell, he had made sure not to lay a finger on her, but he still burned to have her in his bed, and the memory of the sex they had shared still made him lose concentration in meetings. And, yes, so maybe he had mentioned once or twice that he had learnt bitter lessons from being trapped into marriage by the wrong woman for the wrong reasons, but hadn't that made his proposal even more sincere—the fact that he was willing to sidestep those unfortunate lessons and retread the same ground?

Why couldn't she see that?

He had stopped thinking about the possibility that she was still saving herself for Mr Right. Just going down that road made him see red.

'I hate it when you talk about responsibilities,' she snapped, looking briefly at him and then just as quickly looking away. 'And you're driving way too fast. We're going to crash.'

'I'm sticking to the speed limit. Of course I'm going to talk about responsibilities. Why shouldn't I?' Would she rather he had turned his back on her and walked away? Was that the sort of modern guy she would have preferred him to be? He hung onto his patience with difficulty, recognising that the last thing she needed was to be stressed out.

'I just want you to know,' Lesley said fiercely, 'That if anything happens to this baby…'

'Nothing is going to happen to this baby.'

'You don't know that!'

Alessio could sense her desire to have an argument with him and he had no intention of allowing her to indulge that desire. A heated row was not appropriate but he shrewdly guessed that, if he mentioned that, it would generate an even bigger row.

What the hell was wrong? Of course she was worried. So

was he, frankly. But he was here with her, driving her to the hospital, fully prepared to be right there by her side, so why the need to launch into an attack?

Frustration tore into him but, like his impatience, he kept it firmly in check.

Suddenly she felt that it was extremely important that she let him know this vital thing. 'And I just want you to know that, if something does, then your duties to me are finished. You can walk away with a clear conscience, knowing that you didn't dump me when I was pregnant with your child.'

Alessio sucked in his breath sharply. Ahead, he could see the big, impersonal hospital building. He had wanted her to have private medical care during the pregnancy and for the birth of the baby, but she had flatly refused, and he had reluctantly ceded ground. If, indeed, there was anything at all amiss, that small victory would be obliterated because he would damn well make sure that she got the best medical attention there was available.

'This is not the time for this sort of conversation.' He screeched to a halt in front of the Accident and Emergency entrance but, before he killed the engine, he looked at her intently, his eyes boring into her. 'Just try and relax, my darling. I know you're probably scared stiff but I'm here for you.' He brushed her cheek lightly and the tenderness of that touch brought a lump to her throat.

'You're here for the baby, not for me,' Lesley muttered under her breath. But then any further conversation was lost as they were hurried through, suddenly caught up in a very efficient process, channelled to the right place, speeding along the quiet hospital corridors with Lesley in a wheelchair and Alessio keeping pace next to her.

There seemed to be an awful lot of people around and she clasped his hand tightly, hardly even realising that she was doing that.

'If something happens to the baby...' he bent to whisper into her ear as they headed towards the ultrasound room '...then I'm still here for you.'

An exhausting hour later, during which Lesley had had no time to think about what those whispered words meant, she finally found herself in a private room decorated with a television on a bracket against the wall and a heavy door leading, she could see, to her own en-suite bathroom.

Part of her wondered whether those whispered words had actually been uttered or had they been a fiction of her fevered imagination?

She covertly watched as he drew the curtains together and then pulled a chair so that he was on eye-level with her as she lay on the bed.

'Thank you for bringing me here, Alessio,' she said with a weak smile that ended up in a yawn.

'You're tired. But everything's going to be all right with the baby. Didn't I say?'

Lesley smiled with her eyes half-closed. The relief was overwhelming. They had pointed out the strongly beating heart on the scan and had reassured her that rest was all that was called for. She had been planning to work from home towards the beginning of the third trimester. That would now have to be brought forward.

'You said.'

'And—and I meant what I said when we were rushing you in.'

Lesley's eyes flew open and she felt as though her heart had skipped a beat. She had not intended to remind him of what he had said, just in case she had misheard, just in case he had said what he somehow thought she wanted to hear in the depths of her anxiety over her scare.

But now his eyes held hers and she just wanted to lose herself in possibilities.

'What did you say? I can't quite…um…remember.' She looked down at her hand which had somehow found its way between his much bigger hands.

'What I should say is that there was a moment back then when it flashed through my mind—what would I do if anything happened to *you*? It scared the living daylights out of me.'

'I know you feel very responsible…with me being pregnant.' She deliberately tried to kill the shoot of hope rising inside her and tenaciously refusing to go away.

'I'm not talking about the baby. I'm talking about you.' He felt as though he was looking over the side of a very sheer cliff, but he wanted to jump; he didn't care what sort of landing he might be heading for.

So far she hadn't tried to remind him that he wasn't her type and that they weren't suited for one another. That surely had to be a good sign?

'I don't know what I'd do if anything happened to you because you're the love of my life. No, wait, don't say a thing. Just listen to what I have to say and then, if you want me to butt out of your life, I'll do as you say. We can go down the legal route and have the papers drawn up for custody rights, and an allowance to be made for you, and I'll stop pestering you with my attention.' He took a deep breath and his eyes shifted to her mouth, then to the unappealing hospital gown which she was still wearing, and then finally they settled on their linked fingers. It seemed safer.

'I'm listening.' *The love of his life*? She just wanted to repeat that phrase over and over in her head because she didn't think she could possibly get used to hearing it.

'When you first appeared at my front door, I knew you were different to every single woman I had ever met. I knew you were sharp, feisty, outspoken. I was drawn to you, and I guess the fact that you occupied a special place of intimate knowledge about certain aspects of my private life not usually open to public view fuelled my attraction. It was as though the whole package became irresistible. You were sexy as hell without knowing it. You had brains and you had insight into me.'

Lesley almost burst out laughing at the 'sexy as hell' bit but then she remembered the way he had looked at her when they had made love, the things he had said. *She* might have had insecurities about how she looked, but she didn't doubt that his attraction had been genuine and spontaneous. Hadn't he been the one to put those insecurities to bed, after all?

'It just felt so damned right between us,' he admitted, stealing a surreptitious look at her face, and encouraged that she didn't seem to be blocking him out. 'And the more we got to know one another the better it felt. I thought it was all about the sex, but it was much bigger than that, and I just didn't see it. Maybe after Bianca I simply assumed that women could only satisfy a certain part of me before they hit my metaphorical glass ceiling and disappeared from my life. I wasn't looking for any kind of involvement and I certainly didn't bank on finding any. But involvement found me without my even realising it.'

He laughed under his breath and, when he felt the touch of her hand on his cheek, he held it in place so that he could flip it over and kiss the palm of her hand. He relaxed, but not too much.

'Thanks to you, my relationship with Rachel is the healthiest it's ever been. Thanks to you, I've discovered that there's far more to life than trying to be a father to a hostile teenager and burying myself in my work. I never stopped to question how it was that I wasn't gutted when you told me about the pregnancy. I knew I felt different this time round from when Bianca had presented me with a future of fatherhood. If I had taken the time to analyse things, I might have begun to see what had already happened. I might have seen that I had fallen hopelessly in love with you.'

All his cards were on the table and he felt good. Whatever

the outcome. He carried on before she could interrupt with a pity statement about him not really being the one for her.

'And I may not cry at girlie movies or bake bread but you can take me on. I'm a good bet. I'm here for you; you know that. I'll always be here for you because I'm nothing without you. If you still don't want to marry me, or if you want to put me on probation, then I'm willing to go along because I feel I can prove to you that I can be the sort of man you want me to be.'

'Probation?' The concept was barely comprehensible.

'A period of time during which you can try me out for size.' He had never thought he would ever in a million years utter such words to any woman. But he just had and he didn't regret any of them.

'I know what the word means.' The thoughts were rushing round in her head, a mad jumble that filled every space. She wanted to fling her arms around him, kiss him on the mouth, pull him right into her, jump up and down, shout from the roof-tops—all of those things at the same time.

Instead, she said in a barely audible voice, 'Why didn't you say sooner? I wish you had. I've been so miserable, because I love you so much and I thought that the last thing you needed was to be trapped into marriage to someone you never wanted to see out your days with.' She lay back and smiled with such pure joy that it took her breath away. Then she looked at him and carried on smiling, and smiling, and smiling. 'I knew I was falling for you but I knew you weren't into committed re-lationships.'

'I never was.'

'That should have stopped me but I just didn't see it com-ing. You really weren't the sort of guy I ever thought I could have fallen in love with, but who said love obeys rules? By the time I realised that I loved you, I was in so deep that the only way out for me was to run as fast as I could in the opposite di-rection. It was the hardest thing I ever did in my entire life but

I thought that, if I stayed, my heart would be so broken that I would never recover.'

'My darling... My beautiful, unique, special darling.' He kissed her gently on the lips and had the wonderful feeling of being exactly where he was meant to be.

'Then I found out that I was pregnant, and after the shock had worn off a bit, I felt sick at the thought of telling you—sick at the thought of knowing that you would be horrified, your worst nightmare turned into reality.'

'And here we are. So I'm asking you again, my dearest—will you marry me?'

They were married in Ireland a month before their baby was born, with all her family in attendance. Her father, her brothers and her brothers' partners all filled the small local church. And, when they retired to the hotel which they had booked into, the party was still carrying on, as he was told, in typical Irish style. And just as soon as the baby was born, he was informed, they would throw a proper bash—the alcohol wouldn't stop flowing for at least two days. Alessio had grinned and told them that he couldn't wait but that, before the baby discovered the wonders of an Irish bash, she or he would first have to discover the wonders of going on honeymoon, because they had both agreed that wherever they went their baby would come as well.

And their baby, Rose Alexandra, a little girl with his dark hair and big, dark eyes, was born without fuss, a healthy eight pounds four ounces. Rachel, who was over the moon at the prospect of having a sibling she could thoroughly spoil, could barely contain her excitement when she paid her first visit to the hospital and peered into the little tilted cot at the side of Lesley's bed.

The perfect family unit, was the thought that ran through Alessio's mind as he looked at the snapshot picture in front of him. His beautiful wife, radiant but tired after giving birth, smiling down at the baby in her arms while Rachel, the daughter he had once thought lost to him but now found, stood over them both, her dark hair falling in a curtain as she gently touched her sister's small, plump, pink cheek.

If he could have bottled this moment in time, he would have. Instead, still on cloud nine, he leaned into the little group and knew that this, finally, was what life should be all about.

* * * * *

A Baby Scandal In Italy

Chantelle Shaw

Books by Chantelle Shaw

Harlequin Modern

Proof of Their Forbidden Night
Her Wedding Night Negotiation
Housekeeper in the Headlines
The Italian's Bargain for His Bride

Passionately Ever After...

Her Secret Royal Dilemma

Innocent Summer Brides

The Greek Wedding She Never Had
Nine Months to Tame the Tycoon

Visit the Author Profile page
at millsandboon.com.au for more titles.

Chantelle Shaw lives on the Kent coast and thinks up her stories while walking on the beach. She has been married for over thirty years and has six children. Her love affair with reading and writing Harlequin stories began as a teenager, and her first book was published in 2006. She likes strong-willed, slightly unusual characters. Chantelle also loves gardening, walking and wine.

CHAPTER ONE

THIS WAS THE big one. The contract that was guaranteed to show his detractors he was a worthy successor to his father. Rafa Vieri permitted himself a brief smile of satisfaction as he contemplated the business deal he was about to finalise that would cement Vieri Azioni's position as the largest financial holding company in Europe.

He looked around at VA's board members seated at the polished mahogany table. There was a palpable air of excitement and expectation in the boardroom. The white-haired man sitting opposite Rafa was Carlo Landini, who was the head of Italy's most prestigious private bank, Banca Landini. Rafa had used his considerable charm and persuasive powers to convince Carlo to sell a controlling stake in his bank to Vieri Azioni. Banca Landini would continue to operate under its own executive management team, while its assets were protected, and Vieri Azioni would profit hugely from the sound investment.

A few of VA's directors had been doubtful about Rafa's suitability for the joint roles of chairman and CEO following the unexpected death of his father two months ago, pointing to his playboy reputation and the messy divorce from his ex-wife which had been played out in the public eye. Rafa had been a paragon of virtue lately in an effort to impress the board.

Just as importantly he had needed to show Carlo Landini that he'd given up the celebrity lifestyle he had led when he'd been a professional basketball player in America before returning to Italy eighteen months ago to utilise his MBA and work alongside his father at Vieri Azioni.

Rafa knew that Carlo had hoped to pass Banco Landini down to his only son—but Patrizio's body had been found on his yacht in the Bahamas amid rumours that he'd died from an overdose of cocaine. The scandal had been hushed up, but Patrizio's death had left Carlo Landini without a successor. Perhaps unsurprisingly, after the problems with his son, Carlo did not want a whiff of scandal to be associated with his family's centuries-old bank.

Rafa called the meeting to order. 'Are you ready to proceed?' he asked Carlo.

The older man nodded. 'I am ready to sign the deal. You have convinced me, Rafa, that Banca Landini will be safely and successfully managed by Vieri Azioni under your leadership.'

Carlo picked up a pen, but he paused with his hand poised above the document on the table in front of him when the boardroom door flew open.

What the hell? Rafa jerked his head towards the source of the disturbance and stared at the young woman who had burst into the room. His confusion quickly turned to anger. He had instructed his PA that the only reason for the meeting to be interrupted would be if the building were burning down.

The woman froze like a rabbit caught in car headlights when every pair of eyes in the boardroom focused on her. The most noticeable thing about her was her bright pink hair, which clashed violently with her orange tee shirt. Her jeans were ripped at the knees and, to complete the bizarre spectacle, she had a baby in a carrier strapped to her front. All that was visible of the child was a tuft of dark hair and two chubby legs poking out of the bottom of the carrier.

Memories of Lola as a baby flashed into Rafa's mind and his gut twisted. He had been captivated from the moment he had held her in his arms. His princess, his little girl—or so he had believed until his lying, cheating ex-wife had blown his world apart. With a ruthlessness that had made him a champion on the basketball court, and more recently had earned him a reputation as a take-no-prisoners business tycoon, Rafa shoved his past back into a box marked 'do not open'.

He stood up. 'My apologies for the interruption,' he said smoothly to Carlo Landini, disguising his frustration when the deal had been so close to completion.

Rafa's usually unflappable personal assistant hurried into the room. 'Miss Bennett, this is a private meeting. You must leave immediately.' The PA spoke in English to the woman whose garish hair and clothes jarred in the room full of grey-suited businessmen.

'Giulia, *cosa sta succedendo*?' *What is going on?* Rafa demanded furiously.

'I'm sorry.' The PA sounded rattled. 'I explained to Miss Bennett that you were unavailable to see her. Shall I call security?'

'*No*. You can't throw me out.' The woman with the baby ran across the room and halted in front of Rafa. 'Rafael Vieri, I'd like you to meet your son.'

Ivy heard a collective gasp of shock from around the room. She had hoped to speak to Bertie's father in private, but she'd panicked at the prospect of being bundled out of the boardroom by a security guard and blurted out her announcement.

'Is this some sort of joke?' Rafael Vieri's cold voice sent an ice cube slithering down Ivy's spine. She had discovered, when she'd researched him on the Internet, that he was sometimes known as Rafa, and he was a former international basketball superstar and a notorious playboy.

'It's certainly not a joke.' She was angry that he was acting as though he was shocked. After all, her sister had written and informed him that he was the father of her child, but he had not responded. Gemma hadn't told Ivy much about the man she'd had a brief affair with, which had been odd, because they had always confided in each other. All Gemma had said was that Rafael Vieri was the CEO of a financial company in Rome called Vieri Azioni.

Ivy had felt apprehensive about how Rafa would react to her bringing Bertie to Italy. But what else could she have done, now that Gemma was dead? Grief clutched at her heart when she thought of her sister. Technically, they had been half-sisters, and shared the same father, but despite a ten-year age gap they'd always been close.

Gemma had been a confidante and best friend to Ivy after her parents had split up and her mum's complicated love-life had meant she'd had little time for her daughter. Now Ivy was Bertie's legal guardian and her final words to her sister had been a promise to take the baby to meet his father.

The receptionist behind the front desk had been dealing with someone else and hadn't glanced at Ivy when she'd arrived at Vieri Azioni's headquarters. But Rafa Vieri hadn't been in the CEO's office, and she'd been about to return to the lift when she'd heard voices from behind a door further along the corridor.

An elegant woman had emerged from the room and told her that Signor Vieri was busy. Ivy had recognised her voice as the woman she'd spoken to on the phone when she had called to try to make an appointment with Rafa. 'I remember I spoke to you a few days ago, Miss Bennett,' his PA had said. 'But you refused to say why you wanted to see Signor Vieri.'

At that moment, the PA's phone had rung, and while she'd been distracted Ivy had seized her chance and darted into the boardroom.

Now she felt uncomfortable that she was the focus of curiosity from everyone in the room, although only one man held her attention. Rafa Vieri was looking at her as though he could not quite believe what he was seeing. It was her pink hair, Ivy supposed. On a dismal, wet day in England, she'd impulsively dyed her hair bubblegum-pink to cheer herself up.

She flushed when she saw him glance at her old jeans and trainers. Three months ago her life had changed irredeemably when she'd become responsible for her baby half-nephew, and since then she hadn't had the time or energy to think about herself. Every morning she pulled on her jeans and got on with the job of caring for Bertie, and most nights she cried herself to sleep grieving for Gemma.

Rafa's online profile stated that he was six-foot-four. His height hadn't been exceptional when he'd played in the American professional basketball league, where some of the players were seven feet tall, but he towered over Ivy, and she had to tilt her head to look at his face. Photos of him on social media did not do justice to his stunningly handsome features. In those pictures, his mouth had invariably been curved in a wickedly sexy smile, and the gleam of sensual promise in his grey eyes had made Ivy understand why Gemma had been swept off her feet by him.

In the flesh, Rafa was even more gorgeous, more compelling, more *everything,* despite the fact that he was not smiling and his eyes were as hard and uncompromising as steel. Ivy's body responded to the irresistible pull of his magnetism. Her skin felt too tight, and heat radiated from her central core in a surge of sexual awareness that confused and horrified her. How could she be attracted to the father of her dead sister's baby? It was *wrong*!

She exhaled slowly when Rafa released her from his penetrating stare. He looked across the room as an older man, who had been sitting at the table, stood up.

'Rafa, what is the meaning of this interruption? The boardroom is hardly the place to conduct your private affairs. I may have to reconsider our deal.'

'Once again, please accept my apologies for the disturbance, Carlo,' Rafa said smoothly. 'We will take a short break for refreshments.'

He put his hand on Ivy's arm and she felt a zing of electricity shoot through her. 'Come with me,' he ordered curtly, steering her towards the door. He paused next to his PA and said in a low voice, 'Giulia, tell the caterers to serve the champagne and canapés while I deal with this situation.'

Ivy's nerves jangled as she walked beside Rafa along the corridor. His initial reaction to his baby son had not been promising, but she needed his help. The eviction notice she'd received from her landlord, giving her two weeks to move out of her flat, had prompted her to set aside her shock and grief over Gemma and take Bertie to his father. She had used the last of her savings to pay for a budget flight to Rome and had booked to stay for two nights at the cheapest hotel she could find.

'In here,' Rafa growled as he ushered her into his office. It was a masculine room, all marble and chrome with a black, glass-topped desk set at an angle in front of the floor-to-ceiling windows that gave a panoramic view across Rome. Despite the air-conditioning in the building, sweat trickled down Ivy's spine and her tee shirt was sticking to her. It had been a twenty-minute walk from her hotel to Vieri Azioni's headquarters and Bertie was heavy. The straps of the baby carrier were digging into her shoulders. Bertie was stirring and soon he would want another feed. Ivy had packed formula milk, nappies, wipes and all the other paraphernalia necessary for a four-month-old infant in her backpack.

Tenderness swamped her when she looked down at Bertie. She loved her half-sister's baby with all her heart and was determined to do her best for him, but she had struggled without any family to help her. Gemma's mother had died many years ago. Their father was divorced from Ivy's mum and had a new family. He had only seen Bertie once and wasn't interested in his grandson. The same was true of Ivy's mother, who had not been close to her stepdaughter and was not involved with Gemma's baby.

Rafa Vieri followed Ivy into his office and slammed the door shut. He looked grimly forbidding, and her heart sank, knowing that she must try to persuade him to acknowledge Bertie as his son. She lifted her hand to push her hair off her face and caught sight of the tiny butterfly tattoo on the inside of her wrist.

Gemma had been fascinated by butterflies and their symbolism of hope when they emerged from a cocoon and were free to fly away. When Ivy had been diagnosed with cancer as a teenager, Gemma had hung a butterfly mobile above her bed in the hospital and had told her to imagine the future when she was free from the illness that ravaged her body. The butterfly tattoo was in memory of her sister. Ivy took a deep breath, and a sense of calm came over her.

Rafa scowled at the woman with crazy hair whose untimely interruption threatened one of the most important deals of his life. She was making crooning noises to the baby as she lifted him out of the carrier. If it hadn't been for the child, Rafa would have instructed a member of his staff to escort Miss Bennett out of the building.

The baby let out a wail and the sound evoked more poignant memories for Rafa. He remembered the nights he'd spent walking up and down the nursery, rocking Lola in his arms to try to soothe her to sleep. Once he'd believed he had everything he could wish for, but his happiness had been an illusion built on Tiffany's deception. After the divorce, he had vowed never to trust any woman. And he was adamant that he did not want a child. When he'd discovered that Lola was not his daughter, he'd felt as though his heart had been ripped out, and he could not bear to experience that intensity of pain again.

Rafa strode round his desk and threw himself down onto the chair. He was desperate to find a semblance of normality in a situation that felt increasingly like the implausible plot line of one of the very bad films his ex-wife had starred in.

'Are you an actress? Is this a stunt?' Maybe it was someone's idea of a joke. Or could a business rival have paid Miss Bennett to sabotage the deal-signing meeting with Carlo Landini?

Her eyes widened. Despite himself, Rafa noticed that her eyes were startlingly beautiful, huge and dark brown, fringed by impossibly long lashes.

'I'm not an actress. I used to be a show dancer on a cruise ship, but I can't do that job now I have Bertie.'

She shrugged off her backpack and dumped it on Rafa's desk. 'I need to prepare his milk,' she explained as she rummaged in the bag and took out a feeding bottle and a carton of ready-mixed infant formula. Holding the grizzling baby against her shoulder, she deftly unscrewed the lid on the carton with her free hand and tipped the formula milk into the bottle.

'I'm Ivy Bennett. Gemma's sister.' She looked expectantly at Rafa. 'You must remember her. She wrote to you four months ago.'

'I don't know anyone called Gemma. More to the point, I have never met you before,' he drawled as he moved his gaze over her. He had intended to sound dismissive, but his voice was annoyingly husky. Ivy had taken off the baby carrier, and he could not help noticing how her tee shirt clung to her high, firm breasts.

He leaned back in his chair and studied her. She was petite and slim, and her tight-fitting jeans moulded her narrow hips. Her hair had been cut into short, wispy layers framing a heart-shaped face. She was nothing like the glamorous supermodel types Rafa went for, but there was something about her elfin beauty that captured his attention. He wondered what her natural hair colour was. Probably mid-brown, the same as her eyelashes, he mused. His gaze lingered on the sensual fullness of her lips, and he felt an unexpected tug of desire.

Celibacy did not suit him, Rafa decided self-derisively. He assumed that going without sex the past couple of months was the reason for his unwarranted reaction to a fragile-looking girl with atrocious dress sense. He had ended an affair that had been going nowhere shortly before his father had suffered a fatal heart attack. Shock, grief and the responsibilities that went with his new role as the head of Vieri Azioni meant that he hadn't had the time or inclination to dive back into the dating pool, and one-night stands no longer held the appeal they once had.

Ivy Bennett had said that she'd worked as a dancer and her toned figure was an indication that that, at least, was true. An image flashed into Rafa's mind of her slender body beneath him, her small breasts pressed against his chest. He watched the rosy flush that appeared on her cheeks spread lower over her throat and décolletage, and silently cursed his libido which had inconveniently sprung to life.

His gaze meshed with Ivy's, and he recognised her awareness of him in her big brown eyes before her lashes swept down. Rafa always knew. It had happened to him since he'd been a teenager, but these days he was less likely to be tempted by an invitation in a woman's eyes. Especially this woman, who had disrupted a vital business meeting and falsely accused him. He was impatient to return to the boardroom and try to salvage the deal with Carlo Landini. His jaw tightened when Ivy walked over to the sofa and sat down with the baby on her lap.

'Do you mind if I feed Bertie while we talk?'

As he watched the baby greedily suck on the teat of the bottle, Rafa's mind flew back to the past. When Lola had been born, he'd tried to spend as much time as possible with her, and during pre-season he had rushed home from training sessions to give her a bath and her evening feed. The professional basketball season ran for six months of the year and teams travelled to every state in North America. The punishing schedule of playing home and away games had been detrimental to his family life. Tiffany had complained that she was bored and lonely while he was away, but she had not stayed lonely for long, Rafa thought grimly. It had been Tiffany's decision to end their marriage and the divorce had exposed her devastating lies.

His gaze narrowed on Ivy, who was undeniably pretty, but demonstrably a liar. 'We have nothing to talk about, Miss Bennett. You know damn well that I am not the father of your baby and I demand you retract your false allegation. You can consider yourself lucky if I decide not to sue you for slander.'

Her Bambi eyes grew as round as saucers. 'I'm not Bertie's mother. But you are most definitely his father. He is my sister's baby. Gemma met you thirteen months ago while she was working on a cruise ship, and you were one of the passengers. She fell pregnant by you, but when she wrote and told you about your child she never heard from you. It's the old story,' she said, bitterness creeping into her voice. 'Men have the fun and women have the babies.'

'Enough,' Rafa snapped. 'I have never been on a cruise ship. Frankly, it's my idea of hell to be trapped on a boat at sea with hundreds of other people.'

Ivy's nose wrinkled when she frowned and for some reason it made her look even cuter. When had he ever found *cute* a turn on? Rafa thought grimly. He was furious that he could not control his unbidden reaction to Ivy.

'Gemma told me she had met Rafael Vieri aboard the *Ocean Star* on a cruise around the Caribbean islands. Usually we worked on the same ship, but I had been promoted to lead dancer on the company's sister ship, *Ocean Princess*. Gem was a social hostess.' Ivy grimaced. 'To be honest, I was surprised that she'd had a relationship with you, because it is a sackable offence for a crew member to become involved with a passenger. I guess she must have really liked you to have risked her career.'

He swore. 'I repeat, I did not meet your sister on a cruise ship.' His exasperation increased when Ivy looked unconvinced. 'It is feasible, I suppose, that Gemma met a passenger on the ship who had the same name as me. Rafael and Vieri are fairly common names in Italy.'

Rafa had been named after his father. But the possibility that his workaholic father could have spent weeks away from the office to go on a cruise was laughable and Rafa instantly dismissed the idea from his mind.

'Gemma said you had told her that you owned a successful

business in Italy called Vieri Azioni. That's how I knew where to find you.' Ivy sat the baby upright and rubbed his back until he gave a little burp. 'His proper name is Roberto,' she explained when she noticed that Rafa was staring at the child. 'Gemma gave him an Italian name, because he is half-Italian, but somehow Bertie stuck.'

'He did not inherit his Italian heritage from me. Roberto, Bertie, or whatever you choose to call him, is not my child,' Rafa said savagely. When he had sex, he was obsessively careful to use protection so there was no risk of an unplanned pregnancy.

Ivy's jaw was set in a stubborn line. 'Pass me my phone and I'll show you a picture of Gemma that might jog your memory.'

Dio! He'd wasted enough time on Ivy Bennett. Rafa was ninety-nine percent sure he had not slept with her sister, but it would do no harm to look at the photo, he conceded. There was a tiny chance that he'd met Gemma, although not in the Caribbean.

Thirteen months ago he had moved into a penthouse apartment close to the iconic Colosseum. He'd worked long hours at Vieri Azioni to prove to his father his commitment to the company and win the approval of the board, some of whom had believed that the vice-chairman would be a better chairman and CEO. But Rafa acknowledged that his life had not been all work and no play. He'd met women in bars and clubs and had occasionally spent the night with them. The nearby port town of Civitavecchia was where the cruise ships docked, and it was a short train ride for passengers and crew members into the city. Could Ivy's sister's ship have been in Italy shortly before or after it had sailed to the Caribbean? If so, it was just possible that he'd met Gemma in a bar in Rome.

Rafa looked away from the baby who was lying, milk-drunk and contented, in Ivy's arms. Undeniably, Bertie was a beautiful child, but not his child. Rejection burned inside him. Never again would he be fooled into believing he was a father. The bottom had dropped out of his world when he'd discovered that the daughter he had adored was not his. In the unlikely event that he recognised Ivy's sister as someone he'd slept with, he would demand proof that Bertie was his son.

He picked up Ivy's phone from where she'd left it on his desk and strode across the room to hand it to her. Seconds later, he studied the picture of an attractive redhead she showed him on the screen.

'I have never seen this woman before.' Rafa's relief quickly turned to anger. Something was going on here and he was in no mood for games. 'I don't know what you are playing at, Miss Bennett. If the baby belongs to your sister, why did *you* bring him to Italy?'

'Gemma's dead.' Ivy's brown eyes were luminous with tears. 'She died when Bertie was five weeks old. My last words to her were a promise that I would find her baby's father.'

'Why?' Rafa ignored a flicker of remorse when Ivy blinked at his abrupt tone. Everything she had told him so far sounded improbable.

'I thought you should know that you have a son.' She hesitated, 'And I hoped you would offer to support Bertie…financially.'

'You want money?' It was what Rafa had expected, and he could not understand why he felt a fleeting disappointment that the English rose with her understated sensuality was so predictable. 'Finally, we are getting to the truth,' he said cynically.

'I don't want money for me.' Twin spots of colour flared on Ivy's cheeks. She had perfected her air of guilelessness, Rafa thought cynically.

'Bringing up a baby is expensive,' she said. 'I told you I had a job as a dancer on a cruise ship, but I haven't been able to work since my sister died and I became responsible for Bertie. When he is a bit older, I hope to open my own dance school, but I've been living off my savings and the money has nearly run out.'

She caught her bottom lip between her teeth and the action drew Rafa's gaze to her lush mouth. A deliberate ploy? he wondered.

'If you don't want to be involved with your son, I will take him back to England and be the best mother I can to him as I promised my sister. But I did some research about you, and I know you are wealthy. You have a responsibility to provide for Bertie and you can afford to set up a trust fund for him.'

'As his legal guardian, you would no doubt have control of the money in the trust fund!' Rafa laughed. 'You must think I am an idiot, Miss Bennett. What I am curious to know is, did you sister falsely tell you that I had fathered her baby? Or was it your idea to accuse me of being the child's father in a bid to get money from me?'

He ignored Ivy's gasp. 'You admitted that you had looked up information about me. Perhaps you do not know who fathered your sister's baby and you thought you could somehow fool me into believing I had slept with Gemma. You are not the first woman to try to pin a paternity claim on a wealthy man.'

When Tiffany had told him she was pregnant, he'd had no reason to doubt that the baby was his, Rafa brooded. She'd later admitted that, after having been rejected by her child's biological father, she'd allowed Rafa to think that Lola was his daughter because he could provide the affluent lifestyle she craved.

'It wasn't like that at all.' Ivy stood up. The baby was dozing and she carefully placed him on the sofa and wedged cushions around him to prevent him from rolling over. 'Everything I have told you is the truth.'

She tilted her head and glared at Rafa. He noticed that her brown eyes were flecked with amber. 'My sister told me that you are Bertie's father and I believe her. It's more likely that you were lying when you denied receiving Gemma's letter.'

'There was no letter.' Rafa growled, exasperated by her stubbornness. 'Admit defeat, Miss Bennett. The child is not mine and if you ever repeat the allegation you will face serious legal consequences.'

His gaze swivelled towards the door when it opened and his PA appeared. 'What now, Giulia?'

'Landini and his team are about to leave.'

Rafa swore. 'Try and stall them for a couple more minutes. I'm almost done here.' He sent Ivy a simmering glance. 'I will talk to Carlo and explain that there was a misunderstanding.'

The PA nodded. 'I had hoped that Sandro Florenzi might help to smooth things over while you were busy, but he left the boardroom immediately after you, saying he had a migraine.'

Rafa frowned. He knew the deputy CEO occasionally suffered from migraines, but the timing was inconvenient to say the least. Giulia left the room and he looked at Ivy, infuriated by the heat that flared inside him.

Dio, how could he be attracted to a pink-haired pixie who had come to him with a frankly unbelievable story? It would have been laughable if he hadn't been uncomfortably aware of his arousal pressing against his trouser zip. Because of his height, he preferred women who were taller than average. If he kissed Ivy, he would probably crick his neck unless he picked her up and plastered her body against his.

What the hell was the matter with him? He swung away from her to avoid the temptation of her lush mouth that right now was set in a sulky pout. Once he'd secured the deal with Carlo Landini, he would take some time off, Rafa decided. He'd been working flat out since his father had died and he needed a break. He would spend a few days at his castle in the mountains. It was the place he retreated to when he needed some head space and wanted to be alone.

And, when he returned to Rome, he'd start dating again. He always made it clear to women that he could offer expensive dinners and nights of pleasure in his bed, but definitely not commitment.

'Are you staying in Rome?' When Ivy gave him the name of her hotel, he said curtly, 'I'll arrange for you and the child to be driven to your lodgings. Wait here in my office until my personal assistant comes to escort you down to my car. I suggest you return to England immediately, and I strongly advise you not to try to contact me again. Stalking is a criminal offence for which there are serious penalties.'

Rafa studied Ivy's crestfallen face. He was certain she was a liar and he did not trust her. There was no reason why he should feel bad about dismissing her claim that he'd fathered her sister's child. But he sensed that her story about her sister dying was genuine, and he felt a reluctant tug of compassion.

'I'm sorry about Gemma,' he said brusquely. 'My father recently passed away and I understand the pain of grief.'

The amber flecks in Ivy's eyes glowed as fiercely as flames. 'Keep your pseudo-sympathy, Mr Vieri,' she snapped 'I *know* Gemma told me the truth, which makes *you* a liar.'

CHAPTER TWO

IVY HATED RAFAEL VIERI. *Hated* him for planting a seed of doubt in her mind about her sister's claim that he was Bertie's father. Gemma had always told the truth. Even when Ivy had been diagnosed with a type of blood cancer, Gemma had researched information about the illness and had honestly answered her questions about what chemotherapy would be like and her chances of survival. Gem had been a rock when Ivy had needed support and now, through tragic circumstances, she could repay Gemma by bringing up her son.

Rafael was Bertie's father, Ivy was certain. But he had refused to accept responsibility for his child. 'We'll be fine on our own,' she muttered, more to reassure herself than the baby, who was dozing in the carrier as Ivy walked back to the hotel. She had declined to get into the car when the driver had held open the door, partly through stubborn pride—she did not want to accept anything from Rafa after the humiliating scene in his office—but also because the car had not been fitted with a baby seat so she'd had no option than to trudge through the crowded city streets.

'Signorina Bennett.'

Ivy turned her head when she heard someone call her name. A sleek, black saloon had pulled up next to the pavement and a man of about fifty or so emerged. He was smiling as he walked towards her, but there was concern in his voice when he spoke.

'Do you have far to go, Signorina Bennett? You must be tired, carrying the child in the midday heat.'

'Who...?' Ivy began.

'Forgive me.' The man smiled again. 'I was in the boardroom of Vieri Azioni when you introduced Rafael Vieri to his baby son. Everyone was surprised by your revelation that the chairman and CEO has a secret child. But I was even more shocked that Rafa dismissed your claim as a joke.'

'As if I would joke about something so serious.' Her temper simmered when she remembered that Rafa had accused her of staging a stunt. She was barely aware that the stranger—had he told her his name?—had led her over to a café where there were tables outside beneath an awning that provided welcome shade from the sun.

'Please, sit down.' The man pulled out a chair. 'May I call you Ivy? I'm sure you could do with a cold drink. Would you like something to eat?'

A waiter walked past carrying an exotic ice-cream sundae. Ivy eyed the dessert wistfully. She was still feeling tense after meeting Rafa Vieri and craved a sugar hit. Her companion— she was too embarrassed to admit that she hadn't been concentrating when the man had introduced himself—laughed. 'Ah, who can resist *gelato*?' he said. 'Allow me to order for you the chocolate flavour with whipped cream and hazelnuts.'

The dessert sounded heavenly. Ivy sat down and gave a deep sigh. Her shoulders ached from the weight of Bertie in the carrier, particularly her left shoulder that she'd injured a few months ago while she had been rehearsing a dance routine.

It felt like a lifetime ago that she had been a dancer on a cruise ship. She felt a pang, thinking of her friends in the dance troupe. She missed her old life, even though it had been hard work, performing in shows twice a night, seven nights a week. But she had Bertie now, and she couldn't spend long periods of time away at sea. She loved him as much as if he were her own baby, and when he was old enough she would tell him about the wonderful woman who had given birth to him.

Bertie stirred and opened his eyes. They had been blue at birth, but now they were grey, the same colour as Rafael Vieri's eyes. Ivy did not want to think about how Rafa's eyes had gleamed with cold contempt when he'd raked them over her. She did not understand why he affected her. Sure, he was handsome, but she'd met other good-looking guys and hadn't felt the intense awareness that had hit her like a tidal wave when she'd met Rafa. She did not like him, and she was angry that he'd refused to accept Bertie as his child. She was confused that, despite his obvious flaws, she was attracted to him.

The waiter set a decadent ice-cream sundae in front of her and Ivy forgot her worries for a few minutes while she tucked in. Thankfully, Bertie had fallen back to sleep. Her companion murmured, 'Rafa denied that he is the baby's father.'

'He told me not to contact him again.' She put her spoon down, feeling slightly sick from the rich ice-cream.

'It seems unfair that you must bear the responsibility and financial burden of bringing up the child alone.'

'I don't know what I'm going to do,' Ivy admitted dismally. She had been prepared for Rafa to be shocked at first, but she'd hoped he would come round to the idea that Bertie was his son. 'I need to find a job, but childcare is expensive, and then there's rent and all the other living costs.'

'There is a solution to your money worries. Newspapers would be prepared to pay you well for your story.' When Ivy looked puzzled, her companion leaned across the table and said in a low voice, 'I can put you in touch with a journalist who works for a leading news agency. All you would need to do is explain that Rafa Vieri has rejected his son and abandoned you. No one could blame you for accepting an opportunity to earn money that you desperately need for the baby.'

Ivy shook her head. 'If I did that, the circumstances of Bertie's birth would be made public. I won't take the risk that when he is older he might find out from an old news story that his father did not want anything to do with him.'

Even though it was the truth. She hoped that in the future, if Bertie was curious about his father, she would be able to think of an explanation for Rafa's lack of interest in his son.

The man got to his feet and handed Ivy a business card. 'Think about it and, if you change your mind, call this number and talk to the journalist. *Arrivederci*, Signorina Bennett.'

'Wait…who are you?' She looked up from the card that bore the name of a well-known Italian newspaper and a contact number for the senior reporter, Luigi Capello.

Ivy watched the man walk back to his car and wondered why his face seemed vaguely familiar, and why he was keen for her to go to the newspapers with a story that did not show Rafa Vieri in a good light. But, by the time she arrived back at her hotel, Bertie was crying, her shoulder was throbbing and she did not give the matter another thought.

Maybe it was the heat. The hotel room did not have air-conditioning. Or perhaps Bertie sensed that Ivy was stressed. Whatever the reason, the baby was unsettled all night and by morning they were both exhausted. Every time Ivy moved, she felt a sensation like a red-hot poker jabbing into her shoulder.

Bertie finally fell asleep after his nine a.m. feed. Ivy held her breath when she carefully placed him in the cot, praying he would not stir. She winced as her injured shoulder protested, and then cursed beneath her breath when there was a loud knock on the door. Concerned that it was the hotel manager to complain about the baby crying in the night, she shot across the room to open the door before whoever was on the other side knocked again.

Her apology died on her lips, and her heart missed a beat as her eyes collided with Rafa Vieri's hard-as-steel gaze. The previous day he had looked suave, wearing a designer suit. This morning he was drop-dead sexy in faded denim that clung to his muscular thighs and a black polo shirt that looked casual but expensive. He had pushed his sunglasses onto his head and his midnight-dark hair brushed his collar.

Rafa Vieri exuded an air of arrogance and power that was exclusive to the super-rich. An expression of haughty disdain crossed his face when he looked past Ivy into her functional but uninspiring hotel room.

He snapped his gaze back to her and frowned. Ivy had spent the morning giving Bertie a bath and she hadn't had time to get herself dressed. She felt self-conscious that her skimpy shorts and vest top left little to the imagination. During the night, when it had been so hot in her room, she had been glad that her pyjamas were made of thin cotton but now she wished she was wearing something that covered her from head to toe, preferably made of thick winceyette.

She was mortified when she glanced down and discovered that her nipples were standing to attention beneath her top. But, while she was intensely aware of Rafa's potent masculinity, he evidently did not feel an answering spark of attraction for her.

'I warned you of the consequences if you repeated your lies about me.' He delivered each word with the deadly force of a bullet fired from a gun.

'I haven't lied.' She kept her voice quiet, desperate not to wake Bertie. Rafa thrust a newspaper towards her and she saw a picture of him on the front page beneath the headline *Il bambino segreto del magnate!*

Although Ivy did not understand the other words, the meaning of *bambino* was obvious.

'The tycoon's secret baby.' Rafa translated the headline between gritted teeth. '*Dio*, it sounds like the ridiculous title of a novel, and the story is a complete fantasy.' He braced his hands on the door frame and Ivy had the impression that it was to stop himself from putting them around her neck. 'By the time my lawyers have finished, you will wish that you had never heard of me, let alone accused me of being the father of *your* baby.'

Before Ivy could query his surprising statement, the door of the room next to hers opened and a young couple emerged. They looked curiously at Rafa. When they had walked past, he said tersely, 'We can't have a conversation while I'm standing in the corridor.' Without waiting for her to invite him in, he pushed himself off the door frame and stepped past her into the room.

'We can't talk in here,' Ivy told him in a fierce whisper. 'Bertie has gone to sleep at long last and I won't promise not to kill anyone who wakes him up.'

Rafa glanced over at the cot wedged between the bed and the wall and his scowl deepened. 'The room is the size of a rabbit hutch.' At Ivy's glare, he lowered his voice. 'What is in here?' He opened the door to the miniscule bathroom. 'This will have to do. I'm not planning on staying long. I want to know why you did it—although, I can guess. How much did you get paid?' he asked in a cynical voice.

'You're not making any sense.' Ivy's thought process was severely hampered by a lack of sleep. Somehow Rafa had manoeuvred her into the bathroom. He was right behind her and he closed the door, standing with his back against it, and folded his arms across his chest.

He dominated the small space. It was not just his height and athletic build, it was *him*. He was truly the most gorgeous man she'd ever met. She was mesmerised by his sculpted features, the sharp cheekbones, strong nose and uncompromising brows above his heavy-lidded eyes. The dark stubble on his jaw was thicker than it had been yesterday, and she had the impression that he had come straight from his bed to find her.

An image leapt into her mind of him naked in a bed with her beside him and the sheets tangled after a night of passion. She wondered if the rest of his body was as tanned as his muscular arms beneath his short-sleeve shirt. He had a tattoo of a fearsome-looking black horse on his right forearm. Ivy remembered from her research about him that a horse was the logo of the California Colts basketball team.

Her eyes were drawn back to Rafa's face. His mouth was full-lipped and promised untold delights. Something urgent and unfamiliar coiled deep in her pelvis. She had been a teenager when she'd first started to explore her sensuality, but she had never gone further than a few kisses with her boyfriend at the time. Her cancer diagnosis when she'd been seventeen had been terrifying and the treatment—a brutal regime of chemotherapy over two years—had pushed her body to its limits. She had lost her hair and sometimes her hope. Her boyfriend Luke had ditched her, and for a long time her sole focus had been to get well and regain her strength.

Nine months ago she had celebrated being cancer-free for five years but, although she'd dated guys occasionally, she hadn't wanted a serious relationship. Partly her wariness stemmed from witnessing her mum's chaotic love life and the opinion she'd formed as a pre-teen that men were unreliable. That had proved to be true when her heart had been broken by Luke. The end of her first romance had been doubly painful because she'd been ill and vulnerable. Since then, she had been reluctant to risk being hurt again.

But as time had gone on, and she hadn't been wildly attracted to any man, Ivy had wondered if cancer had robbed her not only of her fertility, but all aspects of her femininity. The sweet ache between her thighs and her overwhelming awareness of Rafa were signs that her sexuality was alive and kicking. Why did it have to be he who had revived her desire that had been dormant until now? Rafa was off-limits, Ivy told herself firmly. She could not respect him after he had rejected his baby son.

Her dad had been an unreliable parent, but at least he'd mostly stuck around for the first ten years of her life. After her parents had split up, her mum had married twice more, but neither of those relationships had lasted. Ivy had felt unimportant when her mum had poured her energy and emotions into her new romances. Now she had Bertie to consider, and she was determined that he would never feel second-best, as she had when she'd been growing up.

Ivy saw Rafa's gaze flick to the shower screen where she'd hung Bertie's sleep suits to dry after she'd washed them in the sink. For the trip to Italy, she had only brought what she could fit into a backpack, because the airline charged extra for luggage to go in the hold. Draped next to the sleep suits was a pair of her knickers that she'd rinsed out. Of course, they had to be the black lace panties with the slogan *Hands Off!* printed on the front, which Gemma had given her as a joke last Christmas.

Flushing hotly, Ivy reached up to retrieve her underwear and couldn't restrain a yelp of agony as her shoulder muscles spasmed. The pain was so intense that she felt sick and swayed on her feet. Above the buzzing noise in her ears, she heard Rafa swear. He clamped his strong hands on either side of her waist and sat her down on the edge of the bath.

'Lower your head towards your knees to allow the blood to flow to your brain,' he ordered. She complied, and after a few seconds the light-headed feeling eased, but the knot of tension in her stomach tightened when he remained close beside her and she breathed in the spicy scent of his cologne.

'What happened?' His tone was still curt but held a faint huskiness that sent another coil of heat down to Ivy's pelvis.

'Just an old shoulder injury that plays up sometimes,' she mumbled, cringing when she sounded breathless and gauche. 'It's fine now.' Her shoulder was throbbing, but she needed Rafa to move from where he was crouched next to her. He was so close that he was bound to notice the frantic thud of her pulse at the base of her throat and hear her uneven breaths.

He straightened up but could not put much space between them in the cramped bathroom. His laugh was harsh and humourless. 'A lightning recovery or another lie? Did you pretend to be in pain to win my sympathy? The same reason that you made up a tragic story about your sister dying?' Rafa ignored

Ivy's gasp. 'You said you're not an actress, but you have a talent for make-believe.'

'I told you the truth. Gemma is dead.' Shock at Rafa's callous attitude brought tears to Ivy's eyes. She stood up and was conscious of how much taller than her he was, but she refused to be intimidated by him. 'Why would I make up something so awful?'

'You tell me!' he snapped. 'If Bertie is your sister's baby, why is there no mention of her anywhere? Does Gemma even exist? The story is all over social media, as well as the newspapers, stating that *you* are the baby's mother. It is reported that, when you told me I was the father of your child, I sent you away and warned you never to contact me again.'

Rafa's eyes were icy cold as he raked them over Ivy, starting at her bright pink hair and slowly moving down her body to her bare feet and the chipped varnish on her toenails. 'You are not my type,' he drawled. 'I did not make a child with you.'

Shameful images flashed into her head of just what that would entail, followed by humiliation at his scornful rejection. Obviously she wasn't his type. There had been no need for him to remind her that she was nothing like the glamorous and statuesque women he was often photographed with.

Rafa's comment that he had not made a child with her had delivered another wounding blow to Ivy's bruised heart. It was a painful reminder that she would never hold her own baby in her arms. She would have liked a family of her own and, although she was deeply grateful to have recovered from cancer, there had been a lingering sadness in her heart that she almost certainly couldn't have a baby. Becoming responsible for Bertie had given her a chance to be a mother, but at the terrible cost of her sister's life.

Doubt slid into Ivy's mind. Rafa was adamant that he had never met Gemma. She could not believe her sister had lied, but Gemma had been in Accident and Emergency and being prepared for surgery when Ivy had rushed to the hospital after she'd heard about the accident. Their conversation had been hurried and emotional, but Gemma had clearly said that Rafael Vieri was Bertie's father. It had been the last time that Ivy had seen her sister alive, and she could not hold back her tears at the memory of watching Gemma being wheeled away to Theatre.

Rafa muttered something in Italian that, from his tone, Ivy guessed was not complimentary. 'I might have guessed you would cry when your lies were exposed. It's a clever act, but I am not affected by tears.'

'I'm not acting. I can't help crying when you say such vile things,' she said in a choked voice. As a child, she had rarely showed her feelings. There had always been a drama at home, and she'd learned to be stoical about her parents' volatile relationship and her father's absences when he'd become bored of family life. Even when he had left for good, she'd kept her feelings of disappointment and abandonment to herself.

Cancer had changed Ivy. She had recovered from a life-threatening illness, but she felt like an onion that had had its layers peeled away one by one, leaving her raw and exposing her deepest emotions. She found joy in simple things, but tears came easily when she was upset.

'You treated my sister badly,' she accused Rafa thickly. 'You ignored her when she wrote to tell you that she'd given birth to your baby.'

He threw his hands up in the air. 'I did not sleep with your sister. And why did you tell the newspapers that I am the father of *your* child?'

'I didn't.' Ivy swallowed and tried to regain her composure. It was difficult when Rafa loomed over her like a beautiful, dark angel. 'I told him I wouldn't talk to the press.'

She bit her lip when Rafa glowered at her. 'There was a man,' she muttered. 'He came up to me in the street after I'd left Vieri Azioni's office building and said he'd heard that I had introduced you to your son.'

Rafa looked disbelieving. 'What was his name?'

'I don't know.' She couldn't admit that she'd been unable to think straight after the shock of finding herself attracted to Rafa. 'He…the man…was concerned that I'd had to walk back to my hotel carrying Bertie. There wasn't a baby seat fitted in your car,' she said in response to Rafa's frown. 'He took me to a café…and bought me *gelato*.'

Rafa's brows lifted, and Ivy flushed at the sardonic look he gave her. 'He suggested that I could sell my story to the press for a lot of money,' she continued. 'I told him I wouldn't do that because I didn't want Gemma's and Bertie's private lives published in the newspapers.' She frowned. 'Although, come to think of it, I don't remember that I mentioned Gemma.'

'So you allowed a random stranger to believe that I'd got you pregnant and refused to accept responsibility for my illegitimate child,' Rafa said in a dangerous voice. 'Did it occur to you that Gelato Man could have been a journalist?'

She flushed again at his mocking tone. 'I'm sure he wasn't. I have no idea how the story is in the newspapers or why some of the facts are wrong.'

'The entire story is a complete fabrication that has cost me an important business deal and led the board members of my company to question my suitability to be the CEO.' Rafa's teeth were gritted. His withering tone stirred Ivy's temper.

'My sister was not a liar, and neither am I.'

He snorted. 'Frankly, I don't give a damn whether you or your sister are the baby's mother. I am not his father, and I will prove it by taking a paternity test. When I have the irrefutable truth from the lab report, the newspapers will have to retract the story, and I will sue you for making false allegations to the press, Miss Bennett.'

'I have no objection to a DNA test being carried out. In fact, I was going to suggest it,' Ivy said calmly. 'The test will prove that you are Bertie's father. What will you do then?' she asked Rafa. 'Will you be prepared to make room in your life for your son? And will you love him as he needs and deserves to be loved?'

* * *

Ivy was calling his bluff, Rafa assured himself. The baby was not his. Everything inside him rejected the possibility. He had made room in his life and indeed welcomed the birth of a child once before. He'd loved Lola unreservedly, but the revelation that she was not his daughter had almost broken him and made him bitter and untrusting.

He had no recollection of meeting Ivy's sister. It was true he'd enjoyed numerous sexual liaisons with women who understood that he did not want a long-term relationship, but he had always been sober when he'd taken his lovers to bed. He would swear he'd never slept with the woman in the photo who Ivy had told him was the baby's mother. Why then was it reported in the media that Bertie was Ivy's baby? The whole thing smacked of a scam that Ivy was trying to pull. Yet it was odd that she had agreed to his demand for a paternity test without argument.

The bathroom was hot and airless, and sweat beaded on Rafa's brow. He had every reason to mistrust Ivy, but his libido did not seem to care that she was a liar. He roamed his eyes over her grey vest top and matching tiny shorts that clung to her narrow hips and stopped high up on her thighs. Moving his gaze lower, he noted that her legs were shapely, with the defined calf muscles of a dancer. When he'd followed her into the bathroom, his eyes had been drawn to the rounded curves of her pert bottom.

Now she stood facing him and he could see the enticing outline of her nipples pressing against her thin top. If he'd had sex with Ivy, he would not have forgotten her, he brooded. His wayward imagination indulged in an erotic fantasy in which he undressed her and kissed his way down her body. He was intrigued to discover if the body hair covering her femininity was dyed bright pink too.

Dio! Rafa jerked his mind back from going down a path he was definitely not going to follow. At best Ivy had made a genuine mistake in believing he was the father of her sister's baby. At worst—and, to Rafa's mind, more likely—Ivy was a deceitful gold-digger from the same mould as his ex-wife. Why then was his body reacting as if he were a hormone-fuelled teenager on a first date?

Lust for Tiffany had resulted in their marriage, which in truth had been rocky almost from the start. Rafa had been willing to work at the relationship for the sake of their daughter until Tiffany had admitted that another man was Lola's father and that she'd married Rafa for his money. Since the divorce, he had made decisions based on cold logic rather than unreliable emotions.

Proof that Ivy was a liar would be revealed in the result of the paternity test and he would have no qualms about throwing her to the wolves, or in this case the paparazzi, Rafa thought grimly. He'd see how she liked being fodder for the gutter press. He had been woken early in the morning by the constant pinging of his phone as new messages arrived from friends congratulating him on becoming a father. Immediately, he'd flicked to a news stream and blistering hot rage had surged through him when he'd discovered that Ivy had gone to the press with her scandalous story.

It had to have been her. Rafa remembered Ivy's startled reaction when he'd showed her the front page of the newspaper. She'd admitted that she had been approached by a stranger. Surely she could not be so naïve that she hadn't realised the guy was a journalist? She must have arranged to talk to the press after he had refused to believe her story or give her money. Ivy looked as though butter wouldn't melt in her mouth, but he wasn't fooled by a pretty little liar.

When she stepped closer to him, Rafa's muscles tensed, as if he was preparing to defend himself from an attack by an enemy—which she was, he reminded himself. It was entirely Ivy's fault that Carlo Landini had called him an hour ago and cancelled the deal for Vieri Azioni to buy into Banca Landini. Now he was facing the threat of a vote of no confidence by the board, and some of the directors had suggested that the deputy, Sandro Florenzi, should replace Rafa as chairman and CEO.

'I understand that finding out about Bertie has been a shock for you,' Ivy said softly. 'Especially if you did not receive Gemma's letter. I really don't know how the media got hold of the story.'

It was crazy that he wanted to believe her. His failed marriage and Tiffany's betrayal had made Rafa deeply cynical, but he could not look away from Ivy's melting, chocolate-brown eyes. His body tightened as he watched her pupils dilate. The strap of her top had slipped off one shoulder and his fingers itched to slide it back into place, or better still tug the other strap down until he'd bared her breasts with their pebble-hard nipples. His mouth watered at the prospect of curling his tongue around each taut peak.

The atmosphere in the tiny bathroom simmered with sexual tension that made the hairs on Rafa's neck stand on end and his pulse thud hard and fast. His gaze dropped to Ivy's mouth as her tongue darted across her lips to moisten them. He did not know if it was an unconscious action or a deliberate invitation, and frankly he did not care. He wanted to kiss her. It infuriated him to admit that he desired her, but he was confident that he was in control, and kissing her would simply satisfy his curiosity.

A high-pitched cry from the bedroom shattered whatever had or hadn't been about to happen between them. Rafa told himself he should feel relieved when Ivy gasped as if she had been jolted back to reality and spun away from him.

'I can't believe Bertie is awake already. I hoped he would sleep while I had a shower. I have to check out of the hotel by ten o'clock and my flight back to England is at two this afternoon.'

'You will have to reschedule your flight.' Rafa followed her into the bedroom. 'I have arranged for samples to be taken from me and the baby today. The DNA testing company guarantees that the results will be ready in twenty-four hours.'

'The airline doesn't allow changes to bookings at short notice, and I can't afford to pay for another flight or stay at a hotel tonight. It will be better if I go home today. When you receive the test results, you can let me know what, if any, involvement you want with your son.'

'*Dio*, you don't give up, do you?' Rafa said tersely. He wasn't going to admit he was rattled by Ivy's certainty that he was the baby's father.

'Poor little mite. He's wet through.' She scooped Bertie out of the cot and, from the way her breath hissed between her teeth, Rafa guessed the movement had hurt her shoulder. Whatever else she might have lied about, her shoulder injury was genuine, and she'd almost passed out in the bathroom. 'I should have changed his nappy before I put him down, but I didn't want to risk waking him. Will you pass me one of his sleep suits from the backpack? Tip everything out if it's easier.'

Rafa spotted the backpack on the floor. He opened it and dumped a pile of baby clothes onto the bed. Caught up among the clothes was a business card. He picked it up and gave a harsh laugh.

'*Di Oggie!* The most popular daily newspaper in Italy. I hope they paid you a lot of money. You will need a good lawyer when I sue you for defamation of my character. The fine is likely to be thousands of pounds, or you could be sent to prison.'

He refused to be taken in by Ivy's stricken expression. The reporter's business card was proof that he was right not to believe a word Ivy uttered.

'The man I met in the street gave me the card, but I didn't call the number and speak to the reporter. I've done nothing wrong.'

She was good at playing the innocent victim, but Rafa wasn't fooled by her denial. He was exasperated that he could not control his body's response to Ivy's elfin beauty. 'I suppose you told the journalist the name of your hotel,' he accused when he moved away from her and looked out of the window. 'There is a crowd of reporters outside. Did you tip them off that I was here?'

'No. How could I have done? I haven't been out of your sight since you arrived, and my phone is over there.' She glanced towards her phone on the bedside table.

Anger had brought colour to her pale cheeks and there were sparks of fire in her eyes. Rafa preferred her temper to her earlier sadness. He had an intense horror of tears—a throwback to his childhood when his mother had suffered deeply from depression and Rafa would often hear her crying desperately when she'd thought he was out of earshot.

When Ivy had spoken about her sister, Rafa had seen that her grief was raw and, despite his mistrust of her, he'd felt an urge to comfort her. He understood the gut-wrenching sense of loss. His father had died not long after Ivy's sister. Rafa hadn't realised how much he'd loved his *papà* until it had been too late to tell him. Why did this woman stir his emotions that, like a hornets' nest, were better left alone? he wondered.

'Get dressed,' he told Ivy curtly. 'You and the baby will spend tonight at my apartment. Tomorrow, when the paternity test result exonerates me from any responsibility for the child, I will personally drive you to the airport and put you on the first plane to England on the understanding that I never hear from you or see you again.'

CHAPTER THREE

IVY EMERGED FROM the bathroom, where she had gone to get dressed, and found Rafa's driver in her hotel room. The two men were talking quietly in Italian and there was an infant car seat on the bed. The driver gave her a curious look before he left.

'Aldo says it's a scrum downstairs,' Rafa told her grimly. 'When we leave the hotel, stick close to me and do not say anything to the reporters.'

'It's not my fault that they're outside.'

The scathing look he gave her said he did not believe her. His eyes narrowed as he studied her canary-yellow sundress with a shirred bodice that supported her small breasts. Any movement of her shoulder was agony and she'd given up trying to reach behind her back to do up her bra.

She was conscious that her nipples had tightened and hoped Rafa did not notice her body's response to him as his gaze lingered on her breasts before moving up to her pink hair.

'Very colourful,' he drawled.

'I like bright colours,' Ivy said defensively, wishing she was taller and more elegant and could afford to wear designer clothes like the women she'd seen with Rafa on social media. She was angry with herself for wanting his approval and wishing that he found her attractive.

Her heart sank as she wondered if she had inherited her mother's poor judgement in men. Her mum had always fallen for bad boys, convinced that she would be able to make them love her. As a child, Ivy had felt that her mum had cared more about her pursuit of romantic relationships than her. Seeing how her mum had been badly treated by her husbands and lovers had been a warning that falling in love was a risk that too often resulted in disappointment and heartbreak. When Ivy's first romance as a teenager had ended with Luke heartlessly dumping her because he couldn't cope with her illness, it had reinforced her belief that men were unreliable and likely to let her down.

'You are certainly noticeable,' Rafa told her. 'Is that the point, to grab the paparazzi's attention and sell them another fantasy story? Your plan will backfire when I can prove that I am not Bertie's father.'

Frustration at Rafa's refusal to believe her made Ivy halt on her way over to the cot. She was tired of trying to defend herself. 'We could just stop this now,' she said tautly. 'It's obvious that you don't want Bertie. I'll take him back to England and care for him on my own, and I won't ask you to contribute a penny for him.'

Rafa gave a cynical laugh. 'I've been waiting for you to try to back out of the paternity test, but your luck's out, little lady. Your publicity stunt when you involved the press has damaged my personal reputation and my business credibility, and I have lost the support of many of my board members and shareholders. If you refuse permission for the test, I will seek a court order for it to go ahead.'

'Fine.' She leaned over the cot, but as she lifted Bertie out she felt a tearing pain in her shoulder and could not restrain a sharp cry.

'You had better let me hold him.' Rafa crossed the room in a couple of strides and took the baby from her. A curious expression flickered on his face as he looked down at Bertie lying in his arms. Ivy supposed she was biased, but anyone would have to admit that Bertie was an adorable baby, with his olive-toned complexion and mass of almost black hair. Like father, like son, she thought ruefully. But Rafa did not want his little boy and he believed that she had an ulterior motive for bringing Bertie to Italy.

'Have you seen a doctor about the pain in your shoulder?' he asked her while he strapped Bertie into the car seat. His confident handling of the baby was a surprise, as he'd given the impression that he'd never been within a million miles of a small child before.

Ivy stuffed the baby's clothes into the backpack. 'I had it checked out by a medic on the cruise ship. He thought I'd pulled a muscle from a fall while I was dancing. But that was a few months ago and my shoulder still hurts.'

'It might be a rotator cuff tear, although it's more likely to be a strain where the muscles and tendons that keep your shoulder in its socket are damaged. It's a common injury for basketball players,' Rafa explained when she stared at him. 'At one time I considered training to be a sports physiotherapist when my playing career was over.'

'Why didn't you?' Ivy couldn't hide her curiosity. This was the first conversation she'd had with Rafa without tension bristling between them. His deep voice with the hint of an Italian accent was *so* sexy.

He shrugged. 'I always knew that I was destined to succeed my father as the head of Vieri Azioni. After ten years of playing sport at a professional level, I was ready for a new challenge.' His tone hardened and Ivy wondered if there was more to his decision to return to Italy than he'd let on. She had read that he'd been through an acrimonious divorce while he'd lived in America.

'The company was established by my great-grandfather,' Rafa continued. 'I was my father's only son and there was pressure on me to take his place and continue the family's association with Vieri Azioni.'

'Now you have a son to carry on that association.' Ivy spoke unthinkingly. She wished she could take her words back when Rafa's brows lowered.

'Did you find out from your research that Vieri Azioni's revenue for the last fiscal year was one hundred billion euros? Perhaps you discovered that, aside from my family's wealth, I was one of the highest-paid players in the American professional basketball league.'

'That's not why I brought Bertie to you,' she said quickly, stung by Rafa's scornful tone.

'Paternity fraud is an occupational hazard for rich men,' he carried on as if she hadn't spoken. 'There have been numerous cases where a woman has accused a man, usually a well-known figure or celebrity, of being the father of her child. It can have a devastating impact on an innocent man's life and relationships, especially if he has a wife or long-term partner. Fortunately, I don't, but I will stop at nothing to clear my name. The reason for a false paternity claim is always money.'

Ivy felt incinerated by the scorching contempt in Rafa's eyes. She looked at Bertie sleeping peacefully in the car seat and her heart ached with love for him. He was so perfect and innocently unaware of the furore resulting from his birth.

'I hoped you would want to do the right thing for Bertie,' she muttered. 'Although, I don't know why I thought you might be a good father to him. I'm not even sure that good fathers exist. Mine cleared off when I was ten, and neither of my stepfathers were any more reliable. My dad left because he had been having an affair with another woman. Mum continued to chase a romantic dream and she married and divorced twice more.' She glared at Rafa. 'Bertie will be better off without a father than with a reluctant father who takes no interest in him.'

Rafa's expression was unreadable, and Ivy decided that he had been carved from granite. He slung her backpack over his shoulder, picked up the car seat by the handle and carried Bertie over to the door. 'Let's get this over with,' he said tersely.

The driver had parked the car outside the front of the hotel. When Ivy followed Rafa through the door, she tensed as reporters and photographers surrounded them. Flashlights popped and the clamour of voices asking questions about their relationship grew more insistent. Rafa clamped his arm around Ivy's waist and pushed a path through the crowd to where the driver was holding the car door open for them. She climbed into the back and scrambled across the seat to make room for Rafa. He handed the baby seat to the driver, who fitted it to the anchor point in the car. With Bertie safely stowed, Rafa slammed the door shut. The driver slid behind the steering wheel and, as the car sped away from the hotel, a few die-hard photographers ran behind, still snapping pictures.

'They're like a pack of wolves,' Ivy said shakily. 'Is Bertie all right?' Rafa was sitting between the baby seat and her.

'He's still asleep.'

'I can't imagine how. I was worried he would be scared by the cameras and the shouting.'

'It's a pity you did not consider how he would be affected before you opened your mouth and told the press a pack of lies.'

Ivy did not reply. Nothing she said would make Rafa believe that she hadn't gone public with her allegation that Bertie was his child. The paternity test would show the truth, and if she'd been a vindictive person she'd have enjoyed hearing him apologise. But the sad fact was that there would be no winners. Rafa did not want his son and Bertie was destined to grow up without ever knowing his father.

She leaned her head against the back rest and her eyelashes drifted down. Her disturbed night with Bertie caught up with her as the car crawled along in a traffic jam.

'Ivy, wake up.'

The gravelly voice next to her ear jolted Ivy awake. She opened her eyes and found Rafa's handsome face so close to hers that she could count his thick eyelashes. Her awareness of him was instant as her senses responded to the sensual musk of his aftershave.

She was embarrassed by the unsettling effect he had on her and prayed he could not tell that she was fiercely aware of him. *Get a grip,* she told herself. Bertie was her priority, and she hoped that when Rafa had proof he was the baby's father his attitude would change. She flushed when she realised that she must have fallen asleep with her head resting on Rafa's shoulder.

'Sorry,' she muttered as she hastily moved across to the other side of the car. 'I was up with Bertie several times last night.'

'Is he often restless during the night?'

She took it as a good sign that Rafa was showing an interest in Bertie. 'He usually wakes around midnight and nothing I do seems to comfort him.' Ivy turned her head towards the window so that Rafa would not see the tears in her eyes. 'Maybe he misses Gem.' Her voice thickened. 'I do my best, but I'm not his mum.'

She gave a start when Rafa put his hand over hers where it was lying on her knee and gently squeezed her fingers. 'What happened to your sister? Was she ill?'

'There was a road traffic accident. Gemma was knocked down as she crossed the road.' Ivy swallowed the lump that had formed in her throat. 'She had only popped out to buy nappies. I'd said I would go, but she'd wanted to get out of the flat for a while. We lived on a busy main road and the pedestrian crossing was a few metres away. We had got into the habit of nipping across the road instead of walking to the crossing where it was safe.'

Ivy looked down at Rafa's strong, tanned fingers covering her paler ones. It was a long time since anyone had offered her a physical gesture of comfort. Her dad had given her an awkward hug at Gemma's funeral, but he'd rushed back to Scotland, where he lived with his current girlfriend and their two children. Ivy had never been invited to meet her half-siblings.

Kindness from Rafa was unexpected and tugged on her fragile emotions. 'When I saw the emergency services outside the flat, I didn't realise at first that Gemma had been involved in an accident. But she was ages at the shop, and she didn't answer her phone. The police arrived and said that a van had driven around the corner fast and hit Gem, and she'd been taken to hospital.'

Ivy recalled the PC's sympathetic expression. He must have known that her sister's injuries were life threatening. 'A neighbour looked after Bertie and I rushed to the hospital. Gemma was conscious and I was allowed to see her briefly. She told me the name of Bertie's father and made me promise to find you before she was taken to the operating theatre. But her life couldn't be saved.'

'Is it possible that your sister was confused? She was about to undergo surgery and no doubt she had been given medication before a general anaesthetic.' Rafa frowned. 'Perhaps I'd been mentioned in a newspaper article that Gemma had read. Vieri Azioni is a multinational conglomerate, and its dealings are reported in financial publications around the word. Your sister might have muddled my name with the man she'd met on the cruise ship.'

'Gemma didn't read financial newspapers.' But her sister had been fascinated by the glamorous lives of celebrities and had followed many of them on social media. When Ivy had researched Rafa Vieri online, she had found plenty of pictures and gossip about him.

What if she had made a terrible mistake by bringing Bertie to Italy? She had no idea how the newspapers had got hold of the story that Rafa was the baby's father. If the paternity test came back negative, would he carry out his threat to sue her for slander, and could she really be sent to prison?

Ivy turned her head and met Rafa's enigmatic gaze. She wondered what he would do if she leaned closer and pressed her lips against his stubbled jaw. Would he angle his mouth over hers and kiss her? She wanted him to, she admitted to herself. But she resented her intense awareness of him. He had a reputation as a womaniser, and he was the last man she would ever get involved with.

'We're here.' Rafa released Ivy's hand and she felt oddly bereft.

'I thought we were going to your apartment.' The car had slowed outside one of Rome's most famous hotels, the Palazzo Degli Dei. Opposite was the city's iconic historical landmark, the Colosseum.

'I live in the hotel's penthouse suite.'

'Why do you live in a hotel?'

He shrugged. 'I own the hotel, although my interest is purely as an investment, and I am not involved in running it. I like the convenience of living in a serviced apartment.'

There was a crowd of paparazzi near the hotel's grand entrance, although they were kept away from the door by security guards. Ivy tensed, thinking that they would be mobbed by the photographers, but the car drove past the entrance and turned down a ramp that led to an underground car park. Rafa carried Bertie in the baby seat and ushered Ivy into a private lift that took them directly up to his apartment.

She preceded him inside and her tension increased when she took in her surroundings. The penthouse was ultra-modern and sophisticated with black marble floors, and white velvet sofas were arranged in groups in the vast, open-plan living space. From every window there was a view of the ancient Colosseum.

Everything about the apartment screamed serious money, but it felt like a high-end hotel suite rather than a private home, and there was nothing on show that gave a clue to the personality of the man who lived there.

She turned to find Rafa watching her, and her heart skipped a beat as her gaze locked with his. She wished she knew what he was thinking, but his chiselled features revealed nothing.

'I'll show you where you and the baby will sleep tonight,' he said coolly.

Ivy followed him down the corridor and into a room where there was a cot and a baby-change unit. There was also an impressive looking pushchair with a carry-cot attachment suitable for young babies.

'Do you have another child—or children?' It suddenly occurred to her that Rafa might already be a father. Why else would there be nursery furniture in his swanky apartment?

'No.' Beneath his curt reply, there was something in his voice that stirred Ivy's curiosity. 'The hotel provided the nursery equipment, and I ordered the push chair from a supplier.'

'I'll pay for the push chair,' she said at once, not wanting him to think she was after freebies.

He ignored her and opened a door into a connecting bedroom. 'I assumed you would want to sleep near the baby so that you can attend to him if he wakes in the night.'

The room was at least three times bigger than Ivy's bedroom at the flat in Southampton where she had lived with her sister. She would have to move out of the flat in a matter of days, and finding somewhere affordable for Bertie and her to live was another worry to add to her already long list.

Rafa set the car seat down on the floor and lifted a now awake Bertie out. The baby gave a winsome smile that never failed to melt Ivy's heart, but there was not a flicker of response on Rafa's face as he handed Bertie to her.

'The doctor will be here in a few minutes to take samples for the DNA test. I have been assured that the procedure is a simple cheek swab and Bertie won't feel a thing.' He dropped Ivy's backpack onto the bed. 'I will need yours and the baby's passports so that I can book your return flight to England.'

In twenty-four hours they would know the truth, although Ivy did not doubt her sister. Pride made her want to tell Rafa that she would pay for her own plane ticket, but the reality was she did not have enough money in her account for the flight.

She searched in the backpack for the passports. When she pulled them out, a card fell onto the bed. She had intended to throw the reporter's business card into the bin before she left her hotel, but somehow it had ended up in the backpack, and it silently condemned her. Rafa said nothing, but the icy fury in his eyes sent a shiver through Ivy when he plucked the passports from her fingers and strode out of the room.

* * *

Rafa woke the next morning with a pounding headache. His hangover was not surprising, after the train wreck his life had become in the past forty-eight hours. He was in dire need of strong black coffee and he pulled on a pair of sweatpants before he padded barefoot down the hall to the kitchen.

His stomach tightened when he saw Ivy perched on a stool at the breakfast bar, drinking orange juice out of the carton. It had been a mistake to bring her to his apartment, he brooded. He did not want any involvement with her, or Bertie, who he was certain was not his son. He wished he'd arranged for them to stay in a hotel room, but it had seemed sensible to keep Ivy close to stop her talking to the press and making up more lies about him.

'I couldn't find a glass,' she said when Rafa glowered at her. 'I hope Bertie's crying didn't disturb you during the night.'

The inroads he'd made on a bottle of single malt hadn't blocked out the baby's cries, which had evoked poignant memories of when he'd believed he was the father of an adorable little daughter. Nor had getting drunk banished Ivy from his erotic dreams. The sight of her first thing, looking perkily pretty and as sexy as hell in an over-sized tee shirt that kept slipping off one shoulder, did nothing to improve Rafa's mood.

He took two glasses from a cupboard, filled both with juice and pushed one towards Ivy before he downed his drink in a couple of gulps. On the counter was a selection of the daily newspapers that the maid had delivered to the apartment. The front page of many of the papers had a photo of Rafa carrying Bertie in the baby seat, seemingly hustling Ivy out of a run-down hotel and into a car. She looked young and appallingly innocent with her pink hair and Bambi eyes, beneath the headline.

Il magnate, il suo amante e il loro bambino!

'What does it say?'

'It says, *"the tycoon, his lover and their baby"*.' Rafa translated the headline.

'Oh, no!' Ivy had perfected the 'wide-eyed ingénue' act. But, even knowing that she was a liar and that she had obviously been in contact with the journalist whose business card had been in her bag, Rafa felt an intense desire to crush her soft mouth beneath his and taste the orange juice on her lips. Once again, she wasn't wearing a bra, and he wondered if she even possessed one. Every time she moved, her tee shirt brushed against her breasts, and he glimpsed the tantalising outline of her pointed nipples.

'I don't understand why the papers are saying that you and I are...involved.' Unbelievably, she blushed.

'Don't you?' He had every right to be cynical and suspicious, Rafa told himself.

Ivy lifted her hands in a helpless gesture. 'What can we do?'

The neck of her shirt had slipped off her shoulder, exposing the pale, upper swell of one breast. Heat stirred in Rafa's groin, and he could not control the surge of sexual hunger that swept through him. Resting his elbow on the breakfast counter, he leaned closer to Ivy. She tensed but did not pull away. He was fascinated by the frantic thud of the pulse at the base of her throat.

'The media and half the goddamned world believe we are lovers,' he drawled. He did not add, *thanks to you*, but his unspoken accusation intensified the simmering tension in the kitchen. 'I think I'm owed some sort of compensation for the trouble you have caused.'

Ivy's face was a picture as her lips parted to form a perfect *O!* when his meaning became clear. Rosy colour stained her cheeks and throat, and Rafa's fingers itched to grab the hem of her shirt and pull it over her head so that he could see if the flush of heat had spread across her breasts.

'Are you propositioning me?' The amber flecks in her eyes sparked with temper, but her voice was oddly breathless. 'You said I'm not your type,' she reminded him.

'The pink hair is growing on me.' Compelled by the drumbeat of desire pounding in his veins, Rafa traced his finger down her cheek and neck, stopping at the edge of her shirt, where her breasts were rising and falling jerkily. Her skin was as soft and delicate as rose petals and he was intrigued by how easily she blushed.

He should stop this now before he did something he would later regret, such as kiss the sulky pout from her mouth until her lips were soft and pliant beneath his. His common sense told him that he should switch on the coffee machine and get his kick from a hit of caffeine instead of hitting on Little Miss Liar. But he couldn't move away from her.

'We could be lovers,' he murmured. 'At least then, part of the news story would be true.'

He'd meant it to be a joke, a taunt to annoy her. He wanted to provoke a reaction from her, in the same way that she provoked one from him, but his voice thickened as the heat inside him flared into an inferno.

'I've never had a lover.' The lie—for surely it must be a lie?—slipped so easily from her pretty mouth. 'What makes you think I'd want you?'

Rafa would have been more convinced that she was not interested in him if her voice hadn't become husky and seductive. Her eyes had darkened, the enlarged pupils almost swallowing up the brown irises, drawing him in. He resented the effect she had on him even as he lowered his face towards her.

What makes you think I'd want you? Ivy had challenged him and Rafa could never resist a challenge.

'This,' he murmured before he brought his mouth down on hers.

She gasped and he swallowed the soft sound, easing her lips apart with his. The effect on him was instant. He felt as though an electrical current had zapped through his body. Somehow he stopped himself from ravaging her lips with hungry passion. He had felt her slight hesitation and he kept the kiss light, flicking his tongue over the contours of her mouth and taking little sips from her lips.

He felt her mouth quiver beneath the coaxing pressure of his and a nerve jumped in his cheek as it became harder to restrain himself from devouring her. His patience paid off as, with a low moan, she parted her lips to allow his tongue to probe between them.

Dio, she tasted of orange juice and nectar, and he wanted more. He speared his fingers into her pink hair. The feathery strands felt like silk against his skin as he slid one hand round to her nape and angled her head so that he could fit his mouth even closer to hers. He pushed his tongue between her lips and Ivy copied his actions, tentatively at first, but she grew bolder as the kiss became increasingly erotic.

She placed her hands on his bare chest, and Rafa knew she must feel the erratic thud of his heart. His skin felt too hot, too tight. He wanted her naked against his bare skin. Her breasts would be soft and her nipples as hard as pebbles pressing into his chest.

This was madness. She should not be kissing Rafa. Alarm bells rang in Ivy's brain, but her body wasn't listening. The instant he had covered her mouth with his, a fire had ignited inside her, and she was burning in his fiery passion. She was intoxicated by the scent of his body, a subtle blend of the spicy cologne he'd worn the previous day, the faint peatiness of whisky and something uniquely male that triggered a purely feminine response low in her pelvis.

Her bones had turned to jelly the moment he'd strolled into the kitchen, looking like a fallen god, with his almost black hair spilling across his brow and thick stubble shadowing his jaw. His bare chest was tanned a deep olive-gold and covered with whorls of black hairs that arrowed down to the edge of his sweatpants sitting low on his hips.

While she was sitting on the bar stool, her face was almost

level with Rafa's. He tightened his arms around her, and she was powerless to stop herself from melting against his whip-cord body. Her breasts felt heavy and warmth pooled between her thighs. She ran her hands over his chest, fascinated by the feel of satin overlaid with wiry hairs. Her fingertips explored the ridges of his powerful abs as she strained closer to him and parted her lips beneath his, kissing him with a wild passion she'd never felt for any other man.

In truth, there hadn't been many other men, Ivy acknowledged. Her first romance when she'd been seventeen had ended with her cancer diagnosis. In hindsight, she supposed that Luke had been too young to cope, but when he'd broken up with her it had reinforced her belief that all men were like her father and disappeared when things got tough. One day she hoped she would meet a guy she could rely on. But that guy was not Rafa Vieri. He was a playboy who had slept with her sister and pretended that he did not remember.

What was she doing? Ivy tore her lips from Rafa's. Recrimination tasted like sawdust in her mouth. Her wanton behaviour was completely out of character. She felt guilty that she had betrayed Gemma, even though things with Rafa hadn't gone further than a kiss. But for a few moments she had been utterly carried away by their blazing passion and she'd longed for him to lie her down on the breakfast counter and lower his body onto hers.

'No.' She pushed against Rafa's chest, and he backed off immediately.

'Easy,' he murmured.

Ivy slid down from the bar stool and wrapped her arms around her body as if she could hold herself together. She ran her tongue over her swollen lips. 'I'm not easy,' she told Rafa tremulously. 'I realise I must have given you a different impression. That shouldn't have happened.'

He shrugged. 'It was just a kiss. Nothing to get worked up about.'

Evidently he hadn't been affected by the kiss the way she had, and she wanted to die of shame. *Who would look after Bertie?* demanded a scornful voice in her head. Ivy shuddered with remorse and anger at herself. For those few minutes, while Rafa had been expertly kissing her, she had forgotten about Bertie.

Ivy remembered when she'd been a child and her mum had been so wrapped up in her latest romance that she hadn't paid her much attention. Luckily, she'd had Gemma to turn to, but Bertie had no one else. *How could she have forgotten her sister's baby for even one second?*

She stared at Rafa and despised herself for the way her body responded to his potent masculinity. 'I should not have kissed *you*.'

He strolled down the kitchen and dropped a coffee pod into the machine. 'Forget it,' he drawled in a bored voice. 'I already have.'

'Good, that makes two of us.' Pride came to Ivy's rescue and insisted on her having the last word before she walked out of the room with as much dignity as she could muster. The heart-rending sound of Bertie crying piled on more guilt, and when she hurried down the hallway and into his room the sight of his red face and tears on his cheeks made her feel that she was the worst person in the world.

She scooped him out of the cot and hugged his little body. 'I'm sorry, Bobo,' she choked, using her sister's pet name for him. *I'm sorry, Gemma,* she apologised silently. Bertie was all that mattered to her, and she would never forget him again. She wished she'd never brought the baby to Italy or met Rafa Vieri. But when Bertie was older he would have the right to know the identity of his father. Much as Ivy wanted to take him back to England, she had to remain in Rome until the result of the paternity test confirmed her belief that Bertie was Rafa's son.

CHAPTER FOUR

THE AUTOMATIC GATES opened to allow Rafa to turn his car onto the driveway of his parents' villa in an affluent suburb of the city. A crowd of photographers had gathered outside the estate, and they surged towards the car. The same thing had happened when he had driven away from the Palazzo Degli Dei hotel. A few of the paparazzi had even jumped onto motorbikes and chased after his car, hoping to snap a picture that would make it onto tomorrow's front page.

Instead of driving up to the house, Rafa stopped halfway along the gravel driveway and switched off the engine. Before he had left the penthouse, he'd had a difficult conversation with his mother, when she'd tearfully asked why he had kept her grandson a secret. She was upset that she'd found out about the baby from reading the newspapers. Rafa had come to reassure his mother that Bertie was not his child, and Ivy wasn't his lover.

But he had wanted to make love to Ivy. He grimaced as he remembered how she had threatened his self-control with her understated sensuality. He shouldn't have kissed her, and he was furious with himself for coming on to her like a teenager with a surfeit of testosterone. It wasn't his style, and he did not understand why she got under his skin. But she wouldn't bother him for much longer. He was expecting the result of the paternity test, which would prove that Ivy was a liar who had caused him public embarrassment and possibly cost him his position as the CEO of Vieri Azioni.

Thankfully his father was not around to witness his humiliation. Emotion tightened Rafa's throat. It felt strange, coming back to the family home where he had spent his childhood and teenage years, now his *papà* was no longer here. Guilt augmented his grief. His father hadn't wanted him to move to America to play basketball, but Rafa had been driven by determination—and a fair-sized ego, he acknowledged ruefully—to make his own mark on the world.

As a young man, there had been a weight of expectation on him to dedicate his life to the family business in the same way that his father had done. When he had chosen a different path, he'd sensed he was a disappointment to his father, despite his successful career as a professional sportsman. The unspoken accusation that he was not committed to Vieri Azioni had added to Rafa's feeling that he was not a good enough son.

It was for that reason he had decided not to pursue his interest in training to be a sports physiotherapist when his basketball playing days had been coming to an end. Instead he had returned to the fold and discovered that he'd inherited his father's business acumen. The past eighteen months, when he had worked with his father, had been genuinely enjoyable, and Rafa had felt that they had become closer than they'd ever been.

But the sudden loss of his father meant that he'd faced the new challenge of proving to the board and himself that he was a worthy successor to run Vieri Azioni. Progress had been good and after an initial wobble, that had reflected investors' shock at his father's death, the value of the company's stock had recovered as confidence in the new CEO had increased.

That had been until the story that Rafa had refused to recognise his illegitimate baby son had hit the headlines. It was still the most trended topic on social media. But he was about to receive proof that he had done nothing to bring shame on himself.

The ping of his phone alerted him to the arrival of an email. Relieved that he would be able to get his life back on track, he opened the report from the DNA testing clinic and read it several times. His mouth dried and he was conscious of his heart banging against his ribs. The report did not make any sense.

Ninety-nine point five percent probability. Rafael Vieri is not excluded as the biological father of Roberto Bennett.

He had fallen into a nightmare. That was the only logical explanation. The notes accompanying the report explained that the paternity test could prove with one hundred percent accuracy that a man was *excluded* as the father of a child. That was the result Rafa had been banking on. But the high percentage of probability on the results sheet indicated that the possible father, i.e. himself, was most likely the biological father of the child, since all data gathered from the test supported a relationship of paternity.

Hell!

He pinched the bridge of his nose. Only once before in his life had he experienced such a gut-wrenching shock—when Tiffany had admitted that she'd lied, and the daughter he'd adored was not his child. But this was insane. He could not have fathered a child by Ivy's sister. Rafa was sure he'd never met Gemma, yet the evidence that Bertie was his son was in front of him.

His phone rang, and he cursed softly before he answered it. *'Ciao, Mamma.'*

'Why are you sitting in your car? Are you too ashamed to face me?'

'I had to deal with something important…for work.' It was a white lie, but he did not know what he was going to say to his mother. The email had left him reeling. Once again, the result of a paternity test had blown his life apart, Rafa thought grimly as he drove up to the house.

The maid escorted him into the drawing room where Fabiana

Vieri was lying on the sofa. She did not get up, but languidly held out her hand to him.

'*Mamma.*' Rafa stooped to kiss her fingers. His earliest memories of his mother were of her lying in bed or resting on a sofa with her pills and tonics close to hand.

'I have suffered greatly,' she had once told him when she'd explained that her longed-for hope of another child had been dashed by several miscarriages.

'You still have me, *Mamma*,' the boy Rafa had tried to comfort his mother, but her sadness had permeated the house. He had been convinced that he wasn't good enough and that was the reason she yearned for another child, a better child than him. When his mother had cried—often—and he'd been unable to console her, he had felt that he'd failed her and therefore perhaps he did not deserve for her to love him.

Now he was an adult, but the sight of a woman's tears still made him feel as inadequate as he had when he'd been a boy because he did not know how to help. Deep down, he was wary of feeling rejected, as he'd felt when his mother had locked herself in her bedroom and he'd heard her crying.

These days, instead of taking herbal remedies for mostly imagined health complaints, his mother relied on oxygen cylinders to alleviate the effects of the incurable lung disease she had been diagnosed with six months ago. Rafa had assumed that he would lose his mother first and he was still trying to come to terms with his father's unexpected death.

'Why did you not tell me about my grandson?' Fabiana reproached him. 'You know how much I have longed for a grandchild. My heart was broken when you discovered that *l'angioletta* Lola was not your daughter.'

Rafa grimaced. Tiffany had taken Lola to live with her real father, and the abrupt separation from the little girl he had believed was his child had been as painful as a bereavement. It had given him an insight into how his mother must have felt when her pregnancies had ended in disappointment.

He wondered if his father had been as deeply affected every time his mother had lost a baby. Rafael senior had rarely showed his emotions, and when Rafa had been growing up he had tried to emulate his father. Even now he never opened up to anyone about his feelings. Big boys did not cry. The mind-blowing result of the paternity test made him want to punch the wall in frustration, but he answered his mother calmly.

'I have only just found out about the child.' He could not bring himself to refer to Bertie as *his* child. He needed time to process the frankly bizarre situation. He had been utterly convinced that Ivy Bennett was a liar, but it seemed that she was what she'd said she was—a grieving sister seeking the father of her motherless nephew. Except Rafa's gut instinct was that he had not slept with Gemma and then since forgotten her.

'Of course, you will have to marry the boy's mother. You cannot have an illegitimate heir. I have seen the girl's picture in the newspaper.' For some reason, the disapproval in Fabiana's voice irked Rafa. 'She is not one of us.'

He did not attempt to explain that Ivy was not Bertie's mother. The news story had damaged his reputation, but it would not improve matters if he made a public statement that he did not remember having sex with Ivy's sister. His mother had meant that Ivy was not part of Italy's, and more specifically Rome's, social elite. The Vieri family had been rich and powerful since the fifteenth century and Rafa had never been allowed to forget his heritage.

'Ivy is devoted to the baby,' he said curtly. He did not know what to make of Ivy Bennett and her motives for talking to the press, but Rafa had seen the love and care she showed Bertie.

'I am glad your father is not here to witness the shame you have brought on the family.'

Dio! His mother did not pull any punches. Guilt added to his confusion and anger. Fabiana sagged back against the cushions. It was only two months since she had been widowed and the raw emotion in the room was too much for Rafa to take. 'I need to look for some paperwork in *papà's* study,' he muttered before he strode from the room.

It was the first time he had entered the study since his father had died. The room looked as it always had—immaculately tidy, the few items on the desk neatly arranged. Rafael Vieri senior had been a precise, controlled man who had worked hard and rarely taken time off to relax, apart from to play golf occasionally.

Rafa had respected his father hugely, and he missed the friendship that had developed between them when he had returned to Italy. He threw himself onto the chair behind the desk and dropped his head into his hands as his mother's words echoed in his ears. After a few minutes, while he fought to regain his self-control, he opened the drawer in the desk, although he had no idea what he was looking for. He was about to close it again when something at the back of the drawer caught his attention.

Why had his father kept a model ship hidden in his desk? Rafa lifted the model out. It was evidently a scale reproduction of a cruise liner, and his heart gave a jolt when he read the name on the hull. *Ocean Star.*

Gemma told me she had met Rafael Vieri aboard the Ocean Star *on a cruise around the Caribbean islands.*

It was surely a coincidence that Ivy's sister had been a hostess on a cruise ship with the same name as the model ship on his father's desk. Rafa dismissed the preposterous idea that came into his head. His workaholic father was as likely to have taken a trip to the moon as to have gone on a cruise. The model ship had probably been a gift from someone. He wondered why his father had shoved it in the drawer.

'I found this in *papà's* study. Do you know why he had it?' Rafa asked his mother when he returned to the drawing room with the model ship.

'Oh, that thing. Rafael kept it as a memento of the cruise he took last year.'

Rafa's heart crashed against his ribs. 'When exactly last year?' He tried to keep his voice calm. 'I don't remember that *papà* went on a cruise.'

Fabiana shrugged. 'You had gone on a business trip. Somewhere in Asia, I think.'

'That would have been last April. I went to Hong Kong and Singapore before I flew to Perth, and I was away for nearly a month. My trip coincided with when *papà* had been advised by his doctor to take a complete break from work. He left Sandro Florenzi in charge at the office and went to Florida to meet up with his cousin for a golfing holiday.'

'Cousin Enrico broke his ankle on the day your father arrived. Rafael did not want to go to the golf resort on his own and was about to return home. But then he called to say that he had secured a last-minute booking on a cruise ship leaving Miami for the Caribbean islands. It wasn't like Rafael to be spontaneous. I believe the stroke he'd had a few months earlier had affected him more than he'd admitted.' Fabiana glanced at the model ship. 'Your father brought that back with him. It's a cheap trinket, and I thought he had got rid of it.'

'Can I keep the model ship, if it meant a lot to *papà*?' Maybe he was crazy, but Rafa was certain that the mystery of Bertie's paternity was connected to the model of the cruise ship *Ocean Star*.

His mother nodded. 'In return you must promise to bring your son to visit me.'

Rafa avoided his mother's gaze. 'Give me a little time. There are things I need to sort out.'

'I miss Rafael so much.' Fabiana held a tissue to her eyes. 'He was my one true love. My only consolation is that, when this wretched illness takes me, I will go to him.'

Dio! Rafa couldn't reveal that Bertie was not his son, but that there was a chance the baby was his half-brother. His mother would be utterly heartbroken if he told her of his suspicion that his father had been unfaithful with a hostess on the cruise ship.

She had already suffered so much sadness in her life. He needed time to find out the truth, but the situation was already spiralling out of his control. The story in the media that he was convinced Ivy had been responsible for had made everyone believe they were lovers and that she was the mother of his illegitimate son.

Of course, you will have to marry the boy's mother.

Rafa frowned as he recalled his mother's words. There was not a chance in hell he would ever get married again. But his involvement in a baby scandal meant that he was in danger of losing the support of the majority of Vieri Azioni's board members.

And then there was his mother, who he was desperate to protect. The idea that had come into Rafa's head was crazy, but the whole thing was crazy. He felt disloyal to suspect his father of having had an affair, but he had to discover the truth, for his sanity and for baby Bertie's sake. He had emailed the DNA testing clinic and learned that a more in-depth test could solve the mystery, but it would take time, which Rafa did not have. All he could hope was for the press to lose interest in the story that he had fathered an illegitimate child. And perhaps he could make that happen.

The best way to flatten the story would be to announce his engagement to the baby's mother. Suddenly there would be no scandal and no more paparazzi camped on his doorstep. Vieri Azioni's board would have no reason to vote him out and, most importantly, he would prevent his mother from finding out the awful truth.

Rafa raked his hand through his hair. Could he pull off a fake engagement to Ivy? The chemistry between them was real, and he did not doubt that in public they would be able to put on a convincing act as a couple in love, but in private he must ignore his inconvenient desire for her. She might have been telling the truth when she'd said that Rafael Vieri was the father of her sister's baby after all, but Rafa still had reasons to mistrust her, and frankly he did not know who or what to believe any more.

* * *

Where *was* Rafa? It was late afternoon and Ivy had spent much of the day wheeling Bertie in the pushchair around the penthouse. Rafa's disappearance and lack of contact were proof that he did not want his son. She knew he must have received the result of the paternity test and his absence was damning.

Neither of Ivy's parents had taken much interest in her when she'd been a child and nor had her two stepfathers. A year ago, her mum had moved to Cyprus with her latest lover, and had vaguely mentioned that Ivy should visit some time soon when building work on the villa was finished, but a date had never been set.

Ivy had given up hoping for a close mother-daughter bond and accepted that her mum loved her, but she wasn't a priority. Her feeling of being unimportant to both her parents had made her determined that Bertie would grow up knowing that he was loved unconditionally, just as Gemma had loved her. Ivy's flight back to England was in a few hours' time, but Rafa hadn't returned Bertie's and her passports.

Ivy had explored the penthouse and found a room that Rafa must use as his office. Bertie was asleep and, conscious that she should have left for the airport by now, she did something she would never normally do and searched the drawers in the desk for the passports.

'What are you doing?'

She flushed guiltily when she looked up and met Rafa's lethal gaze across the room. She quickly shut the drawer, feeling like a child who had been caught with her hand in the sweet tin. Her chin came up as she reminded herself that she was not the one at fault. 'I'm looking for the passports. You didn't return them.'

He strolled towards her, his deceptively lazy strides at odds with his razor-sharp eyes that pinned her to the spot like a butterfly in a display case. 'I admit, I forgot about them with everything else going on. The passports are locked in the safe, and that's where they will stay for now. I need you and Bertie to remain in Italy for a while longer.'

Ivy hated him for being suave, and confident that she would obey what sounded like an order. She hated herself even more for finding him so devastatingly attractive. The black jeans he was wearing teamed with a black silk shirt emphasised how much taller than her he was. His tan belt and loafers were no doubt hand-crafted from the finest Italian butter-soft leather. He dropped his designer shades onto the desk, and the gleaming gold watch on his wrist sent a message that the wearer was wealthy and powerful, and he could do what the hell he liked.

'How much longer do you want us to stay? A week? A month? You can't try out fatherhood in the way you would test-drive a new car.'

'I am not Bertie's father.'

'Don't you dare lie,' Ivy said furiously. 'I've seen the paternity test report which states that Bertie is your child. Yesterday, when you left the room, I asked the doctor who took the samples for DNA testing to email me the result at the same time as you. I am Bertie's legal guardian and I have a right to know who his father is.'

She spun away from Rafa, feeling unaccountably disappointed that he was as shallow and irresponsible as she'd thought. She was disappointed with herself for being attracted to him even though he was a smarmy liar who used his good looks and charisma to fool people—women, *her*—into hoping he was a better man than her common sense told her he was.

'Ivy, listen to me.' Rafa caught hold of her shoulder and frowned when she gave a yelp of pain. 'You should get that looked at by a physio.'

'I'll make an appointment with my GP when I go home. Please give me the passports.' She stared at Rafa, noticing for the first time the lines of strain around his eyes. His hair looked as though he'd been raking his fingers through it.

'I need you to hear me out. Bertie is not my son.' He held

up his hand when she opened her mouth to tell him what she thought of him. 'It is possible...likely...' he said heavily, 'That he is my father's child.'

Ivy decided that she must have misunderstood him. 'But... you told me that your father is dead. How could *he* be Bertie's father?' Disbelief turned to anger. 'Have you spent the whole day thinking up such a ridiculous excuse?'

'I know it sounds crazy. When the idea first came to me, I felt disloyal to my father.' His jaw clenched. 'I still do. But I think I'm right, and the facts back me up. Your sister was a hostess on the cruise ship *Ocean Star* that set sail from Southampton at the beginning of April last year.'

When Ivy nodded, he carried on, 'The ship crossed the Atlantic and docked in Miami to collect more passengers, including Rafael Vieri. If you remember, I suggested that there could have been another passenger on the ship who had the same name as me, but it did not occur to me that he could have been my father. However, my mother told me today that my father had gone on a Caribbean cruise after his holiday plans in Miami fell through.'

He looked intently at Ivy. 'Did Gemma say anything at all about the Rafael Vieri she'd had an affair with on the ship?'

Ivy shook her head. 'When Gem announced that she was pregnant, she'd said that she couldn't be with the father. I had an idea he might have been married, but I didn't ask, and she never spoke about him. She only told me his name just before she died.'

'The confusion stems from the fact that my full name is Rafael, the same as my father.' Rafa exhaled heavily. 'I can prove that I was in Asia for business when Rafael Vieri was on the cruise ship. I'd already asked my PA to look back at my diary for last April. When my mother revealed that my father had been away on a cruise at the same time that I was on the other side of the world, I could only draw one conclusion.'

'But the paternity test proves you are Bertie's father.' Ivy's mind was spinning. Initially, she'd assumed that Rafa had made up the elaborate story, but the fact that he and his father shared the same name made the whole thing plausible—except for the paternity test.

'If a father and a son are both the possible father of a child, a basic paternity test could give a false positive result. That's what I believe happened in this case.'

If it was true, and Rafa was not Bertie's father, then there was no reason for her to feel guilty that she'd kissed him. The distracting thought slipped into Ivy's head. If Rafa and Gemma hadn't been lovers, it meant that she had not been disloyal to her sister. But she had still been a fool to have responded to Rafa when she knew he had a reputation as a playboy, Ivy told herself firmly.

'What did your mother say when you told her what you have just told me?'

'My mother is unaware of what I suspect,' Rafa said harshly. 'Only you and I and the DNA testing company, who have signed a watertight confidentiality clause, know that I have requested an extended paternity test where more genetic markers are studied. A child inherits fifty percent of their DNA from their mother and fifty percent from their father. The extended test can exonerate me as Bertie's father and prove with a high percentage of reliability that he is in fact my half-brother.

'Together with what else we know, it will be safe to assume that my father and your sister were lovers on the cruise ship and Bertie is the result of their affair. It will take a couple of weeks for the paternity test company to produce a result, which is why I want you and the baby to stay in Italy.'

Ivy did not know what to believe, and tears filled her eyes as the strain of the past few months overwhelmed her. Losing Gemma in such a shocking way and becoming responsible for a tiny baby had been life-changing events. The uncertainty of the identity of Bertie's father was too much to take in.

'Is the prospect of staying in a luxurious apartment in Rome really so bad that it makes you cry?' Rafa asked in a cynical voice.

'It's not that. If what you have said turns out to be true, it means that Bertie is an orphan, and it's just so tragic.' She rubbed her hand across her eyes. 'I hoped he would have a family in Italy who would want to be involved with him.'

'It was falsely reported by the media that you and I are Bertie's parents. That is the story my mother believes.'

Ivy stared at him. 'Didn't you explain that Bertie is my sister's baby and I had thought that you were his father?'

'No,' Rafa said bluntly. 'My mother can never find out that her husband of thirty-seven years of happy marriage had a casual fling that resulted in a child. It would destroy her.' His frustration was apparent in the dark scowl he sent Ivy. 'If you hadn't sold out to the newspapers, I would have been able to manage the situation differently. But, as it stands, my mother thinks she has a grandson who she is desperate to meet, and some members of Vieri Azioni's board are citing moral turpitude as a reason to try to kick me out of the company.'

Ivy glared back at him, infuriated by his unfairness. 'You refuse to believe that I didn't talk to a journalist, but I am supposed to accept your crazy theory that Bertie is your father's child?'

'It had to have been you who spoke to the press. I'm confident my theory will be proved right by the extended test.'

'I don't care about the test. You say you have proof that you were on a business trip and couldn't have been on the cruise ship, so I accept that Bertie is not your son. Why can't we just leave it at that? Give me the passports, I'll take Bertie and you will never hear from either of us again.'

Rafa shook his head. 'Unfortunately it is not as easy as that. For a start, I don't trust you.' He ignored her gasp of outrage. 'Vieri Azioni was entrusted to me by my father, and I will do whatever it takes to save my position as joint chairman and CEO of my family's company.' His grey eyes held her gaze. 'I have had an idea. I think we should announce that we are engaged.'

Once again, Ivy assumed that she had misheard or misunderstood him. 'Engaged...to who?'

His brows lifted. 'To each other, obviously.'

'You've got to be kidding! I don't want to get engaged to anyone, least of all you.'

'It will not be a real engagement.' Rafa roved his gaze over Ivy, and she was conscious that the stretchy material of her top moulded her breasts. She wished she had persevered through the pain in her shoulder and worn a bra.

Rafa's eyes had narrowed to glittering slits. Perhaps he was thinking that he would have expected his fiancée to be a lot more glamorous and sophisticated than her. Ivy did not understand why a tiny part of her was excited at the idea of being engaged to him. But it would be a fake engagement, she reminded herself.

She shook her head. 'What will be achieved by us pretending to be engaged?'

'If I am seen to have accepted responsibility for Bertie, and am prepared to marry the mother of the child who everyone believes is mine, it will make my mother happy and appease the board members and shareholders.' Rafa shrugged. 'Everyone loves a happy ending. We will pose for photos for the newspapers looking suitably enamoured with one another. Without a scandal to fuel the story, it will quickly fade from public interest, and in a month or two we will quietly break up.'

'What will you tell your mother when we end our engagement?'

'I'll make the excuse that you want to bring the baby up in England to be near your family.' He frowned. 'Do you have family who can help you care for your sister's child?'

She shook her head. 'My dad has many children from his various relationships and my mum is living in Cyprus with her latest Mr Right. At least she has stopped marrying men who promise to love her but always let her down. Gemma was not her daughter, and Mum isn't interested in Bertie.'

Ivy wondered how Rafa had moved closer without her realising. She was standing behind the desk, and he was blocking her escape route to the door. 'I'm going to take Bertie back to England,' she said with more confidence than she felt. 'I think you should tell your mother the truth. Lies always get found out in the end.'

'You don't have to tell me.' His harsh and oddly humourless laugh stirred her curiosity. 'I have explained why I can't be honest with my mother and must allow her to believe that you and I are Bertie's parents. Mentioning your sister will only complicate things further. I won't risk her discovering a possible link between my father and Gemma. We must protect my mother's feelings.'

'With a fake engagement.' Ivy backed away when he took a step towards her. But, while her mind was trying to focus on the surreal conversation with Rafa, her body was communicating with him on a different level. Her heart was racing and her breathing was uneven. She folded her arms across her chest to hide the betraying thrust of her nipples through her clingy top, but the gleam in his eyes told her that he was aware of the effect he was having on her. 'Why should I care about your mother's feelings?' she muttered.

'She's dying. Eighteen months to two years at most, the specialist has advised.'

Ivy bit her lip. Rafa had recently lost his father and his mother was terminally ill. She wasn't close to either of her parents, but she had adored her big sister, and she missed Gemma every day. 'I'm sorry.'

He looked at her intently. 'I think you are. Beneath your belligerence lies a soft heart, Ivy Bennett.' His voice had deepened and it felt like rough velvet caressing her skin. The atmosphere between them had altered subtly and prickled with mutual awareness. Ivy's heart gave a jolt as her eyes crashed into Rafa's searing gaze.

'I want to go home.' It was imperative to her self-preservation that she distanced herself from this man who had such a powerful impact on her. 'You can't make me stay.'

'I have been honest with you about the reasons I'd like you to remain in Italy.' Rafa moved closer. He wasn't touching her, but Ivy was aware of him with every cell in her body. With a jolt, she recognised the gleam of desire in his eyes when he lowered his face towards hers. Memories of the passion that had blazed between them when he had kissed her in the kitchen made her blood pound in her veins, and her lips parted in anticipation for him to claim them. Her brain said *no*, but her body said *yes* to the question in his eyes.

CHAPTER FIVE

RAFA SLID HIS hand round to Ivy's nape and angled his mouth over hers. She hesitated while her common sense battled the confusing feelings that only this man aroused in her. She wanted to dislike him, but he had surprised her with his determination to protect his mother from being hurt, if it was true that Rafa's father had been the man Gemma had had an affair with. Rafa had made his astounding suggestion of a fake engagement to spare his mother's feelings. It showed that he was honourable and had integrity, and Ivy felt a begrudging respect for him.

She placed her hands on his chest, still torn between wanting to push him away or succumb to her attraction to him. The heat of his body through his shirt transferred to her palms, ran like quicksilver up her arms and flooded her breasts. Perhaps if he had pulled her towards him she would have panicked but, other than his hand behind her head, he wasn't touching her, and she felt reassured that she was in control and could end the kiss whenever she wanted.

Except that she did not want it to end. Rafa brushed his mouth over hers and, with a soft sigh, Ivy parted her lips. He kept the kiss light at first, teasing the tip of his tongue between her lips and tantalising her with the promise of sweeter delights. With a low moan, Ivy curled her fingers into his shirt and sank into

him, intensely aware of how hard his body felt against her softness, and how big and powerful he was.

He filled her senses. The taste of him was on her lips and she
breathed in his sensual male scent. She heard the frantic thud
of her heartbeat in her ears, and beneath her fingertips she felt
the thunder of his heart. His free hand settled on her waist and,
when he drew her towards him so that his thigh brushed against
hers, she felt a jolt of purely feminine response to the unmistakeable hardness of his arousal.

When at last Rafa lifted his mouth to allow them to snatch
a breath, Ivy stared into his eyes that gleamed like molten silver. He sat on the edge of the desk so that his face was almost
level with hers and pulled her unresisting body between his
thighs. 'That's better,' he murmured, making her wonder if his
neck ached given he was so much taller than she was. But her
thoughts scattered as he claimed her lips again and kissed her
with a mastery that made her shake.

She believed that he wasn't Bertie's father, and without that
barrier she could not stop herself from falling deeper under
his spell. He used his mouth to enchant and entice her, and she
held her breath when he slid his hands up her body to rest just
beneath her breasts. Her nipples felt tight and hot, and when he
brushed his thumb pads across the swollen peaks the pleasure
was so intense that she shuddered.

It was too much, yet not enough. Her eyelashes swept down
as she focused on the new sensations Rafa was arousing in her.
No other man had made her feel so needy. Privately, she'd been
scathing when friends, or her mum, had confessed that they had
been carried away and unable to stop themselves from having
sex with a guy they'd just met.

Surely it was a matter of self-control? Ivy had thought to
herself. But now for the first time in her life she exalted in her
femininity, and she felt empowered, but at the same time helpless to control her tumultuous desire for Rafa.

When he abruptly released her and stood up, she blinked at

him, struggling to comprehend that the kiss was over and the passion that had blazed for her had not burned as fiercely for him. His expression was unreadable and that made things worse. She felt used and discarded, not good enough. Her old insecurities surfaced. From way back when her father had abandoned her for his girlfriend at the time who'd had a cuter kid, Ivy had never met a man who was genuinely interested in her.

'I will prepare a press release to announce our engagement first thing tomorrow.' Rafa's voice was huskier than usual, and his Italian accent was more pronounced. He strode across the room and Ivy wondered if she imagined that he was avoiding making eye contact with her.

She ran her tongue over lips that were still tingling from his kiss, and was intrigued when she saw his jaw clench. It occurred to her that perhaps he had enjoyed the kiss as much as she had but, like her, he was fighting the attraction they both felt.

'Tomorrow evening we will host an engagement party,' he continued. 'You will need some clothes, so I have arranged for you to meet a personal stylist who can advise you on a suitable wardrobe. People will be curious about my new fiancée, and doubtless we'll receive a flurry of invitations to dinner.'

'I can't afford to buy new clothes.'

'I'll give you my credit card.'

Her pride objected. 'I won't use it.'

'I thought it was every woman's dream for a billionaire to provide unlimited access to his bank account,' he drawled.

'It's not my dream. You are not paying for my clothes. I haven't even agreed to your crazy idea of a pretend engagement.'

'If you are thinking of running to the newspapers and revealing the likely true identity of Bertie's father, I strongly advise you against it.'

'That sounds like a threat.'

He exhaled heavily. 'Do you want to break my mother's heart and make her miserable for the time she has left?'

Ivy remembered how devastated her mum had been when

she'd discovered that her dad was having an affair. Ivy did not want to cause Rafa's mother the distress of finding out that her husband had cheated.

Rafa was pretending that Bertie was his son to protect his mother's feelings. But now he faced the loss of support from his board of directors because of the news story that he had abandoned his illegitimate child. It still rankled that he believed she had spoken to a journalist. If she hadn't brought Bertie to Italy, none of this would have happened, Ivy thought dismally.

'All right,' she said grudgingly, turning to face him. 'I'll be your fake fiancée. But I don't want money or clothes or anything from you.'

'*Dio*, are you always so argumentative?'

'Are you always so bossy? Anyway, taking Bertie on a shopping trip would be a nightmare.'

'While you are with the personal stylist, the baby will remain at the apartment with the nanny I have hired.'

She saw red. 'Well, you can damn well un-hire her. I am perfectly capable of caring for Bertie on my own.' Her voice thickened with emotion. 'He is all I have of Gemma, and I refuse to hand him over to a stranger. Bertie needs me...and... I need him.'

Rafa ran his hand through his hair, his frustration palpable. 'Anna is from a highly reputable agency and has excellent references. I met her earlier today and she is charming. She will help out when you cannot be with the baby—for instance, when we are at the party.'

There was sense in his words, Ivy conceded reluctantly. But Rafa was so forceful, and he was clearly used to getting his own way. 'You have no idea how it feels to be responsible for a defenceless little baby.' She was puzzled by an odd expression that flickered across his chiselled features.

'If my suspicion is proved correct, and Bertie is my half-brother, he will not be solely your responsibility,' he said quietly. 'You will have my support in whatever way we decide is best to care for him.'

Ivy watched Rafa stride out of the room. She was startled by his stated intention to share responsibility for Bertie. He had sounded genuine, but she cautioned herself against believing him too readily. Having witnessed her mother's disastrous relationships, Ivy had learned to be wary of handsome and persuasive men—and she would be a fool to trust Rafa.

Rafa fixed the cufflinks on his shirt and slipped his arms into his jacket. The party was an informal event and he decided against wearing a tie with his casual but nevertheless impeccably tailored linen suit from an Italian couture house. He ran his hand over the trimmed stubble on his jaw—he disliked being clean-shaven. A visit to the barbers had resulted in a shorter hairstyle and a sharper look in preparation for the damage limitation exercise he was hoping to pull off.

Many of Vieri Azioni's board members had accepted invitations to his engagement party, although the deputy CEO, Sandro Florenzi, had apologised in advance for his absence due to his wife's poor health. Rafa walked into the lounge and poured himself a generous Scotch before he stepped outside onto the balcony.

It was early evening, and the Colosseum looked even more spectacular with the fiery rays of the setting sun sinking behind the ancient structure. Once, gladiators had stepped into the arena to fight to the death. Fast forward a few thousand years, and Rafa was facing the fight of his life to retain control of his company. But, instead of a sword or spear, the secret weapon he was banking on to secure his victory was a mock engagement to a young woman who constantly confounded him.

He glanced at his watch. Ivy should make an appearance soon, and he acknowledged that he was curious to see what she was wearing. Hopefully the stylist had persuaded her out of her hip-hugging jeans and into an evening dress that was elegant and demure, suitable for his fiancée.

Rafa frowned as he remembered Ivy's agonised expression when she'd placed Bertie in the nanny's arms before going shopping.

'I've never left him before,' she'd said in a choked voice.

'I will take good care of the baby,' Anna had reassured her. 'If I have any concerns about Bertie, I'll call you.' The nanny spoke fluent English, and Ivy had relaxed a little, although she had slunk out of the penthouse like a lamb being led to the slaughter, instead of looking excited at the prospect of choosing new clothes that she didn't have to pay for.

Most women, in Rafa's experience, did not have a problem spending his money. He could not figure Ivy out, and he was perplexed that she had the ability to turn him on so hard and so fast that his control was threatened. It had never happened to him before, not even with his ex-wife. The truth was, he'd convinced himself that the hot lust he'd felt for Tiffany was love, and he had married her without suspecting that the baby she'd been expecting was not his.

There was no danger that his attraction to Ivy was anything more than a physical response to her fragile beauty, which coincided with a dry spell in his sex life, Rafa assured himself. When he had kissed her in his study the previous day, her ardent response had blown him away, and he'd had to force himself to pull back before the situation had got out of hand. Ivy's initial shyness had given way to a fierce, yet touchingly clumsy passion, reminding him that she'd said she had never had a lover.

It seemed highly unlikely for a woman in her mid-twenties still to be a virgin. But he'd been disturbed by the effect that Ivy had on him, and he'd needed to put some distance between them. He'd spent the evening propping up a bar and had accepted an offer from Matteo, an old school friend, to sleep in his guest room for the night.

That morning, when Rafa had returned to the penthouse,

he had wondered if Ivy had taken baby Bertie and fled back to England. He had half expected her to, and if he was honest he'd half-hoped she would have disappeared. He did not know where in England she lived, and it would have given him an excuse not to look for her.

Admittedly, he would have had to think of an explanation about the son he had allegedly fathered for the press and the board members who wanted to replace him. But he would have forgotten Ivy in a week or two. He'd never allowed a woman to have any kind of hold over him. However, the baby was another matter. Rafa was still struggling to comprehend that Bertie could be his half-brother, with the implication that his father, whom he had put on a pedestal, had betrayed his mother.

A faint sound from behind him pulled Rafa from his troubled thoughts. He took a long sip of whisky before he slowly turned around. He was in control, right?

Wrong! He swept his gaze over Ivy and his body tensed as desire ripped through him. Why had he thought she would choose an elegant and demure gown? Some hope!

She was wearing the ubiquitous little black dress, with emphasis on *little*. The sequin-covered dress moulded her slim figure and drew attention to her tiny waist and the gentle curve of her hips, while the low-cut neckline pushed her small breasts high. The creamy mounds would fit into his palms perfectly, and Rafa ached to explore the sweet valley of her cleavage with his lips. *Dio,* how he ached.

He forced his gaze away from temptation and felt a flicker of surprise when Ivy moved into the pool of light cast by the balcony lamps and he saw that her hair was no longer bright pink but a subtle shade of pale blonde. 'Why did you change your hair?'

'This is my natural colour.' She self-consciously ran her fingers through the feathery blonde layers. 'The stylist at the salon stripped out the pink dye.'

Rafa did not know if it was her blonde hair or the fact that Ivy was wearing make-up, making her eyes seem even bigger and her lips even more lush, with a coating of scarlet gloss, that was responsible for turning her into a sex-bomb. All he knew was that he wanted to forget the damned party, sweep her up into his arms and carry her to the nearest flat surface so that he could slake his hunger for her in the most basic way that a man and a woman could communicate. Ivy made him feel like a teenager on a first date, and he resented that she was tying him in knots.

Perhaps she was unnerved by his brooding silence or by the prickling tension that was almost tangible. 'The personal stylist suggested I should wear a full-length gown to the party. But I didn't feel comfortable in a long dress, so I decided on… um…a short one.'

'So I see,' he said drily. The hem of the sparkly dress stopped above her mid-thighs, revealing her slender legs in sheer black stockings and sexy, strappy, high-heeled shoes. He would like to have had her long legs wrapped around his hips. Rafa's jaw tensed as he tried to dismiss the erotic images that had stormed uninvited into his head. 'The dress is fine,' he said brusquely. 'You look charming.'

He immediately regretted his offhand compliment when Ivy's face fell. There was a curious naivety about her, and she was ridiculously easy to read. He realised that she had wanted his approval, and perhaps his admiration, but he'd been so intent on hiding his reaction to how amazing she looked that he had hurt her feelings. Why that should bother him, Rafa had no idea. He wanted to believe that she had her own agenda for bringing her sister's baby to him. She'd said that she wanted him to set up a trust fund for Bertie that she would control. It was impossible that she was as innocent and unworldly as she seemed.

Ivy returned to the lounge and Rafa followed her inside. He put his hand on her arm and led her over to the table, where there was a leather case. 'I arranged for a jewellery company to deliver a selection of engagement rings so that you can choose one,' he explained as he unlocked the case to reveal its dazzling contents.

'Is it really necessary for me to wear a ring?'

'Of course. Our engagement needs to be convincing. It will be best if you choose the flashiest, most noticeable ring so that no one is in any doubt of my devotion to you.' Rafa realised how cynical he had sounded when Ivy's brown eyes widened.

'It's incredible how realistic imitation jewellery looks,' she said as she picked up a huge sapphire surrounded by diamonds.

'They are not imitation. The gemstones are real.' Rafa caught the sapphire ring when Ivy dropped it as if it had burned her. He captured her hand and felt a tremor run through her as he slid the ring onto her finger.

'It must be worth a fortune.' She sounded horrified. 'What if I lose the ring? It would take me a million years to pay for it.'

'The size of the band can be altered.' The ring was much too big on Ivy's finger and the large stone did not suit her small hand. 'Try a different one.' Rafa wondered if her reluctance to choose a ring was an act intended to convince him that she wasn't a gold-digger. 'I hope you will look happier when we are at the party. You are supposed to be madly in love with me.'

'That will never happen,' she told him seriously.

Rafa decided it was good that Ivy was not spinning any romantic dreams their fake engagement might become real. In fact, she seemed to dislike him, and he felt oddly hurt. He was not a monster, but she had accused him of fathering her sister's baby, and he was determined to discover the truth.

He looked down at the precious gems glittering against the black velvet cushion. He'd asked the jeweller to send a mix of contemporary and traditional designs, and the rings were set with stunning emeralds, exquisite sapphires and blood-red rubies, but none of them suited Ivy.

'What about this one?' He hadn't planned to get involved. A ring was only to make their engagement realistic. But a square, yellow diamond with two smaller white diamonds on either side of the centre stone caught his attention. The yellow diamond emitted sparks of fire when it caught the light, reminding him of the golden flecks in Ivy's eyes.

Rafa took her hand and slid the ring onto her finger. As he'd guessed, the delicate design was perfect for her.

'It's not flashy, but it is very beautiful.' Ivy smiled as she studied the ring.

For some unfathomable reason, Rafa felt reluctant to release her fingers from his grasp. He turned her hand over and saw that she had a small tattoo of an orange butterfly on the inside of her wrist. 'Why a butterfly?'

'My sister loved butterflies. She believed they are a sign of hope.' Ivy gave a soft sigh. 'After she died, I often saw an orange butterfly on the bush outside our flat and I felt it was a sign that Gemma would always be nearby.' Her voice faltered. 'You probably think I'm silly.'

'You must have loved your sister very much to have taken on her baby without any help from the rest of your family.'

Just when he'd thought he had worked Ivy out, she confounded him again. He was taken aback by the selflessness that was in stark contrast to Tiffany's self-serving behaviour throughout their marriage.

'Gem was the best sister anyone could have. She took care of me when my mum was too wrapped up in her own life. Gemma's mother died when she was very young, and our father wasn't the best parent, to be honest. Gemma was drawn to older men. I think she'd wished she could meet someone who would look after her.' Ivy bit her lip. 'If she did meet your father on the cruise ship, I'm sure Gemma would not have known that he was married.'

'I find it hard to believe that my father betrayed my mother and perhaps was not honest with your sister,' Rafa admitted. He had admired his father more than anyone in the world but, as had happened with Tiffany, his faith and trust had been shattered by the realisation that Bertie must be his father's child. There was no other logical explanation.

There would be long-term consequences, he brooded. Ivy was the baby's legal guardian, but it was only fair for him to become involved in his half-brother's upbringing. He intended to end his fake engagement to Ivy once the media lost interest in the baby scandal, but Bertie would be a permanent link between them. Rafa was not sure how he felt about that. He had started by despising Ivy, but he could not deny that he desired her and, now he knew a little more about her, he found he admired her devotion to her sister's baby.

He called the courier to collect the case of rings and arranged for the jeweller to resize the yellow diamond ring to fit Ivy's slim finger and return it later that evening. The maid brought in a tray with a bottle of champagne and two flutes. 'Would you like some champagne?' Rafa asked Ivy when they were alone again.

'Just fruit juice, please. I never drink alcohol.'

'It's as well I found that out before our engagement party. We had better run through a few facts about each other and concoct a story of where we met and fell in love,' he said drily. 'People are bound to ask. Whereabouts in England are you from?'

'Southampton, on the south coast.'

'I am aware of where it is, but I have not been there. I know London fairly well and have visited many of the best clubs in Mayfair. We could pretend that we were introduced at a club.'

Ivy's laughter was sweetly melodious. It was the first time Rafa had heard her laugh and it could easily be addictive. 'I've been to London a few times, but never to the upmarket nightspots where billionaires hang out. The chances that we could have met in a swanky club are zero. Besides, for it to be believable that Bertie is our child, we will need to pretend that we were together thirteen months ago. I was working as a dancer aboard the *Ocean Princess* on a cruise from Bali to Singapore.'

'It so happens that I was in Singapore around the same time.

From my hotel balcony, I could see the ships that were docked in the cruise terminal.'

'Did you stay at the Excelsior Hotel?' When Rafa nodded, Ivy said, 'I remember it was a friend's birthday and we went ashore and had afternoon tea at the Excelsior. Do you realise that we could have actually met in Singapore? I believe in fate. Do you?'

'I believe in coincidence. I also believe in meeting problems head on and taking decisive action to deal with them, which is what we are about to do now.' Rafa picked up Ivy's pashmina from the chair and handed it to her. 'Well, that makes a perfectly plausible back story, then. Now, it's show time, *mia cara fidanzata.*'

The hotel's grand ballroom thronged with guests, all of whom Ivy had never met before. 'How do you know these people?' she asked Rafa. 'You must be very popular with your friends for so many of them to have come to a party that was arranged at short notice.'

He lifted his brows in that way of his that made her feel she did not belong in his rarefied world of the super-rich. 'Some of the guests are my friends, but most are business associates. Deals that are signed off in the boardroom are often the result of networking and bargaining over the buffet table at social events. Besides, everyone is curious to see my future wife, who they have been led to believe by the media is the mother of my son,' he said sardonically.

Rafa's hint that he still believed Ivy had been responsible for the news story was hurtful, but it also stirred her temper, so that she forgot her nervousness when he introduced her to a blur of people whose names and faces she doubted she would remember. Many of the guests spoke English, but they were too polite to be openly curious about her, and Rafa smoothly answered any questions about their relationship without actually revealing very much.

Ivy was intensely aware of his presence by her side and the

weight of his arm around her waist burned through her dress. She reminded herself that his charm offensive and the attention he was paying her were part of the show they were putting on of a couple who were madly in love.

He had said they would have to continue the pretence of their engagement for a couple of months. It suddenly seemed a terrifyingly long time until she would be free to return to her old life. A life that had changed beyond recognition when she'd become a single parent to her sister's baby.

Rafa had an unsettling effect on her. She was nearly twenty-five and still a virgin, for heaven's sake. It had never bothered Ivy before. But now she had a sense that the life she had nearly lost when she'd been a teenager and had fought so hard for was passing her by. She'd never wanted sex for the sake of it, but she had decided long ago that she did not want to get married. She was not going to chase the impossible dream of happy ever after, which was what her mum had spent her life doing. But it meant that she was in a curious limbo and, to further complicate things, her response to Rafa's kisses had revealed her sensuality that she longed to explore with him.

Rafa was chatting to an elderly man called Carlo, who apparently owned a bank. Ivy glanced around the ballroom at the well-heeled guests sipping champagne and nibbling on exquisite canapés served by white-jacketed waiters. It felt a million miles away from her rented flat in Southampton that was damp in the winter and cost a fortune to heat.

At least she wouldn't have to worry about finding a new place to live while she and Bertie were in Italy. If the extended paternity test proved that Bertie was indeed Rafa's father's child, Ivy was determined to seek financial support for the baby. She was realistic enough to know that, however much she loved her half-nephew, she couldn't give him the privileges of wealth such as a private education and a comfortable home that, as a member of the affluent Vieri family, should be Bertie's birth right.

She hoped Bertie would be happy with the nanny. She had

liked Anna immediately, and felt reassured by how warm and caring she'd been with Bertie. Anna had been given a private suite of rooms next to the penthouse and had arranged for the baby's cot to be moved into her bedroom for the night. It was the first time since Gemma had died that Ivy had spent more than an hour apart from Bertie, and she felt guilty that she hadn't rocked him to sleep, but Anna had sent her a couple of texts to reassure her that he had settled happily.

She came out of her thoughts when she realised that Rafa's companion was looking at her. 'I almost did not recognise you tonight, Miss Bennett,' the man called Carlo told her. 'I was in the boardroom of Vieri Azioni when you arrived a few days ago and caused quite a stir.'

Ivy had not noticed him among the grey-suited businessmen who had stared at her when she'd burst into the boardroom. 'I only had eyes for Rafa,' she said truthfully, blushing when she realised how gauche she sounded.

The older man laughed and patted Rafa's arm. 'I am glad that you and your delightful fiancée were able to resolve your problems. When do you plan to marry?'

'Soon,' Rafa replied smoothly, tightening his arm around Ivy's waist when she gave a start of surprise. 'I am impatient to make Ivy my wife. But there is something I must do first.'

'What's happening?' she muttered as he steered her away from Carlo and moved towards the dais at one end of the room. As they mounted the steps, the band stopped playing and the bright overhead lights came on. Ivy was a professional dancer, and was used to being on a stage in front of an audience, but when she saw the mass of curious faces staring at her she wished she could disappear.

Rafa kept her clamped to his side while he spoke to the guests. 'Recently there have been false reports and rumours in the media regarding my relationship with Ivy. Tonight, I want to put the record straight.'

To Ivy's astonishment, he dropped down onto one knee in

front of her and withdrew a small velvet box from his jacket
pocket. When he opened it, the yellow diamond ring sparkled
with fiery brilliance.

'Ivy Bennett, will you do me the greatest honour by agreeing to be my wife?'

She stared into eyes that gleamed like molten silver, and for a
few seconds she imagined that his proposal was real and he was
the fairy-tale prince she had dreamed of as a little girl. She had
outgrown fairy tales long ago, Ivy reminded herself firmly. But
she was seduced by the wicked smile that played on Rafa's lips.

Her common sense told her to run as far and as fast as she
could from this man, who had 'heart breaker' written all over
his arrogantly handsome face, but common sense had never
seemed so unappealing. Besides, it was only make-believe, so
why not play along? A fake proposal was the only kind she
would ever accept.

CHAPTER SIX

'YES.' IVY'S VOICE was huskier than she'd intended, and her hand trembled when Rafa slid the ring onto her finger. The yellow diamond made her think of golden sunshine and a warm feeling curled around her heart. He kept hold of her hand as he led her off the dais and onto the dance floor.

As the band started to play, he drew her into his arms, and they danced a slow dance while the guests looked on. At first she felt self-conscious, but the lights dimmed, and the music—an instrumental version of a popular romantic ballad—was evocative.

The spicy scent of Rafa's aftershave ignited the flame of desire low in her pelvis. Through the fine white silk of his shirt, she could make out the dark shadow of his chest hairs. She remembered those moments in the kitchen when he had been barechested and she'd run her hands over his naked torso.

Rafa lowered his head towards her and murmured in her ear, 'For our engagement to appear authentic, I am going to have to kiss you.'

'I hope you won't find it too much of an ordeal,' she said stiffly, stung by how indifferent he sounded.

His chest shook with silent laughter. 'I assure you it will not be an ordeal, *cara mia*. I am simply warning you in advance of what I am about to do because our romance would not be believable if you stormed off the dance floor.'

Ivy stared at him and registered his sexy smile, which made him even more attractive. 'I didn't storm off the first two times you kissed me.'

'No, you didn't, did you?' His smile disappeared and he gazed intently at her mouth.

The ballroom, the party guests and the music faded and there was only Rafa. He pulled her closer to him and dipped her backwards over his arm. Ivy's lips parted beneath his and she gave a little sigh of pleasure when he claimed her mouth with a possessiveness that should not have thrilled her as much as it did.

He was skilled at the art of seduction, and she did not stand a chance of resisting him when her traitorous body succumbed to his potency. This was where she wanted to be, in Rafa's strong arms, and she gave herself up to the intoxication of his kiss. He created magic with his lips and with his wickedly inventive tongue as he explored the moist interior of her mouth. Ivy curled her fingers into his shoulders and kissed him back with increasing urgency, guided by feminine instinct and an untapped sensuality she had not known she possessed.

The sound of applause was an unwelcome intrusion. Rafa lifted his mouth from hers and Ivy wished that a hole would appear in the ground and swallow her up when she realised the exhibition they had made in front of the guests. That had been the point, of course, she reminded herself when she darted a look at Rafa.

'We need to get out of here now,' he said curtly. They were still going through the motions of dancing together while all around them the party guests were filling the dance floor.

'What's up?' Ivy demanded. Rafa looked furious but she did not understand what she had or had not done. Hadn't he wanted her to put on a convincing act that she was bowled over by him? She ignored the voice in her head that taunted her she hadn't been acting.

'This is what is *up*,' he ground out, jerking her close so that her pelvis was flush to his. She gasped when she felt the unmistakeable hardness of his arousal. There had been self-derision in his voice and something else that sent a shiver of excitement through Ivy.

'I don't understand what you are doing to me.' He sounded as furious as he looked. 'Three days ago I'd never even heard of you, and now you are all I can think about.'

'It's the same for me,' Ivy admitted. 'I came to Italy thinking I would hate you, but I don't know how I feel.'

'Let's get out of here.' Rafa kept an arm around her waist as he strode purposefully across the ballroom.

'We can't leave in the middle of what is supposed to be our engagement party. What will the guests think?' She stumbled in her high heels as she struggled to keep up with him and felt the muscles in his arm flex as he supported her.

'People will think that we can't wait to get our hands on each other, and they would be right.' He grinned at her stunned expression, but behind his smile there was an intentness in him, and the hard glitter in his eyes caused Ivy's heart to miss a beat.

They had reached the private lift that went directly up to the penthouse. As soon as the doors closed, Rafa pulled her into his arms and claimed her mouth with barely concealed impatience. He was heat and flame and she was burning up. He pushed her up against the wall of the lift and held her there with his hip while he plundered her lips, making demands that she found impossible to deny him when it would mean denying herself the heady pleasure of his kiss.

Ivy was barely aware of the lift doors opening and gave a low moan of protest when Rafa took his mouth from hers. He caught hold of her hand and led her into the penthouse. Crossing the open-plan living area, he continued down the hallway to his bedroom.

She had looked into his room once before when she'd explored the apartment. The décor, like the rest of the penthouse, was sleek and sophisticated with dark walls and gold accents. An enormous bed dominated the room and was draped with a velvet throw in rich burgundy. The room had been designed for seduction, and a voice of caution inside Ivy's head questioned how her relationship with Rafa had moved so fast that they had got as far as his bedroom.

She watched him shrug off his jacket and throw it onto a chair. He stood in front of her, and she wondered if he could see the pulse that was thudding erratically at the base of her throat, echoing the frantic thud of her heart.

'You are so beautiful, you take my breath away.' His voice was as soft as smoke, and his Italian accent was so sexy that she shivered.

'There is no need for you to give me false compliments now we are not in public,' she mumbled, remembering how he had looked unimpressed by her before the party.

'I should have told you how stunning you look. The truth is, I wanted to keep you to myself instead of attending the party. Don't you believe me?' Rafa must have sensed that Ivy doubted him. He put his hands lightly on her shoulders and turned her to face the mirror. 'Feel how much you turn me on,' he murmured as he pulled her against him so that her back rested on his chest. She caught her breath when she felt the hard ridge of his arousal nudge her bottom.

Ivy stared at their twin images in the mirror and hardly recognised herself. She had been so busy caring for Bertie for the past three months that she'd only ever worn jeans and baggy sweatshirts. Her party dress was more revealing than anything she'd worn before, and subconsciously she had chosen it because she had wanted to make Rafa notice her. She'd been disappointed by his lukewarm reaction before the party, but now his burning gaze sent a lick of fire through her veins.

She wasn't aware of him undoing her zip until he tugged the top of her dress down to expose her breasts. The air felt cool on her heated skin, and her nipples sprang to attention.

His breath hissed between his teeth. 'I had a bet with myself that you were not wearing a bra.'

'My shoulder hurts when I reach behind my back to do my bra up. Anyway, I don't need to wear one, because I haven't got much up top,' she said ruefully.

'Your breasts are perfect.' Rafa was still standing behind her and nuzzled his lips against her neck while he cupped her small breasts in his hands. His darkly tanned fingers made an erotic contrast to her pale breasts as he rubbed his thumb pads across her nipples, sending a sharp tug of pleasure down to Ivy's molten core.

'Every part of you is perfect,' he said thickly, tugging the clingy dress over her hips so that it fell to the floor. Rafa muttered something in Italian as he slid his hands down to the bare skin of her thighs above the lacy bands of her stocking tops.

Ivy trembled as he explored her inner thighs and discovered the damp panel of her silk panties. She had never gone this far with a man before. She'd never wanted to. But Rafa was a magician, and his touch cast a spell on her so that, when he slipped his fingers into her knickers and lightly brushed them over her moist opening, she parted for him, and it felt natural for him to slide one finger inside her. It was new, wonderful and faintly shocking as she watched him caressing her in the mirror. She wanted more, and made a choked sound of disappointment when he took his hand away.

He laughed. 'Bed,' he said thickly, scooping her up in his arms and carrying her across the room. 'I am as impatient as you are, *mia belleza*.'

The satisfaction in his voice pushed through the sexual haze surrounding Ivy's brain and sent a ripple of unease through her. Rafa pulled back the bed cover and laid her down on the black satin sheets. His fingers circled her ankles as he unfastened the straps on her shoes and slid them off.

She watched him tug open the buttons on his shirt and shrug it off his shoulders. In the subtle light from the bedside lamps, he was a work of art, bronzed and beautiful, with his tight abs and the arrow of dark hairs over his flat stomach. Ivy wanted to stay in the moment, to lose herself once more in his smouldering sensuality, but it was too much, too soon, and Rafa was too *everything*. He put his hands on his belt buckle and reality hit her like a ton of bricks.

She levered herself so that she was sitting upright. 'Rafa... I'm not...' Before she could say *sure about this* he interrupted.

'Don't worry if you are not using contraceptives. I am always prepared.' He pulled open the bedside drawer and took out a handful of condoms.

Of course he was prepared for sex. Ivy's heart dipped as he dropped the foil packets onto the bed. She imagined all the women he must have brought to the penthouse and made love to in his huge bed.

'That's not what I meant.'

She forgot what she had been about to say when he knelt on the mattress and bent his head to her breast to take her nipple into his mouth. The pleasure of him sucking on the tender peak was so intense that she was tempted to succumb to the throb of desire and allow him to appease the ache between her legs.

But what would Rafa think of her, and more importantly what would she think of herself? She wasn't a prude, and had not expected to be in love with a guy when she had sex for the first time, but she'd hoped she would be in a relationship where there was friendship and respect. Her fake engagement to Rafa would end in a couple of months. He wanted to have sex with her because she was convenient.

'You are so responsive. I want to be inside you, now.' Rafa stood up and quickly dispensed with his trousers. The sight of his powerfully masculine body in a pair of boxers that did not hide the bulge of his erection filled Ivy with panic. She tensed when he lay down on the bed beside her and drew her into his arms.

'Do you trust me?'

'What?' He pushed his hair off his brow and his eyes narrowed on her tense face. *'Cara.'* His voice was strained, his frustration evident in his clenched jaw. 'That's not important right now.'

'Of course it's important. I don't want my first time of making love to be with a man who doesn't trust me. And I don't think you do.'

'Your first time? *Seriously?'* He blew out his breath when she nodded. Rafa rolled away from her, breathing heavily. 'It would have been a good idea to mention your virginity before now.'

'I told you that I'd never had a lover. It's not my fault if you didn't believe me.' Ivy felt vulnerable and confused. Her body still ached for Rafa's caresses, but she knew she was right to be wary, and tears filled her eyes.

'Why are you crying?' he asked curtly. 'I would never try to force you to make love if that is what is worrying you. I respect your decision.'

Ivy had not doubted that he was honourable, and his shuttered expression made her feel worse. 'I can't help it. I cry when I'm upset, and I wear my heart on my sleeve.' She couldn't bear Rafa to see how he had broken through her defences, and she gave a muffled sob as she scrambled off the bed and flew towards the door.

'Ivy, wait.'

Ivy hesitated and turned her head to look at Rafa. His gut twisted when he saw tears running down Ivy's face, and he knew he was to blame. The boy he had once been had blamed himself when his mother had cried and he had not known how to console her. Deep down, he'd believed that his mother had not loved him, and he was a disappointment to her. Why else would she have been desperate to have another child?

His ex-wife had not loved him. Tiffany had fooled him into believing he had a daughter and that they were a happy family until her lies had been exposed. In his darkest hours, Rafa wondered if he was flawed in some way that meant he was unlovable.

Why was he thinking about love of all things? He desired Ivy and had wanted to have sex with her. He had not intended to upset her. She'd responded to him with a fiery passion that had made his body ache, and he'd been sure she'd wanted him to make love to her. Her revelation that she was as innocent as she sometimes seemed blew his mind. He couldn't blame her for rejecting him. When she chose her first lover, he hoped she would choose a better man than him.

Rafa stood up and pulled his trousers on before he picked up his shirt. He walked over to Ivy and slipped the shirt around her shoulders. 'Here, wear this.'

Black tracks of mascara were running down her face. She looked a heartbreakingly beautiful mess, and he felt guilty that he had made her cry. 'Stay and talk to me. Please,' he said gruffly.

She scrubbed her hand over her eyes. 'You don't want to talk.'

'Yes, I do.' He realised it was true. Admittedly, it was not how he had envisaged the night would unfold. When they had escaped from the party, he had been so turned on by her that he'd almost made love to her in the lift.

To his relief, Ivy did not resist when he took her hand and led her over to the sofa. 'You are a gorgeous, sexy, independent woman, so how come you are still a virgin?'

She sat down and tucked her feet under her. His shirt swamped her tiny frame, and he was struck anew by her fragile beauty. She waited until he joined her on the sofa and said in a low voice, 'I had cancer when I was a teenager and for a while it was touch and go if I would survive.'

Whatever Rafa might have expected her to say, it hadn't been that. He felt a cold sensation on the back of his neck. Ivy was so full of life, and it was shocking to hear that she had come close to death.

'It was a type of blood cancer. To begin with my symptoms

were vague. I felt lethargic and bruised easily, but I didn't think anything was seriously wrong. I'd left home at seventeen because I hated my new stepfather. Gemma had been working for a cruise company based in Turkey and I went to stay with her.'

Ivy smiled. 'It was a perfect summer. I got a job as a waitress in a café, and I met my first boyfriend. Luke was also English. He was a couple of years older than me and a builder on a new hotel development. Every day after work we used to hang out at the beach. He was my first love, and I thought he loved me and we would be together for ever. But then I became ill.'

'What happened?' Rafa prompted when she fell silent.

'By the time I was diagnosed with a form of leukaemia, I was really sick, and I was given huge doses of chemotherapy, which made my hair fall out. I'd had waist-length, dark blonde hair and I was distraught to lose it, especially when Luke decided that he couldn't cope with the way I looked.'

'He sounds like a jerk,' Rafa muttered. How crazy was it that he wished he could track down Ivy's heartless boyfriend and rearrange the guy's face?

She shrugged. 'I was as bald as an egg, and even my eyelashes fell out. But, yeah, it wasn't the best time to suffer a broken heart. I should have expected it, really. My mum had always been let down by the men she'd fallen in love with, including my dad. I was worried that I'd inherited her poor judgement with Luke.'

After a moment, she continued. 'My sister and I moved back to England so that I could complete my treatment. Gem was amazing,' Ivy said softly. 'She looked after me and kept me upbeat when I had bad days. For the next few years, I put all my energy into getting better, and I wasn't interested in dating. I trained as a dancer and performed at holiday camps. Gemma was working on a cruise ship and when a position as a show dancer became available I successfully auditioned for it. I loved travelling, but the lifestyle is not good for relationships.'

Ivy sighed. 'The truth is, I'm wary of being hurt again. I've dated a few guys, but I never know whether to blurt out straight away that I am very likely to be infertile from the chemotherapy. The doctors who treated me in Turkey were brilliant, but because I was so ill there was no time to discuss the possibility of freezing my eggs so that I might have a chance of a family in the future. If I mention children on a first or second date with a guy, it makes me look like I'm hoping for a long-term relationship.'

'Are you holding on to your virginity until you marry?'

She gave him a startled look. 'No. I never want to get married. My parents' disastrous attempts at marriage put me off,' she said wryly. Soft colour stained her cheeks. 'I didn't deliberately lead you on tonight. I don't know why I respond to you the way I do when you kiss me. You make me feel things I've never felt before.'

Rafa gave her a wry look. 'It's called sexual chemistry, *cara*, and I agree that it is inconvenient.'

It was more than that, he brooded. The developments of the past few days were potentially damaging to his position at Vieri Azioni, and more importantly to his mother's emotional state if, as he suspected, Bertie was his father's child. He still believed that Ivy was responsible for the story that had been reported in the media, and he was determined to keep her close so that she could not cause any more harm. But he did not get involved with virgins who had Bambi eyes and a tendency to cry easily. He was going to have to ignore his desire for Ivy. Surely he would not find it too difficult to think with his brain instead of being ruled by his libido? Rafa mocked himself.

He turned to her and saw that her head was resting on the cushions and that she was half asleep. 'I'll take you to your bedroom,' he murmured as he lifted her into his arms.

'I can walk.' But she did not insist that he set her on her feet when he carried her down the hall and into her room. She weighed next to nothing. Once again, he felt an odd pang at the idea that she'd battled a life-threatening illness.

'Are you fully recovered now?'

'I've been cancer-free for more than five years. But none of us can know what the future holds. I certainly never imagined that Gemma would go out to buy nappies and never come back.' Ivy's brown eyes shimmered with tears. 'The reason I wanted to find Bertie's father was in case anything happens to me and I can't look after him.'

Rafa frowned. 'Nothing is going to happen to you.' Her vulnerability tugged on his insides. 'We have to wait for the result of the paternity test before anything can be decided about Bertie's future.' He pulled back the bed covers and lowered her onto the mattress. '*Buona notte*, Ivy.'

'Rafa.' Her sleepy voice made him halt on his way out of the door. 'If I had been more experienced, I would have had sex with you.'

He swore softly. 'You are going to kill me, *cara*.'

Ivy pulled the duvet over her head and prayed that her memories of the previous night were a bad dream. Had she really told Rafa that if she hadn't been a virgin she would have slept with him? Images flooded her mind of how she had been practically naked in his arms, and how she'd kissed him so enthusiastically that it was little wonder he had assumed they would become lovers.

She couldn't even blame her mislaid inhibitions on being drunk. Having beaten cancer, she felt that she'd been given a second chance at life, and she tried to eat healthily and never drank alcohol. It was even more important that she looked after herself now she was responsible for her sister's baby.

Bertie! She jerked upright and saw on the bedside clock that it was past nine o'clock. She had missed Bertie's seven a.m. feed. The nanny would have given him his milk, but that wasn't the point. Guilt churned in Ivy's stomach as she leapt out of bed and hurried into the *en suite* bathroom. She resembled a panda, with her make-up smudged beneath her eyes, and she quickly scrubbed her face clean. She'd slept in Rafa's shirt, but when she heard the baby's cries she did not waste time getting changed.

The nanny was in the living room talking to Rafa while she pushed the baby in the carry cot, evidently hoping that the motion would send Bertie to sleep. But his yells reached a crescendo. Ivy's heart contracted when she lifted him into her arms and he buried his face in her neck.

'It's all right Bobo, I'm here,' she crooned. Gradually his cries turned to little snuffles and she kissed his flushed cheeks.

'I feel terrible for sleeping in so late,' she told the nanny.

'Bertie was fine until a few minutes ago,' Anna reassured her. 'Signor Vieri explained that you were tired after all the excitement of last night.'

Ivy's startled gaze flew across the room and met Rafa's sardonic expression. 'I told Anna that we became officially engaged at the party,' he said drily.

'May I see your ring? It's beautiful,' the nanny murmured when Ivy held out her left hand. 'Congratulations. I hope you will both be very happy.'

Bertie had fallen asleep. He'd probably worn himself out with crying, Ivy thought guiltily as she placed him in the carry cot. 'Shall I take him to the nursery?' Anna offered. She looked over at Rafa. 'I'll go and pack.'

'Why is Anna leaving?' Ivy asked when she and Rafa were alone. Although she had argued against having a nanny, she had to admit that it was a relief to share her worries about caring for Bertie with Anna, who was experienced in childcare and a mother herself to a nineteen-year-old son.

'We need to get out of the city, and I have decided that we will spend some time at my home in Abruzzo. Anna has a few things to do first and she will join us at the castle tomorrow.'

'You own a castle?' Ivy wondered if Rafa's coldness was because she had refused to sleep with him. At their engagement party she had felt a rapport with him, but now she sensed there was a chasm a mile wide between them.

'The castle was originally built as a fortress in the Apennine mountains. The remote location means we won't be bothered there.'

'Bothered by who?'

'The media. I was contacted this morning by Luigi Capello.' Rafa's voice was even grimmer than his forbidding expression. 'The journalist from the newspaper *Di Oggie*—as I'm sure you know,' he said when Ivy looked blank. 'Capello mentioned Gemma. He said he wanted to clarify who exactly is Bertie's mother.'

'I'd forgotten the journalist's name.' She bit her lip. 'How and what does he know about my sister?'

'You tell me.' Rafa's eyes gleamed like tensile steel. 'You must have spoken to Capello. Only you and I know that Gemma was Bertie's mother, and I sure as hell haven't spoken to the press.'

'Neither have I.' Tears pricked her eyes when Rafa sent her a scathing look. 'I swear I threw the journalist's business card in the bin. Oh, it's hopeless for us to pretend to be engaged when you refuse to believe me!' she snapped, her temper bubbling to the surface. 'I only agreed to your crazy plan because I feel sorry for your mother. We will have to call off our fake engagement.'

She tugged the yellow diamond ring, but the re-sized band was a snug fit on her finger, and she struggled to pull the ring over her knuckle.

'Leave it on,' Rafa commanded. He strode over to her and captured her chin between his fingers, tilting her face up to his. 'My mother is in hospital with a lung infection. The doctor has reported that her condition is stable, but every time something like this happens it leaves her weaker,' he said gruffly. 'She wants to meet you—and her grandson.'

Ivy stared at him. 'How can we introduce Bertie to your mother when he might be the result of your father's infidelity? It feels wrong to lie to her.'

Rafa's jaw clenched. 'I agree, but the likely truth will break her heart. We must continue with the pretence that we are engaged, at least until we have the result of the paternity test. I've arranged for us to pay her a brief visit at the hospital before we drive to the mountains. We'll leave in an hour.'

He skimmed his gaze over his shirt that came to Ivy's mid-thighs, and she felt her breasts tauten when his eyes narrowed to glittering slits.

'You had better go and get dressed.' His voice had thickened and sent a shiver of response through her. Without her high heels that she'd worn to the party, Rafa towered over her, and her bare feet seemed to be welded to the floor.

'Damn you, Ivy,' he said harshly. 'My instincts warn me that I can't trust you, yet I still want to do this.'

Ivy watched as he lowered his face and angled his mouth over hers. The sensible part of her said she should move away from him, but she did not listen, and parted her lips beneath his. The kiss was slow and sensual, an unhurried tasting of her lips as Rafa coaxed a response from her that she was willing to give. He was impossible to resist, and he tempted her like no other man ever had. She tried to remember all the reasons why kissing him was a bad idea, but her body did not care if it was right or wrong, and the drumbeat of desire in her veins thudded in a powerful rhythm.

When Rafa finally broke the kiss, they were both breathing hard. 'Go,' he growled, 'Before I am tempted to take this further and do something that one of us regrets.'

The dangerous glint in his eyes made Ivy's heart miss a beat. She was no longer sure she would regret taking her relationship with Rafa to the next level. But perhaps he was less keen to make love to her now that he knew how inexperienced she was. Sleeping with him would only make the situation even more complicated.

CHAPTER SEVEN

RAFA'S MOTHER LOOKED fragile lying in the hospital bed with her hair a silver cloud on the pillows. Her breathing was laboured, and every few minutes she pulled an oxygen mask over her face to help her breathe.

'Is there anything I can do for you, *Mamma*?' Rafa asked in a gentle voice that Ivy had never heard him use before. His affection and concern for his mother was obvious. He leaned forward on his chair next to the bed and stretched out his hand to clasp her fingers.

Fabiana opened her eyes. 'You cannot help me, Rafa. I am not sad that I am dying, for I will go to my dearest Rafael, and my children who I did not meet in this life, but I know are waiting for me in the next.'

Ivy noticed a curious expression flicker on Rafa's face, almost as if he was hurt by his mother's words. When they had driven to the hospital he had explained that his mother had suffered with depression for much of her life, a result of losing several babies during her pregnancies. They must have been the children she had referred to, Ivy supposed. Rafa was a devoted son, but his mother seemed to think more of the children she had lost than her son who was so caring about her.

Rafa glanced at Ivy. 'I think my mother is tired and we should let her rest. Also, Bertie needs his nappy changed.'

Ivy nodded. She had felt awkward, pretending to be engaged to Rafa in front of his mother. Even worse had been having to lie and introduce Bertie as their son. But Rafa was determined to protect his mother from finding out that her husband was possibly Bertie's father. Earlier, Fabiana had admired the baby, but she'd been too weak to hold him.

'The child looks like you,' she had told Rafa. 'You should have called him Rafael. It is a family tradition to give the first-born son his father's name.'

'Two Rafaels were confusing enough,' Rafa had muttered.

Ivy moved towards the door of the private room and paused when Fabiana spoke. 'Rafa, I would like to talk to your fiancée for a little longer. I'm sure you can change the baby's nappy.'

Ivy looked doubtful as she handed Rafa the baby's bag. 'Can you manage a nappy change?'

'Of course he can,' his mother said. 'My son has had plenty of practice at caring for a baby.'

While Ivy was trying to digest that surprising statement, Rafa carried Bertie out of the room. She gave his mother a faint smile, wondering what Fabiana wanted to talk to her about.

'So, you are going to marry my son. It is strange that he had never mentioned you until the newspaper reported that you are the mother of his child. Where did you and Rafa meet?'

'Um… Singapore.' Ivy tried to remember the story they had concocted. 'Rafa was there on business at the same time that the cruise ship I worked on had docked. We bumped into each other in a hotel near the marina.' She blushed, sure that she sounded unconvincing, and wishing she had not mentioned a cruise ship. She hated lying, but she simply could not tell Rafa's mother the truth about their relationship.

Fabiana was watching her closely. 'The baby is four months old, I believe. Did you have an easy pregnancy?'

'Um, it was normal. I had some morning sickness.' Ivy was

floundering. She had been working on a cruise ship for the first few months of her sister's pregnancy, but she remembered Gemma had said that she had been sick a few times.

'Tell me about your family in England.'

'My mum and dad divorced when I was a child, and both went on to have new partners. I'm not close to either of my parents,' Ivy admitted. She felt sad that there was no one in her family she could turn to for support. 'My sister...' She swallowed. 'My sister died in an accident three months ago.'

'Life can be very cruel. You were close to her?'

'Yes.'

Fabiana was silent for a moment. 'Do you love my son?'

'Er...yes, of course.' Ivy fiddled with the yellow diamond ring that Rafa had insisted she should wear to make their engagement appear real.

'Why do you love Rafa?' Fabiana persisted.

Ivy tried to think if Rafa had any loveable traits. He was arrogant, forceful and he liked his own way. But he cared about his mother, and he cared about the company he had inherited from his father. So much so that he'd given up his successful career as a professional basketball player and abandoned his ambition of training as a sports physiotherapist to take charge of Vieri Azioni. He had also promised her that, if the DNA test proved Bertie was his half-brother, he would share responsibility for the little boy's upbringing.

'Rafa is loyal and protective, and honourable.' It was a strangely old-fashioned term, but instinctively Ivy believed it was true. Even though their first meetings had been explosive, when Rafa had angrily accused her of speaking to the press, she realised that she trusted him.

'He is a good son.' Fabiana sighed. 'I know that Rafa misses Rafael as much as I do. He was close to his father and there were no secrets between them.'

Oh, Lord! Ivy could not meet the other woman's gaze.

'The one thing Rafa will not tolerate is deceit. His insistence on honesty is not surprising after his ex-wife deceived him. I suppose he has told you why his first marriage ended? He tried to keep the story out of the media to protect Lola because he still loved her.

'I never thought I would see my son with a broken heart,' Fabiana said. 'Since his divorce, I sense that Rafa has built a wall around his emotions.' She gave Ivy a shrewd look. 'Perhaps he will fall in love with you, as you hope he will.'

Rafa returned with Bertie then, and Ivy was spared trying to think of a response to his mother's astonishing statement while she strapped the baby into the portable car seat. Of course she did not secretly hope that Rafa would develop feelings for her, and she certainly wouldn't fall in love with him, she assured herself.

They stayed for a few more minutes while Rafa chatted to his mother, but it was obvious that Fabiana had found the visit tiring. 'Get some rest now, *Mamma*,' he murmured as he kissed her cheek. He carried Bertie in his car seat, and he looked sombre when they walked out of the hospital. Ivy instinctively reached out and touched his arm.

'I'm sorry your mother is ill,' she said sympathetically. 'It must be hard for you when you recently lost your father.'

He shrugged. 'You heard her. She would rather be with the ghosts of my father and the children she lost than in this world with me.'

Beneath Rafa's unemotional voice, Ivy heard something that tugged on her heart. She wondered what his childhood had been like when his mother had been grieving for her failed pregnancies and perhaps hadn't had much time for him. It would explain why he was so self-contained and enigmatic.

When they walked across the car park, the breeze lifted the hem of Ivy's silk dress and briefly revealed her thighs and the lace bands of her hold-up stockings.

'You look beautiful,' Rafa said tautly. 'That colour suits you.'

The cinnamon-coloured dress teamed with nude heels and a

matching handbag was one of several outfits the personal stylist had picked out for Ivy's new wardrobe and had deemed suitable for the fiancée of one of Italy's richest men. The dress was the most elegant item of clothing Ivy had ever worn. When she'd glanced in the mirror before they'd had left the penthouse, she had been surprised at how nice she looked. Now the gleam in Rafa's eyes made her blush. It was just sexual chemistry, she reminded herself.

He put Bertie into the car and opened Ivy's door before he walked round to the driver's side and folded his tall frame behind the steering wheel. The hospital was in a suburb of Rome, and soon they had left the city and joined the *autostrada,* where the car picked up speed. Rafa had said the drive to L'Aquila, the town close to his castle, would take a little over an hour. Ivy stared out of the window at the lush green scenery. In the distance she could see the jagged peaks of the mountains.

'Are you going to give me the silent treatment for the whole journey?' he drawled. 'Or are you going to tell me what is bothering you?'

She sighed. 'Your mother said that you won't tolerate dishonesty, but you...we...are deceiving her by pretending that Bertie is our child. It feels wrong.'

'The irony isn't lost on me,' he bit out. 'It tears me apart to think that my father was not as perfect as I'd believed. He made a mistake, and the ramifications of his infidelity would be devastating to my mother. You saw how weak she is, and you heard her say how much she loved my father and how happy they were in their long marriage. How *can* I tell her the truth?'

'It's all a mess,' Ivy said dismally. 'I wish I hadn't brought Bertie to Italy. I imagine you wish that too.'

Rafa glanced at her. 'I have a gut feeling that the test will prove he is my half-brother. Bertie is an innocent baby and none of this mess, as you call it, is his fault. You and I are all he has. For his sake we need to be a team and do our best for him.'

A team with Rafa! Ivy was startled by how much she liked

the idea. Her heart warmed to know that he was prepared to help her take care of Bertie and be involved in his upbringing. She had felt so alone since Gemma had died, and sometimes she'd felt overwhelmed by the responsibility of looking after her baby nephew.

She wondered about the logistics of how she and Rafa would be parents to Bertie. Perhaps he would suggest she move to Italy so that they could share custody more easily than if she and the baby lived in England. She would be willing to relocate, but she'd have to learn to speak Italian. Maybe Rafa would teach her. Heat coiled inside Ivy as she thought of other, more intimate things that she would like him to teach her. No doubt he would be an expert tutor in the bedroom.

She turned her head towards him and her heart missed a beat when her gaze collided with his before he looked at the road again. 'What are you thinking?' he murmured.

Too much, she thought ruefully. They did not even know yet if Bertie was Rafa's half-brother. They also hadn't discussed at what point they would end their fake engagement. She looked down at the yellow diamond on her finger and gave a faint sigh. When she had been a little girl, she'd believed in fairy tales, and had hoped she would meet a handsome prince some day. But she had grown up and realised that happy ever after only happened in books and films.

Her mum had spent years chasing a romantic dream, only to have her heart broken countless times. Ivy had decided that instead of unrealistic daydreams she would settle for achievable goals. A billionaire playboy who had the looks and charisma of a sex god was definitely not achievable, she reminded herself.

Her mind turned to her conversation with Rafa's mother.

'Your mother told me about Lola,' she murmured. 'She seemed to think that you still love her.'

Rafa tightened his fingers on the steering wheel. 'It's not easy to simply switch love off,' he said gruffly.

The sharp sensation like a knife thrust between her ribs was *not* jealousy. Ivy was simply surprised to hear Rafa, the master of self-control, talk openly about love.

'You loved your wife even though Lola deceived you?'

He frowned. 'Lola wasn't my wife. I was married to her mother, Tiffany. For two years I believed that Lola was my daughter.'

Daughter! Shock ran through Ivy. 'When I asked, you told me that you didn't have a child. She stared at his chiselled profile. 'What do you mean, you believed? Are you saying that Lola *wasn't* your child?'

'I suppose you had better know the whole story,' he muttered. 'I had been dating Tiffany for a few months before we got married. When she told me she was pregnant, I had no reason to think the baby wasn't mine, and I immediately proposed.'

He frowned. 'I was under a fair amount of pressure from my father to marry and settle down. With hindsight, I can see that one reason why I married Tiffany was to please my father. I knew he had been disappointed by my decision to move to America. He made no secret that he hoped that I would bring my family to Italy and prepare to take over running Vieri Azioni, but I wasn't ready to give up my basketball career.'

A nerve flickered in Rafa's cheek. 'Cracks started to appear in the marriage early on, partly due to the amount of time I spent away from home during the professional basketball season. Lola was born six weeks early. At least, that's the excuse Tiffany gave. I missed the next match and rushed home to meet my baby girl, and I fell in love with Lola Rose.'

He fell silent and Ivy sensed it pained him to revisit his past. 'I tried to make my marriage work,' he said finally, 'But maybe I didn't try hard enough. I was unwilling to give up my basketball career,' he admitted with raw honesty. 'A month or so after Lola's second birthday, Tiffany told me she wanted a divorce. Even then I hoped the break-up could be amicable and we would share custody of our daughter.

'That was when Tiffany dropped her bombshell and told me

that Lola was not my child. Her real father was a well-known film director, Brad Curran, who Tiffany had been sleeping with at the same time as with me. She had known that she was pregnant with Curran's child, but he hadn't been interested, so she'd let me think I was the baby's father. The dates didn't tie up, which was why she made out that Lola was born earlier than the due date.'

Rafa did not try to hide his bitterness at his ex-wife's betrayal and Ivy didn't know what to say that would not sound trite. She sensed he did not want her sympathy and that his pride had been hurt as well as his feelings.

'While I'd been away on tour with the basketball team, Tiffany had met up with her old flame. Following a positive paternity test, Curran accepted that he was Lola's father and offered to marry Tiffany as soon as she'd divorced me. I had no legal right to see Lola and Tiffany decided that a clean break would be best.

'I was gutted,' Rafa said rawly. 'I stood in the empty nursery. It felt as though Lola had died, but I did not have any right to grieve for her, because she was not my child. If that wasn't bad enough, Tiffany tried to sell the story of our so-called love triangle to the tabloids. I didn't want details of my private life in the media, and more importantly I was anxious to protect Lola's privacy. I had to pay my ex-wife a fortune on top of the divorce settlement I'd given her so that she wouldn't speak to the press.'

It was little wonder Rafa was convinced that *she* had told the journalist he was Bertie's father, Ivy thought. But it hurt that he did not trust her and believed she was as deceitful as his ex-wife.

The rest of the journey passed in silence. Rafa's brooding tension did not invite further conversation, and Ivy retreated to her own thoughts. They left the *autostrada* and the narrow road twisted as it climbed higher into the mountains. The town of L'Aquila was a few miles behind them and the dense forest all around added to the sense of remoteness where even the sun did not venture. The mountain peaks were hidden by clouds and the fine drizzle had turned into a heavy downpour. The car turned a sharp bend and in front of them was an imposing, grey fortress.

'Welcome to the Castello Dei Sogni,' Rafa said, and Ivy's heart sank. The building looked like a prison. 'The name means Castle of Dreams,' he told her. 'The story goes that it was built by a man who dreamed of winning the woman he loved by building her a grand castle. But she turned him down because she loved someone else. The man had the castle's walls reinforced and he spent the rest of his life living alone in his fortress so that love could not find him and make a fool of him again.'

'What a sad story,' Ivy muttered as the car splashed through the puddles in the courtyard. 'What made you buy the castle?'

'When I was a boy, my father sometimes took me trekking in the mountains around here. The castle had been abandoned many years ago and we used to explore the grounds. After my divorce, I needed a project, and a bolthole,' he admitted.

'Everyone, including the agent who had been trying to sell the place for years, warned me that it would be a money pit. Much of the restoration work has been completed. There are about forty bedrooms, but apart from a couple of live-in staff I'm the only person who comes here. The remote location ensures that I have privacy from nosy reporters.'

Ivy climbed out of the car. At least it had stopped raining, but the castle still looked like a forbidding fortress. Rafa carried Bertie up the front steps and Ivy walked slowly behind. Hearing about Rafa's failed marriage and how his wife had betrayed his trust had given her an insight into why he had built a fortress around his emotions. Her heart thumped painfully. Was she doing the right thing by bringing Bertie to a castle that looked as grim as its owner?

Standing next to the front door was an olive tree in a terracotta pot. A sudden movement caught Ivy's attention, and her heart fluttered when she saw an orange butterfly land on the silvery green leaves. It hovered there, opening and closing its delicate wings, before it flew up into the sky towards the patch of blue where the storm clouds had parted.

Ivy took a deep breath and a sense of peace filled her. *Good-bye, Gemma,* she said silently. The butterfly had flown away, but she was sure it was somewhere nearby. She followed Rafa into the castle and was pleasantly surprised to find that the interior was much more welcoming than her first impression of the craggy walls of the fortress. They were greeted by the butler, who led the way through a vast entrance hall and into a sitting room where a fire was blazing in the hearth.

'Arturo lights a fire if there is one grey cloud in the sky,' Rafa said drily. 'It tends to be cooler here in the mountains than in Rome.'

'I thought the rooms would be dark and gloomy, but the pale walls and colourful rugs on the floor give a homely feel to the castle.' Ivy felt happier when Rafa showed her around. All the rooms had been decorated in muted shades and the furniture was a tasteful mix of antiques and contemporary pieces. 'I love that it's quirky and unique. The castle is special to you, isn't it?' she said perceptively. She'd noticed that Rafa had relaxed the moment they had arrived.

He gave one of his rare grins that made him seem carefree, as he must have been before his ex-wife's terrible betrayal had left him bitter and mistrusting. 'Everyone said that I was mad to buy a half-ruined castle, but I like a challenge. Although, restoration of the castle is still an ongoing project.' He hesitated. 'I could show you my plans for the unfinished rooms, if you are interested.'

Ivy could not look away from Rafa's searing gaze. When she had met him for the first time—unbelievably, it was only a few days ago when she had burst into the boardroom and confronted him—his eyes had been as hard as steel. But right now his grey eyes were as soft as wood smoke. Warmth stole around her heart when she remembered how he'd said he wanted them to be a team to take care of Bertie. Her mouth curved upwards, and it felt as though it was the first time she had smiled properly since losing Gemma. 'I'd love to see your ideas.'

'Good.' Rafa's smile made Ivy's heart leap, and she could not explain the feeling she had that she had come home after a long journey.

Rafa had intended to base himself in Rome during the week and return to the castle at weekends to maintain the pretence of his engagement to Ivy. But as one week slipped into the next he found himself opting to work from his study at the castle most days and went to Vieri Azioni's headquarters only when it was absolutely necessary.

His conscience pricked that he could not ignore Bertie when there was a strong possibility that the baby was his flesh and blood. More of a concern was his fierce awareness of Ivy. He'd assumed that he would barely notice her presence in the vast castle, but he had been wrong.

She joined him for breakfast every morning, and he could not hide behind his newspaper while she chatted to him about a book that she was currently reading, or a film they had watched together the previous evening. She was always cheerful and charming to his staff, and somehow the castle seemed a brighter place since Ivy had arrived.

For the past four days and nights, Rafa had stayed in Rome to negotiate a business deal. He was frustrated that Ivy had been on his mind a lot. Now his heart rate accelerated in anticipation of seeing her again. The helicopter dipped low over the trees and moments later the castle came into view. The building looked less fortress-like in the afternoon sunshine, although it was still an unconventional home, Rafa conceded. He did not understand why the Castello Dei Sogni was the only place that felt like *his* home. Perhaps it was because the ruined castle had needed rescuing and so had he. They had found each other.

The legend of why the castle had been built reminded him of why he would not risk his heart again. A wife, a child, a family of his own—he had thought he'd had everything until his life had come crashing down. Tiffany had made a fool of him and being separated from Lola had nearly destroyed him. He had missed being a father, but he'd decided never to have a child, reasoning that he could not miss what he did not have. It followed that, if he never fell in love, he could never be hurt.

When the helicopter landed, he gathered up his briefcase and a file of wallpaper samples he planned to show Ivy. She was enthusiastic about his plans for the refurbishment of the library, and most evenings over dinner they discussed ideas for the library and the various other rooms in the castle that were yet to be renovated. Rafa could employ an interior designer, but he was reluctant to allow a stranger to be involved in his private bolthole. The thought struck him that he did not think of Ivy as a stranger, even though he had known her for less than a month.

He strode into the castle and almost stepped in a dish of milk that had been left on the floor in the entrance hall. The dish tipped over and milk ran across the flagstones. *What the blazes?*

The butler came out of the kitchen, whistling a tune that Rafa vaguely recognised was a song from a popular stage musical. *Seriously!* Arturo could best be described as impassive, and he was certainly not prone to spontaneous whistling. He stopped mid-way through the chorus when he saw Rafa.

'*Signor*, I was not expecting you until the evening.'

'Evidently. Arturo, why is there a dish of milk in the hall?'

'It is for the cat, *signor*.'

'Cat?' Rafa decided that he must have landed in a parallel universe when he followed the butler's gaze and saw a fat ginger cat jump down from the window seat and stalk past him into the sitting room.

'Signorina Ivy rescued the cat after she found it abandoned outside the gates of the castle,' Arturo explained. 'The vet thinks that the kittens will be born in the next day or two.'

Kittens! Rafa cursed beneath his breath. It was bad enough that the solitude in his fortress had been disturbed by a gorgeous woman who tempted him, and a cute baby who tugged on his emotions, without the addition of a pregnant stray cat. 'Where is Signorina Ivy?'

'I believe she is in the ballroom.'

The strains of the tune Arturo had been whistling were audible when Rafa neared the ballroom. He opened the door and halted. Ivy was dancing and did not notice him. He leaned against the door frame and could not take his eyes off her as she twirled, leapt and kicked her legs high in the air.

She was wearing tiny, sparkly shorts and a crop top that revealed her taut midriff. Her long legs looked stunning in black stockings with wide bands of lace around the tops of her thighs. Rafa had arranged for Ivy's flat in Southampton to be cleared and her belongings sent to the castle.

Heat unfurled in his groin. Ivy's body was supple and sexy, and he was mesmerised as he watched her. He guessed the routine was one that she had performed when she'd been a show dancer on a cruise ship. The music pumping out of the speakers quickened in tempo, echoing the drumbeat of desire pounding in his veins.

Ivy spun round and saw him, but she did not stop dancing and beckoned to him. 'Come over here, I need you.'

Rafa was uncomfortably aware of his arousal straining against his trouser zip as he walked across the ballroom.

'Stop there,' Ivy told him when he was close to her. 'I need you to be my dance partner and catch me when I jump into your arms.' She spun round faster and faster, keeping time with the music that was building to a finale. 'Ready?' She made a graceful leap, and Rafa quickly thrust out his arms and caught her against his chest. 'Ta da!' She giggled at his stunned expression.

Her brown eyes made him think of molten chocolate, and her laughter was infectious. 'You are crazy,' he told her. A little of the ice around his heart melted and he laughed out loud. He couldn't remember the last time he had really laughed. It felt...good.

'The dance is meant to be a duet. I need a dance partner—I could teach you the steps. I heard that you were pretty quick around the basketball courts.'

'Playing basketball and dancing are hardly the same. It's true that I was the fastest player in the American professional basketball league.' Rafa did not try to disguise his pride. He'd been the best in the game and had been called a legend by the California Colts' legions of fans.

'Do you miss playing basketball?'

He nodded. 'I miss my team mates and the excitement before an important game.'

Ivy was the first person to show an interest in his sporting career since Rafa has moved back to Italy. He had dominated the basketball courts in the US and around the world for nearly a decade, but his father had thought that playing sport was not a serious job, and had put emotional pressure on Rafa to commit his future to Vieri Azioni.

He acknowledged that since he'd joined the company he'd enjoyed the challenges of corporate business. But basketball had been his independence and where he had found himself, instead of being a replica of his father. That was until Tiffany had made him question everything Rafa had thought he knew about himself.

'I guess you miss being a show dancer,' he said, running his eyes over Ivy's sexy costume.

Her smile became wistful. 'It feels like another life when I worked on cruise ships. When my sister died, and I became responsible for her baby, my life changed for ever. But I don't regret being Bertie's guardian. He is my only chance to be a mother after my brush with cancer.'

Rafa stared down at Ivy's pretty face. Her cheeks were pink and she was breathless from dancing. He wished he could carry her up to his bedroom and make love to her. His body tightened as he imagined her naked body flushed with sensual heat.

'I've never met anyone like you,' he said roughly. She was

so full of energy, and she had brought light and laughter into the castle and into his life. He did not only want to take Ivy to bed. He liked talking to her, and being with Bertie and her. Rafa knew he was on dangerous ground. The embittered man he had become after his divorce warned him to keep his distance, but he was drawn to Ivy's shining light like a moth to a flame.

Abruptly he set her down on her feet and silently cursed his rampant libido when his gaze was drawn to the outline of her nipples beneath her top. 'We seem to have acquired a cat,' he muttered.

'Oh, have you met her? Isn't she sweet? I've named her Jasmine.' Ivy's big brown eyes filled with tears. 'The poor little thing had been abandoned and she is about to have kittens. Arturo has promised to feed Jasmine and her family when I'm not here.'

'Why won't you be at the castle?'

She seemed surprised by the question. 'I assume I'll move out when we end our engagement. I didn't tell Arturo that our engagement is fake,' she said quickly when Rafa frowned. 'I mentioned that I will take Bertie to visit my family. I spoke to my mum a few days ago, and she invited me and Bertie to stay with her in Cyprus in early September. That will be about the right time for us to break up, don't you think?'

Rafa did not know what to think. He was surprised by how much he disliked the prospect of Ivy and Bertie leaving the castle. But the baby scandal story in the media would soon be yesterday's news and there would be no reason to continue their fake engagement.

CHAPTER EIGHT

'I must go,' Ivy said as she glanced at her phone. 'Anna has messaged that Bertie has woken from his nap.'

They walked back to the main hall and saw Arturo emerge from the study. 'A file has just been delivered by a courier,' the butler told Rafa. 'I left it on your desk.'

Rafa assumed the file contained work documents and wondered why his PA had not given them to him before he'd left the office. He opened the study door and frowned when the ginger cat wove around his ankles and preceded him into the room.

'Jasmine has been showing signs that she will give birth to her kittens soon, and she seems to like your study,' Ivy murmured. 'I hope you don't mind.'

'What makes you think I'd mind my study being used as a labour ward?' he muttered, but his sarcasm was lost on Ivy.

'Thank you!' Her bright smile had a peculiar effect on Rafa's heart rate.

The cat was curled up on an arm chair in the study and gave Rafa a disgusted look when he walked in. The file on the desk was marked confidential and, when he opened it, he was startled to find several documents and a handwritten note to him from his father's personal assistant. Beatriz had worked for his father for twenty years and had retired soon after his death.

She had been devoted to Rafael. The note explained that she had hidden the enclosed documents when Rafael had died, to protect his privacy.

With a sense of foreboding, Rafa read the first document—a letter that had been sent to Rafael Vieri from Gemma Bennett, informing Rafael that she had given birth to his son.

The second document was a letter that Rafa's father had written to Gemma Bennett. Rafael had accepted that Bertie was his son, resulting from an affair he'd had with Gemma while they had been on the cruise ship.

Dio! Bertie *was* his father's child. Rafa was stunned by the revelation even though he had realised it might be true. Reading his father's confession that Rafael had been unfaithful to his mother was painful. He had respected his father and looked up to him, but now he had evidence that Rafael had been fallible and imperfect.

Rafa's jaw clenched as he read what his father had written to the young woman who had been the mother of his illegitimate son. Rafael explained that his wife had been diagnosed with a terminal illness and he must take care of her. He was unable to have a role in his baby son's life, but he would arrange for a generous financial settlement to be paid to Gemma.

Rafa frowned. Ivy had not said that her sister had received money from his father. The date on the letter caught his attention and he realised that it was the date of his father's death. His father must have written to Gemma literally just before he'd died. The letter had not been sent, which was why it was included with the documents Beatriz had kept.

When Gemma had been killed in a tragic accident and Ivy had become Bertie's legal guardian, she had mistakenly believed that Rafa was the Rafael Vieri with whom her sister had had an affair.

Rafa pinched the bridge of his nose. His priority must be to protect his mother from ever discovering the truth, and for that reason he had allowed everyone to think that he was Bertie's father.

It *must* have been Ivy who had told the story to the news reporter. Other people in the boardroom had heard her accuse him, and it was true that some of the directors had doubted his suitability to be his father's successor. But he could not believe any of them would have risked the company's reputation by involving the press in the scandal. Carlo Landini, the only other person who had been present that day, despised the paparazzi.

Rafa did not know what Ivy had hoped to gain by telling the reporter that she was the baby's mother instead of her sister. He could not trust her. There was a risk that when he ended their fake engagement she might tell the press the true identity of Bertie's father. He would have to keep a close eye on her, but he doubted she would agree to remain at the castle indefinitely.

He stood up and paced around the study. A shocking idea had come into his mind. If he made their engagement real and actually married Ivy, the media would be convinced that Bertie was his child, and his mother would not discover the truth. After his disastrous marriage to Tiffany, he had vowed never to marry again. But he was desperate to protect his mother from learning about his father's betrayal. Rafa grimaced. He had never been able to make his mother happy, but now it was in his power to prevent her from being heartbroken.

And then there was Bertie, who Rafa now had proof was his half-brother. He had a responsibility to the baby, who was an innocent child and an heir to the Vieri fortune. Rafa felt protective of him. Every child deserved to be loved and Bertie was not responsible for the circumstances of his conception.

What the hell was he going to do? He needed a drink and took a bottle of single malt from the cabinet, pouring a generous amount into a glass. Disillusionment had left a bitter taste in his mouth. He was disappointed with his father. Once again, his faith in someone who he'd trusted had been shattered. It reinforced his belief that trust was a fool's game, Rafa thought grimly.

The cat jumped down from the chair and padded over to him. Rafa bent down and held out his hand to the animal, cursing when he felt sharp claws rake across his skin. A hissing noise similar to the sound of a kettle coming to the boil came from the cat before it shot under the desk.

'Very wise. Never trust anyone,' Rafa muttered.

Rafa had returned to the castle in time for dinner. Ivy had spent the last twenty minutes deciding what to wear. She'd settled on a pale blue dress which left one shoulder bare and showed off her slim waist. The hem of the chiffon skirt floated around her ankles when she walked, giving a glimpse of her strappy silver sandals.

Was the dress too obvious? Her reflection in the mirror revealed a hectic flush on her cheeks and a sparkle of excitement in her eyes. She felt like a teenager on a first date, and in truth she had barely any more experience of men than she'd had at seventeen when she'd become ill. But she had recognised desire blazing in Rafa's eyes when he had caught her in his arms in the ballroom.

She knew he had wanted to kiss her. Perhaps he was waiting for her to give him a sign that she wanted him to take her to bed. He had backed off after she'd told him she was a virgin, but sometimes she caught him looking at her with a gleam in his eyes, which had restored the self-confidence that cancer had stolen along with her hair and her first boyfriend when she had been a teenager.

Her seductive dress sent a signal that he would have to be blind not to see, Ivy thought as she gave a final twirl in front of the mirror and the side-split in the skirt opened to reveal her lace stocking top.

The sound of crying from the baby monitor alerted her that Bertie was awake, and when she hurried into the nursery he was red-faced and tears glistened on his dark eyelashes. Usually he went to sleep after his last feed, but he had been unsettled, and Ivy was worried that he was unwell.

'What's the matter, Bobo?' she crooned to the baby as she lifted him out of the cot. Anxiety made her tense, and she winced when her shoulder gave a twinge. It had felt much better since she'd had a few sessions with the physiotherapist Rafa had arranged for her to see, but she must have strained a muscle while she'd been dancing earlier.

She turned her head when the nursery door opened and Rafa walked in. He was still wearing his business suit, but his tie was missing, and he'd undone the top few buttons on his shirt. It looked as if he'd been running his fingers through his hair, and his jaw was tense, but nothing detracted from his devastating good looks.

'It's unusual for Bertie to be awake at this time,' he commented.

'I don't know what's wrong with him. Anna would probably have an idea, but she has driven to L'Aquila to have dinner with friends and will be back later tonight. I've changed Bertie's nappy, he doesn't seem to have colic, and his temperature is normal. He is crying like he does when he's hungry, but he had a bottle of formula an hour ago.'

'He might be hungry. Babies often have a growth spurt at around four or five months old. I read a lot of parenting books when Lola was a baby,' Rafa said in a gruff voice.

Ivy felt guilty that she had stirred up painful memories for him. 'I don't have any experience of looking after a baby and I feel so useless,' she admitted.

'You shouldn't, you are brilliant with him. Is your shoulder hurting? Here, let me take Bertie. Make up another bottle of formula and hopefully it will settle him.' Rafa cradled the baby in his arms and a curious expression flickered on his face. 'I know for certain that Bertie is my half-brother.'

Ivy tipped the contents of a carton of ready-made formula

milk into a bottle. She gave Rafa a startled look. 'Have you had the result of the extended paternity test?'

'I received confirmation in an email from the clinic an hour ago, just after I had seen a letter which my father had written to your sister, accepting that Bertie was his child.'

'Gemma told me before she died that she hadn't heard from Bertie's father.' Ivy handed Rafa the bottle of milk and watched him feed the baby. 'I don't think she was surprised. A few years ago, her ex-boyfriend had swindled her out of her savings that she'd hoped to use for a deposit to buy a house. That's why we were living in a rented flat. Your father abandoned her. It's what men do,' she muttered.

'I have evidence that my father had arranged for a financial settlement to be paid to Gemma, but he would not have known that she had been killed by the time he wrote to her. He never sent the letter because he suffered a fatal heart attack. His personal assistant had kept the letters, but Beatriz decided that I should have them.' Rafa sighed. 'A cruel twist of fate meant that Bertie was an orphan when he two months old.'

Ivy still suffered flashbacks of the terrible night when Gemma had died. Memories of kissing her sister for the last time before she'd been rushed to the operating theatre, and her disbelief when the surgeon had explained that Gemma's life couldn't be saved, would always haunt her.

She gave a low cry and ran out of the nursery. Her feet took her downstairs to the small, informal dining room where Arturo planned to serve dinner. The French doors were open, and Ivy stepped outside onto the terrace. Dusk had fallen and stars pinpricked the purple sky.

A short while later, Rafa joined her. 'Bertie drank all the milk and he is asleep now. Arturo asked if we are ready to eat.'

'I'm not hungry.' Ivy's voice cracked. 'I miss Gemma so much. When I started chemo and my hair fell out, Gem shaved all her hair off. She said we would beat my cancer together. She was the best sister, and I am determined to look after her son the best I can. But I didn't know why he was crying, and I'm worried about managing on my own. It's heart-breaking that Bertie will grow up without his parents.'

'You are not on your own. Bertie is my responsibility too, and we will be his parents,' Rafa told her.

'How can we be his parents?'

'I think we should both adopt Bertie.'

'I don't see how us adopting him will help,' she said wearily. 'For a start, I live in England and you live in Italy. Are you suggesting that we pass him between us like a parcel?'

Rafa's silence for some reason made the hairs on the back of Ivy's neck prickle. 'I am suggesting that we make our engagement real—and get married.'

'You can't be serious.' Ivy was dismayed by the way her heart had leapt at Rafa's proposal. The little girl inside her who had believed in fairy tales until she'd been ten, when her father had left and she'd realised she would have to fight off the big bad wolf by herself, had briefly hoped that Rafa was the prince of her childhood daydreams. Achievable goals, she reminded herself firmly. 'Neither of us wants to get married,' she reminded him.

'In ordinary circumstances, I would not choose to marry again,' he agreed. 'But the situation is far from ordinary. Bertie deserves to grow up with two parents who will love and care for him.'

'We can't lie to him. He has a right to know who his mother and father were.'

'When he is old enough we'll tell him about his real parents. But it will be some years before he can understand. By then, my mother will no longer be here. At least she'll have been spared knowing that her husband had betrayed her.'

Rafa raked his hand through his hair. 'My father was a decent man, and his behaviour was out of character. I believe he would have wanted me to protect my mother's feelings. It sounds as though your sister was a special person.'

'She was.' Ivy brushed a tear off her cheek.

'When the time is right, we will tell Bertie about them. We are his family now. Our marriage will be a sensible arrangement to allow us to be Bertie's parents, and I believe it will work, because we do not have any expectations of each other.'

'We don't have to be married in order to adopt him.'

'True, but I'm not planning to have children of my own and I want to make Bertie my heir. That can only happen if he is legitimate. Under the rules created by my great-grandfather, it is allowed for the heir to the Vieri fortune and the company to be adopted. Would you deny Bertie his birth right?' Rafa challenged her. 'If we marry, he will be my successor as the head of Vieri Azioni with the wealth, privilege and prestige that goes with the position. Just as importantly, we will give him a stable and secure childhood.'

'It's a crazy idea,' Ivy muttered. She must be crazy to contemplate agreeing to marry Rafa even for a second. But her conscience had pricked when he'd asked if she would deny Bertie his birth right. Her sister's baby was related to the powerful Vieri family and his destiny was in her hands.

'How can you be sure you won't want a child of your own in the future?' She could not bear for Bertie to feel abandoned by Rafa, the way she'd felt when her father had left home and started a new family.

He scowled. 'It damn near destroyed me when I learned that Lola was not my daughter. I'd married Tiffany in good faith and believed she was pregnant with my baby. When I discovered how she'd lied to me, I vowed never to trust another woman enough to have a child.'

Ivy moved away from Rafa and stared over the dark garden. It was impossible to think when her senses were assailed by the spicy scent of his aftershave. Rafa knew because she had told him that she was unable to have children. Had he factored her infertility into his decision to ask her to marry him? He had been adamant that he did not want a child of his own.

But what about her? She couldn't deny that over the past

weeks, when they had been living at the castle and she'd spent time with Rafa, her awareness of him had increased. But what she felt was more than sexual attraction.

She liked being with him and discussing his plans for the renovation of the castle. She had seen how gentle he was with Bertie, and she lived for one of his unguarded smiles that made her think she had broken through his barriers. She could easily fall for him, but he had insisted that their marriage would be a sensible arrangement. If she accepted his proposal, it would be like jumping into the abyss. Was she brave enough, or foolish enough?

'Marriage is a huge step. I need to think about it,' she told him.

'You need to think about marrying a billionaire?' The cynicism in his voice chilled her.

Ivy spun round to face him. 'I don't care about your money. All I care about is doing the right thing for Bertie, and I'm not going to rush into making a decision that will affect him for the rest of his life.' She closed her eyes to block out Rafa's arrogantly handsome face. 'I think I'll go to bed. It's been a long day.'

'It's only eight o'clock. Why don't you relax in the hot tub for a while? The jets might help your shoulder.' When she nodded, Rafa took out his phone. 'I've asked the staff to prepare the pool house and spa,' he said seconds later. 'I'm going to my study to catch up on some work.'

The pool house was at the side of the castle in what must once have been the orangery. At night, the glass roof revealed the canopy of stars in the inky sky. Potted ferns and other plants gave the room a tropical feel. The groundsman was leaving when Ivy arrived. He had switched on the jets in the hot tub and the water foamed and bubbled, creating a cloud of steam.

Ivy expected to find her swimsuit hanging on the hook, but it was missing, and she remembered that she had been wearing it when she'd walked back to the castle after her swim the previous day. There was no one around and, after hesitating briefly, she shimmied out of her dress and panties and stepped into the sunken spa.

The warm water was heavenly when she slid lower into the bubbles and positioned herself so that a jet was directed at her aching shoulder. She closed her eyes and tried to block out the debate in her head as to whether or not she should marry Rafa for Bertie's sake.

She had no idea how long she had been in the tub when a shaft of cool air stirred the fronds of the giant fern, and her heart missed a beat when she looked over at the door as Rafa strolled into the pool house.

'The maid thought you might need fresh towels,' he said, dropping the pile of towels he was carrying onto a lounger. 'She must have forgotten she'd brought some earlier.' He looked un-abashed when Ivy glanced at the stack of clean towels on the counter.

'I'm sorry you interrupted your work unnecessarily.'

He came closer to the hot tub and started to undo his shirt buttons. 'I didn't feel like working. Too many other things on my mind.'

He slipped off his shirt and Ivy's mouth ran dry when she moved her eyes over his broad, bronzed chest overlaid with crisp black hairs that arrowed down his flat stomach. He put his hands on his belt buckle and she remembered that she was naked.

'You can't come in the tub,' she said breathlessly. 'I forgot my swimsuit.'

'I promise not to look.' His sexy grin sent a coil of heat through her, and she felt as if she might self-combust when he stepped out of his trousers to reveal black swim briefs that he must have put on before he'd come to the pool house. So much for his excuse of delivering towels!

His body was a work of art from his wide shoulders, tapered torso and flat abdomen. His hips were lean, and his long legs were powerfully muscular from his years of playing sport at a professional level. Ivy noted that his dark body hairs disappeared into his swim briefs that contained the distinct bulge of his manhood. He stepped into the spa, and she inched along the seat to put as much distance as possible between them.

'Mmm, this feels good,' he murmured, stretching his arms along the sides of the tub and dropping his head back against the tiles. He reminded her of an indolent sultan, and she would not have been surprised if half-naked concubines had appeared to fan him with palm leaves. 'Is your shoulder any easier?'

'A bit. You were right, the jets are helping.'

The water sloshed when he suddenly moved across the tub and somehow manoeuvred them both so that he was sitting behind her. She caught her breath when he settled his hands on her shoulders and pressed his thumbs into her muscles.

'I can feel a knot in your trapezius.' He pressed harder on her left shoulder and she yelped, but after a few seconds the pressure of his thumb started to ease the tension in her muscle. 'The trapezius is a big muscle that starts here.' His warm breath stirred the tendrils of hair at the base of her neck. 'It goes across your shoulders and down to the middle of your back.' The brush of his fingers on her sensitised skin was as light as gossamer, yet Ivy gave a shiver of reaction.

Rafa continued to massage her shoulders and she gradually relaxed beneath his magician's touch. Steam from the hot tub drifted up to the glass roof and the low thrum of the jets made her feel as though they were cocooned in their own world, far from reality.

'What exactly do you mean by marriage?' Her voice was husky as she asked the question that had thudded inside her since his proposal. 'Would you want…?'

Words failed her. The knowledge that she was naked, and he very nearly so, increased her intense awareness of him, especially when he continued to massage her injured shoulder with one hand and slid his other hand around her rib cage to cup her breast. He splayed his fingers over the small mound and found her nipple, making her gasp as pleasure spread like molten liquid down to her feminine core.

'Oh, yes, I would want, *cara mia,*' he said thickly, before he lowered his head and pressed his mouth to her collarbone. 'I want to have sex with you.' Bold and to the point. The images his words evoked in Ivy's imagination were shockingly explicit. 'Tell me what you want, Ivy.'

He dropped his hand from her shoulder and drew her closer so that her back was up against his chest. Now both his arms were around her, and he played with her breasts, rolling her dusky pink nipples between his fingers. Ivy could not fight the waves of languorous delight that swept through her as Rafa caressed her. He lifted her onto his lap and she pressed back against him, catching her breath when the hard ridge of his arousal nudged the cleft of her bottom.

'Do you want me to do this?' Despite the hot water in the spa, his gravelly voice brought her skin out in goose bumps. She held her breath when he skimmed one hand over her stomach, and lower, to the cluster of curls at the junction of her thighs.

'Yes.' She was intrigued and could not deny her longing for him to touch her intimately. She felt boneless and her thighs splayed open to allow him to slip his hand between them. He moved her so that she was sitting sideways across his thighs and bent his head to claim her mouth in a searing kiss that added a new dimension to his sensual foreplay.

This time when he pushed her legs apart there was a new urgency in his touch as he unerringly found her slick opening. He parted her and eased a finger inside her, stretching her a little wider when one finger became two. She loved the feeling of fullness, and her internal muscles were already tightening, quivering as he moved his hand with a steady rhythm.

Ivy clutched his shoulders and moaned as her excitement built. Rafa captured her delighted cries with his mouth and thrust his tongue between her lips, mimicking the action of his fingers inside her. It belatedly occurred to her that she should offer him the same pleasure he was giving her but, when she moved her hand down to his briefs and stroked her fingers along his powerful arousal, he lifted his lips from hers and growled. 'Not this time, *belleza*. This is for you to enjoy.'

And then it was too late for her to think of anything but the wondrous sensations he was creating when he gave a twist of his fingers deep inside her and simultaneously rubbed his thumb across her clitoris. She bucked against his hand as her orgasm hit like a tidal wave, crashing over her, and it kept on coming in ripple after ripple of intense pleasure until she was spent and sagged against him.

Water streamed down Rafa's limbs as he stood with her in his arms and carried her out of the spa. Ivy twined her arms around his neck and pressed her body against his when he set her on her feet. What had happened in the tub had been a prelude and, although it had been amazing, she sensed there was more. She wanted Rafa to teach her everything, and her confusion must have shown on her face when he stepped away from her and shoved his arms into a bath robe before he draped another robe around her.

'I thought...' Her voice was thick with mortification. She had assumed he wanted to have sex with her, and his rejection opened the Pandora's Box of her insecurities.

Rafa slid his hand beneath her chin and tilted her face up to meet his glittering gaze. 'I want to make love to you for the first time on our wedding night, *cara mia*.'

'And if I don't accept your proposal? Her eyes widened. 'Are you using sex to blackmail me to marry you?'

Unforgivably, his lips twitched. 'Not blackmail. I prefer *persuasion*.' His expression became serious. 'You know it is the right thing to do—marry me so that Bertie can claim his birth right as the Vieri heir.'

Ivy bit her lip. Rafa was so forceful and resisting him was impossible—in every way, she thought ruefully. Her body became alive to his caresses, but she was aware that, while she had experienced ecstasy in his arms, he had always remained in control. He must have had dozens of mistresses who were more experienced than her, perhaps hundreds. She did not want to think of the glamourous women he had enjoyed before her. Worse was the idea that there might be others when his desire for her faded.

'Honesty is important to you, and it is to me too.' She held his gaze. 'I want a promise of fidelity so that Bertie doesn't grow up in an atmosphere of suspicion.' She remembered the arguments between her parents when her mum had suspected her dad of having an affair.

Rafa gave a harsh laugh. 'My wife cheated and led me to believe that I was a father. I will be totally committed to our marriage and always tell you the truth. Make no mistake, *cara*—if you marry me, I will demand equal commitment and honesty from you.' His eyes glittered. 'What is your answer?'

Ivy took a deep breath and prepared to jump. 'My answer is yes. I will be your wife.'

CHAPTER NINE

'HAVE YOU FLOWN in a helicopter before?' Rafa watched Ivy grip the arm rests on her seat as the chopper took off and felt guilty that it hadn't occurred to him she might be nervous.

'Only once.' She smiled. 'It was so exciting. The cruise ship had stopped in Hawaii, and I took a helicopter sightseeing flight over the island. The scenery was so beautiful. I'd planned to visit Hawaii again…but things changed,' she said with a soft sigh.

Ivy's life had been blown apart by her sister's tragic death, when she'd become Bertie's guardian. But her love and devotion for the baby were genuine, Rafa brooded. He believed her when she'd insisted that she did not care about his wealth and that her only reason for agreeing to marry him was to secure Bertie's rightful place in the Vieri family.

That was one of the motives behind his decision to make her his wife, he reminded himself. The other was his determination to protect his mother from discovering the truth about Bertie's paternity. The reporter from a national newspaper was still digging for a scandal, but Rafa was certain that, once he had married Ivy and claimed the child everyone believed was his, public interest would fade.

But he could not forget that Ivy had been responsible for the story which had been published in the newspaper. Every time he dropped his guard with her, he remembered that she had lied when she'd said she hadn't spoken to the journalist.

His third motive for proposing to Ivy was less altruistic. He wanted her in his bed—beneath him, on top of him, every which way he could have her. It should bother him that he was so desperate for her. It *did* bother him, but he told himself he was in control, although how he'd held back from possessing her fully in the pool house three nights ago he did not know.

She had been so delightfully responsive, and her soft cries of pleasure when she'd come against his hand had sharpened his hunger. But instinctively he felt it was right to wait so that he could make love to her on their wedding night, and he only needed to be patient for a few more hours.

The helicopter was taking them to their wedding destination. Following the civil ceremony, they would return to the Castello Dei Sogni for an evening reception for two hundred guests. The reception was due to finish before midnight and then, finally, he could claim his virgin bride.

'I don't know anything about San Alinara except that it is an independent microstate, famous for its nickname "Island of Love",' Ivy said.

'The island off the east coast of Italy is an ancient principality that has been ruled by the Pellegrini family for centuries. It has become a popular wedding destination because its laws allow couples to marry easily. But so many people choose to hold their wedding on San Alinara that there is a long waiting list.'

'How did you arrange for us to marry with only three days' notice?'

'The current ruler, Prince Stefano, is an old school friend of mine.'

'Of course he is.' Ivy gnawed her bottom lip with her teeth, making Rafa long to press his mouth to hers and kiss her until she stopped frowning and melted against him. 'I don't belong in your world,' she said in a low voice. 'I grew up on a rough housing estate, and I certainly didn't meet royalty at the local secondary school. I'm not glamorous and sophisticated.'

He shrugged. 'It doesn't matter where you went to school. We are marrying so that Bertie will grow up in my world, as you call it.' He studied her pale grey dress and matching jacket and wondered why he was disappointed that she had chosen a distinctly un-bridal outfit for their wedding.

A limousine with the royal standard flying from the bonnet met them at the airport to drive them to the registry office in San Alinara. 'Unfortunately I will be away on state business on your wedding day,' Prince Stefano had told Rafa when they had spoken on the phone two days ago. 'I hope I will meet your new wife and baby son soon.'

The curiosity in his friend's voice had almost tempted Rafa to explain the reason for his hasty marriage. He hated the web of deceit, but he would not risk the truth being exposed that would shatter his mother. He knew how that felt. He remembered the taste of bile in his throat when Tiffany had told him she'd been sleeping with another man. Maybe it had hurt his pride more than his heart, he acknowledged. Love, if it had ever existed between them, had left the building by then. But his ex-wife's betrayal over Lola had broken him, and when he'd put himself back together trust was a missing component in the colder, harder man he'd become.

The registry office was part of a grand old building that provided a charming backdrop for wedding photographs. Inside they were greeted by an official and, once the paperwork had been checked, they were shown to a private suite where they could relax before the civil ceremony. Ivy disappeared into the bathroom with the travel bag she'd carried off the helicopter.

Rafa fiddled with his tie and tried to ignore the inexplicable jangle of his nerves. He checked his watch for the fifth time and wondered when Ivy was going to reappear—or if. It occurred to him that she might have changed her mind. As he was digesting that unwelcome thought, the bathroom door opened and she stepped into the room.

His jaw dropped and his blood heated to boiling point and surged south to his groin. 'You look...' He was lost for words. Beautiful didn't come close.

Ivy was wearing a pure white column dress, utterly simple, yet the flowing lines could only have been created by an expert couturier. The shimmering silk moulded her slender figure, and the halter-neck top exposed her back, shoulders and elegant neck. Her feathery blonde hair framed her delicate face, and subtle make-up enhanced her big brown eyes, flecked with gold.

She looked ethereal and innocent but, when she moved, the dress clung to her sweet curves and hinted at her sensuality that Rafa longed to explore. She was quite simply his every erotic fantasy in one exquisite package. The erratic thud of his heart warned him that the situation was spinning out of his control. He was not meant to feel like this. He did not want to feel anything. But the anxious expression in her Bambi eyes, the need for his approval in her hopeful smile, unfroze a little of the ice inside him.

He returned her smile, letting her see the genuine admiration in his eyes. 'You are perfect,' he assured her. And that could be a problem if he did not remain on his guard.

'These are for you.' Rafa presented Ivy with an exquisite bouquet of pink roses and delicate white gypsophila, commonly known as baby's breath. 'I remembered that pink is your favourite colour. I'm not likely to forget your pink hair when we first met,' he said drily.

Ivy did not want to think about how furious he had been when she'd turned up at Vieri Azioni's offices with Bertie and accused him of being the baby's father. 'Thank you. They're beautiful.' Lowering her face to the flowers to breathe in their scent gave her a few minutes to try to steady her racing pulse caused by the stark hunger in Rafa's eyes when he'd seen her in her dress.

She had been worried he might be annoyed by her decision

to wear a bridal gown. But she was only ever going to have one wedding and, even though their marriage was a sensible arrangement, she wanted to look like a proper bride.

With hardly any time to prepare for the wedding after Rafa's shock announcement that they would marry in three days, Ivy had called the personal stylist in Rome. Sophia had duly arrived at the castle with a selection of dresses, and Ivy had fallen in love with the simplicity of the white silk gown.

As long as the dress was the only thing she fell in love with, she warned herself. Rafa offered her his arm, and her heart missed a beat when she studied his grey three-piece suit that had been expertly tailored to mould his athletic build. The trimmed stubble on his jaw gave him an edgy sexiness that was reflected in his glittering eyes, and the sensual curve of his mouth promised heaven.

When they entered the room where the wedding was to take place, they were greeted by the registrar, who explained that the civil ceremony was legal and binding. The vows they were about to make were a formal and public pledge of their love and a promise of a lifelong commitment to each other.

Ivy felt Rafa stiffen, and fear clutched her heart. She had agreed to the marriage for Bertie's sake, but was she doing the right thing? If only she had some guidance, but the person she would have confided in and sought advice from had gone for ever.

Through a blur of tears, she noticed something fluttering around the room. A butterfly with vivid orange wings must have flown in through the open window, and now it landed on the bouquet of roses Ivy was holding. At Gemma's funeral an orange butterfly had fluttered around the church yard, even though it had been a bitterly cold winter's day.

A sense of peace came over Ivy. She had loved her sister, and Rafa had loved his father and was desperate to protect his mother. They might not love each other, but their marriage was founded on their shared love for Bertie.

She turned her head and met Rafa's enigmatic grey gaze. 'Are you ready to proceed?' he murmured. The butterfly opened its delicate wings and rose into the air. Ivy watched it flutter across the room and out of the window.

'I am ready,' she said steadily.

In the early-evening sunshine, the Castello Dei Sogni was almost pretty. The helicopter landed in the grounds, and Rafa clasped Ivy's hand in his as they walked towards the castle where the wedding guests had assembled for the reception. Huge urns filled with colourful flowers stood on either side of the front door. Inside, the great hall had been transformed into a romantic idyll with arrangements of pink roses and silver cloths on the tables that had been set out for the wedding dinner.

Ivy did not know most of the guests, who were Rafa's business associates, but she had met some of his friends and their wives who lived in the nearby town of L'Aquila. The stylist, Sophia, had become a good friend, and Anna brought Bertie down from the nursery. Ivy hugged his little body and love flooded her heart. Soon he would be Rafa's and her son, and a Vieri, once the adoption was finalised.

Rafa had arranged for a photographer from a popular magazine to take exclusive pictures of the event. The proceeds from the edition carrying the wedding photos would be donated to a children's charity. It was a clever move, for it meant that he controlled the media coverage.

Ivy duly posed beside Rafa while he held Bertie. She knew he hoped the pictures of them as a happy family would put an end to the speculation about their relationship. He'd told her that the board members and Vieri Azioni's shareholders were pleased their chairman and CEO had given up his playboy lifestyle. As a damage limitation exercise, the marriage was a stroke of genius.

The wedding dinner was sublime, and a champagne toast was made to the happy couple, although the bride drank sparkling water. After the meal, the guests mingled on the terrace and were entertained with music played by a fifteen-piece orchestra.

'Rafa is a lucky man to have such a charming bride.' The voice was vaguely familiar, and Ivy turned to see the elderly man called Carlo who had spoken to her at the engagement party. It had been less than a month ago, but it felt like a lifetime since she had arrived in Rome hoping to meet Bertie's father.

Now she was married to Rafa and tonight she would be his wife in every way. When he had bent his head to kiss her at the end of the marriage ceremony, she'd expected him to brush his lips lightly over hers. But, at the first touch of his mouth, passion had exploded between them that had shocked her with its intensity and she'd sensed it had stunned him too.

The memory of his hungry desire had pulsed hot and needy between her thighs for the rest of the day, and she felt a mixture of anticipation and slight nervousness as the clock ticked towards midnight and the end of the reception.

Ivy pulled her mind back to the present and smiled at Carlo. 'You own a bank.' She remembered that he had been in the boardroom when she'd accused Rafa of being Bertie's father. The scandal had led Carlo to cancel an important business deal with Vieri Azioni.

'I used to own Landini Bank,' he told her. 'But earlier this evening I joined Rafa in his study and signed the documents to complete the sale of the bank to Vieri Azioni. I won't apologise for withdrawing from the deal when I doubted Rafa's integrity. If a man becomes a father out of wedlock, it is my firm belief that he has a duty to honour the mother by giving her his name in marriage and legitimising his child. I told Rafa I would not sell my bank to him until he had proved he was worthy to own it.'

Carlo laughed. 'The timing was tight. I am flying to Canada tomorrow to spend six months with my daughter. Rafa pulled off the wedding just in time.'

So that was why Rafa had disappeared during the reception. Ivy told herself it was silly to feel hurt by the discovery that their rushed wedding had been so he could secure a business deal. He hadn't explained why he'd organised the wedding at short notice, except to repeat that, once they were married, the news reporters would lose interest in them.

Rafa had such a forceful personality and he was used to having his own way. Was this how their marriage would be—him giving commands that he expected her to obey? Ivy's chin came up. Her new husband was in for a surprise if he believed she would be a biddable wife.

By the time the reception had finished and the guests had departed, she felt brittle with tension and perilously close to tears. She escaped to her bedroom and found that her clothes had been moved by the staff into the rooms that she would share with Rafa from now on. The master suite comprised a sitting room and his and hers dressing rooms and bathrooms. The adjoining bedroom was dominated by a huge four-poster bed.

Thankfully, Rafa wasn't there. She could not face him when her emotions were on a tightrope. Ivy dashed into her dressing room and searched through the chest of drawers for her pyjamas, thinking she would make up the bed in her old room and sleep there tonight.

'Finally I've got you to myself.' Rafa had entered the suite without Ivy hearing him, and he stood in the doorway of the dressing room. His voice was as deep as an ocean, and he did not try to hide his satisfaction that they were alone. He had dispensed with his jacket, waistcoat and tie, and his shirt was unbuttoned to halfway down his chest. In one hand he held a tumbler of whisky and his other hand rested on the door frame. He seemed to be relaxed, but his eyes were as sharp as rapiers when he studied her.

'Don't come any closer.' She held out her hand as if to ward him off.

'It's understandable that you might feel nervous about making love for the first time, *piccola*,' he murmured.

'It's not... I don't.' She knew from the Italian lessons she'd been having from Anna that *piccola* meant 'little one'. Damn Rafa for sounding as if he cared when all the evidence showed that he didn't. Tears brimmed. She hated that she was a cry-baby. She hated that he was so big, strong and diabolically gorgeous.

'Is something the matter? I didn't imagine that you were sending me bad vibes for the latter part of the evening,' he said drily.

Ivy took a deep breath. 'I know our marriage is a sensible arrangement. But I hoped there would be honesty and respect between us.' Rafa's brows lifted, but he said nothing, and she continued. 'You should have told me that you had arranged our wedding so quickly because you wanted to do a deal to buy Landini Bank before Carlo Landini went abroad for six months. He told me you'd pulled the wedding off just in time. It would have been nice if you had informed me, that's—that's all I'm saying,' she faltered when Rafa pushed off the door frame and came towards her.

He reminded her of a big cat, but if she was his prey she wasn't going to wait around to be eaten. With the advantage of surprise, she darted past him, back into the bedroom. Belatedly she remembered that, as a professional basketball player, he'd been famous for his speed around the court. He overtook her before she was halfway across the room and spun her round so that her back was up against a post on the bed.

'I did not arrange to make the deal with Landini at the wedding. I'd forgotten about buying the bank, to be honest.' His eyes glittered. 'I had other things on my mind. Carlo asked if he could come to the wedding reception, and I invited him, because despite our differences in the past I like and respect the guy. It was a total surprise when he took me aside this evening and asked if we could finalise the deal. He was keen to hand over responsibility of the bank before his trip to visit his daughter.'

He slid his hand beneath Ivy's chin and tilted her face up to his. 'I do respect you and I will always be honest with you. I expect you to do the same.'

The air simmered with sexual tension. Apart from his fingers gently stroking her jaw, he wasn't touching her, but Ivy was so aware of him it *hurt*. She could feel the heat of his body and see the whorls of chest hairs where his shirt was open. He smelled divinely of his spicy aftershave and something earthier and intrinsically male.

'Do you want to know why I organised the wedding in as short a time as possible?' Beneath the bite of his anger was something raw that made Ivy tremble with excitement. 'This is the reason, *gattina*.' He angled his mouth over hers and kissed her with a fierce hunger that seared her down to her soul.

'I couldn't wait another day or endure another sleepless night while I fantasied about making you mine. I wanted the fantasy to be real, and if I could have married you even sooner you would not now be a wide-eyed virgin looking at me fearfully.'

He brought his mouth down on hers again and kissed her with a desperation that lifted Ivy's heart. His breathing was ragged, and she could feel the thunder of his heart when she pushed the edges of his shirt aside and laid her hands on his bare chest. The evidence of Rafa's desire gave her confidence in her strength as a woman and his skill as a lover. Her first and only lover, for she had not made her marriage vows lightly.

'I'm not afraid of you,' she told him huskily when he moved his lips over her cheek and kissed his way up to her ear to gently bite the lobe.

'Good.' His chest expanded. 'If you're not ready to sleep with me, say so. I would never try to force you. I respect your right to choose what to do with your body, *cara*.'

The last vestiges of her tension drained away. 'I'll be twenty-five in a week. If I'm not ready now, when will I be?' She turned her face to his and kissed his stubbly jaw. The slight abrasion against her lips sent a quiver through her and each of her nerve endings tingled. 'My body chooses you,' she whispered.

He muttered something in Italian and captured both of her hands, lifting them so that her arms were above her head. He curled her fingers around the bed post behind her. 'Hold on tight,' he bade her.

Ivy's heart missed a beat when he held her gaze and she recognised the sensual promise in his eyes. His fingers brushed against the back of her neck as he unfastened the halter top of her dress. The shimmering silk fell away from her breasts and he cradled the pale mounds in his hands, brushing his thumbs across the dusky pink nipples until they stood proud and taut.

'Don't let go,' he commanded softly, and she obeyed the deep timbre of his voice, for he was a magician and she was enchanted by him. She tightened her grip on the bed post and gasped when he bent his head and drew her nipple into his mouth.

The sensation of him sucking the tender peak was so intense that she pinched her thighs together, sure he must notice the musky scent of her arousal. He moved across to her other breast to mete out the same exquisite torture until she was utterly molten down below and her legs felt too weak to hold her upright.

With a tug, Rafa pulled her dress down, and it made a pool of white silk at her feet. *'Bellissima.'* His breath tickled her stomach as he knelt in front of her and kissed his way down to the tiny scrap of white lace between her legs.

Ivy's inhibitions disappeared and were replaced by a longing for him to touch her there. Her arms ached but she gripped the bed post tighter when Rafa pressed his mouth against the damp panel of her panties. It was not enough, she wanted to feel him…

'Oh!' The sheer delight of his mouth on her sensitive flesh when he eased her panties aside drew a moan from her. With a flick of his wrist, he pulled her knickers down and spread her legs apart so that he could bury his face between them. His tongue lapped her slick opening and then dipped inside her in a shockingly intimate caress that took her to the edge. She was powerless to stop the shudders that racked her body as he brought her closer, closer…

She climaxed hard against his mouth and the intensity of pleasure was beyond anything she'd ever experienced. How could she have done when this was all new to her? Only Rafa had ever used his mouth on her this way and, as the pulses of her orgasm faded, Ivy was ready for even greater pleasure.

But she was eager to give as well as receive. When he stood and uncurled her fingers from the post, she twined her arms around his neck and pressed her body against him. He lifted her up so that her pelvis was flush to his and she circled her hips over the hard ridge that strained beneath his trousers.

'Witch!' He growled. 'I want the first time to be good for you, *cara*, but if you keep doing that I'm going to disappoint you and disgrace myself.'

She loved the rough tenderness in his voice. Her heart gave a jolt. Where had the L word come from? She quickly banished it and focused on what he could give her, instead of something that was never going to happen. Sex was going to happen, and she was aware of a little flutter of apprehension when Rafa laid her on the bed before he stripped off his clothes. His trousers hit the floor, followed by his boxers, and the awesome length of his erection made her catch her breath.

How was she here with this powerful, arrogant man who she knew did not trust her but nevertheless made her yearn for his possession with his mind-blowing passion? Perhaps he sensed her faint hesitation. He lay down beside her and drew her into his arms, one hand smoothing tendrils of hair off her face.

His kisses were unhurried and beguiling as he explored every dip and curve of her body with hands that were strong yet gentle. He made no demands, and she relaxed again and slipped into a world of sensory pleasure while heat unfurled inside her and licked through her veins, hotter, more intense, as his fingers parted her and prepared her.

When he took a condom from the bedside drawer, Ivy gave him a shy smile. 'It's okay if you'd rather not wear one. There won't be any repercussions.' She had come to terms with being infertile. But now she was a mother to her sister's baby, and Bertie was very precious.

Her thoughts scattered when Rafa hesitated before he returned the condom to the drawer. There was a steely purpose in his eyes when he lifted himself over her and braced his weight on his elbows while he used one thigh to nudge hers apart. He was so beautiful and so big... Her eyes widened when she re-alised that it was actually going to happen, and she would have to take his hard shaft inside her.

He eased forward and she felt the tip of him press against her opening. Slowly, carefully, he pushed his solid length inside her, pausing every few seconds to allow her to adjust to the sensation of him possessing her.

There was mild discomfort rather than pain. She was aware of a feeling of fullness, of being stretched. She slid her hands along his shoulders and felt the strength in his bunched muscles. His clenched jaw told her of the restraint he was imposing on himself, and his consideration and gentleness brought tears to her eyes.

'*Cara*, I'll stop if I'm hurting you.' His voice was gruff with remorse. He began to withdraw, but she wrapped her legs around his hips.

'It's fine, just...new.'

'*Dio*, I knew you would kill me.' He claimed her mouth in a tender kiss that quickly became intensely erotic as he began to move, pushing deeper into her, easing back and pushing again, a little further, a little harder, until the fire inside her burst into flame. They were in perfect accord. Her body arched to meet his powerful thrusts and his lips sought hers again and again, taking and giving, demanding and appeasing.

He filled her senses and there was only Rafa, her husband who did not love her but who made love to her so sublimely that her heart trembled with the beauty of it. He took her higher and her entire body trembled as she strove for some unknown place that she sensed was there but was frustratingly beyond her reach.

'Relax and it will happen,' he murmured. She wondered how he knew when she did not know herself what her body was desperately seeking. He increased his pace, and there was a new urgency in the way he drove into her. Deep in her feminine core, something was happening, little tremors that became more intense with each devastating thrust of his shaft into her molten heat.

He slipped his hand between their joined bodies and gave a twist of his fingers that sent her tumbling over the edge and into ecstasy. She cried out as her climax cascaded through her, pulsing waves that, when they finally started to ebb, left her limp, boneless and replete.

Rafa had waited while Ivy rode out her orgasm, but now he moved again in hard, rhythmic strokes that prolonged her pleasure as his built to a crescendo. He lifted his mouth from her breast and she felt the tension of the muscles in his back as he remained poised above her for timeless seconds before he gave one final thrust and groaned as he spilled inside her.

She wrapped her arms around his big shoulders and held him while the storm passed. It moved her deeply that this powerful man had come apart and she had been the cause of his downfall. Tenderness filled her and she pressed her lips against his throat and tasted his sweat. In the languorous afterglow of their spent desire, she never wanted to let him go.

But she remembered the speculative look in his eyes when he'd joined their bodies and, although her experience was limited, she sensed that he had always been in control. He would not want her to cling, and for her self-preservation she must hide the effect he had on her emotions.

That shouldn't have happened. Sure, the sex should have happened, but not the way his control had shattered when he'd been thrown into a mind-blowing orgasm. Rafa was amazed that he'd kept his hands off Ivy for as long as he had. But he hadn't expected it to be so spectacularly good, especially as she had been a virgin. Part of him, the cold and bitter part, had not entirely believed her until, with a gut-wrenching sense of shock, he'd discovered that she had told him the truth.

Rafa rolled onto his back and stared up at the canopy above

the bed. His heart was still thundering in his chest, yet incredibly his shaft was already semi-aroused. He wasn't done with Ivy. Not nearly. Something inside him warned he would never have enough of her.

Possessiveness was an unfamiliar emotion for him. Before he'd met her, he had enjoyed a healthy sex life and had had countless lovers. Frankly, he had preferred women who were experienced and willing to accept his no-strings rule.

But when Ivy had tensed beneath him, and he'd realised how innocent she was, he'd felt a knife blade slice through his insides at the idea he might have hurt her. She was his. It should not make him feel like a king. He wondered why she had chosen to have her first sexual experience with him. His conscience pricked that he might not like her answer if he asked her. Those Bambi eyes of hers were so expressive. When he'd slipped the wedding ring onto her finger, he had read defencelessness and, more worryingly, hope in their velvet-brown depths.

He would provide Bertie and her with a comfortable life and every privilege that his fortune could easily afford to buy, Rafa assured himself. Ivy would want for nothing—except for his love, taunted a voice inside him. He couldn't give her his heart for the good reason that he kept it behind an impenetrable wall.

He turned his head on the pillow and watched her long eyelashes flutter against her cheeks. She was so tiny and perfect, like a delicate porcelain figurine. Her fragility made something tighten inside him, knowing that she had survived a life-threatening illness. The world would have been a greyer place without Ivy's golden laughter and the way she found joy in simple things.

He ran the back of his hand lightly down her peach-soft cheek. But, when he tried to draw her into his arms, she rolled away from him to the other side of the mattress. Rafa told himself he was relieved that she wasn't all over him, wanting to be cuddled and petted, but her rejection stung.

CHAPTER TEN

'THIS IS THE most amazing birthday present,' Ivy told Rafa happily. She stretched luxuriously on the sun lounger and stared up at the cobalt blue sky through the fronds of the palm trees.

She'd fallen in love with Hawaii on her brief visit a few years ago, and had been stunned when Rafa had told her he had booked a holiday on the tropical island to celebrate her birthday and their honeymoon. She had been persuaded to leave Bertie with Anna at the castle, as the trip was only for four days.

'You deserve some time to yourself.' Rafa was lying next to her on the double lounger. He propped himself up on his elbow and leaned over her to brush a few strands of hair off her face. 'And I selfishly wanted you all to myself, Signora Vieri.'

He lowered his head and claimed her mouth in a slow kiss that made Ivy's heart race. She had not expected being married to Rafa to feel so real. He was charming and attentive, and since their wedding they had barely been apart. They had been on some wonderful sightseeing trips around Hawaii and had walked hand in hand along the white, sandy beaches beside the glistening Pacific Ocean.

He broke the kiss when a waiter arrived to serve them exotic fruit cocktail drinks decorated with slices of watermelon and a little paper parasol. Rafa disappeared briefly and returned with a garland of vibrant pink flowers, known in Hawaiian culture as a *lei*, which he draped around Ivy's neck. She breathed in the exquisite fragrance of the exotic flowers and gave him a dazzling smile.

The fizzing sensation inside her was happiness, she realised. She had believed she would never be happy again after her sister's death, but the past few days which she had spent exclusively with Rafa had been wonderful. Ivy ignored the voice in her head that reminded her she did not believe in fairy-tale happy endings.

She touched the flowers. 'Thank you for these, and for bringing me to Hawaii. It has been memorable.'

Something indefinable moved in his grey eyes. 'I have enjoyed our trip too, *cara*. What would you like to do on our last night here? We could try the fine dining experience or watch a show in the nightclub.'

'Mmm…or we could swim in our private pool and order room service before we have an early night.'

'How early?' Rafa growled, and Ivy giggled when he scooped her into his arms and carried her across the manicured lawn to their luxury suite.

'It's only afternoon,' she reminded him. He gave her a wicked smile as he laid her on the bed and pulled off his swim shorts. The sight of his burgeoning arousal evoked a flood of warmth between her legs, and she shivered in anticipation when he tugged the strings of her bikini. 'You are insatiable, Signor Vieri.'

'That makes two of us.' He groaned as he bared her breasts and closed his mouth around one nipple, sucking on the tender peak until Ivy moaned with pleasure, and he transferred his mouth to her other breast. 'Do you have any idea how much you turn me on?' His voice was rough with desire.

'Some idea,' Ivy whispered as she curled her fingers around his erection. She loved this teasing side to Rafa. She loved his fierce passion and his hunger for her that made her feel as beautiful as he always told her she was.

She was falling in love with him. The thought crept into her head, and she realised that it had already put down roots in her heart. Sometimes she thought that Rafa was as surprised as she was by the intensity of their relationship. It wasn't meant to be like this, and she did not know how she was going to survive when his passion for her waned, as it surely would. She was just ordinary Ivy Bennett, not a glamourous socialite. What did she have that would captivate a billionaire tycoon?

She pushed her doubts to the back of her mind and twined her arms around his neck to pull his mouth down onto hers. He made a muffled sound in his throat when she initiated a kiss that was wild and fierce. Ivy had a desperate need to know that this at least was real, this urgent passion that held them both in its grip.

'Cara?' He lifted his head and stared into her eyes, frowning when he saw the shimmer of her tears.

'I want you to make love to me now,' she told him. 'Please, Rafa.'

'Oh, I will please you, *cara*.' To Ivy's surprise, he stood up and held out his hand. When she got to her feet he turned her so that she was facing the bed and he bent her forward with her hands resting on the mattress.

His mouth was hot on the back of her neck as he feathered kisses down her spine, and at the same time he curved his hands over her bottom and spread her so that he could enter her with a smooth thrust that drove the breath from her body.

She was glad of his almost savage possession. The terrifying truth was beginning to dawn on her that he was the only man she would ever love. But love had no place in their sensible marriage. She could never tell Rafa that she was emotionally invested in their relationship. Instead she sobbed her surrender, urging him to take her harder, faster.

He held her hips and drove deep, filling her and completing her, driving them both towards the stars. It couldn't last, the crazy ride of their lives. Rafa groaned her name as he plunged into her, and the planets collided in a white-hot explosion that ripped through them and made them reborn.

Afterwards he stretched out beside her on the bed and pulled her into his arms. Ivy rested her head on his chest and listened to the gradual slowing of his heart rate.

Rafa brushed his lips over her hair. 'Happy birthday, *piccola*.' And then in a rougher tone, 'What are you doing to me?'

Rafa was surprised at how easily he slipped into married life when he and Ivy returned to the castle after their honeymoon. One morning a few weeks after the wedding he jogged through the forest until the trees thinned and he emerged into sunlight as he neared the summit of the hill. Behind him were the high peaks of the Apennine mountains, and from his elevated position he looked down on the Castello Dei Sogni.

He frowned as he remembered the legend of the man who had hidden away in the fortress so that love could not find him. In the summer sunshine, the castle's grey walls looked less forbidding. Perhaps even the strongest barricades had weak points and vulnerable areas where a slender girl with golden hair and Bambi eyes could enter stealthily and steal the heart of the castle's foolish owner.

He shook his head, amused by his fanciful ideas. He was not a fool, and his heart was safe, Rafa reassured himself. Admittedly, his marriage to Ivy was better than he could have envisaged. The sex was spectacular, and he couldn't get enough of her. But the truth was that what he felt for her was more than a physical response to their extraordinary chemistry.

What he felt for her. He was in dangerous territory, he brooded. But, the more time he spent with Ivy, the more he liked her. She confounded him daily. Her kindness and compassion were evident in everything she did, which was why his study was currently a feline nursery after the stray cat Ivy had rescued had given birth to her kittens beneath his desk.

Rafa grimaced. Jasmine, the cat from hell, clearly had a personal vendetta against him and dug her claws into his ankles every time he stretched his legs out under his desk. But Ivy adored the cat and her six kittens, so he did not complain when he threw away another pair of ripped socks.

He raked his hand through his hair as he remembered more of Ivy's delightful traits. She was funny, and he had laughed more in the past month during which she had been his wife than he'd done in a lifetime. His childhood hadn't been the happiest of times, Rafa conceded. His mother had always been distracted by her grief, and his father had put work above family. The occasional hiking trips to the mountains had been the times he'd felt closest to his father.

Now there was another Vieri heir. He'd never wanted to have a child of his own, but it was impossible not to love Bertie. Sometimes Rafa woke in the night with the thought that, if Ivy had disappeared back to England with the baby, he would never have known about his half-brother. But Ivy must have spoken to the journalist, who had then reported the facts of the story incorrectly. Rafa had married her to prevent the media and his mother from discovering the true identity of Bertie's father.

He always came back to Ivy's involvement in the newspaper story, and it was the reason he could not trust her. But did it matter? Rafa asked himself as he jogged back to the castle. Ivy was unaware that he had some doubts about her, and his misgivings reminded him as to why he should not be tempted to lower his barricades and allow her close.

He headed straight into the shower and then to his dressing room, to prepare for a dinner party they were hosting for some of his friends and their wives, who had quickly become Ivy's friends. It seemed everyone was drawn to her warmth and sparkle.

When Rafa walked into the bedroom, his breath left his lungs in a rush as Ivy did a twirl in front of him.

'You look stunning,' he said huskily. He heard the hunger in his voice, the rough note of need. *Dio*, when had he started to need Ivy? When hadn't he needed her? questioned a voice inside him.

Her gown was navy-blue silk overlaid with chiffon and embellished with tiny crystals that also adorned the narrow shoulder straps. The low-cut bodice did not allow her to wear a bra, and Rafa wished he could slide the straps down her arms and slowly bare her breasts with their rosy nipples that he loved to feast on.

He took a velvet box from his jacket pocket. 'This will be perfect to wear with your dress,' he said, opening the lid to reveal a delicate necklace of white diamonds, and a larger yellow diamond that matched the one on her engagement ring.

'Oh, Rafa, it's beautiful. But you shouldn't keep buying me things.'

'Why not?' He liked spoiling her and seeing her face light up when he gave her gifts. She had been as appreciative of the bunch of flowers he'd bought for her from a market stall in L'Aquila, on one of their regular visits to the historic town, as she was of an expensive necklace. Her guilelessness was genuine, which increasingly made him wonder if he *could* trust her.

He fastened the necklace around her throat and traced his finger over the yellow diamond nestling between her breasts. 'I'm glad you like it. I had it designed especially for you.'

'I love it.' Her smile was brighter than the most dazzling diamond. 'I wish I had something to give you.'

Rafa pressed his lips to the side of her neck so that she did not see his expression in the mirror. He was stunned to realise that Ivy's sweetness, and her laughter that filled the castle and filled him, were the only gifts he wanted. 'I will look forward to making love to you tonight when you are wearing only the diamond necklace,' he murmured, fascinated by the soft pink stain that spread over her cheeks.

It amazed him that she could still blush after he had kissed every centimetre of her delectable body. But the pink stain on her cheeks quickly faded, and during the dinner party he noticed that Ivy was paler than usual. The party was a great success with excellent food, fine wine and the company of good friends. When the last guests had departed, and Arturo had locked the castle doors, Rafa found Ivy had fallen asleep on the sofa in the snug.

'Perhaps I'm coming down with a virus,' she said, yawning as he lifted her into his arms and carried her upstairs. 'I'm so tired.' Her lashes lifted and the gold flecks in her brown eyes were as bright as flames. 'But not *too* tired,' she said suggestively. 'I've never had sex while adorned with diamonds.'

'You have never had sex with any other man but me.' Possessiveness swept through him. She was his. Ivy's blonde head drooped onto his shoulder, and she did not stir when Rafa carried her into the bedroom, undressed her and returned the necklace to its box.

He pulled the bed covers over her and was struck by how fragile she looked. She had been pale and unusually tired for a few days, and Anna had confided to him that Ivy had experienced dizzy spells recently. It was probably nothing to worry about, he told himself, trying to shrug off a sense of foreboding. Ivy had overcome cancer as a teenager and there would be no harm in persuading her to have a check-up with a doctor.

Ivy opened her eyes and focused blearily on the clock on the bedside table. It must be wrong. It couldn't be ten a.m. But her watch showed that she had slept until late. She sat up carefully and was relieved that she didn't feel nauseous, as she had the past few mornings.

She had tried to convince herself that feeling tired was to be expected when Rafa made love to her at least once every night. But her symptoms reminded her of how she'd felt as a teenager when she had been diagnosed with blood cancer. Of course it wasn't that—she was being over imaginative—but experience had taught her that life was unpredictable and happiness was precarious.

She hurried to the nursery, feeling guilty that she'd left Anna to take care of Bertie. Rafa must have left the castle hours ago. He had told her that he had an early-morning meeting at his office in Rome.

Bertie grinned when he saw her, showing off his first tooth. 'I hope he wasn't too restless during the night,' she said when she took him from the nanny.

'I think you should worry less about Bertie and more about yourself.' Anna gave her a concerned look. 'You have felt unwell for a few days.'

'I'm fine.' But she wasn't fine. Ivy gasped and handed Bertie to Anna before she ran into the bathroom just in time to be violently sick. Eventually it passed and she sat shivering on the edge of the bath. Fear gripped her. Suppose the leukaemia had come back? She blinked back tears as she imagined Bertie growing up without her.

At least he would have one parent in Rafa. Her heart cracked. If she had to have chemo and lost her hair again, would Rafa find her unattractive, as her first boyfriend had done? She could no longer deny to herself that her teenage feelings for Luke had been nothing compared to the overwhelming love she felt for Rafa.

'Nausea and tiredness can be symptoms of early pregnancy,' Anna remarked when Ivy returned to the nursery.

'I'm definitely not pregnant. It's impossible.'

'Babies come when they come. I understand that Bertie was a surprise pregnancy,' Anna said tactfully.

Of course the nanny, like everyone else, believed that Bertie was Rafa's and her child. Ivy hated lying and wished she could confide in Anna, who had become a good friend. But she had given her word that she would not tell a soul the identity of Bertie's father while Rafa's mother could be devastated by the truth.

'You can discuss your symptoms with the doctor,' Anna said. 'Your husband has been concerned about you and he arranged for the doctor to visit the castle.

* * *

Doctor Coretti duly arrived for a consultation with Ivy. She had to rely on his discretion when she explained that Bertie had been adopted, that she was infertile and could not be pregnant.

'It is best to rule out the possibility of pregnancy,' he murmured, handing her a test.

With a shrug, Ivy went into the bathroom, knowing that doing the test was a pointless exercise. A few minutes later she stared at the two blue lines in the test window and frantically re-read the instructions.

Two blue lines meant positive. Her heart stopped beating. She had been told that it would be virtually impossible for her to conceive naturally. She couldn't be pregnant.

The doctor spoke to cancer specialists in Italy and the hospital in Southampton, where Ivy had received some of her treatment. Apparently it was rare for fertility to return after the high doses of chemotherapy she'd received as a teenager. But sometimes miracles happened, Doctor Coretti said cheerfully.

Ivy could not absorb the mind-blowing news that she was expecting a baby. She had been so grateful to be alive after she'd recovered from cancer that she had accepted that being infertile from the chemotherapy was a small price to pay.

Her miracle baby. She placed her hand on her flat stomach and wondered if she dared believe there was a new life developing inside her. Rafa's baby. She dared not imagine what his reaction would be when she told him. He was bound to be as shocked as she was. She remembered how adamant he had been that he did not want a child of his own—it was why he had made Bertie his heir. But surely, once he got over his surprise, he would realise that their baby was a million-to-one miracle.

One thing was certain. She could not wait until the evening, when he was due to return to the castle, to tell him about the baby, nor would it be fair to break the news to him in a phone call. Rafa had driven himself to Rome in his new sports car, which meant that the helicopter was available.

* * *

Ivy usually enjoyed travelling in the helicopter, but she felt horribly sick for the entire flight, and was glad to climb out of the cabin after the pilot landed on the heli-pad on the top of the Vieri Azioni office building. The views across Rome from the roof were incredible, but Ivy did not linger. Her nerves were jangling at the prospect of breaking her shocking news to Rafa.

A flight of stairs took her down to the floor where his office and the boardroom were, and she was met by his PA, who explained that Rafa's meeting had finished but he was still in the boardroom. 'I'll tell him you are here,' Giulia offered.

'No, I'll surprise him.' It would not be the first time, Ivy thought ruefully, remembering how she had slipped past Rafa's personal assistant and burst into the boardroom to confront him with Bertie. This time she knocked and took a deep breath to steady her nerves before she walked in.

'Ivy.' Rafa broke off his conversation with another man when he saw her. 'This is a delightful surprise, *cara*.' He must have noticed her tension and his smile faded. 'Did you meet the doctor?' The concern in his voice warmed Ivy's heart.

'That's why I'm here...' She broke off, puzzled when she recognised the man standing beside Rafa.

'Sandro, I'd like to speak to my wife in private,' Rafa murmured.

'It *is* you.' Ivy could not hide her shock as she stared at the older man. 'You're Gelato Man. Don't you remember me? We met outside the office building and you took me to a café and bought me an ice-cream.'

'I'm afraid I don't...' the man murmured.

'It was definitely you.' Her heart was racing. 'I remember you said that you had heard me accuse Rafa of being Bertie's father and suggested I could sell the story to the press. You even gave me a reporter's business card and contact details.'

The man called Sandro looked at Rafa. 'I think your wife must be confusing me with someone else. I'm sure there is a simple explanation.' He gave Ivy a patronising smile. 'Memory can play tricks on us,' he said before he walked out of the boardroom.

'I know he was the man I met,' Ivy insisted to Rafa.

'*Cara*, Sandro Florenzi has worked for the company for forty years. Isn't it possible that you are mistaken?' Rafa said quietly.

'You don't believe me?'

'I have known Sandro all my life. He was a good friend of my father's.' Rafa frowned. 'I admit that Sandro had hoped to become chairman and CEO and he was disappointed when I succeeded my father. But I am sure he would not do anything to harm Vieri Azioni. I trust him.'

'But you don't trust me, even though I am your wife.'

Rafa did not reply, and his silence felt like a knife in Ivy's heart. He raked a hand through his hair. 'I will talk to Sandro and try to get to the bottom of the mystery. Why don't I take you to lunch, hmm?' He ran his finger lightly down her cheek. 'And this afternoon we'll go shopping.'

Ivy wondered if Rafa could hear her heart shatter. He would buy her anything she wanted, but she did not want material things. *You want him to trust you and love you,* whispered a voice inside her. But he would never do either and the fairy tale she had started to believe might come true turned to dust.

'Rafa…' She prayed for a second miracle. 'I… I'm pregnant.'

'Repeat what you just said,' Rafa demanded. He must have misunderstood. Ivy could not really have said she was pregnant. But her stricken expression told him what he definitely did not want to hear. He swore. This was the second time that Ivy had burst into the boardroom and detonated a bomb that would blow his life apart.

'You assured me that you were unable to have a child.' His phone rang, and with a curse he pulled it out of his pocket and switched the device off.

'I believed I was infertile,' she said huskily. 'When I had cancer, my monthly cycle stopped as a result of the chemo. After a few years I started to have sporadic periods, but I was advised that I would almost certainly never fall pregnant naturally.'

'So how did it happen?' He felt sick. It was as though he was revisiting the nightmare when Tiffany had told him she was expecting his baby, and he had been a gullible fool for two years when he'd believed Lola was his daughter. The difference now was that Ivy had insisted it was safe for them to have unprotected sex because she was unable to have children and he had believed her.

Dio, would he never learn that all women were liars? Rafa thought savagely. A few minutes ago Ivy had accused the deputy CEO of treachery when she'd said that Sandro had urged her to tell the news reporter the story that Rafa Vieri had fathered an illegitimate child. Rafa had been tempted to believe her, despite Sandro's denial. Recently he had begun to doubt her involvement in the news story. But she must have lied about being infertile, and it stood to reason that she could have lied about Sandro Florenzi.

Rage burned like acid in Rafa's gut. He had been a fool to have fallen for Ivy's sweet smile that disguised her damning lies. 'I'll want proof,' he said curtly.

Ivy's head jerked back as if he had slapped her. 'Proof of what? That I'm pregnant or that it's your baby? I've shared your bed every night since we married six weeks ago. When would I have had a chance to play away, even if I'd wanted to? You know I've only ever had sex with you.'

Tears sparkled on her lashes like tiny diamonds. Ivy cried easily, but she was quicker to laugh, and she was the most responsive lover he'd ever known. She held nothing back when they made love, and she was open in her adoration and devotion to Bertie. Rafa did not doubt she would love this baby with the same fierce intensity. *His baby.* Ivy's unguarded emotions had led him to lower his guard and even to start to trust her, which was something he had vowed he would never do again.

His jaw clenched when she came to stand in front of him and he breathed in the floral scent of her perfume, delicate yet subtly sensual, like Ivy herself. 'Maybe you don't believe that I had cancer and I pretended that the treatment had left me infertile.' Her voice shook, but her wounded gaze did not waiver from his.

'I don't…' he began roughly.

'Do you think I made it up that my hair fell out?' She touched the feathery blonde layers that framed her face. 'When my hair grew back after I'd finished chemo, it was a lighter colour, and it breaks easily, so that I can't grow it long. My hair wasn't the only thing that having cancer changed. It made me doubt my body, and it taught me that life is fragile. When I started feeling nauseous and tired recently, I was scared…'

The crack in her voice dealt another blow to the fortress that Rafa had built around his heart. 'I thought the cancer had come back and I might not be around to see Bertie grow up.' She wiped away her tears and more fell. 'Perhaps you think it would be better if I was ill instead of pregnant?'

'*Dio!* Of course I don't.' He pinched the bridge of his nose. His tension was off the scale. 'It's a shock.'

Ivy nodded. 'I was worried about your reaction when I told you. But I didn't expect you to accuse me of lying. I know what your ex-wife did, but you can't keep punishing me for her crimes. And I can't stay married to you if you will never trust me. It hurts too much.' She swallowed. 'I deserve better. Our baby deserves better than to grow up with parents who hate each other.'

'I don't hate you.'

'You will resent me and our baby if you believe that I deliberately tried to fall pregnant.' Tears streamed down her face. 'You don't love me.' It was an anguished cry. 'I could bear it if I knew you would love our baby. But you won't, will you? You're good with Bertie, but I've noticed how you hold back from loving him. You are determined to barricade yourself in your fortress so that love can't find you.'

And make a fool of me, Rafa thought darkly. 'You are being melodramatic. When you've calmed down, we'll discuss—'

'There's nothing to discuss. I'm keeping my miracle baby—at least, I hope I will.' Her mouth trembled. 'I'm only a few weeks into my pregnancy. Experience has taught me that life doesn't have "happiness guaranteed" stamped on the box.'

CHAPTER ELEVEN

IVY TIED RAFA in knots, and her vulnerability made him want to hold her in his arms and promise her that the baby would be fine. But he did not know what the future held. One reason why he had been adamantly opposed to fatherhood was because he had suffered the agony of losing a child when his ex-wife had taken Lola away.

He glared at his PA, who appeared in the doorway. 'I'm sorry to interrupt, Rafa, but your mother called your mobile, and when you didn't answer she came through on the office line. She sounded upset and said she needs to see you urgently.'

What else could go wrong? Rafa wondered. He turned to Ivy. 'We need to talk rationally, but right now I don't feel rational,' he said grimly. 'Go to the penthouse and I'll meet you there as soon as I've visited my mother.'

She walked out of the boardroom without saying another word. Rafa called the pilot. It would be much quicker to travel across the city by helicopter, and he wanted to get back to Ivy as soon as possible.

At the hospital, he hurried to his mother's private room and felt a pang to see her looking so gaunt. He leaned down to kiss her cheek and was surprised when she clung to him for a moment.

'What is wrong, *Mamma*?'

'Your father's assistant came to see me.' Fabiana's voice shook. 'Beatriz gave me a letter that Rafael had written just before he died. His death was so sudden. When Beatriz found some of his personal documents and realised they would cause a scandal if they fell into the wrong hands, she hid them to protect his reputation. But she was sure your father had meant me to see the letter. Here it is.'

Rafa read the letter his mother handed him. His father had been completely truthful about the brief affair he'd had while he'd been on a cruise that had resulted in the young woman giving birth to his baby. Rafael had explained how desperately sorry he was for the pain and upset he had caused everyone involved but that Fabiana, his beloved wife, had a right to know the truth.

'I don't know what to say,' Rafa admitted as he returned the letter to his mother. '*Papa* made a terrible mistake in what he did, but he was right to be honest with you.'

Fabiana nodded. 'There were never secrets between us. Rafael loved me, and my love for him has not diminished. He was a good husband. And you, Rafa, are a wonderful and loyal son. Bertie is Rafael's son, isn't he?

'I have been lying here thinking about it,' she said softly when Rafa froze. 'It was too much of a coincidence that Bertie is the exact age that the child from your father's affair would be. But I don't believe that Ivy is Bertie's mother. She is not good at lying, and she knew very little about pregnancy symptoms.'

Dio! Rafa thought of the astounding news Ivy had just told him, that she was pregnant with his baby. His reaction had been diabolical. Remorse shredded his insides as he acknowledged that Ivy was an unconvincing liar because she was innately honest. But she had agreed to be his fiancée and then his wife to protect his mother's feelings. In the end, the pretence had been unnecessary because his father had admitted what he had done.

'Ivy's sister Gemma was Bertie's mother,' he explained. 'But she died, and Ivy became his legal guardian.'

'I suppose Ivy came to Italy to ask you for help to bring up your half-brother. But you instantly fell in love with her and decided to marry her.'

Rafa stared at his mother. He had been about to deny that he'd fallen in love with Ivy, but with a jolt he realised that he was the biggest fool of all time.

You don't love me, Ivy had sobbed, and he'd frozen. Love hadn't been part of the deal. They had agreed that their marriage would be a sensible arrangement. Ivy had admitted that she wore her heart on her sleeve, and he'd sensed that she hoped for more than he could give her. He had made it clear that he couldn't give her love. He'd been honest.

Had he, though? Rafa forced himself to look inside his heart. He had never told Ivy that he loved seeing her face on the pillow beside him every morning. He'd never told her that his once gloomy castle was filled with light and laughter now that she lived there with him. He certainly hadn't told her that he was scared the way she made him feel weakened in some way.

What had he done? Rafa closed his eyes and saw Ivy's tear-stained face. He knew in his gut that Sandro must somehow have been responsible for the news story. And he did not doubt that Ivy had believed she was unable to have children after her cancer ordeal as a teenager. She had called their baby a miracle and that was exactly what her pregnancy was. An even greater miracle would be if she gave him a second chance to put things right between them.

'*Mamma,* I have behaved appallingly to Ivy,' he said raggedly.

His mother squeezed his hand. 'She will forgive you because she loves you. Go to her, *mio caro figlio.*'

Rafa called Ivy as he tore out of the hospital. 'Are you still at the penthouse, *cara*? I'll be with you in a few minutes.'

'I didn't go to the penthouse. I'm on my way back to the castle in a taxi because earlier I felt sick in the helicopter. I'm going to take Bertie to England and make a home for him and the new baby.' She swallowed audibly and Rafa pictured her big brown eyes brimming with tears. 'My phone battery is about to die, but there is nothing for us to say to each other. I want more than you can give me. I need to know that you trust me and... and care for me a little.'

'I do...' Rafa swore when the line went dead.

The journey to the castle in the helicopter took much less time than by car, and he arrived before Ivy. The castle felt empty without her. He wandered through the rooms, noticing how she had made the once gloomy fortress into a happy family home with potted plants everywhere, framed photos of Bertie and pictures from their honeymoon in Hawaii. He had taken the little signs of her presence for granted, but the idea that she might leave and take Bertie with her made his gut clench.

He wanted to persuade her to stay, but there was still a part of him that was reluctant to open up about his feelings for her and make himself vulnerable. Ivy's pregnancy was an excuse to push her into agreeing to continue with their marriage and would give him time to come to terms with the terrifying reality that the walls of his fortress were crumbling.

An hour passed, and then another. Ivy should have arrived by now. Rafa stood next to the window, watching impatiently for the taxi to turn into the courtyard. He replayed the awful things he had said to her over in his mind. He felt even more guilty after he discovered from a source who worked in the media that the reporter Luigi Cappello had confirmed Sandro Florenzi had given him the story alleging that Bertie was Rafa's illegitimate son.

He had misjudged the resentment Sandro had felt at missing out on becoming the CEO of Vieri Azioni. The baby scandal had caused the other board members and shareholders to withdraw their support from Rafa, as Sandro had intended.

He turned away from his vigil by the window when the nanny entered the study. 'Bertie is having his afternoon nap.' Anna's usual cheerful smile was missing. 'Have you seen the news report of the traffic accident on the *autostrada*? At least six cars were involved, and apparently there have been fatalities.' She looked close to tears. 'Ivy called me from a taxi when she left Rome, but I've been unable to get hold of her since then.'

'She said her phone battery had been about to die.' Rafa scrolled to a news site on his phone and read the report of the accident. Photographs showed a tangled mass of metal and wrecked vehicles, and emergency medics were treating the injured at the roadside. Dread felt like a lead weight in the pit of his stomach.

'The road has been closed since the accident happened,' Anna said. 'Apparently the traffic congestion is taking a long time to clear. Ivy is probably stuck in a tailback and will be home soon.'

'Yes.' He looked away from the nanny's sympathetic expression and returned to stare out of the window. 'Please, *piccola*,' he said beneath his breath. 'Please come home. I need you.' He thought of Bertie in the nursery, waiting for his beloved *mamma*, and whispered hoarsely, 'We both need you.'

Ivy shivered when she saw the blue flashing lights in the distance. The traffic on the *autostrada* was at a standstill and several emergency services vehicles had shot past on the hard shoulder. The wail of their sirens brought back memories of the road accident that had claimed her sister's life.

'Do you know what has happened?' she asked the taxi driver.

He did not speak much English, but he must have understood, and the meaning of his reply was clear. '*Incidente.*'

She hoped the people involved in the accident were not seriously hurt, or worse. Lives could be lost or changed irrevocably in an instant. Since she'd lost Gemma, Ivy had tried to live her life as fully and honestly as possible. That was why it had hurt so much when Rafa had accused her of lying about being infertile.

She had expected him to be shocked. After all, she still couldn't quite believe that she was going to have a baby. She held her hands over her stomach where the precious new life was developing. The baby would be a brother or sister for Bertie, for she would always treasure her sister's child as dearly as her own. But, instead of being in a family, she would be a single mother. Rafa had made it clear that he did not want their baby.

Ivy had no more tears left, and she felt angry with Rafa for his refusal to trust her, even though she hadn't given him any reason to think she had lied to him. She had always been honest with him. Although, that wasn't quite true, her conscience prodded her. She hadn't been honest about her feelings for him. She had hidden her love for him because she'd been afraid of his rejection.

Rafa had told her what his ex-wife had done, how Tiffany had tricked him into believing he had a daughter, whom he'd loved. It was not surprising that he had built a fortress around his emotions. Perhaps, if she'd found the courage to offer him her heart, he might have started to trust her, Ivy thought miserably. It was too late now. He had pulled up the drawbridge and love could not reach him.

The traffic was gridlocked and time passed slowly. An hour, two hours. She stared, frustrated, at her phone's black screen. She had told Anna she was on her way back to the castle, and she imagined how concerned the nanny would be when she failed to return. It was likely that the traffic accident had been reported in the news.

Ivy wondered if Rafa was worried about her. Another half an hour ticked by and her anger turned to despair. She wished she had told him how she felt about him. The road accident that had resulted in the traffic jam emphasised that life and love could not be taken for granted. Rafa had been badly hurt in the past, and he deserved to know that she loved him, and that she would love his baby who was part of him. She was desperate to reach the castle and cuddle Bertie. She needed to start making plans for the future. A future without the only man she would ever love.

Rafa rested his forehead on the window pane. His eyes ached from staring into the distance for a glimpse of the taxi and it must be why his lashes were wet. Big boys were not meant to cry. But a stupid, foolish man who hadn't appreciated the treasure he had been gifted until he faced the gut-wrenching possibility that he might have lost his golden girl—he cried. Silent tears leaked from his eyes and burned in his chest.

He should have told Ivy that he wanted their baby, their miracle. A choked sound of agony was ripped from his throat. If Ivy had been injured, would the baby survive? He wanted to protect her from hurt and pain, and he'd wanted to protect himself, he admitted. Who wanted love when it risked tearing your emotions to shreds? He'd thought he was safe in his fortress, but love had found a way in when he hadn't expected it and had captured his heart.

Lights appeared in the darkness outside, car headlamps that turned through the castle gates. Rafa heard his pulse thundering in his ears as he shot out of the room and took the stairs two at a time. He halted, and his gut clenched as he realised that in the dark he hadn't seen if the car was a taxi...or a police car bringing devastating news that Ivy had been hurt in the traffic accident. He wouldn't allow himself to think she might be dead. He could not bear to lose her.

Before Rafa reached the door, it opened and Ivy walked in. He was amazed that his legs kept him upright. She looked confused to see him.

'Why are you here?' she said in a defeated voice. 'I thought you would be at the penthouse.'

Ivy wished Rafa would say something instead of staring at her as if she were a ghost. The expression on his face made her heart thump, but he always had that effect on her, she thought wearily. Somehow she would have to get over him, in a hundred years or so. She wondered if he would try and prevent her from taking Bertie away. They would have to come to an arrangement over visiting rights. Maybe he would want custody.

She felt sick as she added that new worry to the long list in her head. She could not bear to be parted from Bertie.

But she couldn't stay married to Rafa and have his baby when she would never have his love. It was destroying her, destroying the self-confidence she had found since she'd married him. Worst of all, it was destroying the sense of hope that had carried her through her cancer treatment and losing her beloved sister—the hope that she would one day find a man who loved her. She had reached the end of the fairy tale and discovered that happy-ever-after was a foolish dream after all, just as her mum had found with each of her failed marriages.

Rafa strode towards her and Ivy caught her breath at the wildness in his eyes. His skin was pulled tight over his cheekbones and his jaw was clenched. She had a sense that it was taking his immense willpower to hold himself together.

'Where else would I be but where you are, *tesoro*?' His voice was strained, as if it hurt to speak.

'Don't,' she whispered. She was fooling herself to think he sounded as if he cared about her when she knew he didn't. 'I don't want to be married to you any more, Rafa.'

She heard his sharply indrawn breath. 'I know I have given you every reason to despise me, *piccola*. But if you would give me a chance to show you…to tell you…'

'Tell me what?' She did not understand why he sounded so—broken, as if the idea of her not being his wife hurt him deeply.

'I…' His throat worked as he swallowed hard. 'I know it was Sandro who spoke to the journalist.' For some reason, Ivy had had an idea that he'd been about to say something else. 'I should have believed you, and I will spend the rest of my life trying to win your forgiveness.'

'It doesn't matter now.' She'd forgotten about Gelato Man. 'Why should you have believed me? I know your first wife deceived you.'

'You are nothing like Tiffany.' Rafa's eyes blazed. 'You wear your honesty like a badge, but I was too blinded by my prejudices and bitterness to see the beauty of your heart.'

'Please don't.' Ivy could not take much more, and tears brimmed in her eyes. 'There was an accident and people died.'

'I was terrified that I'd lost you.' Rafa's voice broke and, if Ivy's heart hadn't already been in a million pieces, it would have shattered then. He touched her jaw, and she was startled to see his hand was unsteady. The sheen in his eyes turned them from grey to silver and she did not dare attempt to define the emotion blazing from beneath his thick lashes.

Ivy remembered the promise she had made to herself in the taxi that she would be honest about how she felt about Rafa. Everything was telling her that he felt something for her. Maybe what he felt wasn't love, but it was no reason to withhold her love from him.

'I thought I could marry you and not fall in love with you,' she confessed. 'But I was wrong. I was already in love with you on our wedding day, and I have loved you more with every day since I became your wife.' She put up her hand to hold him off when he moved towards her. 'I love you, but I can't stay in this marriage.'

'Because I don't want the baby,' Rafa said tautly.

Hearing him say it destroyed what was left of her composure and she dropped her face into her hands as sobs tore through her.

'*Tesoro.* Ivy, *amore mio.*' Rafa groaned, pulling her into his arms. 'I want our baby more than almost anything in the world. The only thing I want more is for you to love me as much as I love you.'

She opened her mouth but no words came out. 'You said you would never fall in love. I understand, I do. Your first wife hurt you with her lies...' Her voice tailed off and her heart stopped when she saw that Rafa's eyelashes were wet.

'I love you.' He rested his forehead against her brow. Ivy put her hands on his chest and felt the thunder of his heart beneath her fingertips. 'I tried to deny how you made me feel, and I thought I could be happy with the friendship that grew stronger between us every day. But the truth is that you stole my heart from the beginning, and I never want it back. It's yours, *piccola*, and I know you will take care of it because I trust you beyond words.'

'Rafa…' She was afraid to believe him.

'I want our baby and I will love him or her,' he said intently. 'I already do because the baby is part of you. One day we will tell our eldest child that he is special because we chose to be his parents, and we'll tell our second child how lucky we are to have been given a miracle.'

He captured her tears with his thumbs and gently wiped them from her cheeks. 'Every day I will tell you how much I love you, and if I am luckier than I deserve to be then perhaps one day you'll believe me.'

Rafa's hands shook when he framed her face, and the tenderness in his kiss healed Ivy and made her whole, made her believe in a love so strong it would last a lifetime.

'I love you. I can't remember a time when I didn't,' she admitted softly. She smiled against his mouth when he kissed her and told her that she was his world, the love of his life. His wife. Their passion had always been electrifying, and it blazed when Rafa drew her closer and ran his hands over her body as if he was scared she might disappear.

'I don't deserve you,' he murmured as he swept her up into his arms and carried her upstairs to their bedroom. 'I am going to spend the rest of my life showing you how much I love you.'

'Will you start now?' she asked when he tumbled them down on the bed and they undressed each other with trembling hands.

Rafa drew her into his arms and kissed her with tender passion that quickly became urgent as desire and love combined, and each caress felt new and wondrous.

'I will, my love,' he promised.

EPILOGUE

NICOLO VIERI ARRIVED with minimum fuss—although a good deal of stress for Rafa, who would willingly have endured Ivy's labour pains—on a sunny spring morning. The baby was born in the castle and, once he had been thoroughly inspected by his *mamma*, who pronounced him perfect, he was introduced to his big brother. Bertie had grown into a lively toddler who was adored by his parents, and baby Nico was a treasured addition to the family.

When Anna took Bertie off to play in the garden, Ivy carried her newborn son over to the window to give him his first glimpse of the world, but he remained steadfastly asleep. 'He's so beautiful,' she whispered, entranced by Nico's long eyelashes curling on his cheeks. 'I never imagined I could be this happy.'

Rafa came to stand behind her and wrapped his arms around her waist. 'Do you have any idea how much I love you, *curore mio*? You and our children are my world.'

Outside the window an orange butterfly settled on the ivy that grew over the castle's walls. It remained there, opening and closing its delicate wings, before it took off again. Ivy watched it fly up into the blue sky and smiled.

* * * * *

Keep reading for an excerpt of
One Nigjt Before The Royal Wedding
by Sharon Kendrick.
Find it in the
From Courtship To Crown anthology,
out now!

CHAPTER ONE

WHO *WAS* SHE?

A puppet, that was who.

Zabrina pulled a face, barely recognising the person she saw reflected back at her. Because the woman in the mirror was an imposter, her usual tomboy self replaced by a stranger wearing unaccustomed silks and finery which swamped her tiny frame. Another wave of panic swept over her. The clock was slowly ticking down towards her wedding and she had no way of stopping it.

'Please don't scowl,' said her mother automatically. 'How many times do I have to tell you? It is not becoming of a princess.'

But at that precise moment Zabrina didn't *feel* like a princess. She felt like an object, not a being. An object who was being treated with all the regard you might show towards a sack of rice being dragged by a donkey and cart towards the marketplace.

Yet wasn't that the story of her life?

Expendable and disposable.

As the oldest child, and a female, she had always been expected to safeguard her family's future, with her hand in marriage offered up to a future king when she was little more than a baby. She alone would be the one able to save the nation from her weak father's mismanagement—that was what she had always been told and she had always accepted it. But now the moment was drawing near and her stomach was tying itself up in knots at the thought of what lay ahead. She turned to face her mother, her expression one of appeal, as if even at this late stage she might be granted some sort of reprieve.

'Please, Mama,' she said in a low voice. 'Don't make me marry him.'

Her mother's smile failed to hide her resolve. 'You know that such a request is impossible, Zabrina—just as you have always known that this is your destiny.'

'But this is supposed to be the twenty-first century! I thought women were supposed to be free?'

'Freedom is a word which has no place in a life such as yours,' protested her mother. 'It is the price you pay for your position in life. You are a princess and the rules which govern royals are different from those of ordinary citizens—a fact which you seem determined to ignore. How many times have you been told that you can't just behave as you wish to behave? These early-morning missions of yours are really going to have to stop, Zabrina. Yes, really. Do you think we aren't aware of them?'

Zabrina stared down at her gleaming silver shoes and tried to compose herself. She'd been in trouble again for sneaking out and travelling to a refuge just outside the city, fired by a determination to use her royal privilege to actually *do* something to help improve the plight of some of the women in her country. Poverty-stricken women, some under the control of cruel men. Her paltry personal savings had almost been eaten away because she had ploughed them into a scheme she really believed in. She repressed a bitter smile. And all the while she was doing that, she was being sold off to the king of a neighbouring country—in her own way just as helpless and as vulnerable as the women she was trying to help. Oh, the irony!

She looked up. 'Well, I'm not going to be able to behave as I please when I marry the King, more's the pity!'

'I don't know why you're objecting so much.' Her mother gave her a speculative look. 'For there are many other positive aspects to this union, other than financial.'

'Like what?'

'Like the fact that King Roman of Petrogoria is one of the most influential and powerful men in the world and—'

'He's got a beard!' Zabrina hissed. 'And I *hate* beards!'

'It has never prevented him from having a legion of admirers among the opposite sex, as far as I can understand.' Her mother's eyes flashed. 'And you will soon get used to it—for many, a beard is a sign of virility and fertility. So accept your fate with open arms and it will reward you well.'

Zabrina bit her lip. 'If only I could be allowed to take one of my own servants with me, at least that might make it feel a bit more like home.'

'You know that can't happen,' said her mother firmly. 'Tradition dictates you must go to your new husband without any trappings from your old life. But it is nothing more than a symbolic gesture. Your father and I shall arrive in Petrogoria with your brother and sisters for the wedding.'

'Which is weeks away!'

'Giving you ample opportunity to settle into your palace home and to prepare for your new role as Queen of Petrogoria. After that, if you still wish to send for some of your own staff, I am certain your new husband will not object.'

'But what if he's a tyrant?' Zabrina whispered. 'Who will disagree with me for the sake of disagreement?'

'Then you will work with those disagreements and adapt your behaviour accordingly. You must remember that Roman is King and he will make all the decisions within your marriage. Your place as his queen is to accept that.' Her mother frowned. 'Didn't you read those marriage manuals I gave you?'

'They were a useful cure for my recent insomnia.'

'Zabrina!'

'No, I read them,' admitted Zabrina a little sulkily. 'Or rather, I tried. They must have been written about a hundred years ago.'

'We can learn much from the past,' replied her mother serenely. 'Now smile, and then let's go. The train will already be waiting at the station to take you to your new home.'

Zabrina sighed. It felt like a trap because it *was* a trap—one from which it seemed there was no escape. Never had she felt so at the mercy of her royal destiny. She'd never been particularly keen to marry anyone, but she was far from ready to marry a man *she'd never even met.*

Yet she had been complicit in accepting her fate, mainly because it had always been expected of her. She'd been all too aware of the financial problems in her own country and the fact that she had the ability to put that right. Maybe because she was the oldest child and she loved her younger brother and sisters, she had convinced herself she could do it. After all, she wouldn't be the only princess in the history of the world to endure an arranged marriage!

So she had carefully learnt her lessons in Petrogorian history and become fluent in its lilting language. She studied the geography of the country which was to be her new home, especially the vast swathe of disputed land—the Marengo Forest—which bordered her own and would pass into the ownership of her new husband after their marriage, in exchange for an eye-watering amount of cash. But all those careful studies now felt unconnected with her real life—almost as if she'd been operating in a dream world which had no connection with reality.

And suddenly she had woken up.

Her long gown swished against the polished marble as she followed her mother down the grand palace staircase which descended into an enormous entrance hall, where countless servants began to bow as soon as the two women appeared. Her two sisters came rushing over, a look of disbelief on both their faces.

'Zabrina, is that really you?' breathed Daria.

'Why, it doesn't really look like you at all!' exclaimed little Eva.

Zabrina bit down hard on her lip as she hugged them good-bye, picking up seven-year-old Eva and giving her an extra big hug, for her little sister sometimes felt like a daughter to her. She wanted to cry. To tell them how much she was going to miss them. But that wouldn't be either fair, or wise. She had to be grown-up and mature and concentrate on her new role as Queen, not give in to indulgent emotion.

'I don't know why you don't wear that sort of thing more often,' said Daria as she gazed at the floaty long gown. 'It looks so well on you.'

'Probably because it's not really appropriate clothing for being on the back of a horse,' replied Zabrina wryly. 'Or for running around the palace grounds.'

She hardly ever wore a dress. Even when she was forced into one for some dull state occasion, she wouldn't have dreamed of wearing one like this, with all its heavy embellishments which made it feel as constricting as a suit of armour. The heavy flow of material impeded her naturally athletic movements and she hated the way the embroidered bodice clung to her breasts and emphasised them, when she preferred being strapped securely into a practical sports bra. She liked being wild and free. She liked throwing on a pair of jodhpurs and a loose shirt and jumping onto the back of a horse—and the more temperamental, the better. She liked her long hair tied back out of the way in a simple ponytail, not gathered up into an elaborate style of intricate curls and studded with pearls by her mother's stylist.

Her father was standing there and Zabrina automatically sank to the ground, reluctantly conceding that perhaps it was easier to curtsey in a dress, rather than in a pair of jodhpurs.

'How much better it is to see you look like a young woman for a change,' the King said, his rasping voice the result of too many late-night glasses of whisky. 'Rather than like one of the grooms from the stables. I think being Queen of Petrogoria will suit you very well.'

For one brief moment Zabrina wondered how he would react if she told him she couldn't go through with it. But even if her country *didn't* have an outstanding national debt, there was no way the King would offend his nearest neighbour and ally by announcing that the long-awaited wedding would not take place. Imagine the shattered egos and political fallout which would result if he did!

'I hope so, Papa—I really do,' she answered as she turned towards her brother, Alexandru. She could read the troubled expression in his eyes, as if silently acknowledging her status as sacrificial lamb, but despite his obvious reservations what could the young prince possibly do to help her? Nothing. He was barely seventeen years old. A child, really. And she was doing it for him, she reminded herself. Making Albastase great again—even though she suspected that Alexandru had no real desire to be King.

Zabrina walked through the gilded arch towards the car which was parked in the palace courtyard and, climbing into the back of the vintage Rolls-Royce, she envisaged the journey which lay ahead of her. She would be driven to the railway station where King Roman of Petrogoria's royal train was waiting, with his high-powered security team ready to accompany her. On this beautiful spring afternoon, the train would travel in style through the beautiful countryside and the vast and spectacular Marengo Forest, which divided the two countries. By tomorrow, they would be pulling into Petrogoria's capital city of Rosumunte, where she would meet her future husband for the first time, which was a pretty scary thought. It had been drummed into her that she must be sure to project an expression of gentle gratitude when the powerful monarch greeted her, and to curtsey as deeply as possible. She must keep her eyes downcast and only respond when spoken to. Later that night there would be fireworks and feasting as the first of the pre-wedding celebrations took place.

And two strangers would be expected to spend the rest of their lives together.

Zabrina shot a wistful glance across the courtyard in the direction of the stable block and thought about her beloved horse, which she had ridden at dawn that very morning. How long would it take for Midas to miss her? Would he realise that until she was allowed to send for him one of the palace grooms would take him out for his daily exercise instead of her?

She thought about the bearded King and now her cause for concern was much more worrying. What if she found him physically repulsive? What if her flesh recoiled if—presumably when—he laid a finger on her? Despite her jokey remarks, she had read the book gifted to her by her mother, but she had received most of her sexual education from the Internet and an online version of the Kama Sutra. Even some of the lighter films she'd seen didn't leave a lot to the imagination and Zabrina had watched them diligently, fascinated and repelled in equal measure. She had broken out in a cold sweat at the thought of actually *replicating* some of the things the actors on the screens had been doing. Could she really endure the bearded King's unwanted caresses for the rest of her life?

She swallowed.

Especially as she was a total innocent.

A feeling of resignation washed over her. Of course she was. She'd never even been touched by a man, let alone kissed by one, for her virginity played a pivotal role in this arranged marriage. She thought about another of the books she'd ploughed her way through. The one about managing expectations within relationships and living in the real world, rather than in the fantasy version peddled by books and films. It had been a very sobering read but a rather useful one, and it had taught her a lot. Because once you abandoned all those stupid high-flown ideas of love and romance, you freed yourself from the inevitability of disappointment.

The powerful car pulled away to the sound of clapping and cheering from the assembled line of servants, but Zabrina's heart was heavy as she began her journey towards unwanted destiny.

Subscribe and fall in love with a Mills & Boon series today!

You'll be among the first to read stories delivered to your door monthly and enjoy great savings.

WE SIMPLY LOVE ROMANCE